My Perfect Mistake

ALSO BY KELLY SISKIND

Chasing Crazy

My Perfect Mistake

KELLY SISKIND

FOREVER
YOURS

New York Boston

Copyright © 2016 by Kelly Siskind
Teaser excerpt copyright © 2016 by Kelly Siskind
Cover design by Brian Lemus
Cover copyright © 2016 by Hachette Book Group, Inc.

Forever Yours
Hachette Book Group
1290 Avenue of the Americas
New York, NY 10104
forever-romance.com
twitter.com/foreverromance

First edition: April 2016

Forever Yours is an imprint of Grand Central Publishing.
The Forever Yours name and logo are trademarks of Hachette Book Group, Inc.

The publisher is not responsible for websites (or their content) that are not owned by the publisher.

The Hachette Speakers Bureau provides a wide range of authors for speaking events. To find out more, go to www.hachettespeakersbureau.com or call (866) 376-6591.

ISBN 978-1-4555-6542-9 (ebook edition)
ISBN 978-1-4555-6798-0 (print on demand edition)

E3

My Perfect Mistake

One

Shay

You can tell a lot about a woman by the type of bra she wears. For instance, the silky black number clutched in my hand as I swing my skis on the chairlift, the one that makes my girls look some kind of wonderful, this one says: classy, yet conservative.

"How far is it?" Lily asks, her white-blond hair almost camouflaged by the wisps of snow collecting on her lilac jacket.

March in Aspen and the snow is heavier than in midwinter, the evergreens lining the runs sagging under pillows of the white stuff. With each blink, the frosted tips of my eyelashes brush my cheeks. "It's closer to the end of the lift. Trust me, you can't miss it."

"You sure this is a good idea? We could come back tomorrow, and you could wear a different bra and carry this one so you don't, you know, have to ski down without..." Her pale gray eyes settle on my jacket, about midchest. The area housing my braless boobs.

Raven leans forward, her elbows resting on the safety bar, and she nudges Lily's side. "What do you think's going to happen? You think Shay's bra-mando boobs will get caught under her skis and send her hurtling down the mountain?"

The snowboarder at the end of our four-pack chairlift snorts to himself while Lily sinks against the back of our seat, reverting to her quiet-as-a-mouse routine. Grown men have cowered in the face of Raven's snark, but Lily's backbone is lodged somewhere below her tailbone.

I lick the snowflakes from my lips, knowing it's now or never. When we passed the bra tree on our last ride up the chairlift, its branches weighted down with lingerie, I knew what I had to do. It was instinctual. Visceral. My need to shed this bra and all it represented couldn't wait another second. One run and a quick trip to the washroom later, we got in line for this fateful ride. "Thanks for the concern, Lil, but I'm pretty sure my skiing ability won't be affected by my lack of undergarments. The bra tree *will* be getting another ornament."

"You really want to go through with it, though?" she asks as Snowboarder Dude cranes his neck to check out the black silk gripped in my gloved hand. "I mean, it's *the* bra."

She's right. It's not every day a girl comes across the perfect balance of lift and shape, cleavage and support, no extra skin pushing out the sides or back. Since its purchase, this has been my go-to bra. I wore it the day Richard passed the bar. I bought a new red dress, slinky and clingy in all the right places, but Richard did his usual, "Put on the black one I bought for you last month. The one with the lacy sleeves. I like how it slims your hips." I followed his backhanded compliment with my usual, "Yeah, sure. Okay."

When it came to Richard, my backbone slipped even lower than Lily's.

I tip my skis back and forth, remembering another "slimming" dress he picked out for me—a beaded black cut-out number—that I wore over this bra to celebrate Richard's new job working for one of the top law firms in Toronto. It was the same day I was offered a promotion. The design firm I'd apprenticed at was closing shop to focus on their Montreal location, and I was asked to come along and help establish them as the front-runner of Canadian design. That night I wore my *conservative* bra under my *doesn't-make-my-hips-look-huge* dress, agreeing with Richard as he spouted off all the reasons I needed to stay in Toronto to support him and his career.

My spine pretty much disintegrated.

But my favorite event, the moment that inspired this reality, this moment of truth, was the evening I donned *the* bra and a black dress expecting a proposal from Richard. After stumbling across an expensive Tiffany's bill, I just knew. That was it. We were going to take that next step as partners—spouses in support of each other. His promises would be realized, and I'd finally quit my soul-sucking job designing retirement homes and stretch my wings. With his blessing, of course. What I got instead was: I think we've grown apart.

More to the point, his dick grew toward Deena Wanger.

For five years, I put him first. His wants. His needs. I wasn't even second. A distant third, maybe. I dressed how he wanted, kept our apartment how he liked. The man had me on regular juice cleanses, for Christ's sake. The brazen, confident girl who grew up in a small town got swallowed by the city. And Richard.

Such an appropriate name, really. Even from birth, his parents knew he'd be a Dick.

I huff out a breath, sending a cloud of vapor curling through the cool air. "Oh, I'm sure. This forever-tainted piece of lingerie will adorn that bra tree. It will be the crowning jewel."

"You can't just chuck that," Snowboard Dude says, his mouth the only thing visible under his massive goggles and helmet. "There are rules."

Raven turns to him, her charcoal eyes likely squinting. "Rules? It's an evergreen tree on a ski slope covered with a pile of colorful bras and tacky necklaces. She can launch it if she wants."

He shakes his head and leans more heavily on his elbows. "No way. Tradition is tradition. It's gotta come from the evening's conquest. You bag a chick, take her bra, and sling it on the tree to immortalize the moment. Like I said, tradition. So unless you ladies got busy together last night, or at lunch"—a lazy grin sweeps across his face—"then pocket the bra." If he could see the tattoos inked over Raven's olive skin, he'd maybe look a little less smug. One glance at her in a dark alley, and I'd cross to the other side.

"Let me explain something." She squares her shoulders toward him, head cocked in annoyance. "My girl here just got dumped by a total douche, so we three are hating on men. Since you're the only dude on this chairlift, I'd say your choice is simple. She either hurls her bra on a tree covered in bras, or we channel our angry-girl hormones in your direction. What'll it be?"

That sly grin slips from his face. "Whatever. You wanna spit on tradition, fine by me. But that shit is karmic."

Raven's long black ponytail glides along her jacket as she swings her helmeted head my way. "Forget him. That bra will be taking flight."

I nod in agreement, my helmet bobbing with the movement. I may be hurt and pissed about how things ended with the Dick, but the relief is undeniable. Freeing. Both Raven and Lily made it known they thought I could do better, thought I'd lost a piece of myself to him (like two dress sizes), but I was too scared to step out on my own. Status quo was easier than no quo. I reverted to my pre-pubescent self, who stuttered and struggled to fit in. But knowing I might have said yes to a proposal because it was easy has anger bubbling up inside of me. I need to toss this bra, forget the Dick, and stop being such a doormat. I just wish I felt sexier in my equipment so I could get my flirt on with a rugged ski dude.

This helmet is the anti-sexy.

"Look, look, look!" Lily bounces beside me, the chairlift swaying in response. "That's it, right?"

As we crest a rise, the pinks and reds and blues on the bra tree stand out in vibrant contrast to the white-tipped evergreens. A few skiers are attacking the narrow mogul run below us, their skis scraping and gliding between the massive bumps. God, I love that sound. Growing up in a ski town outside of Toronto meant the local slopes were in my backyard. Although our hills are glorified mounds, I practically skied from the womb, the blades an extension of my feet. Flying to places like Aspen never gets dull. Never repetitive. Ski trips with their mile-long runs, hot tubs, bars, and shops are my version of the typical girls' beach vacation.

The Dick only booked all-inclusive yawners.

"That's it, all right," I say, my eyes locked on the tree.

Snowboard Dude horks and spits over the side of the chair, likely aiming for the yeti splayed on the snow, skis crossed, butt in the air, a yard sale of his gear smattering the uniform bumps. *Karma, my ass.* I scan the tree up ahead, cataloguing each brassiere I can make out. The hefty beige one looks more like a straitjacket than a bra, the thick material folded over a lower branch. It screams: dull, trite, supportive, and dead boring. Above it, a flirty number in bright purple and swirling lace dangles, its owner definitely more sassy than mundane. Swallowing thickly, I glance at the black bra I once loved, hating what an easy read it is.

Classy. Conservative. Proper. Poised.

The perfect accessory to pressed suits and silk ties. The chosen undergarment to accent my slimming black dresses. *The Dick.*

At a time in my life when I was struggling to adapt to the city, overwhelmed and friendless and out of my depth, Richard swooped in with his easy charm and charisma. He was larger than life. He took me out, bought me things, and introduced me to his friends. Lily and Raven were away, all of us busy with our own studies, and I latched onto him, needy and desperate to belong. To not feel so alone. To not be the insecure, stuttering child I thought I had banished. Worried he'd move on and I'd have to start over, I molded myself into his perfect girl. I became *that* chick.

Of course I'd rather suck kale through a straw than eat solid food.

Job promotion? Who needs it? I didn't want a real life anyway.

Bring on the vanilla sex. Experimentation and excitement are over-rated.

Every so often, though, I'd toss one of my hidden cookies into his smoothies…carbs and all.

"You better get ready," Raven says.

We're one chair back, and I raise my arm, readying to slingshot the bra, my past, and all things Richard into oblivion. As I do, a red lacy thing catches my eye. This piece of feminine lingerie is the perfect combination of sultry and flirtatious, the elegantly patterned fabric dipping low in the center, punctuated with a red bow. My heart quickens. *That* is the girl I was, once upon a time. The girl that got smothered by the Dick. That bra screams spontaneous and confident, a little wild and a lot of fun. It's the one I'm buying the second we get to town.

"Come on, Shay." Lily nudges me. "If you wait any longer, you're going to miss it."

I clench my jaw, determination setting in.

I draw my arm back, whip my wrist, and let the fabric go. It sails through the air in an elegant arc, my 34Cs taking flight, before being caught up in a gust of wind and tumbling down, down, down and landing smack on some guy's head. Amid his *what the fuck*s, the girls and I giggle as Snowboard Dude scoffs with a snarky "Karma."

It may not have hit the tree, but that bra is out of my life. Along with the Dick.

We push off the chairlift at the top, and I can't keep my eyes from flitting around. *I'm not wearing a bra.* The secret is enthralling, wanton. A shiver of excitement runs down my spine, and a need for recklessness consumes me. Having been in ski racing programs as a kid, I can handle the expert terrain better than Lily and Raven. Right about now, I could use the adrenaline.

"I say we call it early and have lunch in town. Last run of the day?" Lily asks as she zips the neck of her jacket higher to protect her pale skin. She tucks her blond strands into the back.

Raven jumps up and down, her skis smacking the hard-packed snow. "Bet your ass it is. There's a hot tub and glass of wine with my name on it."

I eye the large terrain map at the top of the lift. The girls will want to take an intermediate blue run down, but those expert double black diamonds have my name on them. The bra is gone, my spine is back, and the Dick is out of my life. "Why don't you guys take Ruthie's Run? I'd rather take Schiller over to Corkscrew. I'll meet you at the bottom."

Raven pushes off on her poles until we're almost chest to chest, her skis beside mine. She snaps her goggles onto her helmet and looks into my eyes. "Is that the old Shay in there? Has she come out to play?"

A couple of guys ski past us, practically colliding as they ogle Raven. Even in her anti-sexy helmet, she draws a crowd. As a teen, I'd catch myself staring at her olive skin, wishing I were sexy and striking with a sheath of shiny black hair. I grew to like my unruly mass of brown curls and wore them down to my waist, thick and untamed. Until I met the Dick, that is. The Dick has a preference for straight hair.

So began the era of the straightener and singeing my hair into submission.

"Yes, bitch, I'm back," I say. "With a vengeance."

I grab her goggles and snap them onto her face, eliciting a gratifying "Fuck" from her. She scowls and adjusts the frames.

I tighten my boot buckles then straighten up and grab my poles, eager to feel the wind blast my face. With each movement my breasts move freely, and I grin wider. "I'll meet you guys at the condo." I'm about to push off when I add, "And we're not going to one of those lame pubs again to hang with a bunch of stoners. Tonight, we're picking up hot ski dudes."

Lily tips her head back and groans. "What am I supposed to do while you two are seducing unsuspecting guys? I doubt Kevin would be too happy about me living it up in Aspen."

"That's easy," Raven says. "Join us. Kevin's a good guy and all, but that relationship of yours is beyond incestuous. Lines need to be drawn when you have naked bath-time pictures together."

Lily tightens her lips until they match her alabaster skin. "We were neighbors, Raven. *Neighbors.* And so what if I've known him forever. He gets me."

When Raven yawns in Lily's face, I skate past them and call, "Don't take forever. We're shopping for bras before we head out."

With that, I'm off, snow crunching, gusts of cool air snapping at my cheeks. There's nothing as freeing as carving across the hill, edging into large, swooping turns as my skis dig deeper and my thighs burn. Nothing exists but the movement. The speed. The effortless up and down. And I'm not wearing a bra.

The first section of moguls is tough. I land hard between the bumps, using my poles and the momentum to propel me into each sharp turn. *Smack. Crunch. Skid.* My blood pumps. My muscles grind. It's my second day skiing, and the altitude and thin air are forcing my lungs to work double-time. The rhythm is unrelenting, exhausting, and by the time I finish the second section, sharp pangs slice through my chest. And the boob sweat is undeniable.

I rest my upper body on my poles as a guy just ahead of me bails on his face. I can't help laughing, and he gives me the finger. The snow has stopped falling, stillness in its place. My heart pounds in my ears. I stare down the hill, regretting my decision to do a marathon's worth of moguls on my last run.

My legs are noodles, my breasts hurt from bouncing, and *God*, the boob sweat.

I maneuver my black jacket and press my long underwear top just so, hoping to mop up the uncomfortable wetness. As I shift to the left, I notice a break in the trees. I glance down the till-death-do-us-part run then back at the path. Better to bushwhack through the glades than have my braless and sweaty self rescued by the ski patrol.

Forcing my legs to move, I push forward and squeeze through the opening, dodging the trees as I pick my way toward the next run. There's a steep dip past the last line of branches, the perfect ramp to shoot me onto the groomed trail. A quick breath, a shift of my stance, and I catapult myself forward, gaining momentum. I hit the edge of the run perfectly. My legs relax, the blades on my feet glide, and I'm so relieved not to be pounding the moguls that I let my skis fly. For a moment. Like a second. The length of time it takes for some jerk to blindside me and send me on my ass.

I haven't fallen while skiing since forever. I ski fast and hard but always in control. It's a good thing. Hard-packed snow is about as soft as concrete. My left butt cheek smarts, a bruise no doubt forming, and I immediately regret laughing at that other dude's face-plant earlier. Distant grumbles carry through the frosty air as I gingerly pick myself up and stretch my legs. With all body parts intact, I glance at the idiot a few feet below who skied into me.

My jaw almost hits the snow.

If a hot ski dude is what I'm after, fate just intervened. His helmet is off as he inspects what could be a crack in his goggles, and oh, my God, *that hair*. Dirty blond and shoulder-length, tousled in a careless, sexy way that has me picturing my hands dragging through it. Add the stubble, the wide shoulders, and the tight booty that is unmistakable even in his ski pants, and I'm about to land on my ass again.

Richard looked nothing like this guy. His short black hair was always tidy, each strand gelled in place. He was good-looking in a *GQ* way with his cut cheekbones and Armani style, and Lord knows I found him attractive. When I'd browse his selection of men's magazines in our apartment, though, I didn't linger on the clean-cut images of guys in suits with their button-down shirts and silk ties. I'd pause on the men in the jeeps. The ones climbing a mountain, three-day stubble accentuating a strong jaw. Like hot ski dude right in front of me. Maybe it was because those guys were the polar opposite of the Dick, or maybe I don't have a "type."

When Mountain Guy stops checking over his gear, he swivels his upper body toward me, that shoulder-length hair doing some sort of model thing as he rakes a hand through the layered strands. "Next time you merge onto a run, you should look uphill so you don't run someone down. And you owe me a pair of goggles. These are trashed."

Come again? The throbbing pain on my butt returns, along with a searing anger that has me shaking. He *may* be kind of right, but his tone and righteousness snaps my spine straight. I'm tired of taking crap. Tired of pussyfooting around guys because they think they run the world. Normally, I'd be all *I'm sorry* and *it won't happen again*, but I tossed that bra and that girl off a chairlift. "You can't be serious. You totally blindsided me. Skied right into me. I'm not buying you squat."

He stretches his neck, the shorter strands of hair by his chin falling across his face. He slings his small pack off his shoulders, unzips it, and shoves the damaged goggles inside, then he straightens and flicks *that hair*. "The skier coming down has right of way. It isn't rocket science. If I were a kid, that shit could've been a lot worse than some cracked goggles. So pay attention the next time you barrel onto a hill." He shoots me a blistering look, like the dude owns the freaking mountain. Like I've never skied before. Then he mutters, "Idiot."

Come to think of it, I do have a type. I'm pretty sure it's Ass. Hole.

"Get over it." I jab my gloved middle finger in the air, fist my poles, and push off, skiing past his cute butt and model hair as the word "Bitch" follows behind me.

I don't glance back. I ski hard, taking wide, sweeping turns, picking up as much speed as possible, leaving the Asshole and my anger behind, because *wow*, was that liberating. My skis are barely on the snow, the wind whipping something fierce, my breasts unrestrained. This must be what crack feels like. Or eating the largest bowl of Lucky Charms. Marshmallow-only Lucky Charms. Now I just want to let loose and swear a bunch and speak my mind. And buy Lucky Charms.

And that red bra.

Two

Kolton

Fuck me. I'm in Colorado, on Aspen Mountain, gazing out at a kick-ass view, and I'm wound tighter than a drum. The endless mountain vistas usually calm me. Something about their size, imposing and downright impressive, puts life into perspective, the trivial day-to-day stresses no longer so heavy. It reminds me how lucky I am. To be here. To be able to barrel down a slope, nothing but the wind whistling in my ears and the scenery blurring by.

But today can kiss my ass.

Nico and Sawyer coaxed me into this trip with good intentions, but if I have to listen to them spouting off about my need to get out and live a little, work less, and find myself a piece of ass, shit's going to get real. Although it's been a while, I chased as much tail as Sawyer in the day, and I wasn't the president of my fraternity for nothing. My list of pranks is a mile long. Even at twenty-nine, I have no problem whipping it out.

This winner of a day started with Sawyer smacking the back of my head as he pushed past me into the condo kitchen, saying a groggy, "Morning, shithead. Can't believe you turned down that chick last night. Another few weeks, and you'll be revirginized."

I chucked an empty beer can at his head. "Have you forgotten your scrawny teenage ass would still be whacking off to pictures of Leah Richardson if I hadn't lied and told her your dick was huge?"

A few more insults were traded, enough to get me out to go skiing, a smile plastered on my face. But the day turned into a massive game of dominoes, each irritation fueling the next until they tumbled into a giant pile of frustration.

My ski pass not working at the base of the mountain sucked. Not day-crushing sucked, but I sent the boys to ski on their own and had to wait for twenty minutes while the dude at the wicket stared lamely at his computer to deduce why my piece of plastic lost its data. Once his boss issued me a new pass, I hauled ass to my gear, itching to ski out my tensing muscles. That's when I noticed the dent in my binding. Another hour and I was at the top of the lift with rental skis. Pack on, goggles down, boots buckled tight, I gripped my poles, ready to let my skis fly, but the sound of little-kid sobs stopped me. The boy looked about Jackson's age, and if my kid were by himself at the top of Aspen Mountain, I'd raise hell.

Instead of skiing out my frustration, I spent the next thirty minutes in the lodge, feeding the little dude chips and chocolate to keep his meltdown in check. When his ski school instructor turned up, I copied the fuckwit's name down and made it clear he better not lose any more kids while teaching. The boy's quiet "Thank you, mister" as he tugged on my hand had me missing Jackson hard.

This is the first vacation I've taken without him. The longest I've been away from him in seven years. I've spent every minute wondering if he's tripping on that shoelace he never ties. If he's brushing his teeth. If he's practicing his writing. Missing him also brought back thoughts of Marina and what I've lost. What I might never find again.

Determined to tackle the slopes and dull the pang of missing Jackson and Marina, I went back outside. Skis on *again*, goggles down *again*, and the snow crunched with each fast turn, finally easing the negative energy churning in my gut. Not for long. Halfway down the mogul run under the chairlift, I was resting my legs, cold air raking through my lungs, when a bra landed on my head. A fucking bra. Some girls were laughing their asses off as I fisted the black fabric and flung it into the trees, every cord in my neck ready to snap. Like I needed the reminder my dry spell could rival the Vancouver Canucks' Stanley Cup drought. Sawyer would've busted a rib laughing.

Nearing my breaking point, I skied down hard—quick, aggressive turns until my thighs screamed—only to get stuck on the next chair for five minutes. When I made it to the top, I didn't hesitate. I flew toward the nearest groomed trail and let my skis run, barreling down, holding nothing back. I let loose every little thing eating at me.

Until that chick careened into my side.

I saw her fly from the trees just in time to avoid a head-on collision, but the tips of our skis crossed, sending her on her butt and me hurtling onto my shoulder. My hand and pole smacked into my goggles, the wind knocked clean out of my chest. The irritation festering all day built into full-blown rage; my only consolation was the fact that my weak shoulder didn't dislocate. And *this chick*? No apology. No remorse for causing the collision. She got up and blew past me. Not before giving me the one-finger salute. *Bitch.*

As I stare out at the rugged mountains, trying to let go of the pile of shit heaped on my shoulders, I can't help picturing how she raced down the hill like an Olympian. There's something about athletic girls who can hold their own on the slopes that gets me going. I bet her legs are toned, her ass probably tight. Strip her out of that ski gear, and *man*, could that be the thing to take the edge off my day. If she could keep her mouth from running.

But that would mean casual sex—quick, fun. And meaningless. My gut churns like it did the last time I met a woman at a bar. The girl had mile-long legs and knew how to have fun, and it was. For a time. Until I left her apartment, went home alone, woke up alone, and spent the day with my son. Alone.

I'm done with meaningless. I'm just not sure my dick got the memo.

Swiveling downhill, I jump into a turn, picking up speed as I head to the base. I need a hot tub and drink stat.

* * *

I'm one beer in by the time Sawyer and Nico show up at the condo's outdoor spa area. Sawyer juts his chin toward a couple of girls heading for the reception area. One has on a Moondog jacket, the other a Moondog hat, both items from our fall/winter clothing line. The

Runaway Jacket—with its asymmetrical zipper, thick lapels, and buckles up the sides—fits the blonde perfectly, the deep purple tone even sharper than I remember.

Sawyer wiggles his eyebrows. "Looks good, huh?" He tosses his towel and lowers himself into the hot tub, beer in hand.

I sigh, dreading what's coming. He may be the design guy behind our growing retail chain, but sometimes he goes too far, edgier than I think our clientele will dig. Not every woman wants to be rocker chic. "Do I have to say it now, or can it wait 'til later?"

After a long pull on his beer, he shrugs. "Now suits me fine."

I tip my head back, the ends of my hair sinking into the water. "Sawyer, dude, you're the man."

"And?"

God, I hate when he's right. "*And*…next time I tell you no chick in her right mind will spend six hundred bucks on a jacket with a bunch of zippers and buckles all over it, I give you permission to waterboard me."

"If waterboarding's going down, count me in." Nico grins, his eyes narrowed with an evil glint that should intimidate me coming from this beast of a guy. Especially since the dude carries a gun to work. Luckily, I've seen him passed out with Jackson in his arms countless times, and my champ has peed on him. Twice.

Just as he's about to step into the water, Sawyer raises his palm. "Use the other tub. One step in here, and you'll send the water flooding out."

"Fuck you." With a grunt, Nico walks his massive thighs in, sprawling out just to piss Sawyer off.

Steam rises from the water, a few snowflakes starting to fall. A couple of kids are in the nearby pool jumping around, and my mind is back on Jackson, hoping he's listening to his teacher. Hoping that snot Evan isn't pushing him around.

Evan, the little shit.

Nico runs a hand over his buzzed head and reaches for his beer. "When'd you call it quits?"

I exhale and watch as the cold flakes dissolve on the warm stone around us. "Maybe an hour ago. Not feeling the slopes today."

High-pitched giggles have Nico tipping his beer toward two girls who just arrived, probably too young for any of us to be watching as they strip down to their bikinis and walk gingerly into the tub a few feet away. "Jail bait," I say.

Sawyer snorts. "For fucking sure." He swigs his beer then kicks me with his foot. "But that chick last night wasn't, and she was all over you. What gives?"

Instead of answering him, I put my beer down, duck under the water, and push through the surface. The frosty air hits me like a shot of oxygen. Those kids are splashing each other, the nearby adult warning them to keep it down. I drag my hand down my face and shake out my hair.

Nico's eyes dart to the kids, then back to me. "It's Jackson's birthday next month, isn't it?"

I nod—a quick jerk of my head, no other comment needed. Silence descends between us as we leave the rest unspoken. No one needs to mention Jackson turning seven means Marina died seven years ago. I don't need the reminder. Life was taken and life was given. An even swap that nearly cut me down. If it weren't for Jackson, I wouldn't have made it.

The girls giggle again as they whisper to each other and eye Nico. With his buzzed head, massive build, and the tattoos curving over his shoulders, he looks more Hell's Angels than cop, but the dude is all heart. Not many guys would upend their lives and move in with a friend for eight months to help raise his son. I cringe, thinking what it would have been like if I had to move back home with my dad, stepmom, and the chaos my three stepbrothers inspire. The word *loud* comes to mind.

Nico clears his throat. "Does your recent vow of celibacy have anything to do with that birthday?" Still no mention of Marina. No need to twist the knife in my gut.

I squeeze my beer until my knuckles burn. "Not interested right now. Tons going on with the expansion at work, and Jackson keeps me busy. Time's a commodity." The bubbling water stills, a shriek and a splash from the pool piercing the quiet.

"That's bullshit and you know it." Sawyer leans out of the tub to hit the dial, and the jets roar back to life. "You're living your life for Jackson, which, don't get me wrong, is awesome. That kid deserves the best. But you've gotta get out and live your life, too. Time *is* a commodity. You don't get these years back. And believe it or not, that girly hair of yours won't reel 'em in when it's gray and thinning."

I slap the edge of my hand against the water, spraying Sawyer's face. "So what? Going from girl to girl and never settling down like you is the answer? That's what you call living?"

Using his forearm, he wipes the water from his face. "First. Do that again, and I beat your ass. These pools are nasty. Second. Yeah, I'm living the life. The life *I* want. For *me*. That's all I'm suggesting. Nico here is your relationship guy. That works for him. I happen to like variety. Either way, you need to figure your shit out because one day Jackson will fly the coop. I say have fun in Aspen, let loose, for fuck's sake, then maybe start into the dating again back home."

What's it been? Six months? Seven? Sure, work, Jackson, and life in general make it tough to find the time to date, but these days I can't muster up the interest. Sawyer and I used to take advantage of our Moondog status, bagging chicks more than happy to list us as conquests. After a couple of them turned creepy stalker, we canned that routine and stopped telling girls what we do for a living. With them it was empty sex, anyway, always at their place, never at mine, keeping Jackson away from the temporary girls in my life. Then came dating. Everyone telling me they had *the* girl for me. The perfect match. A month here, a couple there, but no one with any staying power.

No one is Marina. No one ever will be.

Nico moves to use another jet, and the water sways like one of those wave pools. "He might have a point, dude."

I cough on a swallow of beer. "Seriously? You're siding with the guy who slept with your last girlfriend a month after you broke up?"

He cracks his thick neck. "There wasn't much between us, so I gave him the okay. Besides, I knew what a letdown it would be after riding the Nico Train."

Sawyer copies my move and blasts water in Nico's face. "Asshole."

Nico retaliates with a punch to the shoulder that has Sawyer cursing, then Nico turns to me. "We're in Aspen, hot chicks everywhere. You should've seen the two we met on the slopes today. Might as well use the time to get back in the game. Have some fun. Then maybe hit the dating scene with more enthusiasm. Even online or something."

I sigh. "Right. Online dating. Like that works. And if you met girls, why are you here?"

Nico shrugs. "They took off too fast. Something about meeting a friend at the bottom. And don't diss online dating. I've done it. It might not have lasted, but you never know." He points a finger at both of us. "One smartass word from either of you, and I aim for the throat."

Sawyer and I take one look at each other and burst out laughing, beer almost spurting from my nose. "What did your profile say?" I ask. "Searching for Amazonian woman to handle massive dick?"

A slow smile lights Nico's face. "If the shoe fits."

Chuckling, I push up to sit on the edge of the tub, needing a break from the heat. The boys sink lower, shoulders shaking with laughter. The snow is falling harder, hopefully dumping inches on top. A powder day tomorrow would make up for today's fail. Still, I can't stop reliving every aggravating detail. The bra. The careless instructor. That chick with the attitude, and her effortless turns as she blew past me on the slopes. Picturing her again has heat pooling south, my dick nudging me to get some play. Maybe the boys are right. If I stop worrying about meeting the right girl, if I relax and have some fun, maybe I could approach the whole dating thing with a bit more optimism when home. Not measure every girl against Marina.

"Fine. Let's do it," I say. "But not tonight. Tonight, it's steaks and beers in. The way my day went, going out could be painful. We'll hit the bars tomorrow. Cool?"

Nico grunts, and Sawyer says, "Works for me."

I jump up. "I'll head to town for food. You still off asparagus, Nico?"

He gawks at me. "That was what? A year ago?" When Sawyer makes his what-the-fuck face, Nico says to him, "You remember Stacey, the blonde I dated? She cooked the shit out of it nightly.

Fucking baby food. And Bill Gates here"—he nods to me—"filed that nugget away in his mutant brain."

"I don't remember you complaining about my *genius* brain when I'd do your math homework. I'll just get some salad stuff." I grab my towel, looking forward to a low-key night and a better day tomorrow. Checking out the nightlife and getting laid are starting to sound good. Damn good. Between my assistant, Stella, and Marina's mother, Jackson's in safe hands. Work won't implode over the next four days, and the past months of no action are catching up with me. If this trip is about living it up and letting loose, I may as well push the boundaries. For four days. Starting tomorrow. This particular day can still kiss my ass.

Three

Shay

This night keeps getting worse. Sure, I'm wearing the new red bra I bought after skiing. Not a replica of the one I saw hanging on the bra tree, but it has a little bow in the center and does good things for my girls, keeping them perky and smooth in all the right places. And I *am* wearing my favorite black skirt, red leather boots, and a new low-cut top purchased for the occasion. But the hot ski dudes I expected at this swanky restaurant are pathetically absent.

"Our food is taking forever, and if Daddy Warbucks sends us another round, I'm leaving." Raven crosses her lean arms, her ink displayed in the badass rocker tank she bought on our shopping spree. I can't imagine what her art students think of her. Or the faculty.

Lily slips pink paper from her bottomless purse and methodically rips it into strips. Without taking her eyes off her work, she says, "They're busy, Rave. Be patient."

Two kids fly past us, bumping into Raven's chair for at least the fifth time. She grips the table, and her knuckles whiten. "I swear to God, if they do it again, I'll shove their snotty faces through the window. Who takes kids out at this hour, anyway? To an expensive restaurant?"

I bounce my crossed leg, wishing she hadn't mentioned the hefty price tag attached to this meal. I mentally catalogue my bank account, knowing there aren't enough zeros to pay for too many more nights like this. We wouldn't even be in Aspen if it weren't for Lily's folks always offering to send her and her friends away, always being generous with their money. I almost said no. Having finally stepped out from under the Dick's shadow, I vowed I'd never again be reliant on someone. Never let them pay my way. It was just another thing that tied me to him, another reason I stuck around longer than I should have. But it was Lily. And Raven. And *Aspen*. From here on out, it's little old me doing things my way.

First item on that list: getting some action.

When the same kid smacks Raven's chair for the umpteenth time, she glares at me from below her thick bangs. "Remind me again why we chose this place?"

I offer a weak smile. "Because of the hordes of hot guys at the bar?"

We lock eyes with the bald geezer on a nearby stool, his cowboy boots, leather pants, and silk shirt doing nothing to make him look any younger. Neither is the bolo tie.

When he winks at us, Lily shudders. "Creepy." Then she nudges Raven. "Nothing like the two we met on the hill. I think the big guy wanted to ask you out." She returns to her impromptu art project, weaving the torn pink strips into a thick band.

I frown at Raven. "What guys?"

She rolls her knife around. "The last run, before we met you at the bottom, Lil took a spill. A couple of guys stopped to help get her poles and make sure she was okay. She didn't want to keep you waiting, so she dragged me away. But one of them looked like The Rock's stunt double. Serious lady-boner material. The exact opposite of the dudes here. I mean, *look* at this place."

I glance at the older crowd and families filling the mahogany interior. Not the eye candy promised in the obviously out-of-date Internet review. Frustrated, I slouch in my seat, adjusting my weight off my bruised hip, courtesy of the Asshole. Raven's right. There should be guys like him here—model hair, day-old stubble, athletic and fit. Minus the attitude, of course. Instead, we have Daddy Warbucks.

As we wait for our food, I fill the girls in on my collision with the Asshole, then I distract myself with my usual game. In my mind, I wipe the walls and furniture away like an Etch A Sketch, redesigning the space. Modernizing it. I redo the ceiling with embossed gold tiles and hang a funky black chandelier above the bar. The mahogany walls get divided with chair rail, the top painted a soft cream, the bottom an eye-popping hot pink. The barstools become clear plastic, the bar top poured concrete with crushed glass. By the time I'm done, I've nearly forgotten why I'm annoyed.

Our waiter arrives, and Lily puts away the woven pink bracelet she made in five minutes. "Thanks. It looks amazing," she says to the server, all sweetness and sugar as he places plates in front of her and

Raven. She adjusts her hairband to catch the flyaway white-blond strands escaping her messy bun.

"You finished it," I say, nodding to her hair accessory.

Grinning, she touches the slim band on her head. "Just before the trip. It took a while to find the right colored gems to inlay. Ones with softer tones. Not too vibrant."

"It's perfect, but I hope you made one for Raven, too." I'd kill to see something that girly on her.

"Hilarious," Raven says. "You're just jealous I *could* wear something like that. It would take a girdle to hold back those curls of yours."

Lily shoots her the dirtiest look she can manage. "She's never allowed to straighten it again"—she faces me—"*ever*. It's stunning natural."

With Lily's indie style, Raven's in-your-face flair, and my love of trends, we look more like a motley crew than girlfriends. Two tables over, four women are chatting, each wearing jeans and knee-high boots, sporting similar slim builds, straight hair, and red lipstick. Edited versions of one another. If it weren't for art class, I doubt Lily, Raven, and I would have become friends. A design-obsessed hipster, a badass chick, and a competitive skier don't often mingle in high school. Somehow, though, we work.

The girls dig into their food as a different waiter appears with two more plates. He stops, brow furrowed. "There must have been a mistake. I'll be right back."

"Whoa, whoa, whoa." I hold up my hand before the guy can turn away. "Not another step. Those are for me."

He glances again at the lobster risotto and steak frites and then at the table with *one* customer missing her food. The second item on that doing-things-my-way list: eating whatever I want. The Dick, his smoothies, and my slim hips can go to hell.

The waiter sets down my smorgasbord, awkwardly placing both plates so I can dig in without morsels flying. "Enjoy," he says and smirks, leaving the girls to stare wide-eyed as I shove a massive forkful of risotto into my mouth. I follow with a bite of steak.

Raven shakes her head slowly. "If we feed her after midnight, will she sprout horns and terrorize Aspen?"

Lily giggles and presses her fingers to her lips. "I don't know, but I'm glad our place has three rooms. She's going to feel awful later."

"You know I can hear you, right?" I say around a bite. But Lily's spot on. There's no doubt my wallet and stomach will regret this, but it's *lobster* and *risotto* and *steak frites*.

The night the Dick dumped me, I might have snapped. A little. *Just a smidge.* I hollered choice words in the restaurant and told him not to show up at our apartment while I packed. After cramming my necessities into a few bags—the rest to be dealt with when I felt more rational—I had my hand on the door to leave, but I paused. Evil Shay took over. There's no other explanation. I stomped to our bathroom, grabbed the Dick's toothbrush, and headed for the toilet. No hesitation. I scrubbed that porcelain for a good five minutes, then returned it to the sink at the exact angle he liked. Next, I marched to our bedroom and took his underwear from the laundry basket, folded it (neatly of course—*the Dick*), and put it back on his shelf. Un-freaking-washed. Remembering the laxatives in our medicine cabinet, I smacked my hands together and squealed. That almond milk for his morning smoothie most certainly kept him "regular."

I loaded my car and drove eighty in a sixty zone, but on my way to Lily's, I passed McDonald's and pulled a U-turn. A Big Mac, fries, chicken fingers, and shake later, my sugar-carb coma brought me back to reality. Good Shay returned…with one alteration.

Getting dumped by the Dick after suffering through his crazy diets and juice cleanses has made me slightly food aware. A touch obsessed. *Minutely.*

Hence my all-you-can-eat buffet.

Thirty minutes later, Raven gawks as I force another fry into my mouth. "It's like I'm at the zoo," she says.

Lily bites her lip. "You don't have to finish."

I lean back and polish off the last of my Shiraz. "Yeah, I'm done. But I'm taking the rest to the condo." That hunk of steak and pile of fries have breakfast written all over them. Although there *is* that box of Lucky Charms back at our place. "I'm thinking we need to work brunch into our meal rotation. You know, as a fourth meal."

Raven swirls her wineglass. "Shay, babe, you're not a hobbit. You're a twenty-five-year-old woman who's a tad lost and needs to remember she's the same chick who won the Whistler Cup. That chick knew how to get in the zone. That chick skied circles around those bitches. It'll just take some time is all, and I'm not sure eating your way through Aspen is the answer."

I push fries around my plate.

Skiing today was liberating. It was the thing that brought me out of my shell as a kid, too. Gave me confidence. Being part of a team vanquished the lonely, stuttering child I once was. Temporarily, at least. I may not struggle with my words, but my compliance with Richard echoed an unhappy time in my life. And I was blind to it. "I was sixteen at the Whistler Cup," I say. "It was a lifetime ago. Sure, that—"

A waiter passes with a plate of key lime pie, and I watch, entranced, as my saliva gathers. *Man, that looks good.* When Raven, still waiting on me, clears her throat, I continue, "That girl rocked, but I don't even know who she was…who I *am*." Aside from the first known sufferer of ADFD: Attention Deficit Food Disorder.

"You're an amazing interior designer who's going to chase her dreams again when she gets home," Lily says. "You're not living your life for Richard anymore." She reaches over the table and squeezes my hand.

I sigh, the bra-slinging, determined girl from earlier suddenly absent. "But that's just it. What if I'm screwed? What if I passed up the best job offer I'll ever get?"

"You mean designing retirement homes isn't your dream job?" Raven winks at me.

I pull my hand out from under Lily's, fist the napkin on my lap, and toss it at Raven. If I have to go home and face another mothball-smelling gig, I'll lose the plot. Following our firm's strict guidelines leaves me no choice but to offer clients a choice of ugly or uglier, tacky or tackier—everything outdated BCK (before Calvin Klein). And I have to sell that horror show. *No, really, the paisley you chose is perfect with the big. Giant. Floral. Couch.* I can't unsee that stuff. And it's all because I didn't take the golden-ticket job. The cereal-box-prize job. I chose the Dick.

Heat builds behind my eyes, and I face the large windows lining the restaurant. The snow hasn't stopped since this afternoon, thick flakes still tumbling down. A few kids are grabbing handfuls, packing them into snowballs, and pelting one another. I look up again at the fluffy flakes, remembering one of my childhood art projects—learning how each crystal was unique, no two alike. Those kids are mashing each rare flake into one massive, uniform sphere, all individuality squashed, and my breathing halts. I swivel toward the girls. "I'm a fucking snowball."

Raven blinks at me. "I don't follow."

I pound my fist on the table. "A fucking snowball. I mean, look at us." Lily and Raven exchange glances and shrug. "How different we are," I say. "We're all snowflakes. All unique. But we still work, right? Richard snowballed me. That fucker packed me into his world, belittling and molding me until he killed my uniqueness. And I let him." My resolve from earlier returns tenfold. I may not like the girl I became while with the Dick, or the insecure child I once was, but I can be whoever I want now. I tossed my bra, gave that ski dude the finger, and I'm wearing hot lingerie. *Red-hot* lingerie. Picturing the Asshole who skied into me, sexy booty and all, has me pressing my legs together. It's back to that list of mine. Item one: getting some action. "Let's settle our bill," I say. "It's time to hit a bar."

Item one trumps taking home leftovers.

* * *

The first bar is a disaster. When a total stoner corners Raven and doesn't take her "Get the fuck away or your ability to father children ends" as the not-so-subtle hint it is, we trek to the next place we find, music thumping from the door. Then uninvited hands land on Lily's backside. She squeals and drags us out, not that I mind.

Not one guy there had heat pooling between my thighs the way the Asshole did—okay, *does*—but the idea of calling it a night doesn't sit well. The bra and the snowball epiphany still have my adrenaline coursing, and I can't stop thinking that if I return to the condo, if I wash up and go to sleep, I'll wake up as the old Shay. All progress made today will vanish. Poof. Gone. But the girls have had enough, so I agree to head back, no hot men in tow.

I'm dragging my feet as we turn off the street to cut through another group of condos.

"God, it's cold for March." Lily jumps with each step, hugging her arms tighter.

I walk slower still, delaying the inevitable as we inch closer to our place. And Old Shay. The path is lined with single-story condos, some with their lights on and curtains open. A couple is huddled on a couch watching TV, the two of them making out. And I smell…popcorn. *Mmmm, popcorn.* I could totally go for a snack. Something crunchy and salty, like dill pickle chips. Or salt and vinegar. A few windows down, a group of friends is chatting and laughing as they pour drinks and clink glasses; all the while my tongue tingles and my mind chants *chips, chips, chips.* Maybe I should look for a convenience store.

Then I freeze. *Holy shit.*

Raven and Lily are several strides ahead, but I stand, unmoving, my eyes fixed on the next condo, all thoughts of snacks gone. A guy is sitting in the small living area by the window, his legs propped on a coffee table, and this guy is H-O-T hot. His corded neck, strong jaw, and casual yet trendy hair—shaved on the sides and shaggy up top—put every dude we saw tonight to shame. Not as sexy as the Asshole, but still.

"I didn't peg you for the Peeping Tom type," Raven calls as both girls stare at me from the end of the path.

"Get over here," I whisper-yell while waving.

Deep sighs carry across the crisp air, but the girls humor me and trudge back.

"No way," Raven mumbles when she reaches my side and follows my line of sight. "Isn't that the guy from today, Lil? The one who helped you?"

Lily inhales sharply. "Wow. Yeah. God, he's cute."

We both face her, eyes bugging. "Did you just say wow, Lil?" I ask. "Did the girl who claims she doesn't need to look at other guys because she has a boyfriend just gawk at the manly perfection in there?"

She swats my arm and is about to reply when Raven adds, "Unlike Kevin, I don't think your knight in shining armor was on that field trip with you when you first got your monthly friend. Maybe it's time to upgrade."

Lily squints, her white-blond brows pulling together. "I'm not even going to dignify that with—"

"And there's his friend." Raven's dreamy tone sends my focus back to our peep show as she attempts to lift her jaw off the snow.

"Holy mother of God," I say.

Another guy who must've been hidden walks from the living area to the adjoining kitchen, and I have no idea how he fit through the front door. Hercules would have a hard-on for those shoulders, every inch of exposed flesh covered with black ink. The guy's neck is the size of my thigh, his T-shirt clinging to each and every muscle.

Raven stares, transfixed. "That is a lot of man."

Lily nods. "Too bad the bars didn't have guys like this. You two could finally get some action and stop dragging me around."

"Don't talk to me about getting laid," Raven shoots back and crosses her arms. "Not unless you can look me in the eye and tell me the last time you had sex with Kevin. And I mean real sex. Not the kind where you fake an orgasm."

I cringe at Raven's tone. Unlike me, she's grown more confident with age, no thanks to her parents. Growing up in a small town, we all knew a little too much about people's lives. Kids in high school would point and whisper about her father's gambling issues, her Native American heritage on his side, and her mother's excessive drinking. When it got around that her sister, older by ten years, had a different father she never met, the gossips crowed with glee. Instead of cowering, Raven punked out à la Miley Cyrus, leading to bad crowds, drugs, and extensive ink. The ink and an attitude are ever-present.

"Enough, Rave. We all know you cried when Max Sloan called you trailer trash. Stop bullying Lily."

"Bullying? Shay, how many times did I tell you to dump Richard? How many times did I tell you he was sucking the girl I love dry?" When I don't answer, she turns to Lily. "Sorry it was harsh, but the truth hurts. You seriously need to move on from Kevin. For now, us ladies have a golden opportunity." She quirks up an eyebrow. "I believe there's a party in need of crashing."

Lily's eyes flick to the peep show, then back to Raven. "God, *no*."

"Oh, yes."

"You're crazy. What if they're mass murderers?"

"They stopped to make sure you were okay today," Raven says. "And the smaller one trudged halfway up the hill to get you your pole. They were nice guys, and our girl here needs a pick-me-up. You sold this trip to Shay by telling her it was the best way to start fresh and get over the Dick. Love that name, by the way," she says to me, then focuses on Lily. "The hotness in there is her ticket. Do you want to deny her that?"

"But there's only two guys," I say before Lily can reply. "And what if they have girlfriends?"

"The worst they can do is send us packing, and Lily's already said she's standing by her man, so…"

"There's a third!" Lily points and jumps before reining herself in. "Not that it means anything. Just, I could have someone to hang out with. Platonically. And talk, you know, while you guys do your thing. I'm not, like, interested."

I scan the interior but don't see this mysterious third. "Where is he?"

Lily cranes her neck. "He walked out then turned back toward the hallway."

"Was he cute?" I ask.

"Kind of like the smaller guy but with longer hair in a ponytail, and he looks like he spends more time at the gym. But not as massive as the big guy."

The three of us fidget another minute, dancing on the spot to keep warm. A slow smile lights each of our faces as we silently agree to be wild and crazy for the night. I squeal and grab their hands, thrilled I don't have to go to sleep and dread tomorrow.

Tonight, proper, poised, and perfect are out the window.

Tonight, I embody the red bra.

When we get to the door, Raven reaches up to knock but pauses. "You guys sure?" We nod, but she lowers her hand. "Shay, since this trip is in your honor, you should do the deed."

She walks behind me, grabs my hips, and positions me in front of the door. The door housing three hot guys, one of whom might get to see my new lingerie. As I lift my arm, Raven says, "Wait."

Lily and I flip around with a simultaneous "What?"

"I call dibs on the big guy."

I snort. "Shocker. Anything else?"

Raven shakes her head, but as I spin around to knock, Lily says, "We need a signal."

With a huff, I turn my back to the door *again*. "Like what? If Raven and I are about to hook up, we flash an image of a condom instead of the bat-signal?"

Lily rolls her eyes. "*No.* If one of us wants out or, I don't know, feels uncomfortable, we should have a sign that we want to leave."

"Okay, sure." Raven smirks. "If a guy puts the moves on you, or *doesn't* put the moves on me or Shay, and we get bored, we make the sound of a dying giraffe."

We stare at each other, lips pulled tight to keep from laughing, until we lose it. Raven cackles, Lily shrieks, and I bend forward in a fit of giggles as we remember the *South Park* movie Raven forced us to watch during high school. "No, seriously," I say, my cheeks warm from laughing. "Lily's right. We don't know those guys. If anyone feels weird, then just say something like 'I forgot my credit card at the restaurant.'"

"Done," Raven says. "Let's do this."

We share wicked grins as I flip around, my pulse ticking in my ears. I fist my hand and prepare to live in the moment. *Thump thump thump* goes my heart, each heavy beat deafening.

"Go on. Do it," Lily says from behind me, her impulsiveness catchy.

Either Raven's lashing hit home, or she's doing this for me. Whatever the reason, I rap my knuckles on the door and wait, every muscle tensed. Singing drifts from a group of girls as they traipse through the snow behind us, but the knob doesn't twist. Determined, I knock again. As I'm about to pound my fist a third time, the door swings wide. And I nearly swallow my tongue.

"The Bitch," says the guy from the doorway.

My lip curls. "The Asshole."

Four

Kolton

Un-fucking-believable. An hour from this day finally being over, and *this* girl turns up. I don't recognize the other two crammed in our doorway, but the Bitch with her full lips and confident air is unforgettable. The way her eyes flare, snapping with irritation, it doesn't look like she forgot me, either.

"You here to apologize?" I ask. There are a slew of other things I should find out first, like her name or how the hell she found me, but today's frustrations have festered into the evening, and I haven't let go of her carelessness.

"Apologize? Okay. Sure. I'm *very* sorry you skied into me and nearly broke my tailbone. The guilt is all-consuming." Each word drips with sarcasm, her annoyance clearly still as acute as mine.

"*This* is the Asshole? And you skied off?" says the dark-haired one beside her. Her thick bangs hang blunt over charcoal eyes, a hint of the exotic in her olive skin.

The boys are up now, Sawyer leaning over my shoulder. "So *this* is the Bitch. And didn't we meet you ladies on the hill?" I can't see his face, but there's no doubt he's unleashed his Prince Charming smile. The way the pale blonde blushes, I'd say it's working.

"Call her the Bitch again, and you boys will be filming your own *Hangover* sequel," says the dark-haired girl. "And, yeah, that was us. It was nice of you to help."

Nico pushes by me and scans the area outside, his cop instincts on high alert. "Everything okay?"

"We're fine. We were just heading to our condo and saw you gentlemen in here. Seemed a shame not to thank you for your efforts this afternoon. I'm Raven, this is Lily, and this"—she shoots daggers my way—"is *Shay*. Not sure if you're alone, but…" Her charcoal eyes dance the length of Nico's body.

Sawyer doesn't miss a beat. "Absolutely. I'm Sawyer, the giant is Nico, and the 'Asshole' is Kolton. Although I'm open to the name change."

Raven walks right in, Nico following her like he's a compass and she's due north.

Sawyer looks about to hit on Lily when she says, "I have a boyfriend."

He stops short, then shrugs. "Since my boy and Shay have some unfinished business, you're forced to hang with me just the same."

She bites her lip and steps inside, leaving me with the Bitch.

The two of us face off, not speaking. There's no question she looked hot in her ski clothes, but her tight skirt combined with the fuck-me boots have me itching to unzip her bomber jacket and peek inside. And, man, that curly hair of hers is wild and begging to be tugged.

"Mind closing the door?" Nico calls.

"And not ogling me," Shay says. I meet her gaze, and her eyes flare. "If you get out of the way, I can step inside."

Now I'm wishing I could zip her jacket *higher*, hopefully sealing her inside. Instead of biting back, I turn around and head to the kitchen, needing more than a beer to get through this night. Two fingers of amber liquid and an ice cube later, the girls have shrugged off their coats, Nico and Raven talking tattoos while Sawyer goes on about Lily's purse.

Shay leans against the counter, holding the glass of wine Nico offered. "She made that," she says to Sawyer, gesturing to Lily's purse. "Each one done by hand with recycled materials. She sells them to some indie stores."

"Seriously?" Sawyer tilts his head and rubs his jaw, no doubt putting on his Moondog hat, seeing all the funky designs he can base on the concept. "What'd you use for the sides? Is that..." He turns the small bag over in his hands. "Is that from a skateboard?"

Lily leans forward. "Yeah. I mean, I know it's been done before, but I cut the boards into small pieces and sand them down so they're not too thick. I apply them in geometric patterns, you know, like a mosaic? But on top of material I salvage from vintage leather jackets. That way, the purse and shoulder strap are soft. Flexible. The two materials are contradictory, but they work together. I like playing with the juxtaposition." She sits straighter, eyes darting, as if she just remembered she has an audience. "Sorry. I didn't mean to ramble."

Sawyer massages his jaw some more. "No, no. It's interesting. I've never seen it done this way."

He glances up at me and raises his eyebrows, silently asking if it's okay to talk Moondog with these girls. Not happening. The way Shay went Terminator on me earlier, I have no doubt she has the potential to tip the crazy scale. I shake my head and Sawyer glares, but he doesn't break our code.

Lily focuses on our ski jackets. "You guys must be from Vancouver."

"Are you suddenly clairvoyant?" Raven asks.

Lily tips her chin to our jackets. "All their stuff is Moondog. There are three stores in Van, and I think they're planning on opening one in Toronto this summer. Until then, BC is the only place to buy it."

Lily's on the loveseat, Sawyer kitty-corner on the couch, and he inches forward. "So you know Moondog?"

I try to catch his eye, but he won't look my way. *Bastard.* He better not go there.

She shrugs. "They're kind of the hottest thing in outdoor wear these days."

Sawyer drags a hand through his hair. "What do you think of this year's winter line? Of the women's jackets?"

If he didn't ask the question, I probably would have. You can't pay for this type of honest, unbiased feedback. As long as they don't know who we are, I'm all for the intel. But Lily's in no rush to offer her opinion. She picks at a rip in her jeans, until, "I don't know. I mean, it's clever—fashion-forward. But they don't have the pulse on what women want. They design what men *want* women to want, if that makes sense." She cocks her head and studies Sawyer. "Are you in fashion or something?"

I smack the counter and laugh before the dude can screw us over.

The last time we told a random chick we owned Moondog, Nico almost had to get involved; the texts and calls neared stalker level. "*Sawyer?*" I laugh harder. "The guy's in insurance. He just likes to dress nice to impress the ladies."

Nico snorts, but Sawyer seethes. If looks could kill, I'd be riddled with bullets. He plasters on a smile. "Yeah, well, we can't all be fancy hairstylists like you, can we?"

Point and game. *Fucker.* "No you can't," I say, my grin as forced as his.

"What about you?" Raven asks Nico. "Esthetician?"

He chuckles. "Not in this lifetime. I'm a cop."

They're next to each other, on the opposite end of the couch from Sawyer, and she inches closer to Nico. "*That* I can handle."

He hangs his arm over the back cushion, his huge mitt coming to rest on her shoulder. He whispers in her ear, and her hand moves to his thigh. The intimacy of it sends a pang through my chest. Man, do I miss being with a woman. Those quiet moments. The affection. Seeing every season in her eyes and knowing they change for me. Because of me.

"So, hairdresser, huh?" Shay's leaning on the kitchen counter, her hazel eyes no longer stormy.

"Can't deny the passion when it comes calling." I'm going to kill Sawyer.

"Guess not. And you do have good hair." Her gaze lingers on my ponytail, dragging down my long-underwear top and settling on the area around my belt buckle. "Good hair," she says again, her eyes flicking up to meet mine. And *damn*, that look. Lids lowered, lips parted.

The Bitch is flirting.

Maybe today won't be a total fail. Maybe I don't have to wait until tomorrow to break my dry spell. If her quick temper is any indication, Shay is likely a tiger in the sack. I glance over at our friends: Nico and Raven touching any way they can, Lily and Sawyer leaning in close and talking fashion. Sawyer may not be getting any, but I haven't seen him this interested in talking to a chick in forever. They're all going with the flow. I deserve this night as much as they do. Probably more. Shay may be a pain in the ass, but she's easy on the eyes.

I sip my bourbon and step closer, but I can't think of a thing to say. Gripping my glass tighter by the second, I shift on my feet, my neck prickly and warm. Am I this far off my game? Have I lost the ability to flirt? "What do you do?" I ask.

Apparently, I have.

She frowns, the flirty girl nowhere to be seen. "Interior designer," she says, her tone flat. Then she glances over my shoulder, and her eyes spark back to life. "Are those salt and vinegar chips?"

I glance at the bag of Lay's. "Yeah. Help yourself."

A soft sigh later, she's digging into the bag like she hasn't eaten in weeks, and I pour another drink, still on edge. Talking to this girl should be easy. I certainly have no problem giving her a piece of my mind. But she gets me so off balance. And hot. There's something about her charged energy, feisty and unpredictable—one minute barbed, the next teasing. Add to that her moans of pleasure as she eats, and it's getting harder not to press her against the counter and swallow those sounds.

"The plastic isn't edible," I say when she's practically sucking the crumbs from the bottom.

She freezes—jaw set, lips pursed. "I'll eat the plastic if I want, but I appreciate you looking out for my girlish figure."

Holy fucking left field. "Defensive much? It was a joke. I'm sure you've heard of those on the other side of Canada. Man, you're uptight." I want to eat the words the second they're out, but this chick lights me up. I don't talk shit to girls. Ever. Unless it's a friendly back-and-forth, like the sarcastic jousting I do with my assistant, Stella. But today, with the way Shay has hit all my trigger points, I'm earning the nickname Asshole.

"*Uptight?*" she repeats. When the others look our way, she turns her back to them and lowers her voice. "Which one of us is clenching his glass so tight he can barely have a conversation? Your buddies seem pretty nice. Easygoing. But the guy who blindsided me today and can't relax enough to hang out has a serious stick lodged up his ass."

It's one thing to hear this crap from Nico and Sawyer, but to have to take it from a girl who doesn't know me, doesn't know what I've been through? Jesus. I used to be that guy, ditching school to hit the beach, putting off work if it meant more hours sleeping. Now it's all about the schedule—Jackson's, mine. Work dominating every free minute I have. So what if I need a drink to unwind? So what if responsibilities have dampened my ability to let loose? It's called growing up. "That's fresh coming from a girl who can't laugh at herself for downing a bag of chips in record time. I have no problem unwinding when the girl I'm with isn't *Medusa*. And I'm fine with that stick where it is." I may be rusty in the flirting department, but my temper's alive and well.

The air between us sparks, her chest heaving as she crumples the empty bag and flings it in the sink. "You may be hot, but you're just like every other dick who…"

She's on some rant, her voice low and raspy, and I want nothing more than to show her the door, but I can't tear my eyes from the edge of red lace peeking out from the low neckline of her thin, gray top, the swell of her breasts stretching the fabric. The longer she bitches about God knows what, the more her shirt shifts. More red lace. More skin. If I could only grip her hair and expose her neck, I could lick a path until I shut her up with my mouth.

"You're not even listening to me. And my eyes are up here."

Hot and bothered and hard as hell, I crack my neck. "The view's nice down there. Helps me tune out the crazy."

Temper: 2

Flirting: 0

She makes a throaty sound. "God, you're a child. Where's your bathroom?"

"Down the hall. First door on your left. It would be a shame if you got lost along the way."

She snarls at my sarcasm, and I wink.

I've seriously lost my mojo. Marina and I never dated. We fell in love at fifteen and didn't look back. There was no awkward flirting, no need to impress. Aside from our disastrous first year at university where we went to different schools, things were easy. Then with Moondog and the boys, there was never much to it. Sawyer would reel them in, and I'd play along. The past year, though, I'd down at least two fingers of bourbon when out with a girl, always taking a cab so I could relax. I got tired of the effort involved. Tired of never clicking, something missing with each one. *This one hates movies. That one can't ski.* None of them Marina.

But I'm still a guy, and my recent dry spell is taking its toll.

I shift my jeans as I picture that red lace and what Shay must look like beneath it. At least she gets me fired up. Pisses me off, but there's passion there. Maybe enough to block out her tirades and see if there's more behind the eyes she gave me when studying my "belt." Without Jackson and work and my million everyday decisions, I should be able to get my flirt on with her. For one night. I'm in Aspen, for fuck's sake. Putting down my glass, I kick off the counter to catch her when she leaves the bathroom.

Arms crossed, I stand in the hallway and stare at the door, determination setting in. But my mind won't stop spinning.

I'm laid-back. And fun. A fuck of a lot of fun. I'm practically the definition of cool. Another minute passes, and I fist my hands. Another second and I clench my jaw, ready to spit teeth. This chick doesn't know what she's talking about. She doesn't know me from Adam. I'm the guy who spent an entire night slathering butter in the hallways of our frat house and videoed suckers sliding around in the morning. I'm the dude who painted ten plastic tarantulas, making them look insanely real, and planted them at the Sigma Chi house. The boys jumped a mile, their girly screams rivaling any B-horror film.

Shay doesn't know jack about me.

By the time the door swings inward, blood rushes in my ears. She steps toward the hallway, and I'm ready to give her a piece of my mind for, well, *whatever*. She's pushed so many of my buttons; I don't even know why I'm so pissed. Her eyes are downcast, her focus on her tits as she reaches in to adjust that red bra. More lace. More skin.

My anger spins into lust.

Before she looks up, I'm pushing her back into the bathroom and kicking the door shut behind me. I pin her against the counter, our bodies flush, my erection straining, and I'm about to slam my mouth on hers, but reason takes hold. I pull back, unsure why I'm putting the moves on a woman who pretty much hates me. Then she says, "Now's not the time to get shy."

Maybe *hate* is a strong word.

Roughly, I claim her lips. No more talking. No more snarky remarks. Hunger consumes me, every irritation from today releasing as our tongues collide and chests heave. And fuck, *those lips*—even softer than they look, but sure and demanding. I wrap one arm around her waist and cup her breast with my free hand, drawing out a gratifying whimper as I rock against her and tease her nipple through the thin fabric of her shirt. Burning and frantic, we claw at each other. The movement of our hips inches her skirt higher. I grip her waist and lift her onto the sink, her legs falling wide for me, a tease of red peeking out from between her thighs.

Her head falls against the mirror at her back, eyes drifting shut when I drag my hand up her toned leg. "God, yes," she says and shudders as I slip a finger under the lace. Slick wetness greets me.

She rocks against my hand, circling her hips as I slide a second finger in. Gripping my shoulders, she pants, her nails digging through my shirt. I suck a path to her cleavage, and she arches toward me, asking for more. Demanding it. I bite her skin, marking her sensitive flesh, and I pull her neckline lower. Man, that red lace.

"Shit." She jerks forward and rubs her ass where it just hit the tap. I ease my fingers out, eliciting a sigh from her, then she narrows her eyes. "That's courtesy of you, Asshole." She lifts her skirt higher, displaying a purple bruise.

Sharp breaths spike through me as I hike my top and lower the side of my jeans, the yellow tinge on my hip unmistakable. "Back at ya, Bitch."

"Fuck you."

"I thought you were."

She grips my dick over my jeans and gives a squeeze, naughty and damn nice. I sink a hand into her hair and tug harder than necessary, tipping her head so I can taste the smooth skin along her neck. She moans and grips me tighter, and my vision blurs. I grab her ass and haul her to the edge of the counter, her skirt practically at her waist, those fuck-me boots still on, and I'm ready to explode. Fire in her eyes, cheeks flushed, she hooks her legs around my waist and rips the elastic from my hair. Our tongues tangle as I fumble with my belt buckle. When I get it apart, she eases the zipper down, discovering I fly commando. A soft "Jesus" later, she bites my neck, her hand exploring my dick.

And, *fuck*.

My life, this trip, this day, this room…all of it fades. Nothing is left but the heat of her palm fisting me, her needy sounds getting me harder. Reaching between her thighs, I grip the lace, give a solid pull, and tear it in half. I fling it at the door and press my length against her, all that heat and wetness rubbing up and down. *Rocking. Biting. Hands pulling.* Damn right, Shay's a tiger, and I can't wait another second. I inch back just enough, grip her ass, and push in so quick we both gasp. She shoves my jeans farther down and leans back to get me where she wants me. And I want to be here. Right here. I don't ease in and out of her, don't take it slow. I latch one arm around her hips, plant my other palm on the mirror behind her, and drive so hard she clutches my shoulders to keep from falling.

She's barely able to move as I plunge deeper with each thrust. Her leather boots scratch the bruise on my hip, her hand in my hair, tugging hard. Just the tip of her red lace bra pokes out, but her tits bounce in time to our rhythm. Heat gathers at my spine, shooting south. *So fucking close.* Her hips roll, both of us panting heavier. A sheen of sweat glistens on her neck. Knowing I won't last, I slip my hand from the mirror and guide my thumb between us. She squeezes her knees tighter and clamps her teeth on my shoulder. Her muffled cries push me over the edge, her body convulsing. Liquid fire lights through me. I pump into her harder, faster, my knees almost giving out, my mouth in her hair as I try not to scream the *Christ* and *Shay* and *fuck*s I can't swallow. We collapse forward onto each other.

Five

Shay

Oh, my God. *OhmyGodOhmyGodOhmyGod*. What the hell just happened? I mean, besides the best orgasm of my life. Carefully, Kolton pulls out of me, and I have to watch. Every inch. His flesh is still rigid and flushed, the taut skin glistening…the *bare* taut skin.

Oh.

Shit.

My breath quickens again as I shake my head and blink. How could he—*we*—have done this? How could we have been so careless? One night of fun, and I forget my head and everything I know about safe sex. This guy's a complete stranger.

Frustrated with myself and him, I say, "I'm on the pill, thanks. Nice of you to ask."

He glances down at his release spilling down my thigh. "Shit."

"My thoughts exactly. I can't believe I just let some player screw me in a bathroom without protection. Am I at least the first girl you've had tonight?" *Dammit.* I should've used the bat-condom signal, and I can't remember what code the girls and I chose for when we needed to leave. The giraffe sound? Was that it? I hop off the counter, yank down my skirt, and glance around for a washcloth.

"Look, Shay. I'm clean. I don't sleep around. I don't have unprotected sex." He zips up his jeans, grabs a towel off the wall, dampens it, and reaches to hand it to me.

I don't move. "Then what was that?"

"That was…" He places the towel on the counter and rakes his hair—the strands that were tangled in my fingers moments ago. I should be storming out of here, but a delicious ache still throbs between my thighs, my scalp tingling from where he tugged my curls, and I want to feel him again. And *see* him. The thickness of his shoulders, his backside that flexed under my grip.

This guy muddles my sensibilities.

His dark eyes roam my face, almost questioning. "That was…amazing," he finally says. "And spontaneous. And stupid." He leans his shoulder into the wall opposite the sink. "You were a willing participant, by the way. So don't put it all on me. We were *both* careless."

Like I need the reminder. And like I need to stand here and listen to his accusing tone. The same tone I *probably* used with him. When it comes to Kolton, though, my temper flares at will. I snatch the cloth from the counter. "Says the guy who still won't admit he ran me off the hill. Turn around, please."

He rolls his eyes and swivels.

When I'm cleaned up, I crack open the door. "Guys!"

"What the fuck?" Kolton leans over me to shut the door, but I shake him off.

A few *what*s float from the living room, and I lean my head out. "*If* I sleep with your boy Kolton, do I have to worry about where his junk has been?"

"Jesus, subtle much?" Kolton says from behind me.

One of the guys, Sawyer, I think, says, "*Kolton?*" like it's the funniest thing he's ever heard. When his laughter subsides, he continues, "Well, I don't know. Can you get an STD from excessive masturbation?"

"Bastard." Kolton's hot breath hits my ear. "Happy?"

The same voice drifts in as I close the door. "Just go easy on him, Shay. It's probably pretty sore and chafed."

Hooting and hollering persist as I face Kolton. "Nice."

He shakes his head, attention fixed on the ground, then he peeks up. "It's been a while, okay? But when I've been with girls, I've always used condoms. Just not this time." He invades my space, his firm chest too firm, his perfect hair too perfect. With my height and boots, we're almost eye level. "What about you?" he says, his mouth inches from mine. "Should I be grilling your friends to find out if my dick's gonna fall off? What's *your* sexual history?"

Images of Richard on top of me—*only on Fridays and Sundays*—turn my stomach. The lights were always out, my nightgown partly on, and he'd grunt and thrust at the same angle, the same speed, and in the same bed. As many orgasms were faked as were real. It was white-cotton-bra sex, and I'm not sharing that with the guy I just fucked on the counter. "I'll say this. I was in a relationship for five years, and we broke up recently. You're the first guy I've been with since." If I never think about the Dick again, it will be too soon.

This trip is about moving on and having fun, not rehashing this crap. If Kolton and I can stop yelling at each other for five minutes, there's a chance he could help me do just that. "You know what? We were stupid, but it was fun. And I think—"

"Shhhh." He swats the air by my face and cocks his head. "Is that the phone?"

I strain my ears and hear what could be ringing.

He checks his watch, one of those manly jobs with a thick leather band, then he jerks his head up. "Shit." He shoulders me out of the way, knocking me into the wall, and lunges for the door. Then he's gone.

Jesus C.

The guy screws me—*sans* condom—then he blows past me to grab the phone. He wasn't wearing a ring and there was no telltale tan line, but he could still have a girlfriend back home, a relationship like Lily's that's all history and no heat. His buddies could be covering for him, pushing him to get some action. Our bathroom-counter sex was hot. Give-up-chocolate hot. The way my body's still buzzing, there's no denying that. But here I am, brushed aside by another man, arrogant tone and all. Yeah, it was fun. I embodied the red bra. Still, I'm a marionette, my emotions being pushed and pulled by a guy. Moving on means a break from all that. Kolton can go back to jerking off. For the rest of this trip, it's just me and the girls.

I adjust my top again, smooth my skirt, and inhale through my nose, releasing my breath to the count of ten. I square my shoulders and leave the scene of the crime.

Kolton's quiet voice drifts through a closed door, but I keep walking. I stop at the kitchen counter and wait for someone to notice me. I might as well be invisible. Lily and Sawyer are head to head, deep in conversation, both of them gesturing with their hands. At the other end of the couch, Nico whispers in Raven's ear as she inches her hand up his thigh. I clear my throat, and *nada*. "I left my credit card at the restaurant," I say, and all heads snap my way.

Nico sits taller and shifts his massive frame closer to Raven. "There's a phone book by the fridge. You should call."

I lock eyes with Lily, my best ally. "I don't remember the name of the place, and I don't want to wait."

Lily glances at Sawyer and sucks on her bottom lip. *Not* a good sign. "Are you sure?" she asks and unleashes her doe eyes. "Have you checked your jacket?"

Unbelievable. Lily, of all people, should have my back. Always worried about upsetting Kevin, she never flirts. Even when I was with the Dick, I'd smile and engage guys if I was out. Harmless entertainment. Lily, on the other hand, would brush off advances with her *I have a boyfriend*, and I'd get up and go if she was uncomfortable. Apparently, that street doesn't flow both ways. "Yeah, Lil, I'm sure. Never been more sure of anything in my life. We need to go. Now." I glance back, dreading Kolton's imminent return.

She and Raven exchange looks, then both girls get up and offer sad smiles to the boys.

As awkward good-byes are shared, I hurry to my jacket, shrug it on, zip it up, and push back my mop of hair. The curls catch in my fingers. With a grunt, I yank them through, and my scalp burns, reminding me too much of that bathroom, Kolton's hips, and my raspy name on his lips as he came undone. I say something about needing air and push out the door. Calf-deep in snow, I suck back icy breaths.

Kolton nailed it when he said tonight was amazing…and stupid. I let loose, spontaneous yet reckless, proving I can do it. Now it's time to focus on me. My career needs a jumpstart, and since Lily and Raven finished school and moved to Toronto, we haven't hung out as much as I'd like. It's time to get my life together, quit my soul-sucking job, and spend time with my friends.

I'm almost at the end of the block of condos when they come jogging through the snow. Raven grabs my shoulder and spins me around. "You okay? What went down in there?"

The girls know every detail of my mundane sex life, down to that face the Dick makes when he's coming. (We nearly died laughing when I did the impression.) But this, tonight, is too raw. I have to get my head straight before I can talk it out. I kick at the fluffy snow. "Like I said, the dude's an asshole, on the hill and off."

Raven rolls her hand like, *carry on.*

"He's hot," I say, admitting the obvious, and the girls stare at me, unblinking. "And we made out, okay? I thought about taking it further, but we can't talk for two minutes without reenacting *Mr. and Mrs. Smith*. I needed to leave."

"He *does* look a little like Brad Pitt, doesn't he?" Lily says. "Him and Sawyer both. With the sandy hair and full lips, those three could be brothers."

"You seemed smitten talking to Sawyer," I say, jumping on the chance to change the subject. "Like really into your conversation. And you didn't want me to look for my 'credit card.'"

Her eyes dart around as Raven leans into her space. "Yeah. What were you two talking about so intently?"

On a sigh, Lily says, "Nothing. It was nothing. We just talked fashion. Design stuff. He's pretty into outerwear for an insurance guy." She starts walking, clearly as interested in rehashing her night as I am.

"I'm totally into Nico," Raven says as we traipse after Lily. "In case either of you sluts cares to ask. And the six of us are going out tomorrow night. I need to see that man naked."

I stop and grab her shoulders. "Ex-squeeze-me?"

Raven pouts and holds her hands in prayer. "Come on. I never ask for anything. And I promise not to rag on you and Lil about your ex-boyfriend and her current boyfriend for the rest of the trip. I mean, I know you and Kolton are oil and water, but maybe you just need to get to know him better. And I *really, really, really* want to go out with Nico. We came to Aspen to have fun, and it's not like we'll ever see these guys again. Even Lily hit it off with Sawyer. Platonically," she adds when Lily makes a face. "What do you say?"

The snowboard dude on the lift was right. Tossing that bra was all kinds of karmic. How stupid of me to think I could slip out the door and avoid the Asshole Who Fucked Me on the Sink for the rest of this trip. Especially since Raven has her sights locked on Nico. Another notch for her ever-growing belt. Plus, how can I say no to the girl who called in sick for two days to eat ice cream with me after my epic dumpage? I'll just have to be mature and deal with Kolton like an adult. People have casual sex all the time.

I release her shoulders. "Fine. Groveling doesn't suit you. But I'm sitting at the opposite end of the table from the douche. I need a break from guys. So don't play matchmaker with him and me or anyone else." I blink frost from my lashes, the steady snowfall unrelenting. "I'm catching first tracks tomorrow. You guys in?"

Lily shakes her head. "I'll stick to the groomed trails. I don't think my thighs can take it."

"Yeah. I don't want to tucker myself out before tomorrow night," Raven says, a sly grin rounding out her cheeks. "Is it okay to meet for lunch?"

"Fine by me. I'm not missing the good stuff."

We hunch lower and finish our trek to the condo. Earlier, I was worried I'd go to sleep and wake up as the old Shay, poised and proper. Meek and passive. If I'm going to get through another night, and possibly more, hanging out with Kolton, I better not have buried that girl too deep. Our combustible chemistry leads to poor choices. If I rein myself in, I can endure a few nights with him and his bad attitude—*and killer lips and rock-hard build*. He says one thing to piss me off, though, and God help him.

Six

Shay

Legs on fire, I push off the chairlift, thrilled there's only one more run between me and a cafeteria filled with greasy food. I can already taste the bacon cheeseburger I'll be ordering. I lick my lips, wishing I'd met the girls for lunch when they texted me an hour ago, but two feet of fresh powder on Aspen Mountain takes priority. And it's been therapeutic. The Kolton fiasco is ancient history—the Absentee Condom Incident, our arguments, and his disappearing act are long forgotten. When I see him tonight, it won't be weird or awkward. I don't care if he has a girlfriend back home. That's his bed to sleep in. I don't want to know a thing about him or his history, and since we've worked out whatever sexual tension was between us, maybe we'll even get along. Anything for my friends.

Aiming for the run under the chair and the untracked snow I

spotted to the left, I urge my burning thighs on. I lean back just enough and float downhill. Snow flies up midchest as I bounce through the fluffy powder. The stuff of dreams. At home, skiing through a snowfall this thick would be like plowing through sludge. In Aspen, it's like dancing a waltz. My tired thighs fade to the background, each turn making me giddy. My bad choices last night and my crappy job and the Dick don't exist out here. Out here, it's just me and the slopes.

By the time I make it down and rack my skis, my belly rumbles. The smell of charred meat drifts from the lodge, and I hightail it inside as fast as my ski boots will allow. *Clunk. Clunk. Drag. Clunk.* Elegant I am not.

With all the basic food groups present and accounted for in the cafeteria—salty, greasy, sweet, and breaded—it's hard to know where to start. Ten minutes later, my biceps ache under the weight of my tray. I scan the busy space, taking in the massive windows and cathedral ceiling. Whoever designed this lodge checked all the country-chic boxes.

Thick wood beams. Fireplace. Accented stone wall.

Predictable. Tired. Done to death.

In my mind, I swap the beams for detailed ironwork, the dark wood walls for a sleek white stain. I replace the chairs with barnboard benches, their wide legs made up of the same funky iron. In my mind, I rock the shit out of this room. My strained arms dip as I shake the images away. I plop my lunch on an empty table and toss my helmet and gear next to it, then I take my seat. I'm dying to stuff my face, but this type of meal requires planning. The fries have to be last. That's a no-brainer. And the burger needs to be in and around my mouth now…so burger, then chicken fingers, pizza, Mars Bar, and the fries for the big finish. There's no chance I'll finish half of this, but I couldn't resist tasting it all.

Credit cards were invented for a reason.

I double-fist the burger, juice dripping on my tray as I ease the beefy, bacony awesomeness toward my mouth. And *God*, that first bite. The salt and char mingle with the cheese and doughy bun, and I've landed in heaven.

Then I hear, "Where's the rest of your ski group?"

I'm pretty sure the Asshole doesn't have the password to get past my Pearly Gates (last night aside). The chewed lump of meat settles in my throat as I try to gulp it down. Two massive sips of my *non*–Diet Coke later, I manage to swallow. "Can I help you?"

"Just wondering where the ski team is that's sharing all this food." Without an invitation, Kolton sits opposite me, eyes twinkling. He puts his helmet and jacket beside mine and leans on his elbows. His perfect hair flops forward.

He may be teasing me about my smorgasbord, but it touches too close to everything that is the Dick.

I take the biggest bite I can and tip my head back, chewing and moaning in ecstasy. Still hamming it up, I put down the burger, wipe my hands, and plant my elbows on either side of my tray, mirroring his position. Without a word, I stick to my plan and grab a chicken finger. I roll it around the plum sauce and take a massive bite. "*Mmmmmmm…*" Sounds of pleasure escape as I chew, never breaking eye contact with Kolton. His full bottom lip drops open. Next, I tear a section from the pizza and deposit it on my tongue, making sure to suck every drop of grease from my fingers. Then it's a bite from the Mars Bar and a handful of fries, and Kolton is watching me like he paid fifty bucks at a peep show.

His hand disappears below the table as he shifts on his seat, my irritation suddenly less pronounced. There's something down there I'd like in my mouth, too. It's an involuntary reaction, almost animalistic. Until he extricates his hand, reaches across the table, and grabs some fries.

I smack his wrist, but he doesn't drop them. "Hands off, buddy."

He shoves the bounty into his mouth and chews slowly, matching my glare. "You should share. Wouldn't want you to…what did you call it last night? Harm your 'girlish figure'? I think you said it before we had sex in the bathroom, which was before you took off without a word. Maybe you remember?"

This guy. Just like last night, being around him gives me whiplash: I hate him, I want him, then I hate him again. "Yeah, I remember. I think I said that when you got all up in my face about eating the same chips you probably devour, like it's okay for a guy but not a girl. And I'm pretty sure it was before you dropped me to answer the phone, which was *after* you fucked me on a sink. Without a condom. Is that the comment of which you speak?" I pick up the Mars Bar and inhale another bite.

He pulls his head back and winces. "Shit. I'm sorry. The phone call threw me off. It was—"

I hold up my palm. "Not another word," I say around a mouthful of chocolate. "I don't care. Seriously. Last night happened, and it's over. I don't care who was on the phone. I don't want us to sing 'Kumbaya' and hold hands as we share our deepest and darkest. Apparently our friends have hit it off, which means we have to pretend we don't hate each other for"—I squint as I do the mental math—"another four nights, if they insist on hanging out, and then we can return to our opposite sides of Canada and forget we ever met. Sound good?"

He flexes his jaw and taps his fingers on the table. "Sure. No problem, *friend*. Wouldn't want a repeat of the bathroom, anyway. Jerking off is more fun."

His irate tone flips my childish get-in-the-last-word switch. As a kid, I was shy and insecure with my friends. Not with my family. Road trips rolled to the sound track of my mother's "That's enough, Shay," as I'd nudge and taunt my older brother, Thomas, often singing in his ear. He'd never rise to the bait, but my ability to annoy had no bounds.

Any thoughts of acting mature and getting along are *so* done. "Says the guy who used the word *amazing* in the aftermath. At least one of us got off."

"Says the girl whose teeth tore through the shoulder of my long-underwear top to stop from screaming. And since we're *friends*, I'm sure you won't mind sharing some of the heart-attack-on-a-tray you're inhaling." He grabs the pizza, ignoring my *what*s and *hey*s and *get your own*s.

Twenty minutes later, having not said another word to each other, all that's left is a bite of burger and two chicken fingers between us. He tries to eat the last few fries, but I'm faster. I shove them into my mouth, eliciting a deep belly laugh from him. His cheeks crease and the corners of his eyes crinkle, the softening of his features sending a flutter up my spine. An unwelcome flutter. Last night's lesson was loud and clear: *Keep away from boys.* Then Kolton unleashes his sexy laugh, and I'm ready to muzzle the rational voice in my head.

I stand, knocking my knee into the table, and hurry to the bathroom to get some distance. Not the best choice. One look at the sink and tap, and I'm back in his condo getting thoroughly fucked. *God.*

One second I want to smother him with a pillow, the next I want to make him laugh just to hear that sound and maybe visit another restroom. And I have to spend the night with him.

Damn karmic bra.

Taking my sweet time, I retie my ponytail, apply some lip balm, and leisurely heel-toe it over in my ski boots, fingers crossed Kolton's gone. But he's still here, all six feet of him, gear on, leaning that fine booty against *my* table.

He tosses me my anti-sexy helmet. "We should take another run before we head down."

I catch it and shake my head, unsure I heard him right. "Sorry, *we*? Shouldn't you be skiing with your buddies? It's bad enough you hijacked my lunch and I have to sit at a table with you again tonight. Now you want to ski together? Thanks but no thanks."

He lifts his arms over his head and stretches from side to side. A sliver of skin peeks out below his jacket. "The guys called it quits early. Worried you can't keep up?"

As fucking if. The dude's obviously egging me on, but he snaps my self-control. Everything between us is action, reaction. Spark and flame. What's his deal, anyway? Why sit with me and ski with me when we're worse than cats and dogs? If he thinks firing me up means he's getting a replay of last night, he's mistaken. Still, I need to beat his ass on the slopes. "Fine. I'll take that run. It's about time I put you in your place. But let's be clear. We can have lunch and ski together, but there will be no sex." A teen walking by stops midstride and doubles over in a fit of giggles.

"I didn't catch that." Kolton leans forward and cups a hand around his helmeted ear. "Do you mind speaking up?"

What a total douche.

"Everyone is wise until he speaks," I mumble, recalling my grand-dad's words.

Kolton straightens, a question passing across his face. "Are you Irish? My granddad used to say that all the time. Along with, 'Shut your mouth and eat your dinner.'"

I laugh, abrupt and maniacal, the sharp sound catching me off guard. The energy shifts between us, like the first time I understood my Spanish teacher—the foreign becoming familiar. I frown, unsure I want Kolton to feel familiar. "Yeah, I am. The first curse I learned was *feckin' arse*, and I'd kind of like to use it now."

He smiles to himself, as though we're friends who would sit and talk and laugh about our shared upbringing. Ruffled, I cram my helmet on, get geared up, and try to stomp out of the lodge all *look out, buddy*, but with the boots and Martian head, it's a fail.

Skis on and goggles down, we race to the lift. He arrives first, making like he's been waiting forever with a dramatic yawn. I roll my eyes and push past him. The lift line is empty, so it's just him and me on the four-person chair.

"Mind not doing that?" he says partway up as I swing my skis.

The chair sways in response, and I rock my legs harder. "This?"

His olive skin grays. "Yeah. That." He leans his elbows on the safety bar and closes his eyes.

If he pukes, I'll likely toss my cookies, too. When my brother got food poisoning from China House's all-you-can-eat buffet, it wasn't pretty. I hadn't eaten a thing there, but the second he threw up, I proceeded to reenact that pie eating scene from *Stand by Me*: projectile vomit, solid stream, fire hydrant force.

I still my skis and stop bouncing.

We pass one supporting tower, then another, before he opens his eyes.

"You regretting that lunch?" I ask, smirking.

He flexes his hands, and the poles dangling from his wrists knock around. "No. I'm regretting getting on this chair with you."

Such a charmer. "Then you shouldn't have taunted me with the thrill of skiing circles around you." He goes to fling his hands in exasperation, but his poles smack the bar. "And if you've actually skied before," I say, "you would know to take your straps off when getting on a lift." I motion to the poles tucked under my thigh.

"That's bullshit."

"No. That's safety. If a pole gets stuck getting on or off a lift, it could drag you along with it. But you wouldn't know much about safe *anything*, would you?" I don't say sex, but I don't have to.

Our eyes meet at my acknowledgment of our illicit encounter. His tongue skims his lips, and my body heat congregates between my thighs. He doesn't reply. "That's what I thought," I say as I struggle to sit still. This guy is too sexy for his own good. And mine. I may want to throttle him, but I want to kiss him, too. More than I ever remember longing to lock lips with Richard. But kissing Kolton leads to recklessness.

Muttering to himself, he tips his head back and then grabs his left pole and tries to yank it off. The loop around his wrist snags on his gloves. The Good Samaritan I am, I reach over to help. Unfortunately, we move at the same time—me pushing and him pulling—and the pole slips…then falls.

"Fuck." He leans over, arm extended, as it sinks into the forest below us. He jerks up and swivels toward me. "What is wrong with you?"

There's that tone again, the know-it-all gene that must only survive in overactive testosterone. With him, though, our heated words send my libido into overdrive. "Me?" Eyebrow cocked, I jab a gloved hand at my chest and attempt to ignore the moisture developing south of the border. "*I* was just helping out. If you had your poles off from the start, this wouldn't have happened."

He snorts out a laugh, one of those angry, she-can't-be-for-real laughs. He lowers his voice in challenge. "So this is *my* fault? You crawling up my ass about removing the straps and then flinging my pole off the chair is somehow *my* fault? How do you figure?"

When he puts it that way…

But fighting with Kolton isn't about right or wrong, true or false. It's about knocking his Y chromosome down a peg, the one he shares with the Dick. Either that or I sign up for one of those self-defense classes where I get to beat the crap out of a dude in a sumo suit. Unfortunately, our aggressive banter also inflames my lust. "If you stashed your attitude and weren't yanking at the thing to prove a point, I could've grabbed it."

"Right. Attitude. That's rich coming from a girl who fucks me, explodes around my dick, and claims she didn't get off." He adjusts his pants, but he can't hide the thickness pressing against his zipper.

Not good.

Rage powers my lungs, and my nipples tighten in response, undermining my Y-chromosome attack. Like each sharp word between us is foreplay. His chest rises as fast as mine, the air around us snapping with desire, and I need those full lips against mine. Now. I need his hands between my thighs, the urgency all-consuming. (Apparently, my no-boys motto jumped ship with that pole.) No longer caring about last night or potential regret, I grab his jacket and try to kiss him. Thanks to our goggles and helmets, my spontaneous move has us bouncing off each other like bumper cars. That doesn't stop Kolton. He adjusts and leans forward, clutching me awkwardly. His teeth scrape my lip as we connect in a desperate kiss, our groans rising and falling with our breaths.

He pulls me closer, our bodies twisted toward each other, his remaining pole getting in the way. He presses into me with so much force I almost have to lie down. Thank God the couple chairs in front and behind us are empty. Although I doubt I'd stop if we had an audience.

"Touch me," I say, the words escaping on gasps of air.

He goes to grab my thigh, but his pole rattles around again. "Fuck it." He shakes the strap off his wrist and drops the thing over the side, not bothering to watch it fall. He reaches between my thighs, and I wiggle on the chair, rocking against the movement of his hand, but it's not enough. "Unzip my pants, Kolton. Please."

He steals another kiss and seems about to make his move but pulls back. "First admit I rocked your world last night."

Cheeky bastard. "What if you didn't? What if I'm that good at faking it?"

He presses his hand exactly where I'm aching for him, the rhythm and heat and dampness too much, then he scoots away, taking those skilled fingers with him. "Then I guess we're done here." But his dark eyes flash with hunger.

I try to hold out. Really, I do. I replay every stupid argument—how he comments on my eating like the Dick, that exasperated tone he uses. The phone call that had him leaving me in the lurch. But I'm not that strong, and needs are needs, so...

Since I can't grab his hair or straddle him to rock against the hard-on he's sporting, I drag the poles from under my thighs and let them join his in the abyss below. I scoot right beside him and palm his erection over his ski pants. "I still kind of hate you, and talking to you is up there with memorizing Shakespeare, but last night? I've never come so hard, and if you don't stick your hand down my pants, I'm sending you after those poles."

He grins. "Knew it."

He removes his glove, shoves it into his jacket, then his mouth crushes mine as he undoes my zipper and wiggles his hand beneath my long underwear. "God, you're wet," he says against my lips, the most delicious sounds humming from his chest.

I clutch the safety bar and roll my hips into his fingers, the circling and rubbing making it hard to sit still. He presses his helmet to mine, whispered words floating between us. "Last night," he says. "That red lingerie and those boots." Two thick fingers plunge inside of me, finding the spot that's been neglected far too long. "I had to fuck you. I couldn't stop." He changes the angle of his fingers and my insides clench, my calves so tight they cramp. "Does this feel good, Shay? Do you like it?"

His thumb strokes harder, and I whimper. "So good. Don't stop."

"I won't, baby. I won't stop. I want to feel you explode around my fingers. I want to hear you scream my name this time."

I place my hand over his, increasing the pressure. One stroke later, my hips buck—my movements no longer voluntary. Electricity ignites my nerves. Air traps in my throat.

"Come for me. Let go."

"God, Kolton, *yes*." The second I say his name, a wave of pleasure rushes through me. I keep my hand on his as my hips jerk and he whispers, "Yeah, that's it. So fucking hot."

When the tremors subside, I release my hold on him and he eases out his fingers. And what does he do? He slips them past his lips and sucks on them like they're a Shay Popsicle.

"That was…" At a loss for words, I zip up my pants.

"Mmhm, yeah." He nods and puts on his glove. "I guess we don't have any poles."

We both look down, our equipment long gone.

What do poles cost these days? Fifty? A hundred bucks? That credit card of mine is getting a workout this trip. I glance at Kolton, the outline of his cock still pressing against his pants. If we weren't near the end of the lift, I'd lean over and wrap my lips around those thick inches. I should be hitting the regret stage of this incident, but I still haven't *seen* Kolton in all his naked glory—those shoulders, that backside. His rock-hard chest. The whole no-boys thing might have to wait until after this trip.

He adjusts his new Oakley goggles, the cost of which alone would put my account into receivership. "Now you owe me a pair of goggles *and* poles," he says. "If you don't get your hostility in check, I'll have to keep a running tab."

Hostility? He smirks as though congratulating himself for his clever wit.

"When you admit you ran me off the hill, I'll pay for the goggles." There's that tone of mine again, always hovering below the surface. Always within biting distance. The Dick left his mark on me, all right. One hint someone's bending me to their will or trying to tame me sends my hackles up.

"Jesus. I was joking. Have you always been this stubborn? Let it go already."

A heartbeat ago, I wanted to strip him naked and ride him like a rodeo queen; now I'm wondering if I'd be blamed if I raised the safety bar and he "slipped" off the chair. "I'm not stubborn. It's called having an opinion."

"Or being bull-headed."

"Excuse me?"

"Let's see…you didn't even glance uphill when you merged onto my run and won't admit it. I make a *joke* about what you're eating, and you rant at me for twenty minutes. You launch my pole over the chair and won't cop to it. And it takes blackmail for you to admit you got off last night. So, yeah, the word *bull-headed* comes to mind. And obstinate. And ornery." He leans close, his voice just a whisper. "And passionate. We can add to the list later, if you want." With a wink, he sits back.

He should use his mental thesaurus to look up words for *asshole*. "Now who's not letting go of stuff, huh? Now who's the bull-headed one?" I hate how childish I sound, how irrational, but it's like I've lost control. Like I'm watching myself from afar, unable to tame my outburst.

He groans and grips his helmet, then flings his hands in the air. Carefully, he wraps his fingers around the safety bar. "Just forget it, okay?"

I grunt. "Move."

He gawks at me. "What?"

"*Move*," I repeat. "Unless you want to be stuck together for the trip down. We need to raise the bar."

He looks forward and cocks his head, as though he didn't realize how close we were to the top.

We slip our skis from the footrests, hoist up the bar, and guilt rockets through me. The sweet way he smiled at me when talking about his granddad festers. The confessions he whispered while getting me off linger, too. Another time in our lives and we'd maybe get along. Maybe even go on a date. Kolton's teasing doesn't warrant my biting attitude and irate replies. He doesn't deserve to be my target practice. But he's here and the Dick isn't, and my anger has taken on a life of its own.

Five seconds from the top, I say, "We have to tolerate each other at dinner tonight, but there will be no sex of any kind. Ever again. We don't exactly bring out the best in each other." Then I add, "I'm skiing down on my own." Avoiding eye contact, I push off the lift and ski as quickly as I can (without my poles), leaving him behind.

I'll get through tonight and the next few days, but hooking up is off the table. No more sex. No more fooling around. Clearly, I'm not in the right mental state to be with a guy. Kolton will only get caught in the crossfire.

Seven Hours Later

"Lift up from the snow, Shay…a bit higher and…fuck, yes. Like that. Damn, you feel good."

The Next Morning

"*Leg, leg, leg.* Move left. Jesus, Kolton. Just…yeah. *Harder.*"

In the Trees

"I'm so deep inside of you. So fucking deep."

Bathroom, Round Two

"Quiet. They'll hear us. No, no…don't stop…"

Somewhere in Aspen

"Faster."
  "Deeper."
    "*Shay.*"
    "Kolton!"

Seven

Kolton

"You have a race today?" Shay smiles at the young girl between us on the chairlift as if we didn't just fuck like rabbits in the trees thirty minutes ago.

"No, just training. Season's pretty much over." The girl hunches forward, her tight racing suit pulling at her shoulders.

I don't participate in the conversation. My mind is still on Shay's ass in the air, her hands wrapped around that tree, my body covering hers. It's a good thing this kid's between us.

Shay sighs as if caught in a memory. "I hated that part. Knowing that dry-land training was all I'd have to look forward to over the summer, itching for it to snow again."

The girl tilts her head in Shay's direction, sunlight glinting off her helmet. "You raced?"

"Yep."

My ears prick up. The way Shay skis, I'm not surprised she raced. We just don't spend much time talking. Arguing, yes. Groping, fuck yeah. Talking, limited. I've glimpsed easygoing Shay. When we had to ride the lift with a couple of ski-school kids, she was sweet and charming and chatted with them the whole way. When the six of us went out last night, she joked with Raven and Lily, her quick wit and raspy laugh infectious. But with me, the second she relaxes and lets me in, I say or do something wrong. Then she bites and I bark, and we can't grope each other fast enough.

Dynamite is less explosive.

The girl between us laughs. "I'm totally the same. Hate the summer. Love the winter. Wrenched my knee recently, so I'm just doing basics now. Lots of physio."

Shay winces. "I had a bad knee injury the year before I won the Whistler Cup." She nudges the girl's arm with her elbow. "Maybe next year will be your year."

I can't take my eyes off Shay now. Ski racer. Whistler Cup winner. Who is this woman? Instead of picturing my dick sinking inside of her, I'm imagining her barreling down a race course, skis chattering in ruts as she holds her line into her next turn. I want to know more, ask more, but I don't want to shut her down.

The two of them talk racing the rest of the ride, and I listen, riveted. We push off at the top, the area almost empty. Last chair of the day, last run. I'm about to ask Shay where she wants to head when my phone buzzes. I pull it out of my pocket and frown at Nico's text:

Hate to do this, but I gotta get home. Shit's going down with Josh. Again. I'm flying out in an hour. We'll connect in Van. Best to Shay.

"Nico's flying home," I say.

"Seriously? Why?"

By the time I pocket my phone and look up, she's glaring at me like *I* just split on her. "He has some family stuff going on. Needs to get back."

Still, she levels me with a scowl. "What about Raven?"

I shrug. "Don't ask me." Nico's brother is always getting into trouble, the two of them like night and day. Nico going home means whatever Josh did it was bad, and Nico's going to rake him over the coals.

She curls her lip in annoyance. "Boys are oblivious. I think she really liked him."

"*I'm* not oblivious. I know for a fact you like me."

Her eyes practically roll to the back of her head. "I can tolerate certain parts of your body."

Personally, I'd like to tolerate a whole lot more of Shay. I've seen so little of her skin. We're always so harried and frantic, it's all we can do to get naked enough so I can push into her. *Jesus*, do I want to see her, though; laid out under me on a bed, her curls fanned over a pillow.

Aaaaaaand now I'll have to ski with a hard-on.

But riling her up is too much fun. "Which parts, exactly?"

Her gaze drifts down my body, skirting the bulge in my ski pants. "You might have a hot ass."

"You might have the most beautiful eyes I've ever seen."

The hazel stunners in question widen, a burst of cold air curling from her lips. I'm not sure why I said it. I'm not sure why I don't want to take it back. There's not much I understand about my feelings toward Shay.

Her uncharacteristic silence doesn't last long. "I can't accept compliments from men who watch infantile movies in which explosions outnumber scenes with dialogue."

Back on the movies again. She overhears one conversation I have with the boys about our love of the Rambo series, and it's like tossing a dog a steak. She won't let it go. "There's a reason movies like that do well in theatres. Blowing things up is cool."

"For sixteen-year-olds, maybe. You seriously like that stuff?"

I push closer and lean into her space. "It's all about the climax. The big detonation. Matter of fact, watching you ignite is up there with watching *Rambo*. I'd never lie about liking that."

And she can't lie about the flush of her cheeks and the smile she's barely hiding. Avoiding my heated stare, she dusts off her ski pants, swiping at the snow and bark lodged on her knee from our extracurricular activities.

I've had good sex before. *Great* sex. But I've never experienced the kind of desperation she inspires, the heat that drives our frenzied hands and mouths—raw and rough and spontaneous in the trees, the snow, or a bathroom. Most of the time, I can't decide if I want to throttle Shay or fuck her, but there's a pull between us, an elastic force that's got me hooked. In three days.

"Where to?" I ask, needing to get skiing before I *do* detonate in my pants. One light touch from her is all it would take. But now I'm envisioning her naked ass again, so I add, "Unless you want to skip the skiing and find another wooded area."

I hold my breath, waiting for her to bite my head off. Instead, she winks at me. "I think you're sporting enough wood for the whole forest."

My dick twitches, always up for a challenge. She spins with a laugh and skis off.

I skate after her, pushing off on my poles, working my legs to gain momentum. I pick up speed until I'm a ski's length behind her, matching her turn for turn, rising and falling in time. I'm entranced, fixated on her effortless movements—up, down, up, down—like we're dancing, together but apart. As we near a precipice, the hill dropping into the unknown, she gathers speed, leaning forward to rocket off the edge. Her skis leave the snow. I mimic her moves, catching air. Time suspends—a beat where I flash back to the trees, her cries, and how good she felt. Then I land. Hard. Wrong. Random mounds dot the top of the slope before it narrows into an intense mogul run. Not what I expected. The tips of my skis crank into one of the bumps, sending me onto my side. Onto my shoulder. The one that pops out.

Shit.

My strangled cry explodes before I can stop it. No matter how many times I dislocate my shoulder—this makes four—the sharp pain always winds me. For a moment, I can't breathe. Tingling crawls up and down my right arm, now limp at my side. I imagine a gunshot wound would hurt less. Slowly, I swallow and open my eyes.

"Kolton!" Sounds of ski boots crunching on snow follow Shay's frantic voice. "Are you okay? Are you hurt?" She falls to her knees beside me, goggles on her helmet, her long hair falling toward my chest. Her eyes, those green and brown and gold eyes, dart over my prone body.

"I'm fine," I manage. "Just a dislocated shoulder. I've done it before." I should be embarrassed I fell (although it's her fault for distracting me), but it's all I can do to grit my teeth as I prepare for the agony that will follow. Every time I pop my shoulder back in, I nearly puke, and Nico calls me a pussy. Cold sweat builds at my temples.

She frowns. "*Just* a dislocated shoulder? Should I ski down to get help?"

I shake my head, my rounded helmet rolling over the hard-packed snow. "No. I can fix it. I just need your help."

Determined, she nods. "At your service." She removes my poles and clicks off my skis, jamming them upright into the snow behind us—a caution sign for any skiers barreling down. Then she's at my side again, gloves off, her soft hands on my face. "What do you need?"

Gone are her snarky remarks and biting tone, genuine concern in their place. Holding my arm to my side, I sit up, dreading the imminent jolt of pain. "You have to anchor me," I say. "Hold my elbow and hand, and rotate my arm back and outward, then pull. If I can actually relax, the ball will pop into its socket."

Lines crease her brow. "If?"

"Yeah, if. The fixing part is worse than the dislocating part. Feel free to call me a chick. Nico always does."

She doesn't. She leans into my ear and whispers, "First, that would be a compliment, you chauvinistic bastard. Second, you may have long hair, but nothing about you is feminine." Then, more quietly, "We've got this."

We. My heart rate spikes. For some reason I like the sound of that.

She removes my glove to grip my hand, then guides my arm into position. "Like this?"

I grunt my approval. Instead of closing my eyes, I focus on her face—the worry in her gaze, the fullness of her lips as she says, "Tell me when."

I suck a breath. "When."

On an exhale, she rotates and tugs…and it pops back in.

Jesus Fucking H Christ.

The pain is instant, like a nail hammered through bone. I clench my jaw and fall back onto the snow as the jolt eases into a throb. I stare at the cloudless sky, Colorado blue. My neck tingles the way it does, nausea building at the base of my throat. Shay still has my hand in her grasp, and she lies down next to me.

"I had a dog when I was little," she says. "Snoopy. He was a cute mutt with brown-black fur and a white belly. Looked nothing like the cartoon character. He was a sweet guy and hated getting in trouble. If one of us raised our voice, he'd slink away, tail between his legs."

My lungs swell and shrink more slowly as she talks, her voice a soothing balm. She shifts closer. "So one time, we were all out, and he must've had a bad stomach. Knowing we'd be mad if he had an accident in the house, he crawled into the bathtub and did his business in there. Shat right in the thing. But he must've slipped on his way out or something, and he fell, you know, *in it*. Then he proceeded to rub his fur on every surface of the house."

I chuckle, still focused on the cobalt blue sky, a wisp of cloud marring its expanse. "Is that supposed to make me less nauseous?"

I can't see her face, but I sense her smile. "Good point. Maybe that wasn't the best story." Eventually, she goes on, "Snoopy was my best friend growing up, until I started racing. It changed everything for me—belonging to a team, fitting in. School wasn't easy for me back then. Can't imagine what I'd be like if my folks hadn't pushed me into it."

I'm not sure why she's opening up, sharing her past. To distract me? To connect? I don't ask questions. This much information from Shay is rare. "Kids can be mean," I say. Whatever the reason for her childhood exile, I know how cruel kids are. How tough things are for Jackson. When you're older, being different is often a badge of honor. When younger, when your skin has yet to thicken, it's a curse.

My nausea dissipates, my shoulder good enough to get up and ski down, but I don't want to move. I don't want to get Shay naked or yell at her, either. I just want to *be* with her. Like this. The day near its end, the snow cold and hard beneath us. The few times we've talked about our shared heritage and tossed Irish jokes back and forth, she's let her guard down, even laughing with me. Never losing it, but teasing me with her softer side. Instantly, oddly, I wanted to be the one making her laugh so hard she'd snort. Now I want to freeze time. And I've only known her three days.

"Bucket list," I say to keep her from getting up. "What's your dream ski trip?"

Eight

Shay

Kolton shifts closer when he asks the question, and the snow beneath my hips suddenly doesn't feel so cold. "Chile," I say. "Something about skiing above the tree line in the Andes appeals to me. The old-school lifts. None of the flash and money you see in places like this. It would be awesome."

"Tell me you're fucking around."

I make to sit up, but he puts a hand on my arm, like he wants me here, beside him. I settle against his shoulder. "No, genius, I'm not fucking around. Why?"

"Because that's mine. Chile."

I roll my eyes. "Am I supposed to believe that line? Do other girls fall for that level of Velveeta?"

"I'm serious. I've always wanted to go to Chile. Portillo, actually.

Have you seen pictures of that yellow hotel on the slopes with the outdoor pool right in the mountains?"

I nod, even though he's focused on the deep blue sky. "Yeah. Skiers do jumps into it in the spring. Great resort for big mountain skiing."

"The best. And crazy steep. Lots of backcountry terrain, too."

I sigh. "One day." When I'm not scratching by financially. But I find myself picturing Kolton and me floating through two feet of powder, the dramatic Andes at our backs. Kolton and me in the pool, my legs wrapped around his waist. Kolton and me.

The tips of my fingers are cold, but my palm is warm against his, and his thumb traces lazy circles on my hand. It reminds me of my childhood, my mother writing letters on my back to soothe me when I was sick.

I unlace my fingers from Kolton's hand and write on his palm. A-S-S-H-O-L-E

He smiles, a dimple sinking into his cheek. "Are you trying to tell me something?"

I smile, too. My whole face, my body, feeling warmer than it should on the snow. "As a kid, I used to play this game with my mom. She'd spell words, and I'd have to guess what she wrote. Usually when I was sick. But I loved it. Loved her hands tracing along my back. It was the best part about having a fever. That and missing school."

He takes my hand then, his cool fingertip gliding over my palm, my skin still damp and tepid from pressing against his. B-E-A-U-T-I-F-U-L

Heat shoots through me, like I'm a Canada Day sparkler, colored flames burning bright. The sensation concentrates below my ribs, as if trying to expand. Not wanting to lose this feeling, I take control. I feather my index finger across the expanse of his upturned palm.

Me: S-E-X-Y

Him: F-I-E-R-C-E

Me: U-N-E-X-P-E-C-T-E-D

Him: F-A-S-C-I-N-A-T-E-D

I want to write all over him now, on his powerful forearms, his muscular thighs, the breadth of his chest. Is his heart beating as fast as mine? Has he turned into a sparkler, too?

He laces our fingers, unzips his jacket, and presses my hand against his breastbone. To warm our hands? To answer my unasked question? *Yes, yes, yes* comes his reply, his heart's own Morse code. For right now, nothing matters. Not work. Not the Dick or my dwindling bank account. All that exists is the steady rhythm of Kolton's heart, the racing of mine.

A tree groans, one of the tall white-barked Aspen trees lining the run, breaking my reverie. Reality sets in. "We should probably get going. You okay to ski down?"

He doesn't answer, and I don't move. We lie on our backs, wet snow seeping through our jackets, my hand against his chest.

"Shay," he whispers.

"Umhmm."

"This is nice, don't you think?"

"Yeah," I say before I can catch myself. Too nice. I'm not ready for nice. Tender Kolton is a beast I'm ill-equipped to handle so soon after the Breakup of the Century. One month on my own after five years with Richard is hardly time to heal. I don't know why I told Kolton about my unenjoyable youth, why I let him in just now. Something about his vulnerability, lying here in pain, has me itching to heal him. But this intimacy is suddenly too *intimate*. Too much, too soon. I pull my hand from his.

We're likely the last ones on this run, no stragglers skiing down while we rest. Eventually, Kolton repeats my "We should probably go."

"Do I need to find one of those toboggans to drag your ass down?"

He sits up and rubs his shoulder. "I'm good. In fact, I could still smoke you in a race."

I sit up, too, and glance his way. His profile hasn't changed: strong jaw, the generous curve of his lips, the crease at the corner of his eye. Visually, he's as sexy as ever, like those rugged male models hiking up a mountain, but instead of unzipping his fly, I want to curl into his arms. Instead of yelling at him, I want to kiss his cheek. Instead of doing any of that, I kick his boot with mine. "How about a wager?"

Those chocolate eyes of his shine, his focus on me now, his perusal drifting lower. And lower. Okay, maybe I still want to unzip his fly.

"What's up for grabs?" he asks.

I lean so we're nearly nose to nose, our helmets touching. "If you get to the bottom first, I'm yours for the last day and a half of this trip. If not, them's the breaks." A race I'm happy to lose. I may not be ready to pursue emotional intimacy, but no way am I giving up the best sex I've ever had for the remainder of this trip. In three days, he's become my conductor, my body his symphony. He knows which strokes make me sing, the chords that push me over the edge. In three days, he's given my body more pleasure than the Dick did in five years.

He narrows his gaze, and I raise my eyebrow.

"Deal." Grinning, he jumps to his feet, still babying his arm. "Hope you don't mind a little snow in your face as you eat my dust."

"Like you have a shot. But since you're crippled, I'll give you a head start."

He balks at me. "Not on your life."

We race to our gear, him all awkward with his arm, me struggling to get my equipment straight. There's a *chance* I knock my skis over on purpose. A slight possibility I struggle more than necessary with my bindings. I *maybe* hold back some power when easing into my turns. I totally let the guy win.

Nine

Kolton

Mumford & Sons pump from the speakers as the bartenders put on a show for the packed room. Colorful drinks are poured into vintage glassware, the guys behind the bar looking like they stepped from a 1930s catalogue—bowler hats, vests, and all. I scan the crowd and spot those wild brown curls, the ones that were tangled in my fingers earlier. Shay, Lily, and Raven have their backs to me on the short end of the L-shaped bar, the three of them talking and laughing.

Shay tips her head back, a wide grin softening her face. No trace of annoyance. No frown. Like the way she was lying with me on the hill yesterday. That afternoon, she insisted on coming to the pharmacy to get some pain meds and chatted the whole time. Even last night, she sat beside me at the pasta place Raven chose, including me in conversation, touching my arm or leg to get my attention. It felt…*nice*. When Sawyer brought up my video game record, she laid into me about gratuitous violence and the state of the world.

Thirty minutes later, we were clawing each other in the bathroom.

A blast of cold hits my back. "They here?" Sawyer asks as he steps beside me. I nod to the girls, and he smiles. "What are you waiting for?"

I shrug as they dissolve into another fit of giggles. "Nothing."

He crosses his arms. "Bullshit."

I shove my hands into my jean pockets but don't bother answering.

"Look," he says. "It's obvious you and Shay are messing around. Those fuck-me eyes that pass between you are enough to make me gag, and you've ditched us every day to ski with her."

"Okay. Fine. We've hooked up. Just don't tell Lily and don't let on to Shay you know. She's hell-bent on *not* talking to the girls about it. Something about telling them she's sworn off guys."

"Sure, whatever." He steps back to avoid a server carrying a tray of drinks. "You two going to keep in touch after this?"

Sighing, I dig my hands deeper into my pockets, the tips of my fingers hitting a stray coin. I roll it around. "Nope. When she hops on her flight in four hours, that'll be the last I see of her." Sawyer studies my ticking jaw.

I'm dying to get home to Jackson, but the last four days have been…*unexpected*—the last word Shay wrote on my palm. Lying beside her on the hill, easy and comfortable, is the type of connection I've struggled to find dating. And when she said skiing in Chile was on her bucket list, I almost came in my pants. Just last month, I'd been clicking through the Internet, dreaming about that trip. Then there's the mind-blowing sex.

"Dude, I know Toronto's far, but you'll be there for a couple of months this summer to build out the new shop. I mean, how many times have you bitched about how hard it is to meet chicks? It may have only been four days, but I haven't seen you this interested in a girl in ages. You can't keep your eyes off her."

A pretty blonde with a long black apron tied around her waist steps in front of us. "If you're looking for a table, the wait's pretty long. At least forty-five minutes."

I shake my head. "We're good, thanks. Just meeting some friends at the bar." She smiles and walks off, but Sawyer and I don't budge. I roll the coin in my pocket. "I'm into her, okay? Something about her gets under my skin. But long distance is bullshit. You know what happened with Marina. There's no point pursuing it. And I'm pretty sure this is a vacation fling for Shay. She's probably using me to get over her ex."

"Have you told her about Moondog? Maybe the hairdressing thing isn't working for her."

Sawyer grins, and I jab my elbow into his side. "No, asswipe. I haven't. You didn't say anything to Lily, did you?" He looks down and kicks his foot on the wood floor. *Motherfucker*. "I asked you to keep a lid on it."

He scrubs a hand down his face. "You should hear her, bro. Her design ideas are sick. Really fresh. I couldn't keep listening to her and not engage about Moondog. We're actually planning to work together on some of her ideas, which, by the way, means you need to get the paperwork going to hire her as a freelance designer. She'll work remotely from out east. And before you tear me a new one, she promised not to tell the girls. You can trust her."

I shift on my feet and attempt to rein in my temper. I get where Sawyer's coming from. Lily's designs are innovative and having her on board might do good things for our accessories. Hopefully, he's right when he says she's trustworthy. If she tells Shay what I do and Shay contacts me, my wealth putting dollar signs in her eyes, it would ruin whatever this thing is we have. Or she could be royally pissed I lied to her. "You're a dick, but fine. Does that mean you've charmed your way into Lily's pants?"

He widens his stance and narrows his eyes as two dudes make their way over to the girls. "She's not like that."

I glance over my shoulder and turn in a three-sixty. "Who the hell just said that? The '*I don't work chicks unless they're a sure thing*' Sawyer wouldn't be caught dead speaking those words. Did your balls get snipped?"

"Seriously. I'm not working her. I just…I don't know. I like hanging out. She's different. And anyway, she's got a boyfriend. This is all business."

Business, my ass. His stance is as rigid as mine as those two fuckwits flirting with the girls move in for the kill. Without a word, we push through the crowd. I tap the first guy on his shoulder. "They're with us." Shay rolls her eyes but doesn't contradict me, and Lily's straight spine relaxes. The guys shrug and take off. We hang our jackets on nearby hooks, then Sawyer slides his arm around Lily's high-backed stool.

Raven leans so she can see me from behind Lily. "Territorial much? What if I wanted my breasts ogled?"

Sawyer wiggles his eyebrows. "I thought your type was six foot four, two hundred and seventy pounds, and covered in tats."

Raven winks. "I'm all for diversity. Any word on the big guy?"

It's a casual question, but she asks it too fast. Like she's worried I'll tell him she's poking around. "No," I say. "But no news is good news. When it comes to his brother, Nico's always putting out fires."

Wanting to spend my remaining time with Shay, I turn from the group and lean into her ear. "You packed?" I rub my nose in that spot she likes.

She presses into me and shivers. "Mmmhmm."

I don't ask for her number. Or her e-mail. Or her last name. There's no point. This is the final time I'll see this girl, and for some reason, my chest aches. I nod at her bright green martini. "Is your plan to get drunk enough so you pass out for the flight? Redeyes are a killer."

"Something like that. And redeyes are cheaper, so…" A pause, then, "How's your shoulder today?"

"Tender, but fine. I had a great nurse."

That earns a smile. "Maybe I missed my calling." She holds her drink to her lips, her long hair reaching her waist as she tilts her head to take a sip. I slide my hand along her back and step closer. She doesn't shrug me off, doesn't get snarky. I'd swear her breath catches.

"Today was fun," I whisper as I wrap my arm tighter around her waist. The sound of her crying my name earlier while our skin slapped is filed away for future reference.

She turns her face into my neck, her lips grazing my skin. "I'll take that memory over the ones of you spouting your know-it-all bullshit."

And there's the Shay I know and hate. Not tonight, though. Not for these last hours. Tonight she can goad me all she wants, but I'm not ending this wild fling with an argument. "Agreed," I say.

She pulls back to look at me. "That was refreshing."

I don't reply. Too often, my responses invoke Terminator Shay. Instead, I lean down and kiss her lightly on the lips, the taste of apple lingering from her drink. I don't know why I do it. Aside from that moment on the hill, Shay and I don't do soft and intimate. We don't do affectionate. And the girls are beside us. But it's our last night, and the thought of her leaving is getting more painful by the second. She reaches up and threads her fingers through my hair, pulling me into a deeper kiss. Either she's feeling something similar, or she's responding to my shift in behavior. Whatever the reason, I take full advantage. Lily's "I knew it!" registers, but we keep kissing, slow and intense, as if exploring each other for the first time. The noise and the music and the crowd disappear. There's nothing but us and her soft moans as we move against each other.

I nip her bottom lip, then dip so we're eye to eye. "It sucks you live in Toronto, Shay." She slides her hand from my neck and chews the lip I just had between my teeth. I imagine I'll spend a lot of hours in the coming weeks picturing Shay on the chairlift as she came, as well as in the snow and the bathroom. *Both* bathrooms. But it's the way she lay next to me on that run, talking quietly about her dog and writing on my hand, that lingers now. *Fascinated.* There are so many things about her life I never got to ask.

"Actually," I say, my words leaving before I can contain them, "I might be in Toronto this summer. Maybe we could pick this back up while I'm there?"

She inhales deeply, then her breath rushes out. "I can't even think about that. I don't want to get into it, but my last relationship messed with my head. It's kind of why I've *maybe* been a bit irritable with you. Although you can be a real ass sometimes." She winks.

"I've got a lot to figure out when I get home, including a massive job overhaul."

I nod, almost relieved. Shay and I have a connection I can't quite figure out. I wake up thinking about her and go to sleep reliving our time together. My chest twists tighter as our good-bye approaches. But if there's one thing I've learned about myself, it's that long-distance relationships are a no-go. No point getting in any deeper. "Okay," I say and kiss her cheek. "It's been fun while it lasted."

I step to the side, angling so we can talk to the group. Lily catches Shay's eye and mouths *Oh, my God* and *we'll chat later* in reference to our PDA, then the five of us shoot the shit about ski trips—the places we've been, the mountains we've conquered. Just to make me look like a dick, Sawyer retells how I skied into Laura Millner to get her attention. And broke her arm. Eventually, Shay gets up to use the washroom. I watch her ass in her tight jeans, until a heaped bowl of sweet potato fries passes. Knowing she'd be all over that, I place an order with the bartender, smiling in anticipation. It's refreshing being around a girl who doesn't eat like a bird. The last chick I took to dinner pushed food around her plate.

A few minutes after she returns, my fries arrive.

Her eyes widen. "You didn't."

"I did." I grab a few, dip them into the chipotle aioli, shove them into my mouth, then groan like she did that day in the ski lodge. "Better than sex," I say.

She pinches my side. "I'll be the judge of that."

Five minutes later, Lily, Raven, and Sawyer are staring at us and the empty bowl. "Do you guys have worms?" Raven asks.

I pat my stomach. "I offered. You guys didn't want any."

"We ate dinner an hour ago."

Shay and I shrug at each other. "And?" she says.

They all laugh, when Lily suddenly bounces on her seat. "Oh, Shay. I forgot." She dips her hand into her massive purse and emerges with a journal. "You almost left this at the condo."

She reaches to hand it to Shay, but I snatch it first. "Is this a diary?" Holy fuck, if it is, that whole don't-argue-with-Shay-during-our-last-hour thing is history. I'm not missing the opportunity to read her thoughts from the past four days.

"Give it here, Kolton. It's not a diary. It's my drawing journal. I scribble in it, like ideas and stuff. There's been lots of inspiration in Aspen." She puts her hand over her heart and leans toward Lily. "Thank God for you, Lil. I'd be screwed without this."

Before I hand it over, I flip through the pages, pausing on the ones with shading and color. If this is what Shay calls scribbling, my drawing skills are up there with Jackson's. Some pages show sections of a room, others a full panoramic view, each three-dimensional sketch bringing the spaces to life. One of them has a suspended wall leaning at an angle, modern but edgy. Something like this would kick ass in our new store. "These are great. Really good. Where'd you say you work?" I hate how little I know about her. How superficial most of our conversations have been. But she did tell me about Snoopy.

Her hazel eyes darken. "I didn't say, and it doesn't matter. I'm quitting when I get home, and I won't settle until I land a decent job."

"Judging by this, I don't imagine you'll have much trouble."

She tries to yank the book from my hands, but I pull it closer, amazed by the next page, the space filled with a skull dissolving into a flock of birds. I pause, sure I've seen the image before. "Isn't this on your shoulder, Raven?"

Raven lifts her arm, twisting it to show off her ink. "Sure is. Both Shay and Lily designed something for my sleeve."

"It's amazing," I say more to Shay than Raven.

Shay's eyes spark back to life as she plucks the book from my grasp and tucks it into her purse. "Thanks. I'd kill to incorporate the idea into an actual room. Like design a modern tattoo shop or funky store. One day," she says, frustration edging into her tone.

My phone buzzes, and I nod to Shay, stepping away to get a bit of quiet by the back wall. "Is that you, bud?"

"The spelling show's on, the one we always watch, and they're doing H, Daddy. *H.* And I'm not tired. Not one bit. I probably don't even need to sleep tonight. Or ever. And Aunt Stella said I can stay up as long as I want. So if I stay up *all* night, like the *whole* thing, will you be here soon? They're doing H!"

Jackson and his show. Marina was smart, planning on a nursing degree, and I can work Excel with my eyes closed. But neither of us were language geeks, obsessed with words and dictionaries. We weren't the types to separate our clothes by color or only eat green foods on Thursdays. If Jackson didn't have my brown eyes, the mailman would be having a conversation with my fist.

I check my watch. They're one hour behind at home, only a few minutes past the little guy's bedtime, but Stella will likely let him stay up as long as he wants. Asking my assistant to babysit a couple of years ago wasn't my finest decision, but I was desperate and Jackson knew her. Now, if I ask anyone besides her or his nana Caroline, he starfishes in the kitchen and won't get off the floor. "I'll be back tomorrow, bud, but not early. I suggest you get some sleep. Can you do that for me?"

Static fills my ear then, "'Kay."

"Thanks for being such a big boy. I'll be home tomorrow by dinner. Can't wait to see you. Love you tons."

"Love you, too."

I pocket my phone and turn to find Shay's eyes on me, her lips turned down. I walk over. "You okay?"

She furrows her brow. "Fine."

Her body language says otherwise.

Ever since the phone-call incident the first night we hooked up, she gets weird and distant when I step away to take a call. Each time, I try explaining it's not some girlfriend, but she shuts me down with her *I don't want to know*. Considering we're about to say good-bye for good, there's no point trying again.

Tomorrow, it's back to Vancouver, and although I'll have piles of work to deal with, fires to put out, and an expansion to Toronto to plan, I get to see Jackson. And maybe Sawyer and Nico are right. This whole thing with Shay doesn't have to be a total loss. I'll likely forget about her in a couple of weeks, and having a taste of something more than the casual stuff I gave up makes the idea of returning to the dating pool less painful. I need more balance in my life, more than work and Jackson. Shay showed me that. When I get organized at home, maybe I'll give in and let Stella set me up with the girl she's always going on about.

Sawyer checks his watch. "You ladies need to leave soon if you want to make your flight."

"Yeah, we should go." Shay nudges Lily's thigh.

That twisting in my chest starts up again.

Taking my time, I help Shay with her coat, hug her, and bury my nose in her hair. *Peppermint.* I may have to buy new shampoo at home. "Thanks for skiing into me," I say.

She chuckles, her shoulders shaking in my tight hold. "Thanks for tossing your poles over the chairlift."

I press a chaste kiss to her lips and step aside so she can leave. Sawyer and I watch as the girls zip their coats and open the door. Shay pauses. She glances back, our eyes meeting one last time, then she's gone. When I turn to Sawyer, he looks like someone punched him in the gut. "So you're not into Lily?" I ask.

"Fuck you," he mumbles and orders a double bourbon on the rocks.

"Make that two," I say.

Ten

Shay

Two Months Later

I should've left work fifteen minutes ago. Normally, the store is tidied and mopped by now, but every time I refold a bath towel or fluff the pillows on the display bed, I zone out. Finding my landlord's eviction notice pushed under my door this morning hasn't exactly won me Salesperson of the Day. Five times tonight, customers have had to ask if I heard their repeated questions. I'd apologize, then glaze over again.

Evicted. Me.

As I rearrange the vases on the table the way Natasha likes, I catalogue the timeline of my impending doom: fourteen days' notice, two to four weeks until a court date, then eleven days to pay up or move out. If I'm lucky, I still have seven and a half weeks to come up with the money.

This is temporary, I remind myself.

I just need to turn these shifts at Sass & Style into cash by working harder for commission, and before I know it, my nine-to-five internship at Concept will be a paid designer gig. I'll scrape together enough to keep my head above water. I can totally pull this off.

Natasha puts down her pen and rubs her eyes, then she runs a hand down her straight red hair. She leans on the checkout counter. "You don't have to stay, Shay. I'll cash out tonight. When you're done tidying, you can go."

"I don't mind," I say, wanting to make up for today's shoddy performance. If Natasha wasn't such an understanding boss, she would've given me hell for being late this morning and sucking with the customers. I'd blame my tardiness on the eviction notice, but, really, it's all Kolton's fault. If I hadn't dreamed about him (*again*) and woken up flushed and flustered, I wouldn't have closed my eyes while my hand journeyed downtown. I wouldn't have brought myself to orgasm. Twice.

Yep, it's the Asshole's fault.

Yawning, Natasha arches over the back of her chair. "You're sweet, hun. Really. But you deserve to get out. I've got this."

"You sure?"

"Yes. *Go*. And get some rest. You look exhausted."

I force a weak smile.

Purse over my shoulder, I push out the front door and lock it behind me. A block away, I lean my back on a brick building as the weight of the day settles on my shoulders. Streetcars grind and pedestrians march, everyone in a hurry to get somewhere. Lives moving forward. Constant motion.

Mine traveling in reverse.

I steel myself for my night ahead with Lily and Raven. If I let it slip that my meager paycheck at Sass & Style isn't enough to cover my rent, Raven will yell at me for not telling them sooner, and Lily will have me staying with her and Kevin before I can blink. Or she'll offer me money.

The last thing I want is to be someone's charity case.

I inhale deeply and—*cinnamon*. Man, that smells good. Wafts of spice and coffee curl out the café door to my left, and my belly gurgles. These days, I'm not one to skip meals, but dinner out means something's got to give. At least it was my turn to choose tonight's restaurant. Kwong's chicken lo mein won't bleed my wallet dry, and their portions are huge. As another person leaves the café, I glance through the door. In the length of time it takes for it to close, I've mentally rearranged the décor, covering the walls with vintage metal utensils and kitchen gadgets. I hang old cheese graters from the ceiling as funky light fixtures.

Too bad the most design work I do these days consists of choosing my outfit.

I kick off the wall and hurry with the throng of commuters bustling along the sidewalk. Six blocks later, I push into the tiny eatery half filled with people bent over and slurping noodles. Raven smiles, and Lily stops biting her nails to wave me over. Lily's all styled out in a loose cream top and layered knit vest, tone on tone, three necklaces hanging to her waist. Familiar necklaces.

I slip into the seat opposite them and tug Lily's leather and beaded jewelry. "Aren't these from that high school trip to Tobermory?"

She runs her fingers down their length. "Yeah. I took some old pieces apart and mixed them up. Just fooling around."

"It's cool, but if you don't toss some of these relics, your apartment will end up on an episode of *Hoarders*." These days, her pack rat tendencies straddle the crazy line, her craft room alone on the verge of exploding.

She sticks her nail back into her mouth.

Raven pours me some green tea, her dark hair and thick bangs fanning forward. Next to the whitewashed walls, oddly decorated with kitschy cat drawings, her charcoal eyes and black wardrobe are more striking than usual. "How are things?" she asks.

I signal the waitress. "Can we order first?" If the sounds from my belly persist, people will wonder if there's a troll below our table.

We rattle off our orders, and Raven's about to engage me when I call the waitress back to add a side of spring rolls. As I devour the fried noodle snacks on the table, Raven tries again. "How are things? How's work?"

The handful of deep-fried goodness turns to sludge in my mouth. I coax the glue down with a sip of tea. "Which job, exactly? The one where I fold towels and sheets like Bed Bath and Beyond's employee of the month? Or the one where I've conquered the photocopier and have finally remembered how many sugars Cruella de Suck-myass likes in her coffee?" I lean back and fiddle with my wooden chopsticks.

Burning the money I spent on my design diploma would've been less painful than watching my degree wither as I stock shelves and boil water.

"It's not that bad," Lily says. "Your internship at Concept is a stepping stone, and I love Sass and Style. Most of my apartment's from there." The second the words are out, she reverts to chewing on her bright blue nail polish, likely kicking herself for bringing it up.

I didn't talk to her for a week after she came in and bought up half the place…the day after I told her I work on commission. Like I'm a child. Like I can't make it on my own. It was bad enough I let the Dick pay for everything, knowing, *believing*, he loved me. Or at least the skinnier, steadier, calmer version of me. The black-bra version. But for my friends not to have faith that I'm smart enough to support myself stung.

Now I'm about to get evicted. So much for self-sufficiency.

Swallowing hard, I say, "I appreciate that, Lil, but it's tough. You've scored a gig designing for Moondog, which I still have no idea how you snagged, and Raven finally got that school transfer she's been after, you know, both of you getting your lives together. I'm stuck in reverse."

Raven *pfffft*s me. "This is just a blip. It's only been a couple of months. And if it makes you feel better, that transfer fell through. Not that it really matters. I don't think teaching wealthy brats will be any better than teaching in the projects."

Lily cringes. "Sorry, Rave. That's too bad." Then she pats my hand. "Things will turn around. Soon. I know it. What about your apartment? You need to invite me over so I can give you your house-warming gift."

Yeah. That. "It's great"—*not being able to afford the rent*—"I love the space"—*that's decorated à la starving student*—"but it's still a mess. I'll have you over soon."

My bullshit meter just blew a fuse.

God, when did I start lying to my friends? *My apartment's great.*

I'm not strapped for cash. Their success isn't my failure. Life isn't a competition. So why am I so afraid to admit the extent to which mine's stalled? Every time I pick up the phone or open my mouth to confess my money woes, shame thickens in my throat.

Before Lily can grill me further, the waitress returns with our dinner, and I don't breathe or speak for the next five minutes.

"How do you eat like that and not weigh a thousand pounds?" Raven asks.

I finish off my spring roll and glance down at my hips, happy with my curves since terminating my juice cleanses. "I still run. It's the only option. Never again will I diet for a guy. Nothing is worth giving up fries and pasta."

Lily scoops noodles into her mouth and then dabs her lips with her napkin. "Speaking of which, have you been dating?"

I love my friends. I really do. They don't grill me or ask questions to build themselves up, or as a way to turn the conversation onto them. They want me to succeed. When I got offered my promotion, before the Dick convinced me to let it go, Lily was the first to scream, shouting *ohmyGod* for fifteen minutes. Raven offered to drive me to Montreal and help me apartment hunt. Even now, both girls stare, eyes twinkling, as they wait for me to dish about the nonexistent guys in my life. I know they love me, but this game of Twenty Questions isn't helping tonight. "Haven't been dating. Nothing to report. How's Kevin?" I ask Lily—*deflect, deflect.* "How come he hasn't proposed yet?"

She picks at the label on her Diet Sprite. "Things are fine."

"That's girlspeak for things are crap," I say. "What's going on?"

Raven pauses, forkful of noodles midair. "Please tell me you guys broke up."

I glare at her. "A little tact wouldn't kill you." Then to Lily, "Ignore her. What's up?"

I take another few bites of lo mein while Lily shrugs and sighs and peels her label. "I don't know," she says. "Things are just…fine. Good, I guess. Yeah, they're good." She nods as if convincing herself. Her gaze flicks up, that twinkle still sparkling. "What about Kolton? Do you still think about him?"

Always. "Rarely." Did it just get warmer in here?

"Even"—she lowers her voice—"the sex?"

Twenty-four/seven. "Nope." I stretch the neck of my top as heat crawls up my chest.

"But he's *so* hot."

That model hair, those full lips, his dark eyes that flared with hunger. "Barely remember what he looks like." Yep, the temperature has spiked to steamy.

Raven leans on her elbows, inked birds spiraling up her skin. "You're so full of shit."

Apparently, there's no hiding the blush creeping up my cheeks. "Okay. Busted. Yes, I think about him. Often. But he doesn't live here. There's no point pursuing things."

Why I haven't been able to shake thoughts of Kolton is a mystery. I spent five years with the Dick and never looked back, never wondering, hoping, pondering if I said or did the right things. I'd spike his almond milk with laxatives all over again if given the chance. Two months after spending four short days with Kolton, regret needles me—a chain of what-ifs plaguing my thoughts.

Lily pouts. "But you two were so cute together, and he'll be in Toronto this summer."

Toronto. Here. This summer. I've replayed his whispered words, asking me to hook up again, along with my quick reply, shutting him down. What's done is done. Better to move on. I shove the last bite of noodles into my mouth...but pause mid-chew. I never mentioned to Lily that Kolton was planning on coming here this summer. Not one word. I drop my chopsticks on my empty plate. "How do you know he's coming here?" I lean forward. "Are you still talking to Sawyer?"

She pushes her partly finished food away. "No. Yes. I mean...sometimes. I could get Kolton's number, you know, *if* I speak to Sawyer."

"So you no-yes-sometimes speak to Sawyer, and things are *fine* with Kevin. What part of this story am I supposed to believe?" I ask.

She picks at her cuticles. "Okay. I *do* talk to Sawyer, but it's professional. He helps me with my design stuff."

Raven cackles. "The insurance guy helps you with your design stuff?" She glances out the front window. "Did a pig just fly by?"

"Anyway," Lily says, deflecting my way, "Sawyer might have mentioned that Kolton talks about you."

My ears flame. Kolton talking about me means he thinks about me. Maybe he touches himself while lost in memories of us tugging at each other's clothes. At least, that's what I do. Almost nightly. "Talks about me? Really? Like how? What does he say?"

Lily grins. "You *so* have it bad. Come on. You need to get his number."

I force thoughts of Kolton and the way he kissed me that last night out of my head. I don't replay how cute it was of him to buy me those fries, or the hopefulness on his face when he asked to see me again. Or how right it felt lying next to him on the cold, wet snow after he fell. I shake my head. "What's the point? He may be

in town for a bit this summer, but he doesn't live here. I can't afford
to fly back and forth to Vancouver. I doubt Kolton's hairdressing job
affords him that type of lifestyle, either."

Lily's eyes wander around as she taps her fingers on the table. "Is
it the job?" she asks. "Is that what's holding you back?"

Like I'd judge others on their vocation. "No. I could care less
what he does or how much he makes. Look, after everything with
Richard, it was hard for me to really love myself again. It's not like
the guy was abusive, but if you're around someone who talks down
to you for that long, you kind of start believing them." Lily's eyes
fill and Raven frowns, but I swat the air between us. "It's okay. I'm
feeling good, maybe not careerwise, but my confidence is back, and
I'm ready to date. To meet someone. I'll never let a guy get in the
way of my career or influence me or my life like Richard did, but I
think I'm ready to get back out there. Still," I say before she inter-
jects, "Kolton's not the guy for me. I'm not uprooting my life for
a man again. I won't put myself in that position. Besides, with our
chemistry, one of us would wind up in a body bag."

Lily raises her hands in defeat. "Fine. I won't push. But now we
get to set you up! There's this guy who owns one of the shops where
I sell my purses. A little older, but super nice. And cute. Can I set it
up? Pretty please?"

Raven hooks an arm over the back of her chair. "I don't know
why you guys bother. So much more fun playing the field."

Lily's face falls like a disappointed puppy. "Don't you want to fall
in love? What about Nico? Have you heard from him?"

"I'm happy to watch you girls fall in love. I'll cheer from the sidelines, but it's not for me. And no, thankfully, I haven't heard from
Nico. The guy's an idiot." The way she traces the rose tattooed inside

her wrist, I'd say things aren't so cut and dried. Just last month, when stressing about her job, her finger looped over the thing a dozen times. But I don't get why Nico would inspire anxiety. When I ask her about their time in Aspen, she shrugs and says he's not worth talking about.

Lily picks at her nail polish—*her* nervous tic—but I'm not sure what she's all fidgety about, either. A moment later, she fists her hands. "I bet Nico had his reasons for not getting in touch. Anyway, Shay, what do you say? Can I arrange a date?"

Before I can answer, the waitress gathers our plates and drops fortune cookies on the table. I crack one open and pull out the paper: *If you want the rainbow, you have to tolerate the rain.* Fitting. I'm reaching for my golden-ticket job, slinging coffee and running errands at a decent—albeit not top—design firm, waiting for my big break. It won't happen overnight, but at least I'm on the path. As long as I don't end up homeless between now and then. With my career on a (glacial) trajectory upward, I may as well venture into the wilds of dating. Toronto is a big city, lots of single guys. If I put myself out there, I'm bound to meet someone cool. Someone who gets me as fired up as Kolton does, minus all the arguments.

"Okay," I say. "Let the dating begin."

Eleven

Kolton

A stack of sketches lands on my desk, and I roll my eyes, wishing for the millionth time we hadn't set up shop in this old warehouse. I'd kill for actual walls, even one of those life-sucking cubicles. But we swore when starting up this business, we wouldn't become corporate slaves wearing suits and ties in a fancy office.

Sawyer plants both palms on my desk, and I look up. "Can I help you?"

Before he answers, the intercom on my desk buzzes. The fucking intercom in this wall-less warehouse. Half the space is filled with racks of samples, our three desks—mine, Sawyer's, and my assistant, Stella's—closer than necessary. "Sawyer's here to see you," she says and grins. Her high-pitched voice rings through the space in stereo, her pink glasses and *pinker* hair so glaring I have to blink.

I hit the button on my intercom and lean my lips so close they're nearly touching it. "Send him in."

She drops her head to her mouthpiece. "Sure thing, boss."

She cackles as I curse Nico's office-warming gift. I would've tossed it if he hadn't threatened to stick me in jail. Every time he visits, he checks that his precious intercoms are connected.

I slump in my chair and grip the armrests. "That never gets old."

Sawyer shakes his head at my sarcasm. "Never. You think Nico would notice if we chucked them?"

"Notice?" I cock an eyebrow. "Last time he was here, he played an imaginary spy game with Jackson, the two of them hiding under the desks intercomming each other. We're fucked. Forever."

My intercom crackles with static. "To be fucked you'd have to be getting action."

We both glare at Stella. She retaliates with a wink.

Maybe I can hang curtains from the ceiling.

Sawyer swings back to me. "Speaking of Goliath, you heard from him lately? I feel for the dude."

"We talked the other day. He's driving himself mad over this shit with Josh. If he spends any more time at the jail or doing his own detective work, the guy's gonna implode."

He grunts, I grunt, a moment of silence, then Sawyer says, "Anyway, Lily and I have been brainstorming, and I think you'll dig what we've come up with."

He sits on the corner of my desk, arms folded, while I grab the sketches and flip through them. "I assume Lily drew these." Sawyer nods, not that I need the confirmation. Each sketch centers on an exotic girl with straight black hair and thick bangs or a wild beauty with a mass of curls. Brown curls. Eyes so large they're cartoonlike.

Lips so full you could kiss them for days. *Shay*. It's been two months, and I think about her more, fantasize more. Imagine how she'd look without the layers of clothes that were always between us.

Terminator Shay.

"They're good, huh?" Sawyer grins, smug as usual.

I blink and focus on the sharp lines and asymmetrical cuts coming to life on the page. I glance up from the sketch. "You know they are."

"I'm telling you, Lily has her pulse on what women want. What's fresh. We're gonna kill it this season. The timing is perfect with the expansion." He picks up a couple of sketches, beaming while he studies the designs.

I push the sketches around, my fingers settling on one of Shay in a vibrant green jacket, bold black lines breaking the color into intricate patterns up her slim sides. Something about the hard lines reminds me of her sketchbook—the edgy images I remember each time I turn down another design firm for our Toronto expansion. I rest my hand on the curve of her cheek and tap my fingers once, twice. A third time.

Shay.

Last night was a repeat of too many evenings since our trip. Her torn red lace underwear in my hand. My eyes closed. My dick hard. My hand sliding as I pictured her soft lips, her wild hair, her hips eager against mine. It's getting creepy as fuck. Like I'm some perv stealing underwear from department stores, horny and deviant. I don't know why I kept her trashed lingerie. I've tried to throw them away a few times, but the longer it goes, the harder it gets. The thought gnaws at me, unwelcome.

I tap my fingers a fourth time and draw my hand back.

"You still think about her?" Sawyer's eyes burn into mine.

"Too much." Gripping my armrests again, I study the exposed piping along the ceiling. "I don't know. It's probably because I haven't gotten out. After the trip and everything, I thought things would be different. I'd be different. Like I'd suddenly have all this time to get out and date and meet someone new." I glance at Jackson's pictures on my desk. The two of us in a go-kart. The two of us apple picking. The two of us at the beach. Each photograph is an awesome memory, each one a reminder I don't have anyone to share them with.

"Or maybe it's because you guys were good together." Sawyer drops the sketches on my desk. He drags a chair over, flips it around, and straddles it, facing me. "You can't deny the chemistry you had."

"I never denied it. But we live on opposite sides of the country, and Shay made it clear that whatever happened in Aspen stayed in Aspen. She needed a break from guys or something."

"*Needed* being the operative word."

My heart stutters. The way he rolls his pinky ring, there's no question Sawyer knows more than he's saying. I should probably let him in on his tell, but poker night wouldn't be nearly as much fun. "What does that mean?"

"My understanding is she's decided to jump back into the dating scene."

I nearly crush my armrests. "Your understanding?"

He nods. "Yep." Still twisting that damn ring.

"Does your understanding have something to do with Lily? All those design hours we get billed for…how much of that time is spent with you two gossiping?"

His jaw tics. "She doesn't charge for the hours we chat."

"Hours? So, what…you guys stay up late at night whispering to each other? I bet her boyfriend thinks that's swell."

"You can fuck off. And stop diverting. Lily mentioned she's setting Shay up on a date, so maybe it's time to kick your pride to the curb and call her. Unless you'd rather take one of these sketches home and fuck it with more than your eyes. I could cut a hole in one if you want." He smirks.

The intercom on my desk buzzes. "How's ten tomorrow for that sexual harassment in the workplace support group?"

I slam my thumb onto the stupid fucking intercom. "Sure, but book two spots." I release the button and turn to Sawyer. "I'll fuck that poster when you stop jacking off while talking to Lily. I'm guessing you got that new cell because the old one with her picture on it got sticky."

Stella's voice sounds through the intercom, "Booked."

Sawyer and I continue our staring contest, until he snorts. "Whatever, bro. Like I've said a thousand times, Lily and I are all business. You, on the other hand, are moping around when the girl you're obsessed with might finally be ready to give things a shot. Especially since she could get free haircuts." The bastard tips forward, laughing.

I've been close to calling Shay more times than I'd care to admit. Sawyer dropped her number on my desk shortly after we got back, and I entered it into my cell, where it's festered, taunting me. That time I bailed skiing and ended up with a cast up to my elbow with an ever-present itch below the plaster was less irritating.

But we still live three thousand kilometers apart.

"Look, my life is here, in Vancouver. Jackson is here. My dad, stepmom, and stepbrothers. Marina's parents. I may be spending the summer in Toronto, but that's all it is. A summer. If I get involved with a girl, I don't want it to be casual." I glance again at the picture frames on my desk. "I'm done with casual."

Sawyer drums his thumbs on the back of the chair. "Okay. So what's stopping you from dating? If you won't pursue anything with Shay, then get out there."

"With all my spare hours?"

"Jesus. I'm getting whiplash. Shay's a no-go because you want something more permanent, but you're not willing to make the time to date. Throw me a bone here."

Sawyer and his persistence.

It's not like I haven't run in the same mental circles, chasing my tail. Wishing I had the time to work on my personal life, but always feeling like something's going to suffer—Jackson, work. In Aspen, with Shay, I felt alive. A piece of me long forgotten sparked to life, then I came home without her and fell back into the same patterns. The same ruts. I vowed to find balance this time around, and I haven't even tried. "Okay," I say. "Fine. If I thought I'd be going out with someone decent, someone with potential, I'd make time for it. Now shut up and leave me alone."

Stella's voice crackles through the intercom. "Permission to approach the bench."

This time I chuckle, that damn machine so annoying it's almost funny. I press the heels of my hands into my eyes. "Permission granted," I say without talking into the mouthpiece, then I drop my arms.

She clicks over in her heels, her full hips swaying with each step. Today's outfit is on the tame side, but her pinup image is alive and well. Between the pink hair piled on her head, the tight polka-dot blouse, and her fitted skirt, it's hard to know where to look first. Having witnessed her toss a drink in a guy's face at last year's Christmas party for staring at her tits, I don't focus on the shirt.

She plants a hand on her hip and fixes her attention on me. "My friend Emily is still single, and I think you guys would hit it off."

Sawyer snorts. "Does her hair look like it's been dunked in Kool-Aid, too?"

She purses her pink lips. "Another joke about my hair and Lily will get an anonymous tip in her in-box about a certain sticky cell phone."

Sawyer matches her thin lips and raises her a glare. "Don't you dare." Then he juts his chin toward me. "You're on your own with this, but I say go for it. Even if she looks like one of those troll dolls. Stella wouldn't risk her job by setting you up with a nut job...or by sending that e-mail," he adds before muttering, "We really need walls in here."

Still intent on me, Stella rubs her hands together. "So?"

Right away, I'm wondering if Emily will argue with me and push my buttons. If she'll tell me to fuck off like a certain fiery Irish girl. If she'd be the type to lie on the snow with me, tracing letters on my skin.

Volatile. Combustible. Unpredictable.

Aside from our few intimate moments, those four days with Shay were like a retelling of Jack White's song "Love Interruption," a passion so intense a knife to my gut, a punch to my face, or a shotgun to my temple would maybe simulate the level of emotion she inspired. In four days. But the thing that has my eyes widening and my heart pounding is that I'm not worrying Emily won't compare to Marina. My benchmark. The one true thing I know. I'm sure as shit she won't hold a candle to Shay.

When the hell did this happen?

Shay has lived at the edges of my thoughts the past two months. She's hijacked every one of my dreams, and the idea of her going on a date with someone else has my molars grinding. Fighting my pull toward her is only stalling my life. No matter how many excuses I offer up, I can't ditch that underwear, and I can't get her off my brain.

"Nope. Not going on a date." I shake my head, a plan forming with every twist of my neck. If I sit on my heels and ignore these feelings, I'll always wonder *what if*. Distance apart can be dealt with. Somehow. Separating Jackson from Marina's mother could be tough, especially when he's all she has left of her daughter, and I have no idea how I'd be able to work long term in Toronto. But that doesn't mean we can't figure this out. In time. *If* things go as I hope. For now, I'm tired of thinking five steps ahead. With work I'm always forecasting: bank statements, bills, expansion. With Jackson it's after-school programs, daycare, babysitting, never living in the moment—organization and planning my Holy Grail. I need to shake things up, grab the reins of life, and convince Shay to go out with me.

Stella pouts and returns to her desk.

Sawyer shrugs. "So much for my pep talk."

As he swings his leg over his chair and stands, I say, "We still have to hire a design firm for the Toronto expansion. The ones you've sent me aren't jibing. If we don't find someone in the next few weeks, we'll be screwed."

"Yeah, sorry. I've been drowning in work."

"No worries. I'll take it over. I have some ideas." *That include Shay*, I don't add.

"Cool." He leaves our office with a wave.

The new shop needs to knock people on their asses. Not one of those fancy firms Sawyer has spoken with has given any indication they get our edgy, rock-and-roll image. They hear things like "ski jackets," "outdoor gear," and "hiking shorts," and each one tries to guide us toward country chic, designs packed with log beams and rustic décor. I may not get overly involved with the creative side of our business, but image is everything. I've pored over architecture and design magazines, hoping to feel the same excitement I felt when I studied Shay's sketches in Aspen—that cool hanging wall, how she talked about funky tattoo-inspired spaces.

I straighten up, determination setting in. Her edgy designs are exactly what the new shop needs, and I'm clearly not over her. She'll be pissed I lied about Moondog. For a short while, at least. Seeing her eyes flare and cheeks flush with anger would be an added bonus. Safer not to tell Sawyer. Throw off my scent before my intentions make their way from him to Lily to Shay, tipping her off through their broken telephone. Wouldn't want to miss any of her righteous indignation.

I nod, mind reeling, feeling in control of my life and emotions for the first time in two months. Shay may freak when I show up at her design firm, her stubbornness a bridge I'll have to cross, *carefully*. But chemistry like ours doesn't exist if it's one-sided. She was as into me as I was her.

Reaching for my jacket on the back of my chair, I fish out my cell and pull up Shay's number, thankful Sawyer dropped it on my desk all those weeks ago. I type a message and hit send before I can think twice:

Every time I'm in a bathroom, I think of you.

My phone buzzes a second later, the air suddenly electric.

Because it burns when you pee?

I laugh—a bark of a sound that has Stella looking at me like I've sprouted horns. I'm an idiot for putting things off this long. Quickly, I type:

Did you lie about your sexual history?

I *may* have fibbed.

Bitch.

Asshole. Then: Actually, I'm in a bathroom right now. I'm on a date.

I grip my phone tighter. Toronto is three hours ahead, her night just starting. With another man. I type: What's he like? Because I'm a masochist.

All I get is radio silence, and immediately I regret pushing her.

Until: His hair is too short.

I played basketball in school, and the high I'd get when I'd sink a three-pointer would carry me for hours. But this? Right now? This is a basket from half-court, nothing but net. Warmth surges through my chest.

Tell me more.

He's way too polite. And he blinks a lot.

I chuckle. Time to quit while I'm ahead. Keep things light with Shay. Avoid freaking her out. I hope you have a shitty night.

She replies with a smiley face.

When I put my phone down, Stella says, "Took you long enough."

Her grin is so wide, there's no point denying it. "Agreed. Not a word to Sawyer."

She salutes me.

I check my watch. I'll need to get out of here in the next ten minutes to pick Jackson up from Caroline's—Marina's mother always eager to watch her grandson—then it's off to the library before it closes. We're still on E in the Encyclopedia Britannica, and I promised him we'd get to F by the time we leave for Toronto. I push back from my desk and gather my things. In three weeks, I'll be in Toronto with Stella and Jackson—Stella having agreed to help me out with my son. That's twenty-one days to text Shay. Soften her. Remind her how intense our chemistry is. Then comes the ambush.

Twelve

Shay

"Crap." I duck behind my grocery cart as the Blinker stalks down my row. Thankfully, he finds what he's after and walks back out the way he came before noticing me. Never again will I trust Lily and her "This guy's awesome. I promise. You'll really like him."

Running errands for Cruella de Suckmyass is more pleasurable than listening to the Blinker drone about his carwash run-in (*blink*) and the "negligent asshole" (*blink*) who scratched his precious BMW. (*Blink. Blink. Blink.*) I barely refrained from shoving eye drops in his hand as I lied about needing to get home early...

So I could reread Kolton's texts.

The Blinker must have thought I was nuts, smiling like a loon after I returned from the bathroom. Why, two months after the fact, Kolton decided to reach out, I have no idea. And the timing of it?

While I was on my first date since Aspen? It was like he knew I couldn't stop thinking about him. Still, stubborn as always, I wasn't ready to give up on my dating quest.

I should have.

The dude who chewed cinnamon gum (who chews cinnamon gum?) and the Suit who looked way too Richard for my liking had me ready to slit my wrists. Last night's guy was the worst. He was funny and cute with no serial-killer tendencies, but his eyes were too blue, his opinions too agreeable. He wasn't Kolton. I kicked myself (literally) the second I realized how messed up that was. My date, David, asked if I was okay as I winced and rubbed my ankle. My honest reply slipped out before I could stop it. "No. I am not okay."

For the next twenty minutes, he checked his watch a dozen times, and then we left early.

Not that I blame him. I blame Kolton.

Kolton and his perfect hair and full lips and obnoxious attitude.

Kolton, *the Asshole*, who's coming to Toronto. He hasn't mentioned seeing me, and I've avoided the subject, too. We joke. We tease. But, for some reason, over the past three weeks, neither of us has taken a step forward.

At least something's buzzing at Concept, enough whispers and excitement circulating in our small design firm of four to keep my mind off Kolton, my crappy dates, and my housing dilemma. I've earned some killer commission during my extra shifts at Sass & Style, but I'm still short on cash. With my court date approaching, that leaves me three weeks before I'm lounging on the street, cup in hand, a cardboard sign reading *Too Ugly to Prostitute*. Maybe whatever's brewing at Concept is big enough that I'll get to show off my skill, something to catapult me from intern to associate designer. Secret meetings have abounded the past few days, talk of some amazing account about to be signed. Cruella de Suckmyass, aka Maeve, has been barkier than usual, her clipped tone sending me off this morning for raw cane sugar and gluten-free cookies. God forbid white sugar or flour should touch the tongue of an important client.

I'm at the cash register, sifting through my purse to extricate my wallet, when I hear, "Shay?"

The hairs on my neck stand at attention, that voice flowing through me like molten lava. *Kolton.* What the…? I whip my head up and oh, my God, it's him. Here. In this store. Right now. Staring at me. He opens his mouth, closes it, then he steps closer, but there's an old lady behind me putting her groceries on the conveyer belt.

One. Item. At a time.

"Shay," he says again, a statement now. The syllable rolls off his tongue seductively, like we're back in Aspen—on that chair, in the snow, kissing in the bar. No two-hundred-year-old lady between us. He looks the same, maybe better. His worn jeans hug his hips, his just-tight-enough blue T-shirt showing off the chest I never got to see. His dark eyes are warmer, his shoulders thicker. I want to reach around Granny and pull the elastic from his hair to check if it has grown.

"Kolton," I whisper as the cashier asks something about cash or credit.

How perfect to meet him here, fate intervening on my behalf. After my string of bad dates, Kolton constantly lurking in the back of my mind, this feels right. Destined. My own fairy tale. Three months ago, I wasn't ready for our chemistry, then I made excuses to Lily about where he lives. But each guy I've dated has amplified my regret. My what-ifs. What if I messed up with Kolton? What if he's the guy for me?

Now he's here.

Good thing I wore my best red blouse and gray skirt for today's meeting.

Smiling, I push my loose curls over my shoulder and am about to admit how great it is to see him when a kid with the same brown eyes as Kolton, the same sandy hair, tugs on his hand. "Daddy, you won't believe it. You won't. They have an urban dictionary." I stand, frozen, my smile slipping, as the boy waves the book in Kolton's face. "And it says right here an F-bomb isn't a bomb at all. It means *fuck*. But that F isn't in the big *Bri-ta-nni-ca* book. Can we get it? Please? I need it *so* bad." Then he pushes his glasses up his nose, turns to Granny between us, and hollers, "Did you know an F-bomb wasn't a bomb?"

I want to laugh at this crazy kid and the old lady whose eyes are the size of saucers, but this young boy said "Daddy" while tugging Kolton's hand. *Daddy*. The butterflies that swarmed when I first saw him rush out at once, leaving me nauseous. "Credit card." I turn to the cashier. "Credit card, okay? So type as fast as you can in that machine of yours. I'm in a rush. We're talking life and death here." Of course Kolton has a family. Every phone call he ran to grab while in Aspen had "I'm married" written all over it.

I bounce my knee as I dirty-look Cashier Boy for no good reason, until he *finally* instructs me to insert my card into the machine. Then I wait and wait and *freaking* wait for the minicomputer to ask me for my PIN.

"Shay." Kolton's voice slices through me as I tap the side of the stupid piece of metal.

"Shay."

I don't turn.

"Did you stick it in?" Cashier Boy asks.

I glare at him. "Yes. I stuck it in."

"Stick it in harder."

Kolton laughs, his deep chest rumble curling around me. "Go ahead," the Asshole says. "Stick it in harder."

I swivel, ready to tell him exactly where I'm going to stick something harder when I remember his *son*—Kolton's mini-me—who's watching our interaction with wide eyes. I clamp my mouth shut and slam the heel of my hand against the card. The terminal wakes up.

PIN in, receipt given, and I'm about to bolt when Kolton says, "Come on, Shay. You never let me explain in Aspen. Just wait, okay?"

The truth in his words stops me midstride. Every time Kolton hung up his phone, he sensed my unease and tried to explain. I'd always shut him down. Why bother now? What's there to talk about? He has a kid. A *family*. Not one of his texts hinted at a duplicitous life. Each message was light. Short. Not that he owes me anything. Still, after our texts and spending the last few months reliving our four days together, heat stings behind my eyes.

"Shay," he says again, softer this time.

My name on his lips keeps me rooted. Maybe he's divorced. He could be here for a short stay with friends or family. He could be available. I turn, hope expanding in my chest as the ancient lady places her last item on the counter. My shoulders relax and my erratic breathing regulates, until a hot pinup chick puts her hand on Kolton's shoulder and says something I can't hear.

I glance from her to him and back again. No family resemblance.

She has flawless skin, pink hair, vibrant tattoos snaking down her arms, and stunning blue eyes. She's breathtaking, which would maybe explain the loss of air in my lungs.

That rat bastard.

I could deal with the idea of him having a girlfriend or something while in Aspen. Makes me a class-A bitch, but it was a vacation, and he was a guy I was never going to see again. Not my finest moment. But seeing him with this burlesque girl, who makes Lady Gaga look tame, brings the Count Chocula I ate this morning closer to my throat than I'd like.

I mouth *fuck you*, as Kolton calls, "Wait! It's not what you think!"

Which means it's exactly what I think.

Since he's blocked by the three-thousand-year-old lady, I'm able to get in my car and speed off to work without facing him and his *explanation*. Thank God we have that big meeting this morning. Anything to help me forget I slept with some woman's husband. Some boy's father.

A total, frigging asshole.

* * *

I'm so on edge by the time I pull up to the small brownstone that houses Concept that I drop my keys twice on the way inside. I set my coat and purse at my desk by the back window, then I hurry to the kitchen to brew coffee and plate the cookies I just *had* to buy where I *had* to run into Kolton. Like I needed to be reminded what a fine piece of ass his lying-sack-of-shit self is. Which means tonight I'll be sliding under my sheets, my fingers rubbing, my thighs clenching, as I relive that stupid trip to Aspen for the buttzillionth time.

Damn him and his skilled hips.

I lean forward and peek over the saloon-style doors into the conference room. No sign as to who this new client is. No overt posters tipping me off. The team is gathered in the glass-walled space, this once-old townhouse modernized by Hilary, our president. She sits at the head of the table while Cruella de Suckmyass (Maeve) and Stuart eyeball each other on either side of her. A month ago, Hilary let it be known one of them would be promoted to partner, the potential advancement inciting talons and pecking, a cock match imminent. Stuart sucks in his cheeks—legs crossed, hands folded—his elflike pointy shoes twitching with every narrowed gaze launched at Maeve. Maeve taps her French-manicured fingernails on the marble table, her sharp bangs and sleek bob framing the scowl she aims at Stuart.

They can bicker all they want. He can smack the collagen from her lips. She can mess with his perfectly matched shirts and ties. There can only be one victor, and when one of them gets promoted, I will, hopefully, become Concept's newest associate designer.

Helloooo, paycheck.

I gather the coffeepot and tray of cookies, but my hands are shaking. Today's run-in with Kolton has me jittery and off my game. Visions of me stubbing my toe, coffee everywhere, haunt each inhale. Hands on the counter, I slump forward, trying to calm my racing heart, and I shiver. The air conditioner must be on the fritz again. Last time this happened, I had picked up a wool blanket for a client that I *may* have used before delivering. Teeth clacking at the memory, I make a mental note to get the AC repaired, barely registering the front door opening and the greetings passed around.

"Shay," Maeve calls, but it sounds more like *Shy*. I don't know who she thinks she's fooling. Nobody retains an English accent from one year living abroad...six years ago. "The client's here, *Shy*. Don't dawdle." She snaps her fingers, *snaps*, and I want to break each digit.

"Be right there," I call as the glass door to the conference room screeches shut, the sound like nails on a chalkboard. My growing to-do list now includes: Get the stupid door fixed. I'm not sure why a big client has chosen our small firm for their design needs. Hilary has been vibrating with excitement the past few days, and by the look of things around here, I'd say she needs the work.

Plate and coffee in hand, I push my back into the saloon doors and ease out of the kitchen without dropping anything.

Kolton Kolton Kolton. Don't think about Kolton.

Eyes focused on the hardwood floor, I prepare to smile and nod and take notes during the meeting. Like the consummate professional I am. I blow out a breath, ease my death grip on the coffeepot, and glance up to check out our new client. That's the precise moment the Count Chocula makes itself known again.

The dude in the conference room looks a heck of a lot like Kolton.

But it can't be. It. Just. Can't.

I blink repeatedly, doing my best impersonation of the Blinker. No matter how many times I squeeze my eyes, that familiar back and stance look too *familiar*—legs apart, left foot turned out, hands probably tucked in his front pockets. My Asshole Alert perks up, all synapses firing. There's no doubt to whom that ponytail and fine booty belong, and he's in the conference room talking to my superiors. I strain my ears but can't hear a word through the glass. I stand like an idiot, *blinking*, unsure why the hell he's here. Maeve diverts her gaze from Kolton to me, her missile glare making a direct hit.

Her collagen lips thin.

Blink.

Her tweezed brows pucker.

Blink.

Her fisted hands shake.

Blink. Blink. Blink.

Whatever Kolton's saying has her fuming.

What kind of dick chases me to my place of work? To what? Explain? If I were that kid of his, I'd look up the word *stalker* and remind him I could share every detail of Aspen with his pinup girl. And where's the client Maeve said arrived?

She's on the verge of a stroke, Kolton still talking, Stuart and Hilary both nodding. I stand, apoplectic, while Maeve's silent tantrum graduates to full hysterics. She's waving and pointing and stamping her foot, all while glaring at me. The whole thing plays out like chimpanzee sign language. When the Asshole finally turns, his mouth drops open, and I follow his gaze.

To my tipping coffeepot and the liquid pooling at my feet. All because of him.

Waking from my daze, I hurry back to the kitchen to drop the tray and pot and grab a wad of paper towel. I fist it and scream internally. What the hell is he saying in there? Any minute, our important client will appear from wherever he disappeared to, and he'll have to wait while I apologize for allowing my personal life to follow (stalk) me to work.

What if I get fired?

The conference door makes its ear-splitting sound, and Maeve's heels *clickety-clack* furiously toward me. "What. Was. That? All I asked, *Shy,* was that you pick up cookies, make coffee, and take notes during the meeting. Not spill coffee all over the floor. Hilary instructed me to guide you. Train you. When you misstep, it reflects on me, and I can't have that. Not when the owner of Moondog is in the conference room about to hire us to design their new space. So clean up that mess and get it together. There's too much riding on this."

She stomps her foot sergeant-style, swivels, and marches back to the conference room. Not one fake-accented word was said about me needing to keep my personal life *personal*, and there was no mention of my ex–fuck buddy lingering in the conference room. But I didn't hear much after she said Moondog.

Because that makes no sense. None. Nada.

Kolton's the only person in there aside from our team, and last I heard, he styles hair for a living. And my best friend Lily (soon to be ex-bestie) has never, not once, mentioned Kolton having anything to do with Moondog, the company she works for. I chew my cheek, frowning. But she *has* mentioned she talks design with Sawyer. *The insurance guy.* I sensed something was off there, but Lily never volunteered an explanation, and I never pushed. Now Kolton, the apparent owner of Moondog, is standing in the conference room. Steam builds between my ears, an explosion imminent.

My jittery nerves turn to steel, the lies of the past months unfurling in their eloquence. The edges are fuzzy, the details and motivation unclear, but what is plain as day is the fact that Kolton has lied about his relationship status, having a kid, and what he does for a living. Okay, *technically*, he just lied about his job, but hiding that other stuff isn't cool. Now he's here, where I work, messing with my fragile livelihood. Lily will be dealt with later. For the next hour, I have to find a way to be present in that room.

Without killing Kolton.

Head held high, I march out to the hallway and don't glance through the glass walls. I feel eyes on me, likely the brown stunners I stared into while having one of many mind-blowing orgasms, but I don't look up. I wipe up the coffee and scrub the floor, practically taking off the top varnish. I return to the kitchen, smooth my fitted red blouse, then I grab our premium java and gluten-free cookies, making sure the raw cane sugar is neatly on the plate. Swaying my hips in my gray pencil skirt, I approach the glass door. Each step feeds my fury, distilled anger bleeding through my veins.

Pure. Potent. Lethal.

This isn't Aspen, though. This is my place of work.

I will breathe the same air as Kolton, smile at my colleagues, and take notes. I'll ignore the lump building in my throat at the thought of him with that woman and of my complete ignorance. Too wrapped up in our chemistry, I couldn't see him for what he was and thought, for a moment at least, that we shared something beyond the physical. Consider me schooled. I won't look at the Asshole or acknowledge him. I will reenact the childhood game that served my brother well when in the car together. I'd insist on playing Gotcha Last with him—smacking his arm if he brushed by me—and he'd pretend I was never born.

As of right now, the Asshole doesn't exist.

Thirteen

Shay

Once the door screeches closed behind me, I walk around the table where the group is seated. Avoiding Kolton's gaze, I set up the coffee and cookies on the back counter as Hilary finishes pitching Concept to him.

"We listen to our clients' needs," she says, repeating the same speech I've heard a few times. "We're here to bring your vision to life, not force our ideas on you. Concept is small, intimate. I, of course, would lead the project, but considering the timeline, Stuart and Maeve would be assisting, and our intern, Shay, is available to scour the city as needed for samples when choosing finishes."

She nods toward me, and I smile *at her*. One glance at Kolton and my armor may slip. I'll remember how it felt to have him inside of me, working me over, making my body sing, because the man still looks *fine*. Eyes diverted, I channel my hurt and disappointment into an Oscar-worthy performance. We'll title this short film *The Invisible Man*.

As far as I'm concerned, Kolton's not in this room. Or on this planet.

Hilary's at the head of the table, Stuart and Maeve flanking her, Kolton seated at the opposite end. I settle into the chair next to Maeve as she clucks her tongue. She's been colder than usual today, no doubt reliving yesterday's debacle. I raced across the city, dodging construction zones and cyclists, arriving at Grecko Tile in record time to acquire an emergency sample. Apparently, it was the right shop, but the wrong location. Maeve didn't care to mention I shouldn't go to the store I'd been to numerous times the past month. Still, it was *my* fault for assuming they only had one location. A million red lights later, I got the sample, but her frustrated client couldn't wait and threatened to hire another firm if it happened again.

Stuart had beamed as he rose a notch higher on their imaginary leaderboard.

"By choosing Concept," Hilary says as she wraps up her speech, "you're choosing style and cutting-edge design, but integrity and our clients' needs come first."

Stuart bats his pale blond lashes. "We'll make Moondog the talk of the city."

Never one to let him have the last word, Maeve tips her bright red lips into her "sincere" smile. "With your vision and our guidance, Moondog will set the standard for retail shops everywhere."

"So," Hilary says, leaning back in her leather chair, "is there anything you'd like to discuss before we sign the papers?"

I shiver as the AC blasts into the room. Maeve, however, clicks her manicured nails on the table, looking like she's in her natural habitat. The Ice Queen. Stuart's twitchy shoe taps one of the table legs, all of us waiting on Kolton. The longer he stays quiet, the tighter I fist my cold hands. A guy doesn't show up where a girl works, three months after hooking up, unless he has an agenda. But I can't figure out his angle. I glance over, hoping to get a read on his intentions, and our eyes lock.

Is he smirking? And why does his shirt have to fit so snug?

I'm about to look away when he opens his mouth. "Shay, how nice to see you again."

So much for *The Invisible Man.*

Shifty-eyed, I glance around the table, sure they all know I've fucked our biggest client ever in a bathroom (make that *two* bathrooms). Our *married* biggest client. Hilary sits forward, her long blond ponytail fanning across her back. "I didn't realize you knew our intern."

If he didn't mention me when he got here, why the hell is he acknowledging me now? What is he playing at?

Steam builds between my ears again, the pressure about to blow. "Yes, well…" I start, anger and confusion wiping my confidence.

The ignore-Kolton act was easier to perform.

"We met at a conference in Aspen," he says before I can conjure an appropriate lie.

Maeve's nails stop their endless ticking. "Conference? I don't remember a conference."

Kolton waves a hand in the air. "Not design specific. It was a spur-of-the-moment industry ski thing. It's actually why I've chosen Concept. Shay shared some ideas during one of the meetings I haven't been able to forget." He leans on his elbows, all of that rugged handsomeness focused on me. "I'd like to revisit the finer points of our discussions. Maybe add on to the basics debated." He licks his lips.

Motherfucker.

"Well," Hilary says as Maeve huffs out an exasperated breath, "Shay is a promising young designer. We count ourselves lucky to have her. She'd be happy to pick up where you left off."

Like hell. I sit taller, shoulders back, knowing the red bra I'm wearing has my girls cradled perfectly, leaving a hint of cleavage visible through my unfastened top button. "I'm not sure I'm the best person to revisit that particular conference. Personally, I found it tedious." I tilt my head toward Maeve as if sharing a secret. "You know when you're partway through and all you're thinking is, *God* when will this end? I barely remember a thing from those monotonous discussions." I smile sweetly at Kolton, pleased I'm back in control of my speech. Until the AC blasts and the temperature drops like ten degrees, perking up my nipples. I don't slouch or fold my arms across my chest. That would look meek. Timid. Not a way to stand my ground.

With my nipples nearing diamond-cutting territory, his gaze lowers on target. Gruffly, he clears his throat and drags his eyes up. "Funny, I could have sworn you enjoyed the meetings. You were rather vocal in a few."

A quiver racks my body, but I don't know if it's from the subzero temperature or his heated look. "I'm skilled at faking interest. Wouldn't want the meeting leader to feel inept."

The rest is a dizzying verbal tennis match.

Kolton: "He seemed proficient to me. Quite experienced."

Me: "Didn't care for his delivery."

Kolton: "I've never heard complaints about his delivery before."

Me: "Maybe those attending had low standards."

Hilary studies us, eyes narrowed, probably wondering why I'm giving our potential client such a hard time. And I can't understand why he's flirting with me when he's married. I study his ring finger. Like in Aspen, there's still no gold band. No telltale tan line hinting at his marital status. The burlesque beauty from earlier with her bubblegum hair and candy lips must be a girlfriend. Or his call girl. "Maybe you're thinking of the pink-haired girl who was there," I counter as my teeth chatter, hypothermia imminent. "She seemed keen. A real go-getter."

He shakes his head. "Nope. Definitely not. I specifically remember your comments, and that design book of yours." He turns his focus to Hilary. "I like your firm and everything you've said, but, to be honest, I chose you guys because of Shay. She has some specific designs and ideas that I'd like to use in the shop. If I'm going to sign on here, she'll have to be the lead designer."

There's no mistaking Cruella de Suckmyass's "Fuck me," said under her breath, or how Stuart's jaw drops.

But it's Hilary's "I see" that has me shrinking in my seat. "I'm not sure Shay has the experience needed to pull together a job of this magnitude." Her leather chair squeaks as she clasps her hands on the table.

"I appreciate that," Kolton says. "But she's the reason I'm here, and I'm sure you can support her as we plan the space."

First, the Asshole ambushes me at work after I meet his son and whoever the hell that pink-haired woman is. Now he's bribing my employer to promote me. My eyelid twitches as my mind whirs. If he thinks meddling in my life will win him any favors, he's mistaken.

If I get a promotion, it'll be on my merit, not because some guy wants another slice of my pie. Hilary taps one hand on the table. "If Shay's up for the challenge, I can't think of any reason not to oblige. I, for one, would love to see her designs."

All eyes are on me, that damn twitch unrelenting. I dig my fingernails into my palms and do my best not to hiss out my words. "Thank you for the vote of confidence, Hilary. But do you mind if I speak with Kolton in private to discuss his proposal?"

Her gaze flicks from Kolton to me. Then she says, "Take all the time you need. I'll run over the logistics with Stuart and Maeve while you two iron out"—her sharp blue eyes land on me—"whatever issues you have. This is an important opportunity for us all." Hilary is polite as always, but her meaning is clear.

Lose this client, and I lose my job.

"It sure is," I say. *Twitch, twitch, twitch* goes my eyelid.

Kolton and I stand. He follows me to the door, and I hold it open for him to exit first. I drag it shut, wincing from the grinding sound, making sure it's securely closed. No need for anyone to hear the shit storm about to go down.

I march toward the (*slightly* less frigid) kitchen with Kolton on my heels.

Once through the doors, I swivel and shake my finger at his smug face. "I don't care that you lied about having a kid, or a girlfriend, or your job. You didn't owe me anything in Aspen, and you don't owe me anything now. But you waltz in here with your 'conference' talk, manipulating things so I'm designing your new store, so what? So you can get into my pants again? I may need this job, but I have my pride."

I heave so hard, another button pops open on my blouse. Kolton's eyes scorch a trail down my neck to the more-than-ample cleavage showing. He steps closer. Too close. "I want you for the job, Shay, because your sketches are the best I've seen." He makes eye contact and softens his voice. "I want you for the job because I think you can work those cool tattoo designs you did for Raven into the theme. You said yourself how much you'd like to use that concept to transform a space. That's exactly what I'm after."

His acknowledgment of my work loosens something in my chest, but I'm not letting him off that easily. "So why not mention it? We've been texting. Silly, nothing texts, but you could've let me in on this plan of yours. Maybe even told me what you really do for a living. What kind of moron springs this on someone?"

He scrubs a hand down his face. "Look. I'm sorry I lied. It can be a bad scene when girls find out what Sawyer and I do, and since we weren't pursuing things after Aspen, I didn't see the point in telling you. And based on the Shay I met there, I figured if you knew my intentions, you'd find a way to shut me down, so I kept my texts light."

"Okay. Fine. Whatever. But why now, why like this?"

He sighs and brushes a stray curl off my shoulder. "I want you for the job because of your designs, but...I also want to pick up where we left off. As much as I've tried, I can't forget you. Not just our *conference meetings*." His dark eyes skim every inch of me, nearly melting my skirt. "Your skiing. That afternoon I dislocated my shoulder. The few times you forgot to yell at me and smiled. I've lived with you in my head the past three months, and I'm done brooding. I'm done lusting after some chick across the country. And yeah, I have a son," he says before I can cut in. "I'm sorry I didn't mention him, but I tried to tell you about Jackson in Aspen, and—"

"And a girlfriend," I interrupt, more hurt than angry now. Remembering that colorful girl with her blue eyes and soft curves makes swallowing a challenge.

His jaw twitches like it does *after* we fight and *before* he claims my lips in a kiss. But he doesn't lean in. "If you'd let me finish my sentence, then you'd know the chick you think I'm sleeping with is my assistant. She's here to help me with work and Jackson. My wife, if you're wondering, died seven years ago. The day Jackson was born."

His last whispered words deflate my remaining anger, guilt blooming in its place. He lost a wife and is raising their son on his own, an explanation he tried to offer on multiple occasions in Aspen. Each time, my hand would go up, my "not another word" the first thing I'd say. Kolton's face would fall, but he'd recover quickly and snark back with his own I-could-give-a-shit reply.

Regret tarnishes my memories.

He steps forward and I step backward, until he has me cornered against the island. "Take the job, and go out with me. On a proper date. I won't walk away this time. It's been three months, and I only think about you more. If you turn me down, I'll just try harder." To make his point, he grips the countertop, caging me between his arms.

I've replayed our time together ad nauseam the past three months. I've brought myself to orgasm countless times since Aspen (last night included) while reliving our "meetings." I've compared every crappy date to him, spending each aftermath rereading his texts. With Kolton's mouth inches from mine, I want nothing more than to suck his tongue and grab his hips, desperate for him to ease the ache building under my skirt. But this is my life he's messing with, my fragile livelihood.

"I'm sorry about your wife, and I've thought about you, too. A lot." He presses closer, barely giving me room to breathe, to think. "But any way you work this out..." I struggle to form the words gathering in my mind. "...This situation ends with a no from me." As soon as that one syllable passes my lips, my heart squeezes.

He moves closer still, his unmistakable erection ghosting against my skirt. "I beg to differ."

I place my hands on his chest to gain some stability, some distance, and a shiver runs through him. The sensation conducts through my fingers like electricity, the attraction that spiked between us in Colorado as strong as ever. My knees weaken. My mouth dries. But nothing about this is a good idea. "I can't take a promotion if I didn't earn it, Kolton, and I'd never be okay with a guy using his sway to get me a job because he wants a date. So if you tell me that's all this is, a ruse to get me between your sheets"—I swallow, wishing like heck I could stop picturing him slipping out of me in the bathroom—"then I say: Fuck you. To the job and the date. But if you really think my designs are that good, and this date business is just an added bonus, then I'll take the work. I know I can do it. But it's still a fuck-you to the date. The last thing I need is for the firm to think I slept my way to the top. So, which 'fuck you' do you prefer?"

As he studies my face, unease clenches in my gut. Kolton's sincerity and interest when mentioning Raven's ink and my designs wasn't fake. Not only did he remember my journal, he remembered what I said about incorporating edgy tattoo images into a space. Since Lily took her freelance job with Moondog, I've checked them out. There's no doubt I could sink my teeth into their rock-and-roll vibe. Images flip rapid-fire through my mind, a jumble of inspiration that has me itching to get out my sketch pad. But if he chooses "fuck you" number one, I won't get the chance.

Seeming to come to a decision, Kolton releases the counter and grips my hips, each finger branding me. I whimper.

"I'll take the second fuck-you," he says, and my tense shoulders relax. A fraction. He lowers his mouth to my ear, his hot breath igniting goose bumps across my flesh. My traitorous hips tilt forward. "But it's only a matter of time before I take you out. That's a promise."

The loud screech from the other room sends Kolton spinning away from me as I try to recover from his nearness. His searing touch. He runs a hand over his head and ponytail, the hand I'd kill to have rubbing circles somewhere else. I'm sure my cheeks match the shade of my scarlet blouse, and I just manage to fix the button that came undone before Hilary pokes her head in the kitchen. "Have you two worked everything out?"

"Yes," Kolton says quickly.

She beams. "Wonderful. If you wouldn't mind coming to sign some paperwork, I'd like Maeve to have a quick word with Shay, then we can set up the first meeting."

He lingers a second, then nods at me. "I look forward to working with you. I know we can build on those meetings in Aspen."

His boots thump away as lust knots in my belly. I should be furious with Kolton for barreling into my life, no thought to the damage he'd cause, personally or professionally. But he just confessed he's been thinking about me the past three months. This man who lost his wife and is raising a son sought me out because he couldn't stay away. And he loves my designs. When Richard flipped through my sketches, his condescension bled through each "They're nice" and "Good effort."

Kolton not only saw my work, he saw me. My vision.

Lord knows he's consumed many quiet hours in my head as I've relived our short time together. Already, I miss his closeness. His woodsy scent. His promises of more. If he took the first "fuck you" and walked away, disappearing forever, something tells me it would have sent me face first into a bucket of Ben & Jerry's. But going out with Kolton would seal my fate at Concept. Hilary wouldn't tolerate me, the lowly intern, as job leader if I acquired said job while banging the client.

I can't risk getting fired.

Maeve barges through my thoughts and into the kitchen. She purses her bright red lips. "I don't know how you pulled this off, although I have some idea." Her stealthy gaze peruses my body, and her nose twitches.

Can she smell my arousal? Is it that freaking obvious?

"Hilary asked that I oversee your work so everything runs smoothly," she continues. "It won't be easy. Sketching is one thing; bringing your vision to life for a client is another. I will remind you, *Shy*, that Hilary is promoting me or Stuart to partner shortly. Your performance will reflect her choice. I trust you'll remember that."

Her tone snaps my shoulders back. "I take my work seriously, Maeve. I'm as surprised as you Kolton wants me heading the job, but I'm up for it. I won't let Hilary down, and I know you'll help out as much as needed. For the good of Concept." I match her, glare for glare, the reality of this opportunity buoying my confidence. My once stuttering self would have turtled when confronted by Maeve and her aggression, but I'm not that girl anymore.

Finally, I get to stretch my wings as a designer. I get to prove I can do this.

Two taps of her leopard-print heel later she says, "Good. We'll be meeting Kolton tomorrow at the location. You'll need to put in more hours. Nights. Weekends. Don't expect to have a social life."

With that, she sashays out, my momentary excitement shattering, and all things Kolton fade to the background.

Nights. Weekends. Extra hours.

That means giving up my job at Sass & Style. My paycheck.

I grip the counter behind me to keep from sinking to the floor. I can't pass up this chance. Even in the face of homelessness. This is the gig I've been waiting for, the one that makes the parade of hideous retirement homes worth it and validates everything I've worked toward. Kolton may be the reason behind it, but there's no question I can pimp out his store and rock this project. If I pull it off, I'll have a paycheck and permanent design position in a matter of months.

I'll have to talk to Natasha, ask her to cover some shifts at Sass & Style and pray she doesn't replace me. When I'm there, I'll have to hustle for extra commission. Call the few customers on file who've been delaying purchases. I can totally do this. I *will* do this. If it comes down to it, I'll suck up my pride and ask Lily for help.

What I'm *not* sure of is if I can hold Kolton off that long. The gleam in his eye when promising I'd be dating him soon was predatory. Wolfish. It jacked up his sex appeal to Theo James status. In Aspen, I wasn't able to resist his charms, our sparking chemistry breaking my defenses. If I'm honest, I don't want to resist them now. I want nothing more than to text him my address and pick up exactly where we left off. This isn't a vacation, though. This is reality. There's too much at stake.

Fourteen

Kolton

"Daddy, do you think that man outside the McDonald's lives there?"

I glance in the rearview mirror at Jackson's puckered lips and scrunched face. Always the inquisitor. "Unfortunately, buddy, some people fall on hard times and can't afford a house. If they have nowhere to go, they end up living on the street."

"Does he get cold?"

"Yeah, I'm sure he gets cold."

"Does he have friends to play with?"

"I don't know, bud."

"Does he have a dog? Or a hamster like the one Mrs. Cooper lets us sign outta class? And…And how does he watch TV? And what if no one's there to read him a story? Or what if…what if someone ac-ci-den-ta-lly steps on him?"

Stella adjusts a pin in her pink hair, then she angles her shoulders to face Jackson in the backseat of the Dodge Fucking Caravan the rental company gave me because they lost our reservation. The mid-size Lexus I drive at home may be a barely disguised family van, but there's no hiding the emasculation going on here.

"Jackson," she says, "those are all valid questions, and if we hadn't been driving around for two hours picking up mysterious things for your dad, I'd have the energy to answer all fifty of them. Maybe if you ask your cryptic father to stop dragging us around the city while listening to the *Frozen* soundtrack on repeat, we could sit by the pool at the rental house, and I could field your interrogation."

"You're on a need-to-know basis," I say, my eyes on the road. Last time I shared dating plans with Stella, she called ahead to the restaurant I booked and sent over a copy of *Kama Sutra*. Her reasoning: All girls want to know they won't have to fake it.

Needless to say, she's still single.

She raises a perfectly sculpted eyebrow. "This rental car smells like that chili you bring to work, masked with a god-awful pine air freshener. If you don't at least give me something to do, like expertly advise you on whether the stunt you have planned for Shay will blow up in your face, I might quit and move in with the McDonald's man."

"Me toooo!" Jackson shoots a hand in the air. "Daddy has to come, and we'll all read the Gs in the Bri-ta-nni-ca book, 'kay? Or, *oh*"—he lowers his high-pitched voice into what he thinks is a whisper—"or the urban book, Aunt Stella. Right? Can we? I didn't tell Daddy about the Banana Polish one."

My foot jerks on the brake, and the car jumps. "Last I checked, *Aunt* Stella, I put that book down in the grocery store." I flex my fingers around the wheel, keeping the car in control.

It's bad enough Jackson's with us guys all the time, Sawyer and Nico treating my son like a locker-room buddy, but Stella is an island of her own. A blunt, filterless island. Still, she knows Jackson only eats red apples and has to wear two different socks. She knows how hard it is raising a kid on your own; her single mother deserved an award for weathering Stella's wild teen years. Most important, her defense of Jackson's quirks is mother-bear ferocious. When that little shit Evan started picking on him in school, she nearly got arrested.

She drums her fingers to "Let It Go" playing for the third time. "Kids are growing up fast these days, wonderful-secretive-boss-of-mine. I'm preparing him early, so when a floozy in his first grade class asks if he wants his banana polished, he'll have the sense to say no. Right, Jackson?"

I catch his fist pump through the rearview mirror. "Nooooo polish!"

She grins and says, "See? Trained and ready."

"That book disappears tonight." I try to sound severe, but my barely contained chuckle doesn't reinforce the point.

"It disappears when you stop being all sneaky about these errands, *boss*." Her emphasis on my title drips with sarcasm. And playfulness.

If Stella weren't my employee, I'd probably have asked her out ages ago. But she is, and burlesque clubs aren't my idea of a good time. Plus, her help with Jackson is invaluable.

When she waltzed into Moondog for her interview three years ago, wearing a skintight dress and mile-high heels, and blatantly said it looked like a chimp organized my files, I hired her on the spot. Her résumé was flawless, and my office was a chaotic mess. Under that kaleidoscope skin is a smart woman.

A nosy, smart woman.

I glance into the rearview mirror as Jackson adjusts his glasses. "Should I tell Aunt Stella my plan to woo Shay?" I ask.

He twitches his nose. "What's *woo*?"

I almost offer the easy answer—to make Shay fall for me—but that doesn't apply to this scenario. She's as interested as I am. The way her voice got all breathy when cornered in that kitchen, the way she trembled in my arms, was all the evidence I needed. I know firsthand how wet Shay gets when we fight. I'd bet my left nut she was drenched and ready for me. And I was harder than was decent. There's just something about Shay. After seeing her in my dreams for months, being within biting distance of her soft curves sent all synapses firing. But I wanted to hug her, too. Hold her against my chest and whisper how much I've missed her glare and her lips and how I think about that moment I dislocated my shoulder—the stories she shared, her tenderness. Although I didn't do any of that, I won't walk away from her now. Still, I get why she's freaked, why she panicked about her reputation and being taken seriously on her first big job.

It's only been a week, and already the level of work she's doing proves I made the right choice hiring her. Shay likely stays up all night working on her sketches, and Hilary pores over them each morning, her excitement evident with each approving nod. And I'm blown away. My first look at her rough designs in black and gray, bold splashes of deep purple and wine highlighting the assorted dragons and eagles flying through the space, took my breath away. Dating me won't impact her career; nobody can deny what she's creating.

She just has to see that in herself.

When my GPS announces our destination, I pull over, lucky to find a spot that can accommodate the boat I'm driving. I swivel to face Jackson so I can answer his question. "Normally *woo* means to make someone like you."

He frowns. "Like Evan? Do I need to woo Evan?"

Stella's frosted pink lips flatten. "You need to shove that little—"

"No," I cut in, shooting her a warning glare. "Sometimes it's best to ignore people who aren't nice. The Evans of the world need to make people feel small to feel better. They aren't the ones you woo. But if, say, a girl…"

"Or boy," Stella says, her blue eyes pinning me with judgment.

I sigh. "If you're interested in spending more time with a girl, or *boy*," I say, knowing I'll support Jackson no matter what path he's destined to walk, "then you sometimes have to show the person what they're missing. In Shay's case, I need to show her I'm interested in her for *her*. Not just because she's pretty or good at her job, but because we'd be good together."

I've given Shay as much space as I could handle the past week. After missing her for months, seeing her now and going home alone each night is my own personal hell. I'm ready to explode. Physically. Emotionally. Whatever minty stuff she uses in her hair is an aphrodisiac, each lingering glance a bolt of lightning to my chest. And her curves? I haven't had the pleasure of seeing Shay naked (*yet*), but there's no doubt her breasts are bigger, her hips fuller, and it's sexy as hell. She flaunts her body in figure-hugging jeans and skirts, not afraid of her femininity. Certainly not concerned about the effect her wardrobe has on me.

"How do we woo her, Daddy?"

"Yeah, how?" Stella puts her chin in her hands like an eager schoolgirl.

I roll my eyes. "For starters, we bring her McDonald's."

She drops her hands. "Jackson, don't take dating advice from your father. Ever. You have a question, you come to me."

Ignoring her, I flip off my seat belt. "It's in the bag. If you knew Shay, you'd get it. And anyway, it's stage one. She won't say yes today. Or tomorrow. I'll have to wear her down."

Stella squints at me. "Okay, maybe you're not completely clueless about the mysterious ways of women. But what's with all the other stuff?"

I glance at the brown bags in the backseat and shrug. "Nothing. I can't bring lunch for Shay and not the rest of the team. Unfortunately, that group's not a one-stop-shop."

"Daddy, what's glu-ten?" Jackson leans forward to read the sign above the small store on our right. *Good-bye Gluten*.

With her hand on the door, Stella says, "It's an evil monster that attacks pretentious people, killing their ability to have fun."

The more time Jackson spends with her, the more likely it is I'll find Child Services at my door.

I get out of the car as a truck whizzes by. When there's a break in traffic, I slide open Jackson's door and help him out. "Gluten is found in grain, the stuff that makes bread and pasta and those fish crackers you like. For some people, it hurts their tummy when they eat it."

He puts his hand in mine and repeats, "Glu-ten," cataloguing the word for future reference.

"By the way," Stella says over her shoulder, "Caroline called to remind me that Jackson needs a new pencil sharpener for your library outings." Her cocked eyebrow reinforces what I already know: These two months will be agonizing for Marina's mother. It's the longest she'll have been away from her grandson.

"Roger that," I say, making a mental note to send her photos regularly. I don't let my mind race forward, the future fallout of being with Shay having the potential to crush Caroline. I promised myself I wouldn't worry about what's next. Like Sawyer's always saying: Seize the day. Carpe diem and all that.

We head inside to gather Maeve's fat-gluten-dairy-taste–free lunch, our last stop before we hit the storefront to go over Shay's revised sketches. After she devours the fries in her lunch, she'll find a note from me. The first of many. I haven't been this excited since I used a syringe to squirt habanero pepper extract into every piece of fruit in my frat house. Hopefully, this time, I won't get the piss kicked out of me.

* * *

Shay and Hilary are hunched over a makeshift table at the far end of the room as laborers strip off drywall, exposing a layer of original brick. Little evidence remains of the jean shop that occupied this space. In another month, it'll be unrecognizable. With Stella and Jackson off to the library, I make my way toward the two women at the back, dust billowing with each step. I drop the bags next to the sketches on the table and study the top one—a bird's-eye view of the layout.

I position myself next to Shay. "Love the changes," I say, leaning lower. Her shoulder brushes mine, against the spot her teeth sank into in Aspen. My skin itches with awareness. "I like the checkout counter there, centered but visible from the door." I tap my finger next to the sketched hanging wall instead of dragging my nose up her neck. "Maybe move this left a bit. Leave more room for the accessory section. With Lily's help, we'll be expanding it over the next few years. Once you've done that, scan it and send it to Sawyer. He's got a better eye for this stuff. But I like everything you've done."

Love it, actually. This Moondog location will be a feast for the eyes. Something people will want to be a part of. When they buy a jacket, they're not buying a piece of clothing. They're buying a lifestyle. An image. That's what drives sales. And she's delivering.

A blush blooms on Shay's cheeks, her few freckles disappearing under a scarlet stain. I'd like to think it's my closeness heating her skin. By the way she smiles, though, I'd say it's pride. My ribs tighten. When Jackson looks at me with love in his eyes, when he does well in school or I teach him something new, a glow seeps through me. But this? Being a part of Shay's success stokes the slow burn I've nursed the past few months. I step away before I do something stupid and screw this up.

Hilary squeezes Shay's shoulder. "I'm impressed. Make a list of samples you need Maeve and Stuart to pick up so we can finalize finishes. They should be by shortly. We'll need a draft done of the hanging wall. With its angle, you'll have to vary the shelves on the acute side. Every millimeter counts. Make sure the lower ones are long enough to line up with the ones above them. But I love how the layered silkscreen prints will pop off the top. It will make people feel like they're cocooned in your world."

We all look up as a guy pounds through the drywall, the sound echoing through the empty space. "Hope you ladies are hungry," I say, gesturing to the bags piled on the table.

Hilary cringes. "That's thoughtful, but I don't eat fast food." She points a manicured nail at the McDonald's emblem.

I wince as the dude with the hammer blasts another hole in

the wall. "That's for Shay." I sift through the bags and pull out the chicken curry sandwich she mentioned going out for the other day. I hand it over, and she peeks inside. "Wow, that's…" Her keen blue eyes roam over my face, as if meeting me for the first time. She runs a hand over her pantsuit. "Thank you. I'm surprised you remembered."

I shrug and lean over the table, separating the other lunches. "There's sushi for Stuart, some gluten-free thing for Maeve, and there's a whack of burritos in here for the guys. And this"—I grab the greasy McDonald's bag and hold it out—"is for Shay."

She's not looking at me, though. Not even a side glance. Her puckered brows are focused on the other food. Shit. Maybe she's gone on some crazy chick diet.

Hilary glances between us, then grabs the burritos and her sandwich. "I'll take these to the workers." She raises her bag toward me in salute. "Thanks again. We'll meet here tomorrow morning."

I nod and look back at Shay, who's watching me, my outstretched hand still clutching her lunch. She cocks her head to the side. "You didn't have to do this."

"No. I didn't. I wanted to do this. You've all been putting in long hours." Her thick-lashed eyes flit back to the other food, and I can't read her worth shit. When she's angry, Terminator Shay is incapable of hiding her flaring nostrils. When she's hot for me, it oozes from her every pore. But this Shay, the thoughtful one, is a blank slate, and if she's not eating fries, today's plan is toast. Frustrated, I start to tug my arm back.

She shoots her hand out to stop me. "Not a move, Fabio. That's mine."

Game on.

I run a hand through my shoulder-length hair. "I'm doing a shirt-less photo shoot later. You should come."

She laughs. "Only if I get to wax your chest."

It's a small chuckle, nothing like how she lost it at our first official meeting. That Maeve bitch barked at Shay about some project the two had been consulting on. Once Maeve left, I turned toward Shay and said, "What's with Cruella De Vil?" *One Hundred and One Dalmatians* had been on repeat in my house—Jackson's most recent addiction, those animated movies like crack for kids. I didn't think my comment was all that hilarious, but she doubled over in hysterics and had to walk in circles as she wiped tears from her eyes.

The second she lost it, I knew. Living in the moment and am-bushing her was the best idea I've ever had. Her throaty laugh bled through me until I was howling, too, my gut aching from the effort. The only woman I've shared those spontaneous flashes with was Marina. Never since. It's one of the things I've missed the most, es-pecially with Jackson's quirks. Marina hasn't been here to laugh with me when he insists on wearing his underwear over his pants. When he won't leave the house unless I put on the crown he made me for my birthday. There hasn't been anyone I've *wanted* to share those moments with. Until Shay.

She snatches the bag from my hand and walks over to a nearby bench. She brushes it off, not that it does much good with the dry-wall dust coating every square inch. When she's settled, she opens the bag, sticks her nose in, and inhales.

Burrito and a couple waters in hand, I sit beside her and chuckle. "Glad you're not on some psycho cleanse."

"I've done enough cleanses to last a lifetime." She pulls out the Big Mac and practically salivates.

I stretch out my legs and cross my ankles. "You don't strike me as the type."

She's about to take a bite but pauses. Something crosses her face—anger? It disappears quickly. "I'm not, at least not now. My ex was all into that stuff. Stupid diets, keeping up appearances. I kind of got sucked into his world more than I should have."

It's the most detail she's offered about the fuckwit who messed with her head before we met. Shay's softer than she was in Aspen. Lighter. Whatever she was dealing with, whatever that dickhead she dated did to her, it seems to have rolled off her shoulders. Made her stronger, maybe? She's still feisty, though. After our first scheduled meeting, she wasted no time texting me: I'm not in the sex trade. Quit staring at my boobs.

My reply: Then stop wearing red lingerie.

The next day, her red bra was unmistakable through her knit top.

Tired of tiptoeing around her past, I say, "This stuff with your ex—how did you let it go on so long? I don't mean to be blunt, but…five years? I can't picture you knuckling down under anyone." I set my food aside and swig my water.

Taking my lead, she moves the bag and burger to the seat beside her and wipes her hands on a napkin. "Coming to the city was a big step for me. Lily went to New York to study design, Raven was in teacher's college up north, and I scraped together enough to get into a design program here. Coming from a small town where everyone knew me, I struggled. Had trouble making friends. Couldn't meet anyone I really clicked with outside of classes. Then I met the Dick."

"The Dick?"

"The Dick. Richard. Lawyer extraordinaire." She waves one hand in a flourish.

I raise an eyebrow. "I see I wasn't the first man in your life to earn a profane nickname."

"Or the last," she says, and I grip my water tighter. "Just guys I dated recently," she adds, and I nearly crush the thing. "Anyway," she continues, "Richard had a way about him, and made me feel for the first time in a while like I belonged somewhere, to someone. I needed that. Too much, I guess. I lost sight of who I was in the relationship. Didn't recognize myself anymore. Didn't particularly like myself. Still, it was hard for me to move on. Then he dumped me for a newer model, and I took off to Aspen...where I met the Asshole." Smirking, she tips her head toward me.

I don't return her smile. "How many guys have you been with since then? Since Aspen."

One beat. Two. She lowers her voice. "I've been on dates with a string of losers."

I don't ask if those losers made it to first base, or further. Not something I care to hear. Gradually, I ease my death grip on the water. "I may not have known you when all that went down, but the girl I know now is strong. Independent. And I wouldn't want her any other way."

Her hazel eyes glaze, her emotion close to spilling over. Instead of replying, she says, "Tell me something about your wife."

I lean back, sifting through the memories, some sharp, some fuzzy. "Marina had just finished nursing school when she got pregnant. She wanted to work in pediatrics. Help kids. She had a big heart—big enough to deal with the anguish inherent in the job. She skied. Not as good as you, but she liked it. We had a bad time apart our first year at university, but, mostly, things were easy. We laughed a lot." By the time I look over at Shay, she's wiping at the corner of her eyes. "Thanks for asking. I don't talk about her much."

She places her hand on my shoulder. "Anytime."

The bench below us hasn't moved, dust still hangs in the air, but the space between us shifts. The way her touch lingers, I'd say she feels it, too.

"You should eat," I say. "Wouldn't want your McDonald's to get cold."

A nod later, she takes a massive bite of her burger, and I can't look away from her skinny jeans and those red boots that were latched around my waist the first night we hooked up. Her gray button-down top dims the often intense green in her hazel eyes, and her long curls are braided down her back. With minimal makeup, she's the definition of beautiful. I've backed off the past few days, kept things friendly between us. Businesslike. But keeping a lid on my feelings for Shay is like stuffing a ten-ton elephant into a dog crate. Especially after glimpsing her past and sharing a slice of mine.

I unwrap my burrito, and for the next five minutes neither of us speaks.

As I crumple my napkin, I sense Shay's attention. I've become attuned to her the past week, my scalp tingling when she looks my way. It happens often. "If you don't finish those fries," I say, "I'm calling dibs."

"The hell you are."

I sit, arms folded, waiting. It won't be long now. When a grin lights her face, I know she's found the note I placed at the bottom of her container. My heart pounds in time to the hammering echoing off the walls. She reaches in, pulls out the piece of paper, and leans back to tuck it into her front pocket. With a sigh, she looks at me and says, "No."

Then she's up and walking away as I expected she would. I'll give her a day to reread my words. A day to let my intent crack the wall she's built between us. A day before stage two goes into effect.

Fifteen

Shay

I've been staring at the computer screen for a good five minutes, the cursor blinking in the same stupid spot. Coming to Concept on a Saturday morning was supposed to help me focus, but it's a lost cause. All because of Kolton. Everything in my life these days revolves around him. This amazing job, the lonely nights I spend wishing he were with me. It's all-consuming, and it reminds me too much of my days with Richard, when my world orbited his. One more reason to steer clear of a certain someone with model hair. If it were only that easy.

I search my desk and find my phone under a pile of sketches. Normally, Lily's an early riser, but seven a.m. on a Saturday is questionable. Still, I shoot her a text. My solo mental "should I, shouldn't I" Kolton Marathon is dizzying.

He gave me another gift. This one was ... wow. I don't know what to do.

I tap my toe, thankful for the quiet of the empty brownstone as I wait to see if she's up. My stalemate with Kolton has me rattled. I'm not sure how to deal with his advances, and the feelings I'm trying to ignore. I also don't want him to stop. Not that it's likely. I've been pursued before. When I met Richard, he planned elaborate dates to fancy restaurants, once booking me a spa day followed by a picnic in the park. His charm was a balm to my lonely soul, his lavish attention more than any struggling girl could resist. Kolton is the Dick on steroids.

My phone buzzes: You're up early.

Couldn't sleep. I'm at Concept. Thought I'd get some drafting done.

A moment of silence, then: I'm so proud of you, and Sawyer loves your work. We can't wait to see it. But back to Kolton and his "wow" gift. Do tell.

Normally I'd latch on to her use of "we" when discussing Sawyer, like they're an item. A pair. Today, however, I'm too confused to tease her.

He's outdone himself, I text.

I find it hard to believe he topped the video.

Consider it topped.

I'm dying. TELL ME.

I start to reply but delete my message, unsure how to describe this last gift and the extent to which it's affected me. At first, I thought this was about the chase, a cat-and-mouse game that brought out Kolton's caveman instincts to pursue. But the thought he puts into each offer, each note, says otherwise. When I saw that McDonald's bag a couple of weeks ago, I figured he was trying to seduce me with fries. An easy win for him. A burst of pleasure swirled across my heated skin, as often happens in his presence, but it was the other lunches that sealed the deal. He knew what each of us liked, down to making sure Stuart's cucumber rolls had the rice on the outside. He waved it off like it was nothing, but it was far from nothing. Most people pay cursory attention to those around them, too focused on themselves or how they're perceived. Kolton isn't most people.

He notices things—likes, dislikes—cataloguing them for future reference. At first, I was unsure why he was here instead of Sawyer, Sawyer being the creative of the two, but it's clear someone capable of delegating single-mindedly was needed to control the renovation. Bills minded. Details tended to. In other words, Kolton.

Now all that meticulous intensity is focused on me.

He knew I'd save my fries for last, and the note at the bottom caught me off guard: *I have five bathrooms in the house I'm renting. Go out with me.*

I said no.

N. O.

Two letters strung together, hardly containing the *yes yes yes* that wanted to spill free. That night, I relived our two bathroom escapades from Aspen. I could almost feel Kolton's hard body against mine, his hips punishing as they drove into me. My fingers moved south, and I closed my eyes as I imagined his hands as mine. His length filling me. I fell apart in seconds, his name on my lips as I rode the end of my orgasm.

Then I got pissed. Like Artemis pissed. That Greek goddess and her slaughtering of innocents on a whim suddenly seemed fair. Righteous, even. (Thank you eleventh-grade English.) Who was Kolton to force memories on me when I couldn't act on them? Who was he to dangle what I couldn't have in my face? An asshole, that's who.

But assholes don't crisscross the city to make sure everyone has exactly what they want to eat. They don't follow up with four more gifts over the next two weeks, each more meaningful than the last. They don't share intimate details about their deceased wife.

You still there?

I blink at my phone. Yes.

Was it better than the PEZ?

I smile. How he remembered the two-second conversation we had three months ago is beyond me. In Aspen, we walked into a pharmacy to find medication for his shoulder, and when a display of PEZ candy caught my eye I mentioned how my brother used to get it for me when I was upset. I didn't go into detail. Didn't mention it was when I stuttered and would come home after being trailed by Sue Anne Hinkley at lunch, her *Sh-Sh-Shay* parroted for all to hear. My brother would give me a new PEZ dispenser and list every famous person who stuttered: Winston Churchill, Nicole Kidman, Lewis Carroll. James Earl Jones's smooth baritone once *clip-clip-clopped* like a lame horse. He told me it was a sign of intelligence. He said it meant I'd do great things.

I didn't give Kolton any of these details to make the candy meaningful. It was a blip of a conversation, and he remembered.

Yes, I write. Better than the PEZ.

Fine, but I don't see how he could top the movies.

Before yesterday, I'd have agreed. The movies were pretty awesome. Another nothing moment Kolton held onto from Aspen. One of our many fights centered on movies. The dude watches nothing but action flicks, particularly those boring kung fu films and everything *Rambo*. I ranted at him about gratuitous violence, and how art like the *Before Sunrise* trilogy are what people should watch, raw and real cinema.

What did he do? He gifted me all three movies, but in typical Kolton fashion, he taped his favorite quote to each one. He actually watched them.

Before Sunrise: "Isn't everything we do in life a way to be loved a little more?"

My resolve to keep him at a distance weakened.

Before Sunset: "I don't want to be one of those people that don't believe in any kind of magic."

My willpower joined my stomach in a free fall.

Before Midnight: "You're fucking nuts! You are. Good luck! Find somebody else to put up with your shit for more than like six months, okay? But I accept the whole package, the crazy and the brilliant. I know you're not gonna change, and I don't want you to. It's called accepting you for being you."

The last one nearly broke me, my resolve turning to mush along with my heart. It's everything I didn't have with the Dick. I changed myself for Richard and vowed I'd never let that happen again. And here comes Kolton, offering me everything I want in a relationship. It cracked the already weakened floodgate to my emotions, my barely tethered feelings for him overflowing. It was a freaking tsunami.

I didn't break, though. I kissed him softly on the lips, said no, then walked away. I could feel his eyes on me for each of the thirty-two steps it took to get to my car. Could still feel the press of his lips as I sat for five minutes before pulling away from the curb.

Now he's topped the movies.

Needing a voice of reason to confirm what I'm doing is right, that not dating Kolton is for the best, I answer Lily: Remember the first night in their condo? The bathroom sex?

Yes...

Remember the red lingerie I bought that day?

YES...

We were kind of frantic, and he tore off my underwear.

AND????

And I figured they got trashed. Totally forgot about them. But...

No.

Yes.

He kept them?

Apparently. And the note packed with them hurt my heart. Even back then, he couldn't let me go. What do I do? If I say yes, I could mess up everything with this job.

I don't mention how desperate I am for the promotion and the raise that comes with it. Not a word about my dwindling cash flow now that I've lost shifts at Sass & Style. Natasha's barely getting by, working extra hours to cover for me. Who knows how long she'll let this go on? My life these days is balanced on a fraying wire.

Lily would help me if I asked. She'd invite me to her apartment, but she and Kevin have been struggling lately, their long relationship no longer as solid as it was. Even if I could swallow my pride, that's not a scene I want to crash. And Raven's place is tiny. Like one-cramped-room tiny. Still, if a miracle doesn't happen in the next twelve days, I'll have to ask Lily to borrow money. I'll have to be *that* friend.

Are you interested? Lily texts. If the job weren't in the way, would you go out with Kolton?

I reply without hesitation. Yes.

If you don't give in, do you think you'll always wonder, what if?

This time, I pause. Then, Yes.

There's your answer. You've done nothing but amazing work on this project. I can't imagine Hilary would hold it against you.

My resolve wavers, so I pile on the excuses: But it's like he's too entrenched in my life. My job is because of him. He may have hired me because he thinks I'm right for the work, but he's still the reason for it. I don't want to feel reliant on a guy again.

A moment passes before my phone lights up. I look down, expecting Lily's reply, but it's not Lily. It's Kolton. I'd swear a cool breeze whispers across my neck, a visceral reaction I can't blame on the no-longer-broken air-conditioning. Worried he can hear the rapid beating of my heart, I place my hand over my chest and read his message.

Hate to ask this, but I'm in a bind with Jackson. Stella's taking him to a morning pottery class, but she has to leave early. I have a few things to do and might not make it to pick him up. Any chance you can grab him for me? At 11:00? I can meet you at the library when I'm done.

Disappointment rolls through me at his businesslike tone.

Candid. Friendly. Detached.

After I left the construction site yesterday, his unopened gift clutched in my hand, I'm sure he was expecting a reaction from me—a call, a text, anything. When I pulled the neatly folded red lace from the tissue paper, I sat, unmoving, for who knows how long. Then I read his note:

I'm so consumed by you. I don't understand why, but I've stopped trying to figure it out. You're the first woman in forever to get under my skin. And it's not just the attraction. This torn lace holds some delicious memories, but I kept it because it reminded me of you. It's the only thing I had to remember our time together, and keeping it meant there was a chance it wasn't over. That I'd see you again. Don't let this be the end, Shay. We're too good together. It's too wild and too much fun and I, for one, would like to know how much better we could be if we do this right. Please, take a risk on me.

He took a risk, admitting just how much he's thought about me since Aspen, and that he's a bit of a perv for keeping my torn red thong. Still, the sentiment and words crept under my guard, and my heart nearly burst. Too overwhelmed to even crack a joke, all he got in return was silence. *Have you been wearing these daily?* I should have texted, or, *The fabric smells kind of salty.* But I said nothing.

Now he's distancing himself.

My lungs struggle for air, like on the day my supposed best friend Christine did an impersonation of my stutter in front of our class, the feeling like swallowing burning tar.

Lily's reply to my text comes through then: I don't think Kolton is the type of guy who'd want a mindless Barbie doll girl. He gave you those gifts, each unique, each representing the real you, because that's the girl he's fallen for. The real Shay I know and love.

She's right, and I'm tired of fighting my feelings. If I don't go out with Kolton, potential regret and what-ifs could snowball until I'm a bigger and hotter mess than I was after Richard. I'm done sitting on my heels. I text Kolton: Sure. Forward the address. I hit send, even though I haven't finished drafting the changing rooms for the shop. Even though I'm wearing ripped jean shorts and an oversize Wildcats T-shirt, and I have a shift at Sass & Style this afternoon. Time to play my hand at the Game of Life.

* * *

I enter the storefront on Yonge Street. Ten or so kids are covered in drying clay, paintbrushes in hand as they finish decorating their works of art. Among the khaki-and-white–wearing parents, Stella stands apart—a Jackson Pollock painting among a room of Michelangelos. In a tight black bodice with two thin straps, every inch of swirling color on her arms and chest is emphasized. The kaleidoscope continues down her calves, the area visible below her white pedal pushers and above her pink slingback shoes. I bet she's not even wearing a bra.

She waves as Jackson runs over to her, some atrocious clay piece in his hand. He pushes his glasses up his nose and frowns down at the ugliest I-have-no-idea-what-the-heck-it-is thing I have ever seen. "The glaze is wrong," he says. "If I did the yellow one like I wanted, it would've been better. And I told the teacher I wanted to do yellow, but she said red would be nicer, but it's not, and now I'm stuck with red."

Stella picks up the maybe-ashtray and turns it around in her hands. "You're right. You should've done yellow. Know why?"

He slumps forward and stares at his sneakers. The sneakers encasing one yellow and one white sock. "'Cause my ideas are different.

And different is unique. And unique is the best." He huffs out a breath and looks up at Stella. "I broke the rule, didn't I?"

She nods. "Let this ugly red glaze remind you to always go with your gut. Especially when it comes to style. Most people wouldn't know style if it bit them in the derrière."

He squints as she hands him back his maybe-ashtray. "De-rri-ère? That's, like, bum, right? Uncle Sawyer says *ass*, but Daddy always gets mad."

"Hey!" I do some weird waving thing, my impression of Queen Elizabeth on acid, as I hurry over to meet them. Hopefully, my awkward moves are enough to distract this PTA group from commenting on Jackson's language. The way the gray-haired teacher narrows her eyes at us, I'd say we've been caught.

He turns toward me, his eyes widening behind his Coke-bottle glasses. "Shay! You're here!" Then he turns to Stella and attempts to lower his voice. Unsuccessfully. *"She's here."*

I'm sure he was told I'd be coming, but there's something about the charged excitement in his tone that sets off my Kolton radar. But he's nowhere to be seen. "I'm here," I say, glancing around again.

"Can I ask her?" he says to Stella, like I'm not right beside them.

"Go for it," she says.

Sharp scents of musty earth cling to the air in the shop, the warmth from the running kilns radiating through the space. I grab the hem of my top and shake the fabric to create a breeze. "I'd say now is the perfect time to ask. What can I do for you, Jackson?"

His eyes flit up to Stella again, then he swallows and addresses me. "Have you been wooed?"

I stop shaking my shirt. "Wooed?"

Jackson nods vigorously. "Wooed. Did you say yes? Are you gonna date my dad?"

The smells of clay and fire press in around me. I raise an eyebrow at Stella. "Wooed?"

She shrugs. "Wooed."

At least coming from her corseted-wearing self, it doesn't sound so out of place. But that old-fashioned word in this modern-day pottery shop has distracted me from what's really going down. Kolton is using his kid to get to me. "Sorry," I say to Jackson. "I didn't say yes. Sadly, I am not wooed."

Total freaking lie, Batman. But I can hold out a little longer, long enough to find out what Kolton has planned. Hopefully, curiosity doesn't kill this cat.

Instead of looking upset or unleashing those impossible-to-resist puppy-dog eyes all kids stock in their arsenal, he jumps and grabs the maybe-ashtray from Stella and holds it out for me. "I made this for you, but it's not the right color. It was s'posed to be yellow like I wanted, but I didn't follow my rule and painted it red so it's not as nice as it coulda been, but…" He holds it up higher.

Hesitantly, I take his offering. "Thanks, Jackson. It's the nicest"—bowl? Vase? Cup?—"gift I've ever gotten. Even though it's red." I run my hand over the rough, wonky edges, then look inside and the dust-filled air solidifies in my throat. I should have expected this. Kolton warned me the first day he wouldn't back off.

In uneven black strokes, Jackson has written: *Please date my dad.*

The teacher calls for the kids to clean up, and Jackson runs off. I blink a few times, then turn my likely shocked face to Stella. "Does he do this sort of wooing often?"

She chuckles and smooths a few pink flyaway hairs into her bouffant do. "Listen. I've worked for the boys for three years. I've watched them date and flirt, and raise this kid, and build their business. But I've never witnessed the wooing. Kolton's not a player. He goes through phases with women, wanting to meet someone, then getting fed up. But he wouldn't put this much time and energy into just anyone. I mean, look at this." She points to the maybe-ashtray and rolls her eyes.

Taking my silence as rejection, Stella places her hand on my arm. "I don't know the details, and I don't want to overstep, but"—she winks—"I will. I'm sure you've noticed I don't look like your typical high-profile personal assistant." We glance around at the Stepford Wives who are doing their best to pretend we don't exist. "Getting a good job wasn't easy," she says. "I'm smart. I aced my bachelor's degree, and I can tame any computer program thrown at me. I'm also organized to a fault. But I wasn't willing to wear some granny pantsuit and cover up who I am to prove that. Kolton and Sawyer never judged me. If they had, I'd have moved on." When I don't say anything, she continues, "You're a good designer, Shay. Great. Who you do or don't date won't change that. Don't compromise yourself to please others."

After Lily's "regret" speech, that one word—*compromise*—confirms my decision to date Kolton. Here I've been worried I'll compromise myself with *him*, lose my identity, my wants and desires, in a relationship again. I haven't stopped to think about how *not* being with him is denying my most basic needs. Trading off romance, great sex, and potential love to fit into Hilary's view of what's appropriate is me, once again, molding myself to be what someone else wants.

I turn the maybe-ashtray in my hand and run my fingers over Jackson's words. "I am so wooed."

"Glad to hear it. Just know it takes a lot for a single father to bring a woman into his life. Don't take that lightly. Anyway, I have to split. I have a tattoo appointment."

I study her exposed flesh, unsure where she'll squeeze another design. There is, of course, the intimate skin below her corseted top and pedal pushers. I blush at the thought.

"Jackson," she calls, "I'm heading out. Shay will take you to meet your dad at the library." She hands me a small backpack.

With one last wipe of his table, he walks over and places his small hand in mine. "'Kay."

As Stella sashays her full hips out the door, I glance down at Kolton's mini-me—his sandy hair and warm brown eyes unmistakable. Stella's right. Kolton's risking more than me by pursuing us. Emotionally, at least. If I date him, I'll be part of his son's life, and I'm suddenly unsure I'm qualified for the job description. Getting deeper means being in an open and honest relationship, putting aside all the baggage the Dick heaped on my shoulders. Baggage I haven't fully sorted yet. But denying my feelings for Kolton is like saying I don't like cupcakes. Hopefully, I won't mess this up.

Sixteen

Kolton

I can't remember the exact symptoms of a heart attack. Something about an uncomfortable pressure in the chest that comes and goes, like squeezing or fullness. I'm pretty sure there's shortness of breath, too. Either I'm about to drop to the ground, or seeing my son's hand in Shay's as they walk toward me is messing with my blood flow. She looks stunning as always, but the relaxed fit of her ripped shorts and oversize T-shirt kicks her sexy up a notch. Jackson's dog-ugly pottery is clutched in her free hand, his small backpack slung over her shoulder.

He's talking up a storm, and she tips her head back, those long curls catching in a breeze as she laughs.

She stops in front of me, and the smile slips from her face. "Your kid's really shy. You need to work on that."

"Yeah," I say, playing along with her sarcasm. "Hard to get a word out of him."

Flipping the pottery in her hand, she holds it so I can read the center: *Please date my dad.* "You know anything about this?"

I pull my head back, shocked. "Jackson gave that to *you*? Wow… this is awkward. He was supposed to give that to his teacher."

Jackson giggles and tugs on her hand. "No I *wasn't.* It was for you."

She bats her eyes at me. "Didn't peg you for the older-woman type. How very Oedipus of you."

"Ee-di-puss?" Jackson says.

"Yeah, buddy, Oedipus. He was a Greek guy from a long time ago." Who married his mother, I don't say, because it's creepy as fuck. I keep my focus on Shay. "I'm more of an Athena type. Goddess of war and wisdom. I prefer my women feisty and smart. So"—I nudge Jackson—"did it work? Did she give you her answer?"

Jackson sucks a massive breath and heaves it out on a sigh. "Sorry, Daddy. She didn't say. I think it was the red paint. I wanted to do yellow."

Those heart attack symptoms return.

I knew it would take a while to break Shay, to get her to realize this thing between us is bigger than a job, but she's holding out like a commander in the Thirty Years' War. She hasn't said a thing about the scrap of lace I saved from Aspen, or the note I wrote. No hint of cracking. Looking at her now, though, with her breath coming faster and her brow creased, her eyes so full of everything she's not saying, I know she's fighting her feelings for me. She can't hold out forever. "Let's head in," I say, tipping my head toward the door.

Jackson steps forward, attempting to pull Shay with him, but she doesn't budge. "Actually," she says, "I *do* have an answer."

Forget heart attack. This is a full-on stroke. "Will I like it?"

She licks her lips. "I'm considering being wooed."

"Considering?"

"Maybe you can pick me up from work tonight so we can discuss said wooing? I have a shift at Sass and Style starting at one thirty."

Fucking A. "I'll take that maybe." Which is a total yes. "And that gives us an hour and a half to hang out."

She stubs her toe into the pavement. "With both of you?"

I nod, knowing what she's thinking. It's risky bringing Shay into Jackson's life. If they get close and things fall apart, it would be hard on him, but dating her only works if she's cool spending time with Jackson and doesn't judge him. Anything less is a deal breaker. I lean closer, my elbow brushing hers. "Don't stress. We're going to spend a bit of time in a library with Jackson and a dictionary. And since I didn't get a firm yes from you, I might even find an older librarian to give his pottery to. You really want to miss that?"

She chuckles. "Fine. But I get to choose the lucky recipient, Fabio."

"As you wish, Buttercup."

Her bottom lip drops open, no doubt picking up on my *Princess Bride* reference, another film she mentioned in Aspen when ranting about my taste in movies. At least this one had sword fighting and André the Giant. But I'd be lying if I said the Sunrise series didn't hit home. There's something about that Julie Delpy chick and her accent, but it's the years that couple wasted, denying themselves when they could've been together, that sat with me. Years apart. Years you don't get back. I've already lost three months with Shay, and I have no intention of losing another minute.

Wordlessly, she follows us into the library.

Scratching pens, whispers, and shifting chairs greet us, familiar scents of parchment and lead hanging in the stuffy air. Light filters through the tall windows, dust particles caught in its glow. I head toward a free table at the back. Once Shay and Jackson take a seat, I kneel beside him. "What voice do you use in here, bud?"

"The inside one," he says on cue.

I wink at him and turn to Shay. "Be right back."

A couple minutes later, I return with *Encyclopedia Britannica*'s volume G tucked to my side. Jackson's swinging his legs as he tells Shay about the pool and sauna at the house I've rented, his "inside" voice drawing irritated glances their way. I sit beside him, Shay across from us, glad I can watch her for the next ninety minutes. "Pass me his pack," I say as I heft the massive book onto the table. She slides it across, and I sift inside for Jackson's journal and colored pencils, then I place them in front of him. "Where'd we finish last time?"

He clucks his tongue against his teeth as he flips the pages of his journal, and I stretch my leg out until the side of my calf presses against Shay's. She doesn't move, and I don't move.

"Here!" Jackson points to our last entry. A reedy girl a table over shushes us.

"Yeah, okay, bud. But inside voice, remember?"

"*Here*," he says again, maybe a fraction more quietly. "The gaboon viper."

Shay leans forward and whispers, "What's a gaboon viper?"

Her calf rubs against mine.

Jackson pushes his glasses higher, puts on his serious face, and proceeds to read the entry. "A big snake with long fangs and triangles on its body. It lives in Africa. It's a nice snake, but if it gets mad, it shoots poison." He looks up. "The gaboon viper."

"Cool." She reaches over and places her fingers on the edge of his book. "Mind if I take a look at this?"

He bites his lip, anxiety radiating from his hitched shoulders, three *um*s filling the awkward silence. Sensing his turmoil, Shay pulls her hand back. "I don't need to see it, but maybe you can explain how it works. Do you record *all* the words?"

I rub his back until his arms relax, the same circular motion I use when he has a nightmare. It soothes me as much as it does him. "Not all the words," he says, excited again. "Just the best words."

Shay props her chin on her hands. "How do you know which are the best?"

He shrugs. "I just know. Daddy runs his finger down the page, and I say stop when I see one of 'em. Then Daddy says the word and then I say it and then he reads the de-fi-ni-tion, then I hafta say how I wanna write it and *then* I write the word in orange and Daddy writes the de-fi-ni-tion in purple, unless it's a Sunday." Finally, he takes a breath. "Then we use red and blue."

I watch Shay for any sign of judgment. Jackson's eccentricities are confusing for some people. Caroline is great with him. Patient. Understanding. Exactly how Marina would've been—like mother, like daughter. When *my* mother's in from Arizona, she spends her time trying to fix him, like he's broken. Like I've done something to fuck him up. She begs him to wear the same socks and insists he not walk backward into the kitchen on Tuesdays. But Jackson is Jackson. I used to stress about his idiosyncrasies and OCD behavior, many hours wasted in doctors' offices wondering if there's a magic pill or something to make my kid "normal." The first medication I tried dulled him. Diluted his personality, watering down everything that made him *him*. A month in, I tossed it and vowed never again to lose sight of how awesome he is. How perfectly unique.

It's not as easy for outsiders to understand.

Shay drops her hands under the table, her attention still fixed on Jackson, but her fingers find my knee. "Can I help today? Can I maybe write some definitions for you?" She squeezes my knee, and I slip my hand below the table to cover hers. Of course she gets it. Of course this girl with the wild hair and mad temper and stubborn streak doesn't question my son's quirks. Hopefully, she's done questioning us, too. I rub my thumb over her smooth skin until she pulls back. But her leg stays pressed to mine, her cheeks and neck a soft pink.

I lean over Jackson, who's scrunching his face. "What do you say, bud? I've seen Shay's writing, and it's pretty neat. We could give her a different color to use." I should make him write it all, but after a year, it's hard to let go of the tradition—my measured writing next to his looping letters, each word gradually getting neater.

Straighter.

Older.

More scrunching, more *um*s, until he says, "'Kay. But we'll have to find the green for you. It's not in the pack." He shakes the incomplete set of pencils.

Shay drags the bag toward her and practically sticks her head inside. She emerges with the lost green pencil…and the book I thought Stella tossed. "*The Urban Dictionary*?" She cocks her head at Jackson. "Is this yours, too?"

His eyes get as wide as his glasses. "Yeah. Aunt Stella said I could keep it but Daddy's not s'posed to know, so we should put it back before he gets mad."

She, of course, doesn't. She flips through the book and lands on a dog-eared page. "Banana polish," she says slowly, her left eye squinting like it does when she's puzzling something out.

That's when Jackson shouts, "Noooo polish!" his fist in the air.

Not only does the shushing get emphatic, but we invite the wrath of the librarian. I've been to this library a few times, the front desk always staffed by an older lady who looks like she hasn't seen sunlight in years. Today, however, a different woman is working. With her pencil skirt, high heels, and low-cut blouse, the chick approaching the table could star in every teen boy's naughty-librarian fantasy. Her sleek black hair is in a bun, her arms crossed defiantly over her ample chest. "There are people working in here. You need to respect the silence and speak in hushed voices, or I'll have to ask you to leave. Understood?"

Shay's eyes dip up and down the woman's body. She blinks a few times, then moves her leg away from mine under the table, her warmth from moments ago spiraling into hostility. As if she's jealous. As if she thinks this chick's why I come here.

I really hope she's jealous.

I reassure the librarian we won't cause any trouble. When she leaves, Shay leans toward Jackson. "You guys come here often?" When Jackson nods with a quick yes, she glances back at the retreating hottie and huffs. "Guess your dad wasn't joking about the pottery. He must enjoy the view in here."

Fuck yeah, she's jealous. Perfect time to reel her in. "The view's great. Best it's ever been." I reach under the table and grab her knee with both hands, inching my fingers up her bare thigh. Her head jerks my way, her breasts rising on a shaky inhale. I stop at the hem of her short shorts. "This view's better than the mountains in Aspen and Kitsilano Beach at sunset. It's the view I've fallen asleep imagining every night for three months. I'd like it to be the view I wake up to in the morning. The pottery was for you, Shay, and no one else. And I look forward to your real answer tonight."

Jackson fidgets in his seat while pens scratch and whispers drift and feet plod along the worn carpet. She moves her leg back to mine and is about to speak when Jackson says, "Can we start?"

I press my leg to hers, *harder*, but turn to Jackson. "Sure, bud."

Tonight can't come soon enough.

* * *

An hour later, we've added four words to Jackson's journal, Shay writing out the first two and me the next. As I finish the definition for *gaffer*: the person on a movie set who's in charge of lights, her throaty chuckle floats across the table.

"Daddy." Jackson tugs on the side of my shirt. "Can we please add some words from the *Urban* one? Pleeeeease."

I glance up. Shay's flipping through that damn book, a look of pure delight on her face. Why does everyone want to corrupt my son? "No, Jackson. That book isn't appropriate." When she looks up, I narrow my eyes and mouth, *thanks*.

She pouts, pushing out her bottom lip. The one I'd kill to take between my teeth. "Come on, Dad, *please*," she says, turning the book toward me. "This is an awesome word."

Jackson is practically on the table, his head pushing against my cheek as he reads along with me. "*Glomp?*" he says. "Glomp! Oh, we hafta, Daddy. It's perfect. I need it in my journal so bad."

Warring with my instincts to shove this asking-for-trouble book on a random shelf never to be heard from again, I sigh. Saying no to Jackson is never easy. Add Shay into the mix, and I'm a goner. Plus, it is an awesome word. "Okay, fine. Read it aloud then tell me how you want it written down."

He pulls the book toward him and pushes up his glasses. "Glomp. A running tackle-hug from behind to show spon-ta-ne-ous affection." He scans the sentence a few more times, mouthing the words silently, then says, "A attack hug made of love. Can we write it like that?"

"Sure, but it's *an* attack hug, not *a*. You want me or Shay to write it?"

"I want Shay."

So do I, buddy. So do I.

I pass her the journal, unable to look away while she squints her left eye and chews her lip, making sure to write neatly.

"Found another one."

A chorus of shushes reply to Jackson's not-inside voice, the sexy librarian shooting daggers our way. "Quiet, buddy." I turn to him. His finger is dead center on a page of *The Urban Dictionary*, his eyes shining bright. So absorbed in Shay, I didn't realize he was scanning it. I lean forward to read his choice and curse inwardly. Forget hiding it, I should've burned the book. Time for Shay to learn how curious my seven-year-old can be. "Why don't you field this one?" I push it toward her and point at Jackson's word.

G-spot.

She chokes on nothing, and her cheeks flame. "Maybe we should put that book away."

"But what's it mean when it says it's harder to find than proof of God? Is it a treasure?"

Damn right it is. I'm pretty sure I found Shay's pot of gold in Aspen, but I'd happily spend a solid month searching to be sure. The thought sends my blood pumping south. She looks to me for saving, but I shrug. The smart parenting decision would be to nip this in the bud and tell Jackson we'll discuss these words when he's older. But this is too much fun. "Your can of worms," I say to her. "And don't be feeding my kid misinformation."

Now she's glaring, her eyes darting around like the non-embarrassing answer is written somewhere on the table. "It's…" More glaring, more avoiding. "It's…" Terminator Shay has been unleashed, flared nostrils and all. With a huff, she leans on her elbows, making eye contact with my way-too-curious kid. "It's a spot girls have that makes them happy. But it's personal and not something you should ever mention to your friends. Like ever."

"But…" He rereads the definition, glances at Shay then at me, then back at her. "Is that why you're not wooed? Did Daddy not find your G-spot? Did he not make you happy enough?"

Jesus, you can't script this stuff. I cock an eyebrow at her. "Yeah, Shay. Did I not find your special spot?"

She mouths *you're dead* and pushes back her chair. "Nope. He didn't find it. And I need to go." *Dead*, she mouths as she stands.

But that means she's leaving before our time is up. "We still have forty-five minutes," I say. "Lots of time to search for your treasure."

She doesn't smile at my joke. She glowers. Without replying, she beelines for the exit.

As she nears the door, Jackson calls, "Don't worry, Shay. I'll help Daddy find your G-spot!"

Holy shit. She stops dead and then practically runs for safety. Unable to decide if I should crack up or get mad, I shove his book and pencils in his bag, avoiding the shocked glances from every set of eyes in the place. I grab Jackson with one hand and his pottery with the other, and I hightail it to the door as the sexy librarian gives me the evil eye.

Guess we won't be returning to this branch.

I hurry outside and catch Shay as she's shuffling for her keys. "Come on, Shay. Don't go. We can head to the park for a bit." When she ignores me, I add, "I'd really like to hang out."

She steps so close her hot breath brushes my ear. "I should kill you."

I love how tall she is, how I barely had to bend down to capture her lips in a kiss all those months ago. "Why would you do that?"

She looks down at Jackson, who's tucking his pottery into his backpack, and she lowers her voice. "You fed me to the wolves for your own amusement."

"You have to admit, it was hilarious."

Her mouth twitches as she fights a smile. "Hilarious until someone calls Child Services."

"True. But now there are two questions I need answered."

"Two?"

With one eyebrow cocked, she looks equal parts amused and annoyed, but there's no backing down now. "Yeah, two. The wooing for starters. Then we need to discuss whether or not I found your happy spot. You may have noticed I'm a pretty determined guy when I know what I want. I'm happy to search for hours."

Her gaze glides down to my dick, and he, of course, wakes up. "I never stood a chance," she says. Then to my face, "How far is the park?"

I take her hand and usher Jackson along. "Just around the corner."

Seventeen

Shay

Jackson skips ahead of us, the domesticity of the scene not lost on me. The last hour has solidified what a big deal this is. Kolton inviting me into not only his life but into *Jackson's* life is a massive responsibility. That's three hearts in this relationship. Three people who can get hurt. Kolton's trust in me is astounding, and we're not even dating. Flirting, *yes*. Smoldering, *yes*. But dating, no. Until tonight, that is.

Kolton rubs his thumb along my hand as we near the park. "Thanks," he says.

For pushing him away for so long? For always giving him a hard time? "For what?"

"For taking Jackson's quirks in stride. Not everyone gets him."

"You mean they don't like when he shouts about their G-spot?"

He chuckles. "That's one for the history books."

No book I'd like to revisit, but, where Jackson's concerned, I know what he's getting at. My heart squeezes for the little guy. He's sweet and hilarious in his always-candid way, but kids can be cruel. His two different socks and eccentricities must be magnets for bullies. With my stutter, I lived through the taunting and ridicule only nine-year-olds can inflict. Hitler? Stalin? Piece of cake. One minute cornered in the schoolyard with Sue Anne Hinkley's insults, and my confidence would bleed onto the ground. I'd choose death by fire ants over reliving that time in my life. Jackson can't have it easy.

"I get him," I say. "At least what it's like to be different. And I love that you and Stella teach him to own who he is. That's invaluable."

Jackson runs toward a swing set, but Kolton pulls me to a stop. "From you, it means a lot."

His tone—so sincere and heartfelt—has me listing toward him. Kolton may have poured his heart out to me in that note and done silly things to get my attention, but this is a man, a father, sharing his deepest self. "I'm glad I came," I say. "Glad you didn't give up on me." I so badly want to rise to the challenge of being with him. Finally know what it's like to be in a healthy relationship.

"I knew you'd cave. The sex was too good." His cockiness resurfaces, along with playfulness, covering the intensity of the moment. And damn it all to hell if he isn't right.

"Will you push me, Shay?" Jackson tugs at a swing as two kids sprint past him and race up the red-and-blue jungle gym. The park is small but clean, a large geometric dome anchoring the center. Parents and nannies chat on the far side, occasionally yelling at kids to slow down or lower their voices. Jackson is yelling for me.

"Is it okay?" I ask Kolton, unaccustomed to the sense of well-being swelling against my ribs.

He nods. "Looks like I've been replaced."

As if. But Jackson tosses his backpack to Kolton and wiggles into the swing, smacking his shoes together while I move behind him. I pull him back and say, "I'll push on the count of three."

"Actually," Kolton calls, "I count to four."

Pausing, I squint at him. "Four?"

"Four."

"Who counts to four? In the history of jungle gyms, no one has ever counted to four."

"I'm pretty sure there isn't a swing-set rule book stating the precise number a person must reach before the big push."

He's getting feisty with me. Or maybe we're getting feisty with each other. "But that's like singing 'Happy Birthday' *after* the candles have been blown out. It's just not done."

He widens his stance in a familiar show of authority. Like he's right. Like I won't argue this until I'm blue in the face. And maybe that's okay. Maybe we'll always be this way with each other: challenging and fiery. I'm all for fiery. Kolton's usual exasperation is hidden by the gleam in his chocolate eyes. "In this family, we count to four, and we sing 'Happy Birthday' *after* the wish and the candles."

I almost let the swing slip through my fingers. "You can't be serious. How am I supposed to date you now? I mean, it was one thing—"

"Shay?" Jackson kicks his legs, jostling the chain in my hands. "Can you push me now?"

Right. Jackson. The adorable boy who asked me to play with him. I peel my eyes away from the sex-on-a-stick pushing my buttons and focus on his son. "There's nothing I'd love more. What number should I count to?"

"Four," he says, and Kolton smirks like he just won the World Series of Poker.

Ignoring him, I grip the swing. "One," I sing, pulling Jackson farther back. "Two." He leans into me and tenses. "Three." I force myself to wait. *"Four!"*

Jackson squeals as I launch him forward, the sound spiraling through the air, followed by a string of giggles. With each shove, he laughs harder and Kolton grins wider and I'm no longer sure it matters what number we reached.

As I'm getting into my groove, Kolton's cell rings, and he steps away to answer the call. He ducks his head and rubs his neck. He nods, then glances at us and waves the phone at Jackson. "Nana wants to say hi."

Jackson tips forward as the swing dips, reaching for his dad before he's come to a stop. Visions of a face-plant complete with bloody nose and missing teeth have me latching my arm around his waist. Unaware I just saved his life, he's off running the second I loosen my hold, but my heart has leapt into my throat. Already, protectiveness for this boy surges through me.

As he chatters to his grandmother, my pulse slows, and Kolton nods to a nearby bench. I want to tell him how grateful and honored I am to get to know his son, but he's gazing at me in that sexy way of his, and the words turn to steam in my throat. I sit beside him, my knee brushing his, his arm slung over the back. His thumb comes to rest on my shoulder. We're barely touching, but I am *aware*. So freaking a-*ware*. Little kid shrieks and the occasional passing car punctuate the tension.

"So you really count to four?" I ask.

Chuckling, he says, "Give it up." But he moves his thumb closer to my neck. My very warm and tingly neck.

I tilt my head back to soak up the sun…and maybe get closer to his hand. "Which grandmother called?"

"Marina's mother. My stepmom's three boys run her ragged, and my mother isn't exactly involved. She loves Jackson; she's just busy with her life and doesn't like to meddle."

"But Marina's mother does? Like to be involved, I mean."

He shifts closer, the expanse of his hand moving to my shoulder, covering it with warmth. I keep my eyes closed. "Yeah," he says. "She's always offering to babysit and goes out of her way to pick him up from school, and she spends hours with him reading and doing puzzles and making the food he likes. She's a godsend, really."

It's easy to forget what Kolton's been through—the hardship, losing Marina and raising their son on his own. Shading my eyes, I glance at Jackson. He's sitting on the grass, pulling out stalks as he chatters on the phone, unaware of how much joy he brings to the people in his life. How much joy he could bring to mine. "Does she call often?"

"Is every day often?" I turn to find concern in his creased brow. He scrubs his foot over the earth, back and forth, steady yet tense. "I knew being away would be hard on her. I just didn't think it would be *this* hard. Marina was an only child, so Jackson's the only grandchild she'll ever have."

My body shifts closer of its own volition, my hand skimming across his thigh. "It's nice that she calls. That she cares. And it's a good thing Jackson isn't a typical seven-year-old who runs screaming when handed the phone."

His focus drags from his son down to my hand, to the curl of my fingers along his inner thigh. "It is." He swallows. "It's also really nice to have you here, Shay. Nice to finally spend time together."

So nice, I can't remember why I've put him off. "Am I still being wooed?"

"Do you want me to stop?"

I'm done fighting this thing between us. Done pretending I can get over him. He'll need to respect my opinions and not impose himself on me like the Dick, but he's here. We're together. If Aspen proved anything, it's that our chemistry, although volatile, is hot enough to scorch the sky.

"No," I say. "Don't stop."

And God, *that look*. We're in a public space, his son in visual distance, but Kolton's hooded gaze and parted lips read SEX SEX SEX.

Sex we haven't had in months.

His eyes burn into mine. "If we were somewhere private," he says, "if Jackson weren't with us, I'd kiss you right now." His admission hits me in my lower belly, a lightning bolt of desire. "Question is, Shay…would you let me?"

I'm pretty sure I'd let him throw me over his shoulder and have his caveman way with me in the middle of the tundra, but all I say is "Yes."

Our chests rise in unison, air expanding with lust. He wets his lips and I taste mine, wishing like heck I was tasting something else. Wishing his tongue were sliding against mine, desperate moans traded as we finally give into this blazing attraction. An attraction heightened by the day with his son and our silly arguments and the complete rightness of *being* with him. Also, SEX SEX SEX.

An eternity later, Kolton shakes his head. "That was intense."

I pull my hand back and rub it down my thighs, a lame attempt to tame my goose bumps. "As far as imagined kisses go, that one deserves an Oscar." I glance at my watch and, reluctantly, push to my feet. "I need to head out."

He rests his elbows on his knees and looks up at me. "I'm still picking you up tonight, right? From work?"

"If I'm still being wooed, then you better." He winks, then I say good-bye to Jackson, unsure how I'll get through my shift.

Eighteen

Kolton

I glance inside the large windows of Sass & Style. Even though it's near closing, the place is bustling. Shay is pulling out a duvet for a woman, a few couples are milling around, the line at the cash register is three deep, and someone's letting their kid run around the place. The young boy is moving things on the shelves, things Shay will have to fix later. I push through the door and amble through the space, listening as Shay explains the washing instructions for the purple comforter in her hand.

The lady at the register must be the owner, Natasha. Shay's mentioned her bright red hair, and the fact that she's been accommodating these past weeks since Shay's had to give up hours. With my back to Shay, I glance at a wonky blue bowl on the square dining table, the ceramic uneven but funky. A masterpiece compared to Jackson's ugly-ass pottery. An artist my kid is not. I'm about to pick it up when my scalp tingles, my body always attuned to a certain woman's attention. I don't turn around. I wait. I run my fingers over the bowl until heat radiates behind me.

Shay.

"That imaginary kiss of yours," she says, "has left me brain-dead for my shift. You should come with a warning label."

Instead of turning, I slide a hand behind me to her hip. "I'll come however and whenever you'd like. And that imaginary kiss has nothing on the real thing."

"I wouldn't remember."

A phone rings as the last customer in line files off. Natasha picks it up, cradling the handset with her shoulder. I spin, needing to see each shade of green and brown in Shay's hazel eyes. "I do. I remember every detail. But I think this time will be even better." Man, do I need to get her out of here, get her alone, and finally kiss her senseless. "You ready to head out soon?"

"Shay," Natasha calls, "we need to talk."

"Okay…" Shay draws out the word, a frown puckering her brow. Then to me, "I'll meet you outside."

But I don't move. Shay fists her hands and approaches Natasha hesitantly, as if preparing for bad news. The women exchange whispered words, Shay's posture shrinking with each passing second, her arms gesturing as if in a plea. I can't hear a thing. There's one last woman still milling around, the one with the rambunctious son. I cringe as he reaches for what looks like an expensive vase on a coffee table.

"That's a fragile piece." At Natasha's stern tone, the boy's mother scolds him to put it down. Natasha turns back to Shay. "I'm sorry," she says. "I wish I could help you out, I really do. But I'm strapped. I'll need your key before you leave."

I can almost hear Shay swallow. "Okay. I'll get it from my purse. And Natasha"—her voice breaks—"thanks for trying."

Natasha offers her a sad smile and then catches my eye. "I assume you're waiting for Shay?"

I nod, but Shay doesn't glance my way.

The mother and son leave while I wait, my jaw tensing with each passing second. If I didn't know better, I'd say Shay just lost her job. Did she screw up? Did something bad go down with a customer? I've been here three weeks, giving her PEZ and videos and flirting with her, not a clue to what's really going on in her life.

Shay emerges with her purse and walks like she's wading through molasses, each step dragging. I wait for her to acknowledge me, but she doesn't. She returns her key, shares a few more words with Natasha, then she leaves the store.

I hurry after her and push outside. She's barely made it a few steps. Her back is to me, her right hand on the brick wall past the shop as if she needs it for support. A car honks, brakes screech, and a man bumps my shoulder as he strides past me, but it's the slump of Shay's shoulders that nearly knocks me over. I come up behind her and loop my arm around her waist. "I've got you, Shay. Whatever this is, we'll work it out."

She falls into me, her spine curved into my chest. She rests her head against my jaw. "I thought I could do it on my own, and now it's all fucked. I'll have to grovel to Lily, or maybe I should just quit and go home. I'm such a failure."

I don't know what happened to the feisty girl who's turned my world upside down, but if she thinks she's leaving the city and me behind, she better think again. For three months, I pined for her. For three weeks, I've chased after her. I even used my son to soften her. She's not going anywhere. "Tell me what happened."

She slumps lower. "I'm about to be evicted, and I just lost my paycheck."

Evicted? Jesus. "I can give you the money. Or a loan, if it makes you feel better. I'm not letting you sleep on the street."

Her whole body tenses. I can't see her face, but I'd bet her nostrils have flared. "I don't want your charity, Kolton. Lily will help me if I ask. I just don't want to put her in that position. I don't want it to affect our friendship. Money does weird things sometimes."

No shit. The way girls used to get when they found out what I do always altered the dynamic, and Sawyer no longer speaks to a cousin who borrowed money for some bullshit next-big-thing. I'd go it alone, too, for as long as possible before asking friends for cash. But Shay needs help. And, come to think of it, I have the answer. The perfect solution. It would mean bringing her further into Jackson's life, opening him up to potential hurt. But after being with them at the library today and seeing how good she was with him at the park, I can't help but want her more permanently in our lives, her in the pictures on my desk. With only six weeks left together, may as well go the whole nine yards. I latch my arm tighter around her. "Come to my place. The house I've rented is huge. You can have your own room if you want."

"No." One word, sharp with irritation.

Typical, bull-headed Shay.

I lean over her, covering her hair, her shoulders, her body with mine. "You can't do this on your own. You need help. I'm offering it."

She sags against me then, whatever fight she had in her gone. "It's too much. I can't live with you. Live *off* of you. And we both know if I move into your place, there won't be separate rooms. I bet this turn of events fits right into your wooing plan."

The bitterness in her voice stings. "Ten minutes ago, you were okay with the wooing. More than okay. I get that what happened is a big deal, but nothing's changed between us."

"Everything's changed." Her words hit me square in the chest.

I spin her around until we're almost nose to nose. "No, Shay, it hasn't." I wince at my harsh tone. Her words cut deeper than I'd like to admit, but she's the one who's been dealt the bigger blow. Schooling my hurt, I smooth her hair and lower my voice. "I want you in my bed. I want you under me, over me, next to me. I want you like I've never wanted anyone. But if I need to put that on hold while we make sure you get things sorted, then I will. Just don't shut down on me." After all these years, after countless dates, this girl has knocked me on my ass, and she's pushing me away. Again.

She studies a spot over my shoulder. "There's so much for me to figure out. Maybe we aren't meant to be. Maybe the timing will always be wrong."

Yep, shutting down. I can't imagine what she's going through, but to end this now after we've both admitted how strong our connection is doesn't make sense. I can deal with putting us on hold, but I'm not letting myself or Jackson get in deeper, only to be shoved aside when the going gets tough.

I walk until her back is pressed to the wall, my hands on the rough brick, caging her. "I don't know what's going on with you, but I get why you didn't ask Lily for help. I'd have to be pretty fucked to ask my friends for money. What I do know is how I feel. Seeing you upset doesn't sit well. I *want* to be with you. I *want* to be in your life. But only if you feel the same. If you don't, now's the time to tell me. Tell me to my face that you don't feel every little thing I feel. That you don't think about me when I'm not around. That you haven't lost minutes, hours, days reliving our time in Aspen. Tell me that, and I'll walk away. Tell me that, and I'll swap places with Sawyer so you can work with him on the space. Tell me that, and I'm out of your life...*after* you've sorted out this apartment thing." There's no way in hell I'd leave her in the lurch, but fuck. *Leave her.* Saying it, thinking it, tightens my throat.

We're so close, my chest nearly grazing hers. I can't stop from pressing closer. Closer still. "Tell me, Shay. Say the words."

No words. Only breaths. Deeper. Faster. Her breasts brushing my chest.

"Tell me," I say again.

She doesn't speak. Not one syllable. I see everything in her eyes, but I need to hear the words. Then she says, "Don't go." Her voice sounds small, desperate. Her hands curl into my hips, and I'm done for. I press my lips to hers before she can take it back, before I wake up another morning alone in my bed. Her tongue slides against mine, both of us groaning at the contact. She grips me tighter, and I cup her head. Bodies flush, we move against each other, hungry hands searching for more. Her warmth bleeds into me, through me, until I have to push away, panting. "Fuck."

She blinks repeatedly. "Yeah."

Behind me, boots smack the pavement, voices rise and fall—the sounds of the city rushing back. I can barely look at her swollen lips. Barely maintain the small distance between us in this very public place. If we were back in Aspen, I'd yank her into the nearest public bathroom or dark alley, unable to wait a second longer to be inside of her. But this isn't Aspen. Not even close. The next time I have Shay, it will be slow. Deliberate. Not an inch of her left unexplored or unseen. "Come to my place so we can talk this out." The timbre of my voice is gruff.

Dazed, she nods. "Give me your address. I'll grab a few things, then meet you there." Her fingers float to her mouth, as if checking it's still intact.

Following the line of her finger, I drag my thumb across her bottom lip. Because I can. Because, finally, she won't push me away. I kiss her once, softly. "Okay." I text her my address and walk away before I pin her back against that wall.

Nineteen

Shay

Sitting. Waiting. Barely breathing. Aside from the drumming of my thumb on the steering wheel—a relentless *tat tat tat*—my body seems to have disconnected from my brain. *Move*, I think. My legs don't twitch. Kolton's rental house is huge, the circular driveway I'm parked on something you'd find at a castle. The landscaping alone belongs in a botanical garden.

One minute.

Two minutes.

Tat tat tat

Five minutes.

Ten minutes.

Tat tat tat

The massive front door opens, the dark wood pulling back under soft lights that illuminate the detailed stonework of the exterior walls. And Kolton. He leans his shoulder into the doorframe and crosses his arms. His hair hangs loose, brushing his shoulders. He doesn't move, and I don't move. Every inch of me burns for him. Our kiss from earlier lingers on my lips, his breath still mingling with mine.

Tat tat tat

Earlier today, after Kolton had his kid shouting in front of the world about my G-spot (which, dear Lord, the man found), and before my life imploded at Sass & Style, I couldn't wait for this moment. Finally, I'd put aside my bullshit and go out with Kolton. This isn't just a date, though. He asked me to move in with him. To help me, but the look in his eyes said he wanted more. Everything. I could try to fight it, cave and ask Lily for cash, but I want everything, too. With him. When hot coals burn for months on end, a faint spark lights an inferno. Not the kind that goes out quickly. The kind that catches, eating everything in its path.

Now he's there and I'm here, but my legs won't move.

My feelings for Richard were juvenile compared to this. This need. This want. This sense of wholeness when Kolton's around. Still, I grip the steering wheel.

Tat

Tat

Tat

Who will I become with Kolton? Another version of me? Will I lose myself again? Get snowballed into his life? His world?

Or will I stay a snowflake?

Probably tired of waiting, he pushes off the doorframe and takes long strides toward me. His jeans hug his hips, his bare feet sure on the interlocked stone. When he gets to my car, he leans his elbows through the open window, and I barely refrain from touching his toned arms.

Tat tat tat…

Tat

"Hey." He brushes a loose curl from my forehead.

"Hey," I say. One breathy syllable.

"When I said I wanted to talk, I didn't mean in your car."

"Thanks, Fabio. I'm just using my GPS to figure out how to find the front door amid all the elaborate shrubbery."

He hums to himself. "If you don't come out, I'm coming in."

I release the steering wheel in defeat. "Back away, then. Wouldn't want your hair to get caught in the door when I close it."

His rumbling laugh fills the night air. And my chest. "Noted, Connor. But I distinctly remember a certain woman's hands enjoying this hair."

More than he knows. But I'm too jumpy to play nice. Shoving the door with my elbow, I rack my brain, needing to match his obscure nickname with one of my own. Eighties hair bands and my brother's first Guns N' Roses album come to mind. "You certainly have a keen memory, *Axl*. The details you hold onto are impressive. Are you one of those idiot savants? And who the hell is Connor?"

Another laugh. "More idiot than savant. And if you don't know who Connor is, you aren't watching the right movies."

"I watch cinema. You watch trash." Squinting, I rack my brain for the movie reference so I can defend myself against whatever fun he's poking. *Connor. Connor.* Damn him and his cryptic self. I get out of the car, and Kolton barely backs up. Barely gives me space. His warm brown eyes are heavy on me, passing over my breasts, my hips, and my legs in the short shorts I put back on in my apartment. "I came here to talk, Bon Jovi. Stop with the sexy looks."

Not backing away, he watches me a breath longer, knowing I'm full of crap. Knowing I won't be able to stay away from him tonight. Then he says, "If I'd known about your shit taste in music, Connor, I would've made a mix tape and bought you a Walkman."

It's my turn to laugh. "*That* would've been awesome. You can thank my hillbilly brother for my love of cheesy eighties rock."

He nods. "Noted. Come on. Let's go inside."

Stepping away from me, he heads for his mansion, and I pause, enjoying my unimpeded view of his tight booty. Soon, maybe tonight, I'll see all of this man in the flesh, no heavy winter clothes between us. Suppressing a moan, I follow him inside.

A massive chandelier hangs above the large vestibule, a Persian carpet draped over the marble floor. In my mind, I break up the cream walls with sections of wood, swapping the ornate trim with clean lines. The elaborate front bench lowers, taking on a geometric, Japanese simplicity, lime accents on a cushion, bamboo lining one of the walls.

Kolton waits at the base of a spiral staircase. He juts his chin toward the second floor. "Stella and Jackson sleep upstairs, and there's another spare room up there. As well as three bedrooms in the lower level. I sleep in a room on the main floor on the other side of the kitchen. I got you some food. We can talk while you eat."

My motor skills cease again, all but my hammering heart. *His room.* How long until we end up in there? Until I move in there?

I follow him into the kitchen, where he has, of course, laid out one of my favorite meals. "Am I this predictable?" I ask, eyeing the mushroom-stuffed chicken breast next to the Anton's bag—the restaurant I mentioned loving a week ago.

"I just pay attention to things I'm interested in." He walks close and reaches around me, pushing something out from behind the takeout bag.

No he didn't.

The masterpiece that is the cookie dough cupcake has me salivating: vanilla cake filled with fudge, garnished with cookie-dough frosting and a chocolate chip cookie.

Sex disguised as cake.

I groan at the sight of its perfection, and Kolton's on me in seconds.

His mouth swallows my sounds, which are getting louder. And louder. So much for talking. Or breathing. I've relived my moments with him countless times, but the real thing…

He drags his hands all over my body as he presses my back into the island countertop, then he lifts me onto the stool and nudges my legs open for him. Like they need the assistance. His lips are soft but firm, demanding me. Devouring me. "Shay," he murmurs. "Shay, Shay, Shay…"

"Kolton," I answer, my head tipping back as he sucks a line down my neck. How I ever put off his advances is a mystery. His jeans are barely containing him, the hard line of his cock pressing insistently between my thighs. I fist his hair and force his lips back to my mouth. He tastes like sugar and cake and…cookies?

I pull my head back. "Did you eat a cupcake?"

He tries to kiss me again, but I turn my face away. He palms my ass and rubs his raging hard-on against the soft flesh scarcely covered by my short shorts and underwear. *Wow.* When my eyes refocus, I notice Jackson's backpack from earlier today. Jackson's books. With more force, I push Kolton away, both our clothes twisted from our restless hands.

"What?" he says, his voice gruff.

"*What?*" I repeat, straightening my top. "Let's see…we haven't talked yet, haven't even discussed what's going on here—my job, my living arrangements, how this is all going to work. I'm pretty sure your son is upstairs, along with your assistant, who could both walk down here at any moment. And, *and*, I have it on good authority you ate one of my cupcakes. *That's* what."

His jaw works back and forth. "Whose authority?"

"Your tongue's. I'd know that taste anywhere, Fabio, and I don't share cupcakes."

"Maybe I need to be punished." A wicked grin lights his face.

I narrow my eyes and point to the ceiling. "There are people here," I hiss. "Do you have no shame?"

"Jackson's asleep and Stella's probably passed out, too. She had a long tattoo session today. But if you want me to keep my hands off you, I'd suggest not making those moaning sounds when you see junk food. Not even a breathy hum. I'm on a tightrope with you, and those noises of yours push me over the edge."

Sounds? I make breathy sounds? "Don't put your lack of self-control on me."

He steps closer, and I almost reach for him. "I also suggest not arguing with me. When I say I'm close to snapping, I'm not fucking around. I'll stay away from you…for now. Just know it won't be easy." He inhales deeply as if scenting me, then strides around to the opposite side of the island. He leans his elbows on the counter, and I focus on the food. Chicken. Potatoes. Cookie dough cupcake.

When I realize I'd rather taste the remnants of that perfect dessert on Kolton's tongue than eat one myself, the situation I'm in becomes clear: Some naked Twister will be played tonight. First, I need to eat. Then, we need to talk. And then, Lord Jesus, I need to release the caged beast eyeing me from the other side of the island.

He pours me a glass of wine and takes a beer for himself. As I dig into my meal, he says, "Talk."

"Just like that? Talk?"

"Just like that. What happened? How'd it get this far?"

I push the food around my plate, no longer so hungry. "I told you about Richard." He nods, so I go on, "After Aspen, I needed to get my life together, needed to find myself again. Feel in control. I gave up a great promotion when I was with him and ended up designing retirement homes. Not a word, Fabio," I say as his mouth opens. He holds up his hands in surrender and refrains from spewing whatever teasing comment was on the tip of his tongue. "I was gung ho about quitting," I continue, "and did it before I had something lined up. Add a ridiculous credit card bill from my trip, and cash was leaving faster than it was coming in. I had trouble making rent. And"—I glare at Kolton—"some people have said I can be a bit strong-willed."

"Stubborn as fuck," he chimes in.

I ignore him. "I didn't want to ask for money. My folks get by, but they're not exactly rolling in cash. Raven's still paying off her school loans. That left Lily. But every time I'd open my mouth to ask for help, I'd feel sick. I got both jobs—the internship to build my future, the retail gig to put some cash in my pocket—but it wasn't enough. I kept putting it off, knowing I'd be evicted soon, but thinking some miracle would happen, like an amazing commission at Sass and Style. Then I had to give up shifts to focus on your project, and Natasha just found out her sister's having surgery. Nothing serious, but she needs to help her out and can't keep covering for me. She's hiring someone more reliable. Now there's no way I'll make my rent."

He tips his beer back and swallows. "How long?"

"How long until what?"

"Until you're evicted."

"Twelve days."

He leans on his elbows and looks up through his lashes. "Move in with me, Shay. That gives you six weeks to figure something out, and it gives us six weeks to really see if we work."

I'm so close to saying yes, but the same worries gnaw at me. I resume pushing my food around. "There's still a chance Hilary will be pissed if she finds out. Think less of my work. And living with you, relying on you like I did on Richard, brings a lot of bad stuff back. I don't want to repeat the same mistakes."

His brows pull together as he wipes some crumbs off the counter. "And you think that's what you'd be doing with me? Repeating mistakes?"

I replay my conversation with Lily this morning, about his gifts and how each thoughtful offering reflected me. The real me. Not some arm candy with slimmed hips and straight hair, some girl he imagined me to be. He gave me the movies *I* like. The food *I* crave. He even got me an awful My Little Pony T-shirt because he knows I had a collection as a kid. No. Being with him wouldn't be a mistake. It would be dangerous. He doesn't live here, and I'm building a life here. And I'm not sure how to find balance on my own two feet when he's responsible for my job, and now my housing, too. He's not doing any of this to control my life, but it's the net result just the same.

"Nothing about you would be a mistake," I say, trying to find the right words. "But I've spent all this time craving independence." I gesture around the house. "Living here and working for you doesn't exactly scream independence."

He massages his neck, then drops his hand. "That's not what the job was about. I hired the designer I wanted. It happened to be the girl I wanted, too, but that doesn't change your talent and what you're accomplishing. Hilary sees it. Everyone sees it. And you have to know I'm not Richard. I'm not some insecure fuck who's trying to control your life. I like you feisty, Connor." He winks at me.

Again with that damn reference.

"I wouldn't change a thing," he adds, "except maybe give you a few ski lessons, so you don't crash into innocent bystanders."

I mouth, *fuck you.*

He smiles, *okay.* Then, "Let's give things a shot. The large columns outside may suggest otherwise, but this isn't a castle. There's no dungeon below. I won't keep you against your will. Live with me. Go on a date with me. If things work out, we'll deal with the future and how to make it work. It's high time we see if the glass slipper fits."

"Jesus. How the hell am I supposed to say no after that? The glass slipper?"

His chocolate eyes smolder at me. "Say yes, baby."

"Maybe?"

"Fuck your pride, Shay. Fuck your bull-headed nature. Hilary will understand. Live with me for the next six weeks, and we'll see if we've built this thing up between us, or if it's real. My bet's on real."

No way would I take that bet. Real is a racing heart and shaking hands and promises of support, not control. Encouragement, not suffocation. I knew my answer the second Jackson gave me his maybe-ashtray. No point continuing to swim upstream. "Yes," I say.

He straightens. "Yes?"

"Did I stutter?" The irony of my choice of playful insults isn't lost on me and my inner stuttering child who struggled with her words. Not something I'm ready to share with Kolton. "But I need to talk to Hilary about this before you get all needy and clingy around me at work."

He puts his beer down and prowls around the counter, my un-eaten food forgotten. A first for me. His pupils are blown wide with desire, his gaze searing into me as he passes the first corner. Lust, like a long-suffering hunger, pools low in my belly. And I'm ravenous. Insatiable. But as he rounds the last corner, my phone rings.

"Don't answer it," he says.

But it could be Hilary. After losing one job tonight, I'd rather not piss off another boss. I pick it up and frown. Why the hell is Cruella de Suckmyass calling me at this hour? Kolton's in front of me, practically on top of me. He snakes an arm around my waist and repeats his "Don't answer it."

"I have to." I twist in his grasp, because those lips, those eyes…not a coherent word will come out of me if I'm facing him. Still, he flattens his palm on my belly and presses me closer, my back to his chest.

I bring the phone to my ear. "Hi, Maeve, what's up?"

He nibbles on my neck.

"Stuart quit." Her voice barely registers.

Kolton's hand glides

down

down

down

My thighs *burn burn burn*.

"Did you hear me, *Shy*? Stuart quit. No notice. That leaves you and me to get this job done. I'll be taking over his duties."

I clamp Kolton's wandering hand with my own and try to pull away. The man doesn't ease his iron grip. "Okay. We'll make it work. Longer hours. Whatever it takes." His lips travel to my free ear. "Can we discuss this tomorrow, Maeve? I still have a lot of work to do tonight." Like mapping every muscle on Kolton's body.

A pause. Lengthy. Full of…something. "That's fine, *Shy*. But let me remind you I've put in two years at Concept. I know why you got this project. I know why Kolton chose you. That's not enough to make it in this business. Not enough to be promoted to partner."

She hangs up, and my blood runs cold. With more force this time, I yank out of Kolton's grasp and stumble forward. "I'm so screwed."

He grips my shoulders and spins me around. "Why? What did Maeve want?"

"Stuart quit."

He swallows. Nods. "Okay. That sucks, but we can get the space done on time."

"No, you don't get it…Stuart *quit*. Stuart, who was vying for the partnership Maeve's been coveting like a serial killer. She has 'lost' important messages from his clients, switched appointments without telling him. She has messed with his career so she can make it out on top. Now that he's gone, guess who she deems her new opponent?"

Still holding my arms, he shrugs. "So what? Who gives a shit what she thinks?"

I shake away from his grasp, attempting to keep the panic out of my voice. I don't want Jackson coming down here. "I *need* this job. Without it, I have nothing. Literally. Not a roof over my head, not a cent to my name. Sure, I have a family who loves and supports me, and I can go home with my tail between my legs. But that means after Richard and everything, I still failed. That I can't make it on my own. So you...this—we come at a price. There's no way Hilary would promote me to partner at this stage of my career, but Maeve's so paranoid she believes it. She'll find some way to twist our relationship into something ugly and use it against me. Then I'll have nothing."

Kolton takes one step back. Then two. "Just so I'm clear, if you lose this job for some fucked-up reason, but the two of us are together, then you end up with nothing. Is that what you're saying?"

Exhausted, I tip my head back. "I don't know." But I do. I'd have everything. And nothing. Tonight, I lost a job, and now my career is being threatened by a chick with a fake English accent. But there's a man who wants me, who was about to make love to me, and I told him he means nothing. "Kolton," I say, needing him to understand.

His face is stone. One more step back, another, then he's striding across the kitchen to a door at the far side. "I'll help any way I can with your apartment," he says, steel in his voice. "Otherwise I'll see you at the store tomorrow. You know the way out." Without another glance, he closes the door behind him. Between us.

I slump onto the stool at the counter and drag the cupcake toward me. The cupcake Kolton bought at Lush because it's my favorite. I dip my finger into the icing and suck off the sweet perfection, but the sugar sours on my tongue. If the better-than-sex cookie dough cupcake can't make me happy, I really have nothing. I'm so tired of myself and my excuses. Tired of keeping Kolton at a distance. Moving in with him fights my natural instinct to forge my own path, but if I don't try now, I'll never deal with these issues. With Jackson in the picture, he's risking plenty to be with me. Time for me to show him I'm worth it.

Twenty

Kolton

I sit on my bed and fold my arms, then I lie down on top of the sheets and stare at the ceiling. Nights the past few months have been the worst. If I wake up, I can't get back to sleep. Back home in Vancouver, I'd lie in bed wondering what Shay was doing, wondering why I was consumed by her. Hoping she thought about me. Now we're together, but she's not giving us a chance.

Fuck me for being a prick and leaving her in the kitchen so I could tend to my bruised ego. She's the one struggling, her life caving in around her, but I'm the one who needs reassurance. I haven't opened my heart to a woman since Marina, haven't had to risk that kind of hurt. For her, I'm willing to chance it, but she has to meet me halfway.

I close my eyes. I open them. Darkness sinks into the room, the light blue walls muting into navy, then my door creaks.

Silence. Nothing. But Shay's minty scent invades my nose.

She closes the door, sits on the floor beside the bed, and the pressure on my heart eases. I stay lying on my back, one arm behind my head, afraid if I move I'll wake up from a dream.

"Kolton." Her soft voice whispers through the quiet.

"Shay," I reply, just to hear her name.

"I'm sorry."

"Me, too." I study the chandelier on the ceiling, one of the crystals hanging lower than the others. Likely broken and replaced. I don't look at Shay. If I do, my self-control will snap. My body senses her, though. Feels her. Already, my jeans are tight.

"You're not nothing," she says. "You're too much. I'm scared."

The waver in her voice says as much. There's more to this for Shay. More than her job and apartment. For her to open up, she has to know she's not alone. "Don't you think I'm scared, too? I have a life in Vancouver. A kid I have to take care of and look out for. Pursuing you and asking you out wasn't easy for me. Bringing you into Jackson's life is a huge risk. But you're worth it." I'm dying to look at her face, but I'll be dragging her up on this bed if I so much as glance her way.

What sounds like a hand rubbing along the carpet fills the quiet, then, "So why do it? There are lots of girls in Vancouver. Why come here? Why me?"

I wish I knew the answer to that question—that intangible thing known as chemistry. Shay is beautiful. Every construction worker at the shop ogles her, and it makes me want to staple-gun their eyes shut. It's more than her curvy figure, though, her wild hair and full lips. It's the way my ribs tighten when she's in the room. How easy it was to tell her about Marina and hang out together with Jackson. The stuff you can't measure. Can't name. "Because," I say, "you're the one I can't forget. The one who drives me nuts. The one who makes me want to risk things. What exactly are you afraid of? Is it really the job?"

More rubbing of the carpet. "I'm scared I'll lose myself in you."

And there we have it. That asshole Richard did a number on her, all right. I turn my head toward her. She's by the bed, knees tucked to her chest in those tiny shorts. I shift onto my side and smooth my thumb over her cheek. "Losing yourself is the best part." She exhales and presses her face into my hand, but I pull my arm back. "It's the best part, but I won't go down that road alone. You have to trust me. Trust yourself with me. The rest—job, money, independence, distance—we can work out."

This carpe diem thing is getting harder by the moment, my mind already spinning through the possibilities. The future. Long-distance relationships don't work. I tried that crap with Marina our first year at university, and we split up. Briefly. It was a fucking nightmare, really. Not something I'd go through again. Making things work with Shay means one of us has to make huge sacrifices.

Her steady breaths quicken. "I trust you. I'll risk it for you."

Thank fucking Christ.

In one swift move, I swing my legs over the side of the bed and reach for the table lamp. There's no way I'm touching Shay unless I get to watch every expression on her face, every shudder of her body. "Come here," I say.

Slowly, she stands.

She moves between my legs.

She reaches for my head.

She runs her fingers down my hair.

"I've missed you so much," she says.

"So much," I repeat.

Without a word, she grabs the hem of her shirt and yanks it over her head, then she shucks off her shorts, leaving her in a black lace bra and skimpy underwear.

"Finally," I breathe out on a sigh. I drag my hands up her thighs and lean in to kiss her belly.

"Yes," she says. "God, yes…"

I slip off her bra.

With one hand on her ass and the other on her full breast, I flick her nipple with my tongue, and her head drops back. Another groan. Another *yes*. I put my whole mouth on her, and her knees nearly buckle. Needing a better view, I grip her waist and guide her to the bed, laying her out before me, those curls fanning over the white sheets like I've imagined a thousand times. She barely blinks as I lose my shirt and jeans, and then I'm standing naked at the side of the bed.

"Closer," she says, reaching for me.

Her heavy-lidded gaze drops to my cock, which twitches in acknowledgment, but I don't move. "Later. Right now I need to look at you. See everything I've pictured since Aspen. And these need to come off." Leaning forward, I hook my thumbs through the scrap of lace around her hips and drag them down.

My breath hitches.

I almost have to close my eyes and picture my first grade teacher nude so I don't come right here, right now. But I won't close them. Not for a second.

Shay's right hand travels to her thigh, feathering over her skin. Back and forth. Back and forth. I get harder. "If you don't touch me soon, I'm gonna touch myself. I've had lots of practice lately."

I bet she has. "Don't you dare. That pussy is mine."

Her hips move restlessly over the sheets. "But I can't wait."

I'm right there with her, needing to be inside of her, but I'm not rushing this. "I'll take care of you, Shay. You'll be begging me to stop. But we do this my way. Move your hand and close your eyes."

Her gaze runs down my chest and abs, and lower—my want for her on display. She's still restless, still stroking her skin. Then she softens into the bed, clutches the sheets, and closes her eyes. Picking up one long leg, I kneel on the bed and start at her ankle, working my way up, touching, kissing. Memorizing every inch. Each caress produces a deep moan from her. When I get to the apex of her thighs, her beautiful wetness an inch away, she presses her hips up with a desperate "Now, Kolton. Please."

I start on the other leg.

Time dissolves. Seconds become kisses; minutes are measured in tastes, each touch eliciting her throaty sounds. I move to her hips, each breast, her neck, her shoulder, the dip at the base of her throat. So much Shay to explore. "I can't get enough," I say as I hover over her on my knees. Any closer, and I won't last.

Her eyes open, and her hands move. She traces the lines of my pecs and the tensed muscles of my abs, finally reaching around to knead my ass and pull me toward her, but I resist. "Not yet, baby."

Her nostrils flare. "Now you're just being cruel."

When I suck a trail through the center of her ribs, over her belly button, and down to her beautiful, slick, hot wetness, she drops her knees wide and groans with a breathy "God."

Fuck yeah.

I spread her open. Each lick sends her hips into spasm. She pushes into my face, not shy about asking for more. I give her what she wants. I give her everything. I want her to break apart around me, because of me. I want her to forget everything but this. Us. How I make her feel. In seconds, she's chanting my name and convulsing. I grip her ass as I prepare for round two.

More moans. Another cry.

She falls apart while fisting my hair, her *yes, Kolton, God* coming out on ragged breaths. Then she tugs me up.

She brings my mouth to hers, kissing me, tasting herself on me. So damn hot.

"Shay," I say.

Deeper kisses. Throaty moans. Hers and mine.

The air swells with our sounds.

Reluctantly, I pull back. "I was tested after Aspen and haven't been with anyone since."

She reaches down and fists my length, the heat and tightness of her grip halting my ability to speak. Lust for this woman shoots down my spine. "Me too," she says. Then, "No condom needed."

I cover her hand with mine, both of us guiding me to her entrance. Moving back on my knees, I grip her hips and push in slowly, inch by glorious inch, watching as I sink inside of her. Warm. Wet. Perfect. I pull her closer, press deeper. She tries to draw her hips back, forcing me to move. But I don't. I can't. Not yet. When it gets too much, I pull out almost all the way, then *in in in*. Stopping. Waiting. Breathing hard. Dragging out the pleasure of being inside of her, finally. In Aspen, Shay was fit and lean. I may never have seen her body laid out like this, but she has curves going on now that weren't there then. Rounded hips, slim waist, more than ample tits. A fucking vision. This time, I drag out and thrust in harder. Her breasts bounce, and she groans. Or maybe I do. She writhes and tries to grind against me, her unruly curls sliding along the sheets. I want to watch her face, her breasts, but I need to feel my skin on hers, my mouth on hers. I need that hair in my hands.

Dropping forward, I pick up the pace; our bodies flush as I roll my hips. I slide my arms under her shoulders and grip her hair while she scrapes my back and rasps my name. Our lips meet, but neither of us has enough control to connect. We stay, breath mingling, lips touching. Time stops. Evaporates. I tuck my elbows to her sides, and she wraps her legs around my waist, squeezing tight. Closer. Deeper. Until, "I'm there, baby. You with me?" My lips skim hers, still not kissing.

"Yes, God, yes," comes her breathy reply.

Then we're falling.

Shay. Jesus. Fuck. Yes.

Our bodies press closer, a thin sheen of sweat between us, as the last shocks spike through me. I ride the end of my orgasm, panting, repeating her name until I collapse on top of her.

She runs her hands along my back. "Forget Fabio. From now on, you're Thor."

I nestle my nose behind her ear and suck her sensitive skin. "Does that mean you've watched that not-very-deep action movie of your own free will? Lots of shit gets blown up in those films."

"Mmhmm," she hums. "Chris Hemsworth trumps bad cinema."

I laugh, the movement causing me to slip out of her. The sudden loss of connection has my stomach dropping to my feet. If I have to leave after six weeks, and Shay decides she can't do this with me, be with me, it won't be pretty. I didn't lose Marina by choice, and I have no intention of losing Shay. Living in the now is no longer a luxury. Six weeks. Forty-two days. That's long enough to show her we're worth fighting for. If we're going to make this work, one of us will have to compromise in the long run. Move. Change jobs. Exactly what terrifies her. Exactly what I've tried to ignore. But this, right now, losing that bit of contact, tells me everything I need to know: Shay is my future.

The thought knocks me for a spin.

"I like it better with you in me," she says, reading my mind.

I push up onto my elbows and seal the kiss we couldn't finish before. "Good thing it's not morning yet."

* * *

But morning comes, and I'm a mess by the afternoon—the intensity of my feelings for Shay taking my mind to dangerous places. She left before the sun rose, giving me time to explain to Jackson and Stella that she's moving in. Jackson, of course, was thrilled. To him, it's just more time with his new friend, but Stella pulled me aside.

"You sure this is a good idea? I like Shay. I'm all for you guys dating. But isn't it soon?"

There wasn't much I could say to that. "It is, but she was in a bind and we're only here a short while. I *want* this time with her. I know it's sudden, but I'm tired of always worrying about the future."

She agreed to get behind the decision, but the worrying I wanted to avoid has only increased, each passing hour making me edgier.

Needing air, I head on a walk, barely noticing the spectacular homes lining the street, my boots pounding out a steady drone. After last night, I know I want to be with Shay beyond this trip, but acknowledging it and making it happen are two different beasts. Maybe working remotely from Toronto is possible. Sawyer's managed okay so far, and Jackson would adapt. But Marina's mother called again this morning. I knew this trip would be hard on her, but I didn't anticipate the constant phone calls. The worry. Her voice cracks every time she gets off the phone, every time she asks when we're returning. With her husband, Paul, locked into his teaching pension, they'd never move, and Jackson is their only link to their daughter. Who am I to deny them that?

Thoughts of them and Marina spur my confusion, and I pick up the pace, hands stuffed in my front pockets, head down.

Marina and I were effortless. We didn't butt heads or disagree. We both loved to rock climb and watch action movies and spend hours counting the stars. I've dated plenty since then, met girls like her—sweet-tempered women who I imagined would fill my future with a similar contentment, but there was never enough chemistry to pursue them. Shay and I have more chemistry than a NASA lab. I never know when she'll bite my head off for saying the wrong thing or kiss me or push me away. There's nothing easy about our relationship, but she's all I think about, all I want. And she's the opposite of Marina.

I've walked around the block twice, my place in view again. When I reach the driveway, I grab my phone from my pocket and dial Sawyer.

"Miss me?" He offers no greeting.

I settle my hip onto my new rental SUV—that emasculating van finally exchanged—and kick some loose stones. "I'm fucked up."

"And?"

A woman with a pound of makeup on her face speed-walks by as her tiny dog scampers to keep up. I hunch forward and rake my hand through my hair, sweat gathering under my shirt on this warm July day. "Do you think Marina and I were the real deal?"

Pause. Silence. A fucking eternity. "Where the hell's this coming from?"

"Answer the question."

"Give me a sec." A muffled voice—a female voice—carries through the line then, "Seriously, dude, what's going on?"

"Is someone with you?"

"No. It's just Lily. We were Skyping. I got off."

"Her boyfriend know you *got off* while Skyping with her?"

A distant *I swear to God* rumbles through the phone before he comes back on full volume. "Fuck you. Now back to this ridiculous question of yours. I don't know what kind of messed-up shit is going on in your head, but you and Marina were epic. The best together. Why the hell are you questioning that? What happened with Shay?"

I hunch farther forward, shifting my weight from foot to foot, a bead of sweat gathering at the base of my spine. "Shay and Marina are so different."

"And?"

"And I'm in over my head with Shay. Things have been intense. More intense than they were with Marina. Does that mean Marina and I would've grown apart? That we weren't what I thought we were?" We got together so young. People change. Grow. Maybe we would have ended up seeing Jackson on alternate weekends.

Crunching crackles in my ear, Sawyer likely inhaling a bag of Lay's. It reminds me of Shay. Like everything these days. He stops eating long enough to say, "Don't play that game, bro. Nothing good comes of it. What you and Marina had was golden. Untouchable. Nothing you do or don't do will ever change that. So don't fuck yourself over by messing things up with Shay because you're overthinking things like a girl. Live in the now." He pauses, more crunching as I wait for him to continue with his motivational speech.

Apparently, he's done.

But his words ease the churning in my gut. I must sound like an ass, questioning what Marina and I had. Deep down, I know we were solid, but everything about Shay has me twisted up. Especially the part about living for the moment. "What are the odds of me being able to work from Toronto? Permanently?"

His reply takes longer this time. "It's that serious?"

"For me, it is. Shay's still dealing with some stuff over her ex, but I'm pretty sure she feels the same. I can't keep putting off the future. And the more I think about it, the more I want her in that future." So much for that carpe diem crap. I'm a planner. That's what I do best. Acknowledging what I have with Shay could be even better than what I had with Marina has revved my heart to warp speed. There has to be a way to work this out.

Sawyer's heavy sigh isn't the sound I want to hear. "I hate to be the bringer of bad news, but you've only been gone a few weeks, and things aren't pretty here. That shipment of zippers I ordered? I got the quantity mixed up, and it's set us back; two production staff quit, and that guy you deal with on the jacket insulation? Howard something? He's telling me they won't have our order in next month. Since you've got a lot to organize, I was trying to handle things, but I'm drowning."

So much for the business being under control. Moondog is growing faster than we can handle, and it needs us both there to weather the storm. In time we'll hire more people, but even then, if I'm not present, I can't rummage through files to figure things out, can't stop by our production floor to assess damage and delay. From a distance, everything takes longer, gets more complicated. Stressful. Our head office is in Vancouver, and that's where I have to be. It's where Marina's mother is.

That leaves Shay moving to Vancouver.

"I am so fucked," I say.

"That mean the sex is good?"

Ignoring him, I stand from the car and pace. "I'm not sure I can convince Shay to move."

"So do the long-distance thing. Fly down for weekends."

I stop dead and tighten my grip on the phone. "Never again, Sawyer. I can't do it."

"People do it all the time."

"Have you forgotten what happened with Marina? What a fucking disaster that was?" More like the ninth circle of hell.

"Sure, but—" He cuts off the line and comes back with "Give me a sec. There's someone at the door."

He can take as long as he wants; it won't change a damn thing. When Marina and I were applying to university, she had her heart set on a nursing program in Calgary, and I got a scholarship to the University of British Columbia. It meant we'd be a province apart, but it was us and we thought we could make things work. Talk about being young and naïve. We fought. Jealousy got the better of us. Bad shit went down—stuff I can't relive—and, eventually, we broke up. I was destroyed. Fucking obliterated. Since I was on scholarship, Marina offered to transfer her second year, and we worked things out. The lesson, however, was loud and clear: Long-distance relationships are doomed before they start.

Now there's Shay.

For the second time in my life, I'm in deep with a woman whose life is on a different path than mine. Unless we converge.

"Fine," Sawyer says when he comes back on the line. "I won't harp on the long-distance thing, even though you're being a pussy about it, but there's always a solution. Figure out what would hold Shay back from moving, and prove to her you're worth it. Do that charming stuff you do. But back to the insulation, we need to find a new supplier."

We brainstorm a while, then I head inside to make notes and figure out a plan of attack. Two plans, actually. Suppliers I can deal with, but Shay will be a lot harder to manage, but I want this, *us*, to work. If I know Shay, her job at Concept will hold her back, which means I need to show her how much opportunity there is in Vancouver, how much she can thrive there. Pumped, I spend the first of many hours on the computer. I'll gather an arsenal of facts over the next few weeks and, when the time is right, I'll say my piece. Lay it out for her in a pretty package. Until then, I'll have to use my body to convince her we belong together.

Twenty-one

Shay

If I thought my focus was off before I spent five straight nights with Kolton, my current inability to keep my mind on work and off him could land me in a psych ward. While I text Hilary about the changes I've made to the silkscreens, Maeve breezes into the construction zone that will soon be Moondog's new shop. Her sleek bob is freshly blown, her red lipstick glossy, not a wrinkle on her linen pants or silk top, but she appears to be empty-handed.

And she looks smug. Battle ready.

A loud bang rings through the space, dust billowing as drills, saws, and hammers create a symphony of noise. I sneeze, wrinkling my nose in an effort to fight the reflex a second time. Each day I leave here covered in a layer of grime, fine drywall powder invading every pore on my body.

As Maeve approaches, I narrow my eyes. "Didn't you pick up the lights this morning? The electrician needs them today."

Her grin widens; my frown deepens.

"Sorry, *Shy*. I had car trouble and didn't want to be late."

Car trouble my ass. For a moment, I wondered if she would put aside her crap to help pull this project together in the face of Stuart's departure, but Maeve is still Maeve—territorial, insecure. Evil. If stores were open longer, I'd do everything myself. I'd crisscross the city through traffic if it meant not relying on her. Sadly, furniture and design shops don't offer twenty-four-hour drive-thru. "And you didn't call to tell me because…?"

She ignores my snarky tone and studies a manicured nail. "I presumed you'd be busy, *delegating*. I wouldn't want to interrupt your work, *Shy*." Each fake-accented sentence dips at the end, each word elongated.

Kolton pushes through the front door then, and my frustrated reply dries up. Along with my saliva. Visions of our night together burn through my mind. Me, naked on the desk in his room while he stood before me, my backside in his hands, his deep thrusts knocking the furniture into the wall. Him, bent over my back whispering dirty nothings into my ear as he shattered my multiple-orgasm record. (Hence the concentration issues.)

Sunday morning, after our first night together and I agreed to move in with him, I drove home before the sun came up, giving him time to explain the situation to Jackson, giving myself time to adjust. He lent me money to settle things with my landlord and has offered me his home, his bed, his heart. But I'm still guarding mine, worried the second I give him all of me, I'll lose the girl I've worked so hard to find. One blink and she'll be gone. But each day

I offer him another inch, and tomorrow we'll be going on our first official date.

He strides toward me, coffees in hand, barely concealing the hunger in his eyes, like we're back in his room, on his bed, against his wall. He looks delicious with the dusting of scruff on his chin. Worn boots, snug jeans, Moondog T-shirt. I'd take one of him over ten of those cookie dough cupcakes. Maybe.

Behind him, the electrician steps inside, and I curse under my breath. Maeve glances over her shoulder, then back at me, and smiles her Cruella De Vil smile. "Shall I fetch the lights, then?"

"Yes, Maeve. Fetch. And please be quick about it." But it's rush hour, streets overcrowded with drivers fighting gridlock. It'll take her at least an hour to get there and back. The electrician has another job this afternoon, which means he won't be back until after the weekend. Hilary won't be happy.

"Kolton," Maeve says in greeting as she struts by him.

He tips his head. "Maeve." Then he's close enough to touch, his familiar woodsy scent curling around me. "Missed you this morning," he says. "I didn't even hear you get up. Wasn't sure you'd be able to move after last night." He places one of the coffees on the worktable behind me and grazes my arm. A casual brush that is anything but.

A bruise on my left hip throbs as if sensing its creator. "I'm great, thanks. Nice to see you." His face hardens at my formal reply, so I soften my voice. "Hilary hasn't been in yet. I haven't had a chance to speak with her about us. I will, though. This morning."

Every day since I moved in, I've piled on another excuse, a reason not to tell Hilary I'm sleeping with our client. *She was in a bad mood. We didn't have time to talk.* Last night, Kolton rolled on top of me and pinned my arms above my head. "As much as I love our time between the sheets," he said, his knees nudging mine wider, "I hate pretending in public. Please talk to Hilary." He had me groaning *yes* in minutes.

That makes today D-Day.

Appeased, he says, "While we have a moment, I wanted to ask you something." I smile, and he goes on, "Sawyer hired an event company to organize the grand opening, but I think they need to coordinate with you to get a better vibe for the store. Any chance you have time to work with them?"

The electrician tries to catch my eye, so I hold a hand up to let him know I'll be a minute, a minute I barely have. Sighing, I face Kolton. "As much as I'd love to help, I'm not sure I can sacrifice the time. But Lily's great with details and planning, and she knows the business as well as I do."

He nods. "Great idea. You mind asking?"

"No. I'm meeting her and Raven for lunch and can ask then. For now I need to deal with a problem."

I leave him to greet the approaching electrician, readying to admit I don't have everything he requested. After explaining my (Maeve's) incompetence to the man, we make a plan for him to return on Monday. He leaves as Hilary comes in. Like Maeve, she's always polished and put together, her long blond hair in an elegant ponytail, today's pencil skirt and blue blouse likely off a rack at Prada. Based on her flawless skin, I'd guess she's had a treatment or two to delay next year's forty-fifth birthday she'll never admit to reaching.

She glances over the skinny jeans, sandals, and tight black T-shirt I threw on this morning. I'm all for Casual Friday. Frowning, she says, "Why is the electrician leaving?"

I contemplate throwing Maeve under the bus as Hilary places her purse on our worktable. With the Kolton bomb I'll be dropping, I don't want to give her any other reason to question my ability. But I won't stoop to that level. I need to own my position as team leader. "I made a bad call," I say. "I've sent Maeve to get what we need this morning, and the electrician will be back on Monday to run the wires."

Again, she studies me, a contemplative look that has my shoulders wanting to cave forward. I fight the urge to slouch, instead standing taller.

"It shouldn't set us back too much," she says. "But you need to stay on top of things. This is your job. Your project. Things will always go wrong when pulling a space together. It's your responsibility to manage it. People included. Associate designers don't shrink from confrontation."

This is the first time she's hinted at a promotion, and there's something in her tone—appraising, supportive. *Challenging?* Like she wants me to succeed, but only if I prove myself. Like she knows Maeve is a world-class bitch who will do her best to trip me up, and my advancement depends on my ability to govern her. If I owned my own firm, Maeve's the last person I'd trust as partner, but it's not my decision to make.

The confidence I've exuded the past few weeks cowers under nervous jitters as I follow Hilary to where Kolton's waiting. I dig my nails into my palms to calm my shaking hands. Nothing's changed with this project. The designs and plans and momentum haven't altered. But it all feels different. More demanding. More daunting.

Kolton's brown eyes latch onto me.

There's more at risk.

"Shay," he says when we reach him. He keeps a healthy distance between us and juts his chin toward Ben, the largest guy in our construction crew, overalls and workbooks his daily uniform. "You need to review the exact angle of the hanging wall," Kolton says. "Ben started drilling, but it doesn't look like he has the revised drawings."

Shit. Kolton shouldn't be catching this. I should be catching this. "Yeah, okay. I was sure I'd given everyone the changes." Stupid. Stupid. Stupid. Of course Hilary is here to catch the mistake. I hurry toward the worktable at the back and sift through the mass of parchment on top. When I find the folder with the wall dimensions, I check the date on the bottom to confirm they're the ones I adjusted earlier this week. Kolton's chatting with Hilary, sipping his coffee, the two of them in a private tête-à-tête closer to the front door. Paranoia crawls up my neck. Is she asking him about me? Does she know? I'm so frazzled by the time I return to Ben that I drop the papers on the floor.

We both stoop to pick them up, and he places his large hand on my back. "Don't worry about the hole I drilled. It won't be visible when we're done." We often pore over drawings together, Ben always quick to boost my confidence when complications arise.

I force a smile, still angry at myself for the mistake. "Thanks."

When we're standing, his hand lingers on me, his distance closer than Kolton's was a moment ago. "Everything okay? You seem a little off."

Kolton stares at us with tight lips. Last night, while whispering in my ear, he said he couldn't wait to be able to touch me in public; for people to know we're together. Now another man's hand is on my back. Attempting to ignore the brown lasers boring into me from across the room, I face Ben and step out of reach. "Let's just say the ante's been upped on this job, and I'm not playing with a full deck."

"A poker reference." He drops his head and leans into my ear, his deep baritone lowering. "Now I have to ask you out."

More flustered than ever, I shrug with an awkward "I'm sort of seeing someone."

If "sort of" is living together and sharing a bed.

Disappointment clouds his face. "If the 'sort of' part of the equation doesn't pan out, let me know."

Ben returns to work, and, unable to stop myself, I glance over at Kolton and take in his reddening face and stiff stance. Hilary's saying something to him, but he barely looks her way as the coffee in his hand tilts at a precarious angle. A few drops land on the floor, unnoticed.

Man, does he look pissed. And I don't blame him. If a girl were leaning into his side and asking him out, I'd go roller derby on her.

Whatever Kolton says to Hilary ends their conversation. He dumps his coffee in a nearby bin and skirts around the Shop-Vac and tools piled on the floor, aiming right for me. My heart pounds a quickening beat, *thump thump thumping* in my ears. Then he's in front of me. Then his hand is on my back. Then he's leading me toward what will eventually be the back room, the section divided with drywall.

Thumpity thump thump.

He backs me into a dark corner. "Not cool."

"What?" I say, feigning innocence.

"You know what. If Ben knew we were together, he'd never pull that shit. Touching you in front of me. Whispering to you." He grips my hips, the bruise from last night reminding me how punishing Kolton can be. Delectably punishing. "I don't like it," he finishes.

I lean into him. "I know. I'm sorry. But he's harmless." My lips are level with his jaw, and I ghost them along his stubble. So delicious. I want to run my hand up his shirt, over the firm ridges of his abs, and through the dusting of hair across his chest.

He tips his head down and kisses me so deeply I forget where we are. He nips my lower lip. "He may be harmless, but I'm not. I can't watch guys flirt with you and pretend I don't care. It's not who I am. If he makes another move on you in front of me, I'll deck the guy. Is that how you want Hilary to find out we're seeing each other?"

Crap. Hilary. With the associate design position dangled in front of me, my competitive streak from years of ski racing ignites. I deserve the job, more than Maeve deserves the partnership. I'm working my butt off on this project, and unlike a certain gluten-intolerant bitch, I'd never step on others to rise. But if Hilary learns Kolton and I are dating, her looks of approval may turn into frowns of disdain, my capability and talent put into question. Avoiding the subject of our closeted relationship, I say, "I told you not to watch all those violent movies. They're a bad influence."

He breaks away from me and steps back. "Tell her, Shay. We have five weeks left together. That's it. I'm not spending that time hiding like teenagers."

I'm about to open my mouth and spew the same nonsense about work and Hilary and me being taken seriously on this job, but Kolton's right. I want this time with him. He's jumped in with both feet, and he deserves nothing less than my honesty. Besides, Hilary wouldn't consider me for the associate designer position on a whim. The promotion ups the stakes, but it also proves I'm good at what I do. Even if I tell her about Kolton and me and the worst happens, this is my living portfolio. I can use it to get another job. But I can't use it to get another Kolton.

Two steps remain between us. Loud voices fill the gap, a reminder we're not alone. I place my hand on his chest. "I'll tell her today. I promise. And"—I smile, suddenly shy—"Hilary mentioned she's considering me for a permanent position."

His eyes cloud momentarily, then his body softens under my touch. "Thank you. And of course she is. Your designs kick ass." He kisses me softly and presses his forehead to mine. "I hate to leave, but I have an appointment."

"Where?" I tug him closer, dreading losing contact.

"We'll discuss it on our date tomorrow. Have fun at lunch with the girls." He squeezes my hips and leaves me to gather myself before I face Hilary and confess that I'm dating the most important client Concept has ever had.

She's by the worktable, flipping through papers, and I search out Kolton for one last dose of courage. He pauses at the front door, a meaningful glance back before he leaves.

Time to face the music.

"Hil—" I start, but her name lodges in my throat. I clear it and try again. "Hilary."

She looks up. "Yes."

For the second time today, I dig my nails into my palms to steady myself. She won't fire me at this stage. She needs me to complete this job. That'll give me at least four or five weeks to find something else. I can live with Kolton until then.

I roll my shoulders back and face Hilary. "We need to talk."

She wipes a spot of dust from her skirt. "Okay."

Unable to draw out the torture, I say, "Kolton and I are dating."

Better to rip off the Band-Aid.

She crosses her arms, but says nothing.

"I know how it must look," I say to fill the ominous silence, "but that's not why he hired me and the firm. We've known each other for a while but have only recently started dating"—if all-night sexathons are considered dating—"and I don't want my relationship with him to jeopardize my job. It's too important, and I thought you should know." My heart thumps again, this time in my ears.

She walks closer and leans against the table. "I suspected as much. The way you two sneak glances at each other, it's hard to miss. But, tell me honestly…will dating him impact your ability to complete this project?"

"No. Definitely not."

She studies me. "Then we'll deal with it. Kolton seems great. Thoughtful. The type of guy you hold on to." There's wistfulness in her voice, maybe a thread of regret concerning her recent divorce. Whatever the reason, I almost fall at her feet in gratitude.

"You've proven yourself on this project," she says. "I mentioned the associate position earlier because I see a lot of potential in you. You have that natural finesse with clients and tradespeople—a bedside manner, so to speak, which is an important part of the job. We're psychologists as much as we are designers. It isn't ideal to be dating the client, but there are no rules against it. As long as you two can keep that area of your life separate and don't bring arguments or difficulties to work, I have no problem with it." She places a hand on my shoulder. "And that hair really is something." She winks at me, and my neck flames.

Seriously. That hair.

"Thanks for understanding, it means a lot. I won't let you down."

"I know you won't," she says, less playfully. She may have given me her blessing, but Concept is her company, her only child. She won't stand by idly if she feels it's threatened.

I gather my purse and briefcase. "I'll run to the carpenter's to check on the change-room doors after lunch. I'll be back in a few hours."

"Okay. I'll keep an eye on Ben to make sure he follows those designs to the letter. That wall is the centerpiece of the space. There's no room for error." Her raised eyebrow is the only reminder I need to buckle down and make sure no more glitches happen on my watch.

Relieved, I nearly skip to the front door, a gust of warm summer air blasting my face as I step outside. Scents of charred meat float from a hot-dog stand as people brush by me. Brakes grind, phones ring, laughter drifts from a couple walking hand in hand. It's the same street, but different. The same day, but different.

I'm the same, but different.

My shoulders feel light, unburdened, a future with so many possibilities ahead of me. Kolton. My career finally taking off. *Kolton.* But the girls still don't know about my apartment and current living arrangements, and I'm tired of all my secrets. I hurry down the street, ready to come clean.

But a block away, I hear, "Shay? Is that you?"

I frown at the familiar voice and spin around. "Michael. Wow. It's been a while."

Actually, it's been since Richard dumped my ass. Seeing the Dick's best friend dampens my joy, but I offer a smile. It's not Michael's fault Richard hurt me in ways that can't be measured, invisible scars that have me keeping Kolton at a distance. If I'm honest, though, it's not all Richard's doing. I let him condescend to me, belittle me. I let him influence every decision in my life. Including my continued stubbornness.

Michael folds his arms, and his expensive suit tightens around his shoulders. "You look great. Everything good?"

It's a real question, not forced conversation, the brightness in his eyes saying as much. He's always been a nice guy. I broaden my smile. "Can't complain. You?"

"Yeah. Great. Working too much, but aren't we all? You still at that design place? Retirement homes, right?"

I snort, those floral-on-floral themes forever burned into my retinas. "No. The mothball smell got to me. Allergies. Moondog's opening their first shop in Toronto. I'm designing the space for them." Until now, when dishing about this job, I've felt like an imposter. Like I'm living someone else's life. But I'm on track to maybe, *possibly*, becoming a full-time, paid designer. He nods, his gaze suddenly more probing, roaming over me from head to toe. As though he doesn't recognize the girl before him. His eyes linger on my breasts, about a size bigger since quitting my juice cleanses. "Cool," he says. "Love their stuff. Anyway, I've gotta run. It was good seeing you. I'll tell Richard you say hi."

Hi? *Really?* Michael's on his way with the throng of pedestrians, caught up in the flow of the city, before I can squash that nonsense. If I had to pass a message to Richard, a simple "hi" wouldn't cut it. If I had to leave him a token of my regard, I'd add the all-encompassing dumbass after the salutation. Or limpdick. Or jerkoff. I bet Jackson's *Urban Dictionary* has a slew of fitting names.

When the last of Michael's dark blue suit disappears, thoughts of Richard and retirement homes fade with him. I rush to meet the girls.

* * *

"Why do you look like you stuck your finger in a light socket?" When I frown and touch my hair, Raven waves at my face. "Not your curls. You're all fidgety. Like that time you couldn't wait to gossip about Susie Marshall losing her V-card. What aren't you telling us?"

Lily swallows a spoonful of soup. "You do look like you're about to burst."

We come to this café often, the soups, salads, and sandwiches filling and easy on the wallet. But it's been ages since we've hung out. Life's been busy for all of us. Work. Stress. Relationships. The second we sat down, Raven dished about her summer photography classes, and Lily complained, *again*, that Kevin and she are drifting apart, their relationship lingering past its expiration date. I listened and asked questions, all the while excited and nervous to share my news. They might be upset I've kept them in the dark so long.

Raven jabs her fork at me. "Spill it. Unless you want me to inform your brother the dent on his beloved Chevy wasn't a hit-and-run. What did that cost him to fix? Eight hundred…a thousand bucks?"

Raven and her threats. "First, I'm pretty sure you're the reason we took his car for a joyride. And second, that lamppost jumped in front of me." I inhale the last bite of my chicken wrap while we have a stare-off.

Lily pushes her finished soup away. "Come on, Shay. What's got you so wound up?"

Where do I start? My money woes have gone on so long, they've bled into every facet of my life. My job turmoil, my Kolton stress, and my living arrangements are all symptoms of the greater cause: I was too proud to ask for help.

"I'll give you the condensed version," I say, raising my hand to tick the items off one by one. "I've been strapped for cash for a while." *One.* "Natasha fired me from Sass and Style." *Two.* "I'm close to getting a permanent design position at Concept." *Three.* "I was nearly evicted." *Four.* "I've moved in with Kolton." *Five.* "And…"

My mouth opens, ready to list number six before I have the sense to swallow the words. "I could be falling in love."

My life whittled down to six sentences.

Raven and I are both in fitted black T-shirts, but her inked arms look as intimidating as her narrowed eyes. "Let me get this straight. You've been on the verge of getting booted from your apartment, and you haven't spoken to us about it?"

Lily, on the other hand, covers her heart with her hand. "You're falling in love?"

These girls couldn't be more different. Needing to address both topics, I start with the unpleasant one and face Raven. "I should have told you guys, but I was embarrassed and didn't want to ask for money. I kept thinking I'd figure things out on my own."

"You know we're your friends, right? It's our job to help when shit like that goes down."

"I know. I just get so stuck on doing things my way."

More specifically, *not* Richard's way. Seeing Michael was a reminder that I'm still reeling from the side effects of that shitty relationship. It's childish and frustrating, and I'm angry his controlling ways still impact my life. When I conquered my stutter, the fear of its return plagued me for ages. I'd never raise my hand in class and would fake sick when presentations were due. I knew I could speak fluently, but I was terrified I'd relapse. Like now—my fear of falling back into my old patterns has robbed me of the girls' support.

"I'm sorry," I say again.

"You're forgiven. But next time I'll be tattooing the word 'stubborn' on your forehead." Raven blows me a kiss.

"Except for the tattooing, I second everything Raven said, but can we get back to the love part? The living with Kolton part?" Lily's gray eyes sparkle as bright as her beaded necklace.

Once I've filled them in on the wooing, my firing, and my new living arrangements, Raven clicks her black nails on the table. "When does Kolton go back home?"

I shrug. "Not sure. Someone needs to stay a while so things run smoothly at the new shop. With the amount of work Kolton's missed, it sounds like it'll be Sawyer. So five weeks, maybe?"

"Then what?"

Raven doesn't mince words. Words I'd rather ignore. So focused on keeping Kolton away and dealing with my apartment drama and the Moondog project, I haven't allowed myself time to worry about the future. But if we get in deeper, I won't have a choice. I just hope that choice doesn't involve giving up a promotion at Concept.

"One thing at a time," Lily says. "You have five weeks together. Enjoy it. And if you really fall in love, you guys will figure it out. There's always a way to make things work."

She's right, and it's time I shake the shadows hanging over my head. I deserve to enjoy Kolton without stressing about the next step. "Agreed," I say, then I touch Lily's arm. "I almost forgot. Kolton asked if you can help coordinate the grand opening. He needs someone to make sure it flows with the design. Since you rock at detail stuff and can shop anyone under the table, I suggested you."

"Seriously? I'd love to."

Raven coughs on a sip of water. "You know she'll just turn it into a coffeehouse theme and force the guys to grow beards and wear lumberjack shirts, right?"

Lily rolls her eyes. "Better that than a goth party with bats and vampires."

Raven slaps the table. "That's genius. We should totally do a goth event."

As they joke, I let their banter roll over me. I've come clean with my friends, Kolton and I are in the clear, and tomorrow he's taking me on a date. I will enjoy every second we have, in the bedroom and out. I'll try to banish my post-Richard issues and approach this time with a clear heart. Hopefully, I won't sabotage the best thing that's ever happened to me.

Twenty-two

Shay

"Does this mean you've been wooed?"

Jackson's on a stool at the kitchen island, swinging his legs, while Stella finishes plating his dinner. It's the second time he's asked me that question, but I'm too entranced watching Stella to answer. She places a stack of sliced cucumbers in one corner, two chicken fingers in the other, layered just so, five slices of red apple in the third, and in the fourth and final corner she mounds what might pass for peas.

I squint, studying them. "Are those purple?"

Stella, operating like a brain surgeon, places the final pea in place. "Yep. It's Saturday," she says by way of explanation and nods to the beet juice on the counter, probably used to dye them. Jackson and his quirks.

He pokes my arm again. "Are you wooed? Did Daddy woo you?"

My answering grin speaks for itself. "Yes, Jackson. Consider me wooed." And nervous as a schoolgirl for our first date. It's a simple night out, the two of us enjoying a meal together, but we've never done something so couple-y. It took me ages to select my white skirt, the bottom printed with blue blades of grass, and my complementing white tank and sandals. The first five outfits didn't cut it.

Stella passes Jackson's dinner over the counter and then leans on her colorful elbows, rainbowed birds and flowers wrapping her arms. "I've never seen Kolton so happy," she says, her gaze sliding up to meet mine. "I hope you feel the same."

A flutter rolls through my belly, catching me off guard. "Yeah. I'm pretty happy."

And terrified. And excited.

Jackson puts his fork down, a purple pea meandering across the plate. "So…does that mean Daddy found your G-spot? You know, your happy spot?"

Stella snorts while I duck and search for cover. Kolton strides into the room in worn jeans, sandals, and a fitted gray T-shirt. Effortlessly handsome. "What did I say about asking girls that question?"

Jackson hunches and studies his fingers. "It's personal, and it's not polite to ask."

Kolton stops at my side, kisses my cheek, then glares at Stella. "Next time I tell him no, don't play favorite auntie and buy him stuff he shouldn't have. That book will be the death of me."

She doesn't bat an eye. "Like I said, boss, I'm just preparing him for life. Do you know how young kids are when they start experimenting these days? I'm not sending Jackson into those piranha-filled waters unarmed. He'd get slaughtered."

Kolton shakes his head and reaches over to tug a lock of Jackson's hair. "We're going out, bud. I'll see you tomorrow. I'm busy in the morning, but we'll hit the library in the afternoon. Cool?"

Jackson nods, and his glasses slide down his nose. He pushes them in place and picks up his fork, alternating bites between each of the four foods on his plate. With the way I plan my meals—what to eat last, what to savor—I'd say he's my people.

A warm hand slides along my back, Kolton's *let's go* brushing by my ear. He guides me to the front door, but stops and faces me. "Wait here a sec."

"Okay…" I say, drawing out the word.

His eyes twinkle, reminding me of my dad on Christmas morning, often more excited than us kids to unwrap our presents. Instead of returning for something in the house, he slips out the front door and closes it. In my face. I peek out the side window and watch as he gets into his SUV and drives away. Without me. I'm not sure what kind of dates he's used to, but leaving the female half of the equation behind doesn't bode well for future sexy-time. I cross my arms, the flutters from before hardening into lead.

A minute later, he pulls up the opposite side of the circular driveway, parks, and makes his way to the door. He rings the bell. Still unsure what he's up to, I open the door just wide enough to fit my shoulders. "Shay's not here. *No en casa*," I say in my best Spanish accent.

One hand is behind his back, and he scratches his chin with the other. "That's a shame. I'm here to pick her up. Had a whole evening planned. And I wanted to give her these." He produces what's supposed to look like flowers, but they're sticks of candy, lollipops, and chocolate bundled together in a bouquet. The flutters return in torrents, feathers dancing along my skin. He holds them out to me. "You sure Shay *no en casa*?"

I snatch the bouquet. "Well played, Fabio. What else do you have planned?"

"I started with the big guns. The rest is just me and dinner."

He could've said him and a colonoscopy, and I'd follow.

* * *

The sprawling restaurant is dark enough to be intimate, and our waiter leads us to a quieter table along the wall. Usually, I spend the first few minutes in a room redesigning it in my mind, but I wouldn't change a thing in here. Soft red lights flood the dark walls, intermittent paintings of geisha girls spanning the room. Each clear glass table is topped with miniature bamboo plants, understated and sexy. Once seated, we look at each other and smile.

We glance around.

We touch our cutlery.

We arrange our chopsticks.

We shift on our seats.

"I love the décor in here. Warm and cozy." I flip over my fork. Once. Twice.

When naked in bed the past week, our whispered flirting has been effortless. There's never a pause when we pore over sketches and samples. Side by side on the ski hill or eating a hurried lunch at work has always been easy. Here, in this formal setting, the lull stretches.

And stretches.

Melodic techno beats float between us.

He runs his hand through his hair like he does. "The menu's set up as more of a share-plate thing. Considering you like to taste your way through a meal, I thought it would be fun."

More fidgeting. More glancing around.

There's so much I don't know about Kolton, like how he stays in such good shape. Is he a gym rat, a cyclist, or a runner like me? Does he prefer a fireplace or a bonfire? An ocean or a pool? Still, not a question passes my lips. We trade a few pleasantries. Stiff. Formal. Like a couple of strangers. Upon our waiter's return, Kolton orders a bourbon and I opt for a glass of Riesling.

We study our menus as if there will be a quiz.

Knots form around my vocal chords, each word constricted before it escapes. When I can't take it anymore, I blurt, "I stuttered as a child."

Talk about offering up my most vulnerable self.

He exhales, the tight lines by his eyes softening as he reaches across the table to take my hand. "I wouldn't have guessed. Your words flow pretty freely with me, especially when you're pissed."

"What can I say? You bring out the best in me. But yeah, I stuttered. Made for an unenjoyable youth. I clocked lots of hours with a speech therapist." Quiet returns between us, this time warm and cozy. Wine-by-a-fire quiet.

I press my thumb into his palm. "Your turn. Tell me something I don't know about you." I slip off a sandal, maneuver my foot over his, and wiggle my toes inside the cuff of his jeans.

His eyes flare then fall heavy. "I love your hair like that, wild and loose. I love when I notice you looking at me across a room"—I drag my toes higher—"and I'm starting to question why we're in a public place when I could have you in my room."

I ease my hands from his and place them on my lap. My foot stays where it is. "You must have misunderstood the question, Einstein. I asked you to tell me something I *don't* know about you."

The waiter appears with our drinks, places them down wordlessly, and then disappears. We each take a sip. "Okay," he says. "I do some occasional rock climbing, and I'm a black belt in karate."

Not a gym rat. I picture the cut muscles below his shirt, the ridged lines of his abs. The sharp V of his hips. Escaping to his room is sounding better and better. "When did you get into martial arts?"

He swills his glass. "After Marina died. I needed to channel some anger to a more productive place." He doesn't embellish, doesn't get teary-eyed, but my heart breaks. To be on the cusp of what is often the happiest time in a couple's life, and to have it wrenched from you in such an ugly way is unimaginable. It could embitter a man, cut him down. The Kolton in front of me, though, the one who laughs and woos and loves his son, that man has overcome.

More swilling. Another sip. "Unfortunately," he says, "over the last year, I've let it slide. I train at home, but it's not the same. I try to spend as much time as I can with Jackson, and work has exploded." He looks up, brightness in his chocolate eyes. "But I checked out a place yesterday; that's why I took off from the shop. Wanted to meet with the teacher to make sure I liked the vibe. Anyway, I'm taking a class tomorrow morning. I've been promising myself for months I'd find more balance in my life. Figured it was time to make it happen."

"Is Sawyer helping out more with the business end of things, then?"

He snorts. "No. Not his strong suit. Stella's been doing some on-line accounting courses. She'll be tackling more of the workload. She's smart. Knows our business inside and out, and helps more than she should with Jackson. Not sure what I'd do without her."

The waiter returns to ask if we're ready to order, but we wave him off. Kolton leans onto his elbows. "My turn. How is it the girl who can't stand action movies, unless Chris Hemsworth is starring in them, loves *South Park*? That show is nothing but inappropriate and obnoxious. Hilarious, sure, but I can't picture you watching it."

Unable to sit this close without some contact, I trace circles on Kolton's ankle with my pink-painted toes. He shifts his leg closer to me. "*South Park* was Raven's thing. I hated it at first. If she and Lily were watching, I'd spend most of the time hurling insults from the sidelines, averting my attention. Then they'd double over giggling, and Raven would pout and beg me to watch, too. Eventually, I gave in."

He leans back in his seat and cocks his head. "Interesting."

At his judgmental tone, I pull my foot away. "Interesting, what?"

"Put your foot back, then I'll tell you." He stares me down, his gaze darkening like it does when he takes control in the bedroom. My body responds as always. Compliant. Obedient. His to command. In life, I covet independence. Sexually, I revel in his dominance. I brush my foot over the dusting of hair at his ankle, then he says, "I find that nugget interesting, because the Shay I know is often too stubborn to compromise. She holds pretty fast to her opinions, her rules. It doesn't leave much room for growth and change—for someone else."

Meaning him.

He's peeling back my thick hide, exposing the scars Richard left in his wake. The same issue I was stressing over yesterday with the girls. I've made huge leaps forward with Kolton. Still, this morning, when he suggested I read a book instead of my *People* magazine, my snappy reply cut him off midsentence. One step forward, half a step back. I am, after all, a snowflake, unprepared and unwilling to let another man snowball me into his world. But this is Kolton, the guy who celebrates my individuality with PEZ candy and McDonald's take-out. "I'm not that bad," I say, faint and feeble.

"Shay, did liking *South Park* change you for the worse? Did it weaken who you are? Or did it expand your horizons? Your humor? I bet letting go and laughing with your girlfriends felt great."

God, we sound stupid, talking about *South Park* like it's a life-altering show of serious depth, but the analogy isn't lost on me. "Yeah," I concede. "It was fun."

He shifts forward, serious now. "This time we have, the next five weeks…it's important. I want you to let yourself go with me. Not just physically. Emotionally, too."

Wow, can this man read me. Letting go means I may watch an action movie to make him happy. I may try rock climbing because he loves it. I may change like I did with the Dick. There's also a chance, at the core, I'll still be me. Kolton's asking me to try, and I'm running out of excuses. "Are you falling for me, Fabio?" My tone is teasing, my question anything but.

He chuckles. "Yeah, Connor. But I didn't think it required much deduction on your part. Do you need it skywritten?"

I shoot him a mock-glare. "No, *Axl*. What I need is for you to tell me who this Connor is." But hearing him admit his feelings reignites my inner sparkler, heat radiating from below my ribs. I inhale deeply, then say, "It makes it easier to let go if the guy I'm falling for feels the same." Something passes over his face—contentment, relief? I'm pretty sure the sentiment's mirrored on mine. "As long as you don't embarrass yourself on this date tonight," I add, "I'd be happy to test if this mutual 'falling' heats things up in the bedroom." If he only knew what I have planned for later.

He checks his thick, leather-banded watch. "Noted. We should order. And eat really fast."

But we don't. The waiter returns, and we wave him off. Twice. We talk. We touch. We laugh. Eventually, food is ordered, eaten, and enjoyed. The Asian slaw we share is an orgasm on a plate, each bite different and exotic. I moan, and he shifts on his seat. The check is brought, the bill paid, and Kolton nearly gets in a car accident as my hand inches up his thigh.

I run to the front door before the car comes to a complete stop and fumble with my key to get the darn thing open. Kolton presses up behind me and weaves his fingers through my hair, tugging hard enough to turn my face to his. His tongue invades my mouth. My senses. His lips are hungry on mine. When my key clicks in place, I pull away and stumble inside. He reaches for me, but I push at his chest, waiting and listening for Stella.

"Continue with your coupling," she calls from upstairs. "Jackson's asleep."

Before Kolton can resume his groping, I hurry ahead. He may have pulled out all the stops with his candy bouquet—left, sadly, on the front seat of the car—but I have my own plans for this evening. Yesterday, I passed by the sauna in the lower level, and couldn't stop imagining Kolton's slippery skin sliding over mine. I set the timer before leaving tonight.

"Come to our room," he says as I head for the stairs.

Breathless with anticipation, I stay my course. I grip the banister and descend, nearly tripping in my rush. Kolton's hot on my heels, a step behind, and when we make it to the bottom, his hand snakes around my waist. He almost falls on top of me. "You're naughty tonight," he says as he palms my breast. My nipples pebble instantly.

"You haven't seen naughty yet. Tonight, I'm in charge."

He sneaks in another squeeze, then releases his hold. I cross the hardwood floor and run my hand along the pool table in the center of the living space. I don't have to glance behind to know he's following; heat suffuses my back.

Soon, it will get even warmer.

When I reach the sauna door, I don't stop. I don't strip down. I walk in fully clothed, a breathy *Jesus* coming from Kolton. He seals the door behind him, and I flip around. In seconds, his shirt clings to his body, the lines of his pecs defined under the damp cotton. Sweat gathers on his face. "I don't think I can let you take control in here. It's too much." He shakes his head as if to clear it, his eyes locking on my white tank top, the moist fabric no longer leaving much to the imagination.

He doesn't move. And I don't move.

Heat seeps into my bones, dense and heavy, until it's hard to stand.

The sauna's big enough for six people, but Kolton's presence crowds me. Overwhelms me. And I need this. If I'm going to be with him, shatter the last of my defenses, I need to know I can control him, too. Own him. Because I think I'm finally ready to let go. Reaching down, I grab the large sponge from the water bucket and squeeze it over the hot stones. Steam billows, filling the sultry air and shooting the temperature up to scorching. My hair drips down my back. Instead of answering him, I say, "Strip, but don't touch me."

Cedar and eucalyptus invade my nose on each deep inhale.

One beat. Two.

He peels off his wet shirt.

One groan. Two.

My eager sounds fill the room.

Fit but lean, his body is a thing of beauty: broad chest with the perfect amount of hair, abs so defined I could wash my very wet underwear on them (*while* worn), and narrow hips that point to the treasure at the end of this hunt. He undoes his belt buckle, and I thank God for the millionth time that Kolton flies commando. His cock springs from his jeans. Once his denim's off, he steps toward me, but I hold up my hand. My tank top and skirt are a second skin, suctioned to my body. I remove the sodden layer, then my bra and underwear, until I'm bare before him, moving close enough that my breasts skim his chest. He sucks a sharp breath. Like a good boy, though, he doesn't touch me. I press my lips to his ear. "Put your hands on the wall."

He flexes his fingers. "I'll watch a week straight of chick flicks if I can put my hands somewhere else."

Tempting, but I step away and douse the stones with more water. More steam. More heat. It's almost suffocating. As stifling as the emotion gathering in my chest. I wish he could see how fast my heart is beating, how full it is with unsaid words. *Love. Joy. Respect. Devotion.* Finally, I'm ready for it all. With a grunt, he turns around and fans his palms on the wood wall, giving me complete control and the view I've imagined ceaselessly. Rivulets of sweat drip down his skin, hours of karate and rock climbing having cut grooves through which the liquid flows. I could stare at that back and those shoulders forever, but it's his booty that's making it hard to blink. Toned and taut and rising in plump perfection, glistening in the warm light. The Sistine Chapel of butts. A butt I plan to worship shortly. Kolton shifts his feet, his frustration at facing away evident in his bunched muscles.

I run my hand down the length of my wet hair. "I think I need to get a camera."

He drops his head forward. "If you leave here, I'm dragging you back and locking the door."

Point taken.

His ass flexes, and I can't maintain my distance, can barely keep from telling him how hard I've fallen. I come up behind him, wet and slippery, and press my breasts against his back, sucking a trail from shoulder to shoulder. I glide my hands around his ribs, charting the map that leads to his treasure trail and my treasure. So slick. So hard. I grip him, and a pained *fuck* tears from his throat while I slide every inch of my drenched body along his back. "Did you touch yourself while we were apart?" I ask. "Did you picture me when you came?"

He thrusts into my hand, and I bite his shoulder, salt invading my tongue. "Yes," he says. His fingers claw the wood.

"I'd love to watch you." I'm drenched…everywhere, searching for some relief by rubbing my most sensitive spot on his backside. I won't be able to play the role of seductress much longer.

"I'll put on a show, baby. But not tonight. Tonight I need to be inside you."

He moves to face me, but I stop him with a "Don't you dare." I grip his dick tighter and he curses, then he moves with my steady strokes, getting harder, breathing heavier. But there's more of him to explore. Releasing him, I kiss every inch of his back and the expanse of his shoulder blades while I knead his strong thighs with my hands, making my way lower, and lower, until I'm on my knees, worshipping his glorious ass.

"Turn around," I say, my voice tight with desire, longing to take him in my mouth and show him just how hot he makes me.

He does as instructed, but my desire blooms into something else. His dark eyes shine down with so much vulnerability I want to gather him to my chest and hold on forever. He touches my soaked hair and drags his hands to my cheeks, keeping me back from wrapping my lips around him. "Shay...I..."

I...

I...

I...

I know what he wants to say, and I want to sing the words, too. Instead, we stare at each other, me on my knees, him loving me with his eyes, both of us exposed to the core. Then he takes control.

He pulls me up and crushes me to him. Skin slides. Lips bruise. Sweat pools at our feet. Rapture guides our hands. He walks us toward the bench and sits, reaching for my hips. "Wrap your legs around my waist."

His demand inflames me. Sometimes sex with Kolton is sweet and slow, sometimes rough and raw, but he's always holding, pressing, clutching. At night, with him, I let go physically, and I shoot off like a rocket. How intense will it be now that I've opened my heart, too?

I secure my legs around him, and he lifts my backside. With one swift move of my hips, he's inside me. My *oh God* mingles with his *Jesus* as we press together. "So hot," I say. "So wet."

"So perfect," he replies. "But don't move yet."

His mouth travels down my neck and over each breast, the sweat and heat melting us together. My hands are in his hair, on his shoulders, his back. I rotate my hips, grinding against his pelvis. Then we're moving. Our wet lips collide as I pull back and crash onto him. Over. And over. Groaning cuts off our *God*s and *fuck*s. The temperature skyrockets, the heat between my thighs threatening to ignite, the pressure in my chest just as volatile. He slows us down. He speeds us up. Always in control. Always with his mouth on me, whispered words I can't hear dripping down my skin, my silent confessions of love sliding down his. I ride the ledge, rising and falling, until, without warning, I fall apart. I toss my head back, and he drives into me while guiding my hips, knowing I'm nearly boneless from the heat and the high. Then he joins me, my name like a prayer on his lips. I latch my loose limbs around him, and he buries his face in my neck, still connected, the scents of cedar and eucalyptus mingling with the smell of sex.

My pulse thunders. Not from the heat. Not from the exertion. Because this was it. Everything. Whatever happens from here on out, my heart is his.

Twenty-three

Kolton

Things I've learned the past four weeks about kids and living with a girlfriend:

a) If morning sex is on the agenda, set your alarm crack-of-dawn early.

b) Build a pillow fort at the base of the bed to prevent your child from launching himself at said girlfriend. And maiming her.

c) Don't let said girlfriend sleep naked.

The sauna evening was one thing, but after last night's marathon between the sheets, I know better than to wake Shay for another round. I'm up as usual, though, watching her. She burrows into my side, an unconscious twisting she's done every morning since she moved in. She tightens her arm around my waist and tucks her leg over mine. I barely breathe for fear of waking her. If I thought I had it bad for Shay after Aspen, I'm beyond screwed now.

As I smooth a curl from her face, she tenses and then stretches like a cat, her lacy tank riding up. I flatten my palm on her hip. "Morning."

Her tongue flits out to taste my collarbone, soft lips brushing back and forth. "Is it Jackson time?"

I plant a kiss on her cheek. "We should have a few minutes."

She squeezes closer. "Like how many?"

I replay the image of her on her knees last night, my dick sliding into her mouth. Then us on the bed, her back arched in surrender. She let me possess her, but in the end, I think it was she who owned me. "I could be quick."

"You don't do quick."

She has a point, and last night was no exception. I've never dragged out my pleasure so long, never needed to hear a woman fall apart so desperately. And did she ever. The image of her writhing as she chanted my name, wetness on her cheeks, is still lodged in my throat. My chest. Her emotion rushed through me until I was free-falling, and I have no intention of landing. Knowing I can make her convulse and cry my name and lose control is greedy business. It means I affect her as much as she affects me. It means she might move to Vancouver.

My phone buzzes from the nightstand, but I ignore it. Instead I press my index finger over her heart, the scoop of her white tank leaving enough skin to write on. Thinking back to our game in Aspen, I trace the word:

M-I-N-E

She shivers, then she touches my chest.

H-O-O-K-E-D, she writes.

Me: A-D-D-I-C-T-E-D

Her: M-O-R-E

I frown at the word, unsure what it references. More me? More us? More *time*?

I flatten my palm over her beating heart. *Time.* Something dangerously scarce these days. The opening is in one week, my plane leaving in two, and we haven't talked about where we go from here. Something that will be rectified soon.

Again, my phone buzzes. Again, I ignore it.

She nudges me with her knee. "You better get that. What if it's important?" Lifting her head, she glances at my noisy cell and stiffens. "Shit. It's Stella. Get the pillows; Jackson will be here any minute."

Happy for the distraction, I roll to the end of my side and grab the pillows from the floor to create our Jackson barrier. On cue, my little guy barrels into our room and launches himself onto the bed, landing shoulder first into Shay's pillow-shield. She peeks over her white barricade. "Morning, Jackson."

Instead of replying with a polite good morning, he says, "We need to go to the library. I need to finish H and buy more pencils 'cause the orange is too short, but Aunt Stella says I hafta go to pottery, but I really, *really* need to finish H. So can we go to the library? Please? Can we?"

Normally, I'd give him a speech about commitment and finishing things you start, but he's scratching his left knuckle, a nervous tic I've come to dread—the one that started before I found out that little shit Evan was picking on him. He curls his back into Shay's pillow, a puckered frown on his face. I still his fidgety hand with mine. "Did something happen at pottery last week?"

He stops scratching for half a second, then digs deeper with his nails, a spot of blood smearing across his skin. Shay mouths *what's up*, and I shrug. Adjusting my boxers, I sit up cross-legged and drag Jackson onto my lap. Shay mirrors our pose, a pillow clutched under her arms. I try again. "Jackson, if something happened at pottery and you don't want to go back, I need to know what it is. We've paid for the classes, and you're in the middle of building that awesome"—no idea what it is—"piece. I won't get mad, but you need to talk to me, bud."

His narrow shoulders curve inward, then he nuzzles his head into my neck, and his glasses scrape my skin. "The kids there are mean." He resumes scratching his knuckle.

My molars crack together as I wrap my arms tighter around his thin frame. So vulnerable. So helpless. Kids are fucking cruel. "Did someone hurt you? Call you names?" I still his hands again and bring his knuckle to my mouth so I can lick his self-inflicted wound. My little lion cub.

He wiggles on my lap and sighs, an exasperated sound more suited to a forty-year-old. "Samantha said my pottery was ugly and pushed it off the table, but when I told the teacher about it Samantha lied and said it was an accident, but I *know* it wasn't 'cause it was just after she called me a..." His longwinded sentence trails off.

Sun filters through the windows, highlighting streaks of caramel in his brown hair. I nudge his head with my nose. "Called you what, bud?"

"...A freak." He pulls up his socks—one red, one blue. "I don't wanna go back."

My clenched jaw radiates down my neck, my shoulders hitched to my ears. Goddamn kids. Why they have to go out of their way to make my son feel like he's different, less, is beyond me. My cousin, Heather, has cerebral palsy, and the fuckwits in school never let her forget she walked differently, thought differently, and couldn't do gym like the rest of them. I wasn't always there to defend her, but I'll sure as shit be having a word with this bully's parents. "It's okay, bud, I'll come with you—"

"Was it the pigtail girl in the yellow dress? The one fighting with her mom when I picked you up last week?" Shay has on her Terminator face, nostrils flared, eyes narrowed. For my kid.

Jackson nods and goes to scratch his knuckles again, but I whisper, "No, bud. Leave it."

Shay folds over her pillow and places her hand on his knee. "Know what I think?"

He looks up, bottom lip pouting, trembling.

"I think," she continues, "that Samantha's folks maybe don't let her wear two different socks. Maybe they don't make her purple peas and spend time with her in the library. I think maybe she's jealous you get to do and wear all that cool stuff."

The sun burns brighter, casting light across Jackson's pinched face. "You think?" he asks, his voice so quiet Shay tilts her ear toward him.

She nods decisively. "Yeah, I think. I feel kind of bad for her, don't you? It would suck if you couldn't do those things, right? If you had to be like everyone else? You have it pretty good."

Just like that, she twists the problem, making Jackson the cool kid. The lucky one.

Just like that, he stops trying to scratch his knuckles.

Just like that, I fall more in love with her.

He chews his bottom lip. "Should I bring Samantha some peas today?"

She flings her pillow-shield on the floor and smacks her hands together. "Brilliant idea! And…it was going to be a surprise, but I made you some purple apple slices yesterday. We can add those."

He jumps up, whacking my chin with his shoulder. "Purple? Really?"

I rub my smarting jaw as the two of them run from the room, Shay in her white tank top and My Little Pony flannel shorts. Shay with her wild hair and shrieking laugh. Shay with my now-happy son. *Shay.*

Tonight's dinner out was planned as a celebration. The store is almost complete, merchandise arriving Monday along with Sawyer, all of us needed to pull it together, late nights and long hours training staff ahead. This is my last chance before the grand opening next weekend to spend quality time with Shay. To propose my plan for our future and hope she doesn't freak out.

I've researched every design firm in the area, listing them by size, prestige, and style. I've spoken to each one, narrowing the field. I'll lay it out in a neat package so she knows exactly what she stands to gain, personally and professionally. Already, I can picture her features tightening at the suggestion. Her defenses building. All that crap with her ex rearing back up between us. Shay has changed, though. Her tears last night when we made love only mean one thing. She wrote the word *more* on my chest. She wouldn't spend this much time with Jackson, plant herself into his world, if she wasn't as committed as I am to making this work.

I throw off my covers and drag a hand down my face, hoping she doesn't shove my heart through a blender.

* * *

Swanky restaurants aren't generally my deal, the pressed shirts and gelled hair too uptight for my liking. But Shay had to work late, and it's close to the shop. I check the time again, then continue with my people watching. The dude at the back provides ample entertainment. He's in a corner booth with another couple, his arm draped over the dark leather cushion behind what must be his girlfriend, but his eyes haven't left the waitress with the big tits, her tight white blouse sure to rake in tips. I tap my fingers to the crooner tunes drifting from the speakers, chuckling to myself. Either the girlfriend's oblivious to his wandering gaze, or she happily trades that for the rocks sparkling around her neck.

"Hey there, handsome." Shay's voice blocks out the rising laughs from a nearby table. She slides into the seat opposite me. "Sorry I'm late. It took forever to fix the angle of the silkscreens. But, oh, my God, it looks so freaking good. I can't believe how it's coming together. And"—she tries to sit still, but the table shakes from her bouncing legs—"I have news."

I plant my palms on her knees until they still. Her bare knees. The ones above her red fuck-me boots and below that fitted gray skirt of hers. I love when she wears skirts. "Kiss me first, news after."

She huffs out a playful breath. "If I must."

I never used to be one for PDA, or sex in public places, but there's something about Shay. Sliding my hand up her skirt, I kiss her hard and deep and run my thumb along her panty line. She pulls back, breathless. "Hello to you, too."

I extricate my hand and push the glass of Chardonnay I ordered for her across the table. "Why don't we toast your news, Connor?"

My use of her nickname earns me a glare—which is pretty much why I do it—but she doesn't ask for its source again. She's determined to figure it out on her own. Her dirty look transforms quickly, her face scrunching like Jackson's when he's too keyed up to sit still. My lips tug upward, too, her excitement infectious, but as the seconds tick by, I realize there's only one thing that would have Shay so stoked she's bouncing in her chair.

The job. The associate designer position.

Hilary must have promoted her.

As I raise my glass, my heart sinks.

The job.

Everything Shay wants. Everything she'll hate to leave.

Finally, her joy spills out. "Hilary took me aside as I was leaving, which is why I'm late, and she offered me the job. *Associate designer*, Kolton. A permanent position! I mean, I know she's hinted at it, but it's been so nuts I didn't have time to stress over it. And now"—she squeals—"I have a real live job."

She tosses her head back, and I can't help but revel in her success. I've worked my ass off building my company. For our one-year anniversary we held a bonfire on the beach, guitars strummed and booze swilled until the sun came up. When we opened our second shop, we took the crew for a weekend skiing in Whistler, closing down the bars each night. We always celebrated our milestones, but this, seeing Shay achieve her goal, has me swelling with a different kind of a pride. Whatever happens between us, however things work out, I'll make it through as long as she's this happy. "To you," I say, raising my drink higher.

She settles onto her elbows, and we clink glasses. "To the man who thought I could do it and gave me the chance to prove myself."

Eyes locked, we sip our drinks, then chat about the space, the job, and the opening next week. The whole while, she gestures with her hands and sips her wine, only stopping when a plate of steak frites passes our table. Our cue to order. More talking, more laughing. As we eat off each other's plates, we dissect the Sawyer-Lily drama, Shay agonizing over how they'll survive the grand opening—Lily attending with Kevin, Sawyer with his flavor of the week. It won't be pretty. She frowns when I mention Nico will be coming, too. Apparently, Raven gets weird when the big guy is mentioned, but Shay hasn't figured out why.

Our plates are removed, a molten chocolate cake ordered, and my thrill over Shay's happiness takes an ugly turn. I could put off The Talk, but there's no point. One more day or week or month won't make any difference. We need to figure our shit out, promotion or not. She needs to make her choice.

I run my finger around the base of my wineglass. That jerk from earlier still has a loose arm behind his girlfriend, a possessive yet superficial pose, but the couple beside them is different. They sit close and touch and lean into each other. They share meaningful glances, conversations without words. Like Shay and me. Swallowing is suddenly an effort.

"We need to talk," I say.

The glow she's sported all night dulls, the lines between her eyes creasing. "Now?"

Slowly, I nod. Slowly, I sip my wine, the liquid catching on the knot in my throat. "I leave in two weeks. Things are only getting busier. We can't keep pretending we're not on a timeline. I've been thinking a lot, and I have a suggestion."

She bites her lip. Her eyes search mine, imploring, seeking. Something about the desperation on her face reminds me of Caroline. After Marina died, her mother attended church to beg for answers, demanding why her only child was taken far too soon. Not my thing, but it gave her peace. It's almost as though Shay's looking to me that way—to save her. Us. I clear my throat. "We both knew one of us would have to make sacrifices for this to work. We always knew that, and we jumped in anyway. I've tried. I've spoken to Sawyer about me moving and working from here permanently, but the complications are too…complicated."

She winces, a slight twitch of her cheeks. I reach over and grip her wrist, her fingers curling around mine, too, holding on. But she doesn't speak. "It's not just about me, Shay. Caroline has been a wreck without Jackson there. He's a living reminder of her daughter, all she has, and I couldn't live with myself if I took that away from her." When pursuing Shay, I ignored the roadblocks that stood in our way, but I'd do it all over again. Re-experience every argument, touch, and taste, even if it meant losing her. It's all too good, and she has to see that, too. Has to see how much we stand to gain by staying together.

She tries to tug her hand away, but I tighten my grip. "That leaves you," I say as her gaze drops to the table, no longer looking to me for answers. I press the heel of my palm into hers. "There's a great job opening at a design firm in Vancouver, and I've already spoken to them. They've seen your sketches from the shop, and, of course, love them. They want to set up an interview. I know how much the promotion with Hilary means, but this job is pretty sweet. It's a bigger firm. They just finished a lodge in Whistler that would blow your mind."

She studies the table, her nails digging into my wrist. Still, she stays quiet.

"Look," I say, itching to fill the silence. In no time, she'll overthink this to death. "I know you have a life here and friends, but I also know what we have isn't something you find every day. I don't want to lose you. I care about you too much." I don't tell her I love her, not when she hasn't said a fucking word. The only emotion readable is the fear in her flitting downward gaze. "*Shay*," I implore, and finally, she looks up.

"You used your influence to get me a job again." Her tone is flat, disappointment rolling off her in waves.

Jesus Christ. Of course she latches onto the one thing in this equation that reminds her of her asshole ex. Like I'm trying to control her. Like I don't want what's best for *her*. "It's your work they looked at. Your designs. It's your interview to rock or fail. I opened the door because I wanted to help. I want you with me—me *and* Jackson. I knew how hard leaving Hilary and Concept would be for you, and I wanted you to know you have options. That's all. Look for another job, for all I care. Or don't work. I can support us. Whatever you want. Just, please, say you'll consider coming with me. Say you think we're worth it."

The way she's clawing my wrist, I'm pretty sure I'll have a nasty bruise. Our waiter appears and places our chocolate dessert between us, rich, syrupy scents rising on a wisp of steam. She inhales deeply, eases her grip, and lowers her shoulders on an exhale. "I'm sorry. I shouldn't have said that. Thank you for doing the research. I'll think about it. Yes, you're worth it. We're worth it. There's just a lot to consider. Maybe we'll find a middle ground," she says, her eyes suddenly hopeful.

I've told Shay snippets of my disastrous year apart from Marina, always keeping things vague, never wanting to dig up old wounds. All these years later, it's still hard to admit what Marina did. I've never felt so betrayed. Never hated myself more. When everything came to a head, I punched a wall and broke my hand, but it was my heart that shattered. Shay deserves my complete honesty, but when the words rise, bile rises with them. All I can do is swallow them down. A wave of embarrassment, shame, and anger—emotions I thought I'd moved past—surprises me in its ferocity.

I school my face and release her wrist, picking up a fork instead of acknowledging her comment. "Take your time," I say. "We still have a couple of weeks. We'll talk about it again when you're ready." Hopefully, time won't be my enemy. Hopefully, she gives us a chance.

She studies me a moment, thankfully choosing cake over pushing the middle-ground issue. She cuts into the dessert, a thick river of chocolate spilling from the center. "Okay," she says, all her focus directed to her fork.

She scoops up a decadent morsel and is about to place it on her tongue when a deep masculine voice says, "Shay? Is that you?"

Her lip curls before she glances up…at the fuckwit who was ogling the waitress earlier. Not a gelled hair on his head is out of place, his button-down shirt is neatly tucked, and his cologne overpowers the sweet scents curling from our plate.

"Richard," she says, and I nearly stand and deck the guy.

The girl with the sparkly necklace is at the front door, her impatient "Ri-*chard*" drawing a sharp glare from Shay. He seems oblivious. His gaze drags up Shay's body, settling on her breasts the way he leered at the waitress. Yep. I really want to deck the guy.

Finally, he looks her in the eye. "Michael said he saw you recently, said you were doing well. Designing that new Moondog shop, right?"

I don't know who this Michael is, but I don't like that Richard knows what Shay's up to, like he's keeping tabs on her. And he hasn't even acknowledged me.

Shay shoves a forkful of chocolate in her mouth, moaning like she did that day on Aspen Mountain in the cafeteria. As if she's goading him, daring him to make a comment. She drops her fork and fists her hand. "Yeah, things are good. Perfect, actually. This is my boyfriend, Kolton. He owns Moondog." Her words are clipped. Tense.

I offer a curt nod and place my hand back over hers.

His assessing gaze focuses on our hands, on my thumb rubbing circles. Then a smug, trust-fund smile settles on his face. Like he's Sherlock Holmes about to crack a case. "That's great, Shay. I'm happy for you. It's really *nice* of Kolton to let you design the space. Can't wait to see it."

That's great. Let you design. Really nice.

Shay wasn't kidding when she said this douche was arrogant and condescending, insinuating I gave my girlfriend the job as a favor. Not because she had the most creative sketches I'd seen. Not because she's capable. I squeeze her hand. "Shay's an amazing designer. Her work speaks for itself."

Smirking, he studies her breasts another minute. "I'm sure it does. Anyway, see you around."

What a total dick.

He turns toward his girlfriend, who looks like she's had enough of him ogling other women, and I focus on Shay. "So that's the man in the flesh." I release her clenched hand and stuff a bite of cake into my mouth. I glance at her as I swallow, and the chocolate barely makes it down. She's frozen midbreath, her mouth open in what looks like panic, and my heart halts. That wasn't some simple run-in with an ex, one of those blips where chicks flaunt how good they look and how awesome they're doing since moving on. That was Richard reinforcing the very things that plague Shay.

Me, controlling her life. Me, influencing her career.

Her not making it on her own.

Why the fuck did he have to be here tonight?

She recovers quickly, forcing a tiny bite of cake past her lips, followed by a smile that doesn't reach her eyes. "That was the Dick," she confirms and says nothing more.

"You know he's wrong, right? You know he's full of crap."

"Yeah, I know." But there's no conviction in her words. Then more forcefully, "I know, Kolton. I know why you hired me."

Stilted conversation ensues; moving out west is avoided. By both of us. I signal the waiter for our check as Shay shreds a sugar packet.

Just like that, the night's over.

We hardly talk on the ride home. Her continued silence when we crawl into bed joins the unease accumulating between us. Still, she curls her body around mine and drags her hands through my hair, and I'm on her in seconds, pressing my fingers into her skin while I suck a path down her neck and over her heart. Her legs fall wide, and I touch her and tease her and show her how good I can make her feel. We don't need words. We just need mornings at the park with Jackson and days cuddled on the couch and nights like this. I rock my hand, and she fists my length, her hazel eyes brewing with all we aren't saying. *Choose me*, I think when she gasps and shatters around my fingers. *Choose us*. Then I'm pushing into her and pumping into her and kissing her so hard my lips feel bruised. I say her name a thousand times, the tension traveling up my thighs and expanding against my ribs. This isn't sex. This is possession. I can't control my need to move fast and deep, to obliterate anything but us, here in this bed. I thrust and bite and groan. She matches my movements, clawing at my back. Rougher. Needier. Until we fall together, her nails breaking skin, my face buried in her neck, all that hair of hers gripped in my fists.

Still, we don't speak.

I gather her close, and she places her head on my chest. My tangled and twisted chest. I wish I had a formula, a simple equation that could solve our problems. An X and Y and Z that, ordered just right, could lead us out the other side. Together. No blueprint can predict the fallout, though. Love is irrational. Immeasurable. Unquantifiable. I'll either return home happier than I've ever been, or a fucking wreck.

And it's all up to Shay.

I close my eyes, but sleep is a write-off. By the way her breath shudders from time to time, I don't think she rests much, either.

Twenty-four

Shay

The grand opening is in full swing, celebratory sounds drifting from the shop. I should be ecstatic. Flying. On a high to rival my Whistler Cup win. When I skied past the finish line that day, bells rang out in the crowd, the yells and hollers enough to wake a sleeping giant. The blue sky reflected off the snow, my breath coming hard and fast. My legs weren't tired. The knee I'd recently twisted didn't throb. Adrenaline pumped through me as I flung a euphoric fist into the air. After all my hard work—endless training, running, and skiing—I did the impossible.

I won.

Walking into the grand opening of Moondog Toronto should feel the same.

But it doesn't. Not one bit.

Kolton's in there somewhere, schmoozing, smiling for the cameras, and I've let three groups of people pass me on the sidewalk while I stare at the door.

"Excuse me." Another shoulder brushes mine, and I barely budge.

Why can't I go in and celebrate? Why can't I share this accomplishment with him?

"Shay!" Lily runs along the sidewalk, Kevin behind her. Her hair blows off her bare shoulders, the blues and purples of her strapless summer dress flowing, her long beaded necklaces accenting her bohemian style. She flings her arms around me. "I'm so excited. I can't believe you did this. And thank you for suggesting I help with the opening. It was a blast. I ended up organizing the band and helped with flowers. I hope you love it! Is Kolton inside? Is Raven here? Oh, shoot." She twists around, her hands still on my shoulders. "Kev, did you grab my purse from the car?"

He smiles and lifts her recent creation, but his features are tight. Normally, we joke that Kevin could still get carded at twenty-five, his smooth cheeks and small frame more boy than man. I doubt the guy has ever shaved. But here, in the lamp-lit night, he looks drawn. Weathered. His soft brown hair is still neat, but dark, puffy skin cradles his eyes. Tonight, he looks like a man holding onto the last of his strength.

I wonder if I look the same.

He nods to me. "You should be proud. You've done an awesome job. Are your folks here?"

"Thanks, and no. Dad had a last-minute job come through at Dwyer's farm. An emergency build after a storm blew through his barn. He couldn't pass it up." Lily steps back, the three of us forming a circle and shaking our heads, teenage memories transporting us through time. Gord Dwyer has put off fixing that barn ever since Raven nearly burned it to the ground during her punk stage, a night of dares and drinking gone awry. She had to muck stalls for two months as penance.

Kevin chuckles. "We should send Raven to christen it."

"Christen what?" says the devil herself.

Raven walks up behind Kevin. She's not a small girl, a couple of inches taller than me, but her stilettos elongate her already long legs, most of which can be seen in her black mini dress. Next to Kevin's slight frame, she looks like a sexy giant.

"Big night," she says to me. "But why are you out here? I heard a rumor there's a cute dude with a ponytail inside." She winks at me.

I drop my eyes, wondering if there's a manhole I can squeeze through. Anything to avoid Kolton and the conversation we've yet to finish. The past week has been nonstop: meetings, errands, late nights setting up. I've needed every available second to pull the shop together, but Kolton and I both know I've also used every available second to steer clear of the biggest decision I've ever faced. When I was with Richard and got offered the cereal-box-prize job in Montreal, I knew I wanted it. Knew it could do amazing things for my future. But the Dick's reaction pricked my fragile self-esteem, deflating the momentary confidence I'd gained. "I need you here," he said. "Besides, it's too soon to take on something that big. *If* it falls apart, you'll only hurt your career." His weak "if" was a poorly disguised "when." Suddenly, leaving him and starting over seemed too daunting, failure too tangible. So I gave it up.

Regret has shadowed me ever since.

Raven's heels click closer, and she slides her arm around my waist. "Why don't you head in, Kev? Us ladies need some girl time."

I watch, unmoving, as Kevin's black leather shoes retreat.

Raven bumps my hip with hers. "If you're planning on working as one of those frozen mimes, you should put a hat out to collect money."

I snort and look up. Her dark eyes are squinting, like she's trying to see through me, and Lily's soft gray gaze is full of compassion. I opt for sarcasm. "Not my thing. If someone passes with a hot dog, I'll for sure salivate and twitch." The thought alone has me scanning the area for street meat.

"There's my girl." Raven folds her arms. "Now let's have it. Why are you lurking outside the grand opening you helped create?"

Lily's hand shoots to her heart. "Did you decide about moving?"

Evading the subject seems more exhausting than sharing my jumbled thoughts. "No. I'm a mess. And I don't know how to go in there and pretend everything's fine."

Raven folds her arms. "I know it's your life, Shay, and you're reluctant to ask for advice these days, but you're about to get some." She widens her stance. "The negative shit churning in that beautiful head of yours needs to stop. Giving up Hilary's promotion isn't weakness; it's following your heart. Moving to another province isn't subservience to a man; it's allowing yourself to fall in love. Love may not be in my future plans, but I know you. This is what you want. If you're not interested in trying, if the job really means more to you than Kolton, then by all means…don't go. Stay here. But be honest. If not with us or him, at least with yourself. Because if you love him, but your pride and fear keep you in Toronto, the regret you wallowed in after giving up the Montreal gig will feel like a stroll in the park."

Lily leans forward and adjusts the plunging neckline of my red dress. "She has a point." The door to the event swings wide, laughter and guitar licks drifting onto the street. "Do you love him?" she asks.

On the surface, it's such a simple question, and I know my answer. Kolton's proven time and again he's nothing like Richard. He asks questions when I talk about work, like why I choose a certain color or if there's a reason behind a particular design. We'll be out at a restaurant, and he'll instigate my design game, asking me to point out all the things I'd redo if given the chance. Those are the times I want to hit pause, the world around freezing, so I can say, *I love you*. But I've been a coward.

What if I go to Vancouver and hate it there? What if things aren't the same between us? What if we drift apart? What if I resent him? What if I pass up another job and end up designing retirement homes again?

If, if, if…

If I have to endure another round of floral couches, I'll die of ugly.

"It's not a trick question," Raven says. "Do you love the man or not?"

I study a crack in the sidewalk, the meandering fracture running through an R + S carved inside a heart. What Raven and Lily are asking is *if* I don't go, *if* I let Kolton slip away, will regret eat me alive? Seeing Richard the other night sucked. It was a reminder that the bad choices behind me and the tough ones ahead always center around the man in my life. A gravitational pull. But Kolton is the polar opposite of the Dick. He buys me PEZ and watches cheesy movies for me. With him, I could stay a snowflake.

I face the girls. "Yes. I love him. Head-over-heels in love. But I want this job so badly I can taste it."

Lily frowns. "Why do you have to choose?"

I chew my cheek, remembering how Kolton evaded the subject of compromising the night we were out, his stern expression an easy read: my way or the highway.

"Yeah," Raven says. "I know he looked into moving here, but why is this so black-and-white? Why can't you take the job for a year or two and start things with him long distance? It wouldn't have to be permanent."

I place my toe over the top loop of the R on the pavement, the wonky heart now reading: K + S. "Kolton mentioned stuff about doing long distance in university with Marina and it blowing up. I think he's freaked about that. When we talked about things, he made it sound like this was the only way. I move, or we're over."

"Fuck that." Raven looks ready to spit nails. "That was years ago. People do long distance all the time. It's not ideal, but it doesn't mean it can't work. If this is important to you, if he loves you, he'll give it a shot."

I step completely over the cracked heart in the pavement, unwilling to imagine its fractured fate as mine, because Raven is right. Sensing Kolton's hesitation, I've avoided this option, but it makes perfect sense. It would be hard. Missing him after Aspen was bad enough. After the time we've spent together now, a year would be agony. Still, I'd get to build my career, and time flies these days. As a kid, a half hour was a lifetime; now months blur, each year moving faster. Plus, *phone sex*. Kolton will understand. When he sees how much this means to me, he'll give it a shot. I just have to convince him this won't be a repeat of his past.

I smile, my relief palpable. "Thanks, guys. I think I needed that push. I was stupid for not forcing the issue with him earlier. Middle ground it is. I'll take the job for a year or so, build my portfolio, then look into moving to Vancouver." My pulse quickens, nearing light speed. *Me. Move to Vancouver. With Kolton.* "Is this crazy? Hauling my life across the country? It seems crazy."

Raven shrugs. "Crazy is Lily's apartment overflowing with recycled goods. You're in the clear." Lily chews on her nail, and Raven claps. "With that solved, I think it's time to go inside so you can celebrate your design and new job. There's an open bar, and that red dress of yours needs to be seen."

I smooth a crease on the front of my silk dress—the dress I picked out weeks ago. I knew Kolton would go nuts over it: the plunging neckline, the cutaway back, the empire waist and loose fabric that falls below my knees. He came to the event early and hasn't seen me yet, and he doesn't know I'll be moving to Vancouver yet...*after* I convince him we can make long distance work. My excitement builds, nerves buzzing through my shaky fingers.

The girls open the door, and I follow them inside. The voices and laughter and rock band light up the space. *My* space. I've basically lived here the past week, but seeing it come to life pushes all Kolton stress to the background. I did this. Me. No one else. But a tinge of doubt taints my exhilaration. A bruise on a perfect peach. Maybe this is the best I'll ever do. This could be the extent of my creativity, and Hilary will fire me in a few months when I fail to impress. I shake my head, knowing all artists go through this. Nothing and no one, not even the Dick and his insinuations, can ruin this moment.

This is the start of my promising career.

On an exhale, I study the space again. The sharp gray pipes and ductwork on the industrial ceiling stand out just enough, the restored brick walls, graffitied in sections, pop—their tattoo-inspired images echoed on the silkscreens twisting over the hanging wall.

Splashes of purple and wine swirl, the mottled concrete floor shines, and the rusted corrugated metal wrapping the cash counter adds a warehouse feel.

I almost fist-pump Whistler-Cup style.

Among the throng of people, there's no sexy ponytail. Raven waves at me from the bar, so I join the girls, who've, thankfully, ordered me two blue shots. Time to celebrate: this space, my job, my future with Kolton.

Lily raises her glass. "To Shay. I always knew you had it in you."

"To Shay." Raven aligns her shot with Lily's.

"To me," I say, grinning.

Liquid fire slides down my throat, followed by another round. Then I order a glass of wine. Raven stands with me, and Kevin joins Lily at the bar, the energy between the couple thickening with...something.

You could cut the air between them with a chainsaw.

They don't touch. Don't speak. He drains his beer in minutes while Lily examines the crowd. Then her face falls. I follow her line of sight, all that turmoil focused on Sawyer and the girl suctioned to his side. I have half a mind to bitch-slap that blond skank out of here, the alcohol coursing through my blood leading me into invincible territory, but Sawyer hasn't done anything wrong. Unless you count falling for a girl who's struggling to break up with her long-time beau. He must sense Lily's attention. The way his face twists at the sight of Kevin is hard to miss. This date of his is likely a ruse. A desperate attempt to forget Lily, or maybe make her jealous.

That's when Lily loops her arm through Kevin's.

That's when Sawyer whispers in his date's ear.

That's when both couples kiss.

Forget interior designer, I should pilot a reality show titled *Seriously Bad Ideas*.

Lily needs a wake-up call. She and Sawyer are awesome together. This week, while setting up, the two of them worked side by side, sneaking heated glances. Still, she stays with Kevin. With comfort. With safety. The more she rubs it in Sawyer's face, the less likely it is he'll be around if she ever rocks that boat.

"Perfect," Raven says beside me, her tone clipped. I twist my neck to see what she's glaring at. Nico's huge chest, colossal shoulders, and massive neck are larger than I remember. He should have a light on his buzzed head to alert air traffic control. He smiles at me, then nods at Raven, who's already turned on her heels, her hips swaying as she walks away.

He sidles up to me. "Congrats on the space."

"Thanks." I wrench my neck back, back, back to see his face. His dark eyes are fixed on the direction Raven fled. "How long are you in town for?" I ask.

Finally, he looks at me. "What?"

"In town. How long are you staying?"

His gaze flicks over my shoulder again, then back to me. "A couple of days. Just here for the guys." Again, his focus leaves my face.

"You could go talk to her."

"Yeah," he says, and nothing more. Then, "I need a drink."

Not much of a talker.

Taking another gulp of wine, the alcohol having officially transported me to Happy Town, I beam at the crowd, readying myself to mingle. Until I see Kolton.

Sexy, smart, caring, and *sexy* Kolton. Did I say sexy?

Two guys are chattering at him, both in slacks and button-downs, their clothes owning the men. Kolton's doing his outfit a favor. He's not a jacket-and-tie guy, choosing a simple white shirt, top two buttons undone. A hint of chest hair. Broad shoulders. I've never seen him in dress pants before, but the pressed black wool is tailored perfectly to his narrow waist.

His penetrating gaze locks on me.

He barely participates in his conversation. He sips his drink—probably bourbon—then says something to the guys, eyes still on me, before he prowls in my direction. My heart pounds to the rock and roll beats. We've had sex a few times this week. Not daily like before. Not sweet. No sensual explorations. Rougher sex, almost desperate. Like we're sailing into a storm, the rope holding us on course dragging through our fingers. Tonight, the storm will finally break.

He stops in front of me, his hand finding the exposed skin of my back. "You're a fucking vision standing here. That dress…" His heated gaze dips lower than my plunging neckline, the thin silk feeling transparent. Unconcerned with my lipstick, he kisses me, slow but chaste. "If this weren't our grand opening, we'd be finding a dark corner."

I wipe the smear of red off his lips. "Lost your nerve, Axl? What happened to the daring guy in Aspen?" It's probably not professional to flirt with Kolton here, but I'm living in Happy Town, and his manly perfection is too perfect. With how tense things have been, it's fun to let loose. Especially knowing I'm ready to make things work with him, the pieces of my life finally falling into place.

He rubs circles on my back. "That guy took off. He's looking for the girl he met on that trip. You know where he can find her?"

A not-so-subtle dig about my distance this week. "Yeah. I think

I've located her. Maybe we can schedule a meeting later. There's something I'd like to discuss."

He flattens his hand on my tailbone. "Have you made a decision?"

God, do I want to tell him I love him. That I choose him and will work to make sure we last while apart this year. But if I do that, I won't be able to keep from tearing the buttons on his shirt. This conversation has to wait until later. "I have."

He studies me, his eyes boring into mine, searching for a clue. Am I that hard to read? Does he not see how excited I am to be a part of his and Jackson's life?

I spot Hilary over his shoulder and wave. "We'll talk later. I promise. I need to speak with Hilary."

He drags his hand down his ponytail. "Sure. It's a date."

* * *

An hour, and two more glasses of wine, later, there's no sign of Kolton, and I'm lit up like a Christmas tree. Unable to contain my excitement, I told Hilary I'd love to accept her offer, and she hugged me. A first for her. She also gave me the best news imaginable: Cruella got handed her pink slip. I don't know exactly what went down, but it appears Hilary's been aware of Maeve's true nature for a while. Hilary's exact words: "I was about to let her go when Stuart quit, but I couldn't afford to be down two designers. As of this morning, Maeve and her god-awful accent are free to sabotage someone else's firm." Tipsy Hilary is fun.

We toasted my promotion and Cruella's departure.

I should have waited until I talked to Kolton, but the shots and wine emboldened me. Hilary started going on about a new client who loves the work I've done, and I nearly fainted.

Next, I get to share the news with Kolton.

A waiter passes with a tray of chocolate truffles, and I pop one in my mouth. (My fifth, but who's counting?) I slide my tongue over my gums, savoring the decadence, when fingers grip my arm. "Come with me." Kolton's grasp tightens, his sharp tug anything but friendly.

I pull the opposite way and nearly topple. "Aggressive much? Can't this wait?"

"No, Shay. Now."

The music pumps, people busting a move on the small dance floor. A few drinks, and everyone loosens up. Everyone except Kolton. I almost have to run in my heels to keep pace with him as we dodge bodies. He pushes out the side emergency exit and drags me into the dark alley. An overflowing garbage bin farther down alerts the alcohol in my system it might need to evacuate. Up my throat.

Breathing through my mouth, I twist out of Kolton's grip. "What the hell? I don't mind you grabbing me like that in bed, but maybe not appropriate at a public event."

He doesn't flinch. "You accepted the job."

Crap. Hilary. She must have mentioned something to him. I'm so stupid. *Stupid, stupid, stupid.* Alcohol is not my friend. "I'm sorry, I just…I should have told you first, but she kept talking about future work and with the excitement and the drinks…" I press the palm of my hand to his chest. "I wanted to wait until we were alone, so we could celebrate."

He stares at my hand and covers it with his, then his eyes flick up, dark with accusation. "How could you accept a job and tell her without even talking to me? And what do you mean celebrate? How is this a good thing for us?" He steps back, and my hand drops.

The scents of rotting food dissipate, a sudden breeze blowing them the opposite way, but my nausea persists. Kolton scrubs his face, blinking at me like I'm a stranger. I hug my arms around my waist. "Because I want the job, but I want us to be together, too. It'll only be for a year or so to build my résumé. I'll walk away with a portfolio that will guarantee me a good position in Vancouver, and then I'll move there. We can make this work." He scowls, and I press on, "I don't know exactly what happened with Marina. But you're different now. We're different. A year is nothing in the scheme of things. We can totally do this."

His frown turns ugly, a sneer marring his beautiful mouth. He tilts his head back and jabs his toe into the pavement—an internal battle raging. Then he glares, *glares*, at me. "You want to know what happened with Marina? Fine. She cheated on me. We'd been having a rough go of things, fighting, pissing each other off. The longer we were apart, the worse it got. One day, I said some mean shit. Unspeakable shit. Then she got drunk at a party and slept with some dude. It was as much my fault as it was hers. We eventually moved past it. But when I say long distance isn't an option, it's not an off-the-cuff statement. I won't go there again. Especially not with Jackson in the picture. Already, he talks about you when you're not around. I won't let him get more attached only for it to fall apart. So, no, I'd say your news isn't celebration-worthy, because if you choose the job, we're done."

Tears gather—sympathy and anger mixing in a salty cocktail that burns my throat. I fist my hands. "I'm sorry about Marina, but…" Bitter memories of passing up a job for Richard slice through me, a familiar self-hate dredged up from my past. Again, a guy is making me choose. Again, a man's life takes precedence over mine. My pulse thunders until I shout, "I'm not a snowball!"

Really? Snowball? Happy Town just took a sharp left into Crazyville.

He throws his hands up. "What are you talking about? A snowball? What does that have to do with you not giving us a shot?"

"I'm not a snowball," I say more quietly, but I still sound insane. "I don't want to disappear into your life. I'd be giving up everything just to be with you. What does that say about me? What type of person does that make me?"

"Brave," he says.

He scrubs his foot along the asphalt while I blink the sting from my eyes. Determined, I look up. "I am being brave. I'm offering you a compromise. I'd be in this with you, together. If you get hurt, I get hurt. If Jackson suffers, I suffer. I would never cheat on you. I...I love you."

Instead of acknowledging my confession, he stares up at a flickering light, the strobe snapping to a silent beat. "Marina loved me, too, Shay. Distance changes people. I didn't like the guy I became." *Flicker flicker flicker.* "Anyway, it's fine. You made your choice. It would've been nice to hear it from you and not Hilary, but it's your choice just the same."

"Kolton..." Nothing else. No words are adequate. My chest constricts.

"I'm switching my flight," he continues. "Leaving tomorrow. Maybe you should stay with one of the girls tonight. I'll tell Jackson you said good-bye. Sawyer can handle things from here."

Leaving? Tomorrow? Not waiting or caring or trying harder? His acquiescence is like a blowtorch to my heart. And *Jackson*. I didn't weigh his role in our relationship. He added a dimension to my life I didn't know I'd miss. Now I lose him, too.

Suddenly boneless, I crouch on my heels to keep from falling. This is a different Kolton: sterile, clinical. Unfeeling. Gone is the charmer who woos. He's shuttered himself from me. This man who taught me trust and surrender is walking away.

This is what I wanted, right? The job. My career. That's my future. Not Kolton.

His shoes shuffle in front of me, then he says, "Shay," followed by a quiet, "are you okay? Should I get the girls?"

"No," I whisper. "I'll be fine." Total lie.

Steadying my feet, I stand as the side door slams open. Lily and Raven tumble into the alley. "We've been looking everywhere for you." Raven staggers toward me but stops when she sees Kolton. "Sorry. Did we interrupt?"

He shoves a hand into his pocket. "No, we're done."

Over. Finished.

Forever.

He opens his mouth but closes it. "Enjoy the rest of your night, girls." Then he's gone. No backward glance. The door clicks shut behind him, and a tear slips down my cheek. I swipe it away. Damn him for forcing my hand, for making me choose. Next time I date a guy, it'll be on even ground. I won't rely on him for money, housing, or a job. I'll be my own woman, a force to be reckoned with. I'll be brave.

Lily wipes the rest of my tears away. "He didn't like Option Three?"

I shake my head.

Raven squeezes my shoulder. "I'm sorry. We were gonna drag you inside to dance. They switched to a DJ and Pink was on."

My eyes widen. "Was it 'Stupid Girls'?" They both nod, that song always zooming us back to high school: stolen alcohol, a car stereo blasting, and the three of us dancing in the street. I sag forward. "Can't say I'm in the mood for dancing."

"What happened?" Lily asks.

I shrug, my shoulders feeling a thousand pounds. "It's over. The Marina thing was bigger than I realized. She cheated on him during their year apart, and he's not willing to try long distance again. And, I don't know, maybe I shouldn't take the job, but it's so much to give up." My voice trails off. I wish I could be brave enough to leave everything behind, risk it all for the man I love. I could run after him and take it back, but he didn't even flinch when I said, *I love you.* Why put my heart on the butcher block again?

"Give it time." Raven tucks a curl behind my ear. "Maybe you both need some distance to figure things out. This doesn't have to be final."

But everything about Kolton's body language screamed final. I bite my cheek to keep from crying.

Lily nudges Raven. "Did you talk to Nico tonight? He kept watching you from afar."

"Nope. I avoided Hercules. No need to revisit that mistake."

Lily grabs each of our hands. "I think tonight qualifies as a girls' night. I'll ask Kevin to crash at a friend's, and"—she tips her chin toward me—"you can stay with me for as long as you need. Slumber party?"

Grateful, I nod, my tears pushing their way to the surface.

Raven kisses my cheek. "Don't cry, babe. I'll even do my impression of *your* impression of the Dick's orgasm face." She twists her mouth so hideously, I can't help but laugh. My tears leak regardless, our giggles building in a familiar symphony—our teenage years, once again, revived. *South Park.* My first (and only) cigarette. Gossiping about Randy Armstrong's mullet. I've clocked a lot of laughter with these ladies. Amid my streaming tears, I link arms with them to head inside, thankful for our bond. If the hollow in my heart persists, moments like this will be my balm, along with a therapeutic run a few days a week. Surely, this feeling can't last too long.

One Week Later

My half-hour run extends to forty-five minutes.

Two Weeks and Four Days

Sixty minutes six days a week.

Three Weeks, Two Days, 1,152 Minutes

One hour Sunday through Saturday. Twice on Tuesdays.

One Endless Month

Two runs daily, plus one cookie dough cupcake each night, the running and sugar doing nothing to mend my broken heart.

Twenty-five

Kolton

Sawyer assumes his usual position at my desk, legs straddling a flipped chair, elbows hanging over the back. "Have you looked at my layout for the Snow Show?"

I scan my growing stack of papers, more coming in than going out, then I focus back on my computer. "Haven't had time."

He taps his hand against the chair, his pinky ring striking out a chime. "Nico's coming by. You in for a beer tonight?"

"Nope. I'm hitting the library with Jackson, then karate."

"Tomorrow?"

"Rock climbing."

"Next year, maybe? Or are you booked?"

I don't answer, but the inter-fucking-com on my desk buzzes. Stella: "He's pretty tied up. He has a Wallow in Self-Pity class next week, and he just signed up for a Burying Your Feelings web-inar."

Sawyer coughs out a laugh, but I keep my attention fixed on the neat rows and columns on my screen, everything ordered just so. Computers are easy, their formulas predictable. I feed information in, and answers are spit out. Always right. No room for misinterpre-tation. Not like life these days. I roll my chair to the side and face Sawyer. "Is there something I can help you with? Something you want to say to me?"

He nods. "You're an idiot."

"I'd go with moron," Stella says, her voice crackling through the intercom.

I slam my palm on the top button. "If you're taking part in this bash-Kolton session, get over here." I lift my hand and mutter, "Nico and his fucking gift."

Stella sashays over, pulls a chair next to Sawyer, and sits, crossing her legs. "You're a mess," she says.

I smile at her bluntness. "Tell me something I don't know."

She nudges Sawyer's shoulder. "You want to field this, or should I?"

"I say we tag-team him. You start, and I'll come in for the finish."

I can't help but chuckle. "Why do you guys always talk about me like I'm not here?"

She swivels my way. "Are you comfortable, boss? This might take a while."

Tipping back in my chair, I stare at the deflated red balloon stuck in the duct work. It's been there a while, since we hosted Jack-son's seventh birthday. He was having a tough time at school and didn't want to celebrate with friends. We surprised him with cake, balloons, and a slew of books. Nico and Sawyer dressed up as magicians, putting on a horrific show. Their flying dove shat all over my desk. Stella made Jackson's favorite foods, my stepbrothers tore through the place as if it were a jungle gym, and Caroline brought too many presents, spoiling her only grandchild. Predictably, my mother didn't fly in, but that was nothing new.

What I wasn't prepared for, what hit hard, was wishing Shay were with me. It was a few weeks after Aspen, we'd only spent four days together, and still, I could feel her absence. I wanted to share that day with her. Now we've had movie nights, library dates, the sauna...and each day gets harder. But she made her choice. "Nothing you say will change anything," I say, knowing that won't stop Stella.

She folds her hands over her black-and-white-striped skirt. "You gave up. You tucked tail and ran when things didn't go your way. There were other options. Instead, you bailed, and now we have to work with Grumpy Smurf."

"What's done is done." I massage my temples, the ugly truth triggering renewed throbbing. When I shut Shay down and she crouched on her heels, too emotional to hold herself up, I almost caved. I could've pulled her against me and told her I loved her, too. That we'd work through this, long distance be damned. But the butterfly effect of my past shut me down. The way I treated Marina while we were apart, her retaliation, it was all too much.

"Kolton," Stella says softly, "when the wooing started, what did you say to me?"

Releasing my head, I slump in my chair. "I don't know. But I'm sure you're going to tell me."

"I believe your words were, 'Shay won't say yes today or tomorrow. I'll have to wear her down.' That was said by a man willing to fight for his woman. A man who woos. The other guy, the one who walked away as soon as Shay said no, that guy sucks. He gave up."

I look to Sawyer for saving, but the dude shrugs. "Can't argue with the truth."

If I had walls, I'd kick these two out. Not a luxury I have, and I'm tired of being a dick. Tired of cutting Sawyer off when he mentions Lily or Shay or Toronto. I pick at a loose stitch on my leather chair. "You both know I looked into moving, and you know how hard it would be on Caroline if she couldn't see Jackson regularly. It was a dead end. And Shay chose her job over me. What was I supposed to do? Abduct her?" A sudden image of Shay in her red dress has me wishing I'd done just that. Toned calves. Cleavage. Hair spilling down her exposed back.

So damn beautiful.

"Here's the thing, bro." Sawyer leans more heavily on his elbows. "You're a smart guy, but bailing on Shay was just plain stupid. You didn't even try to see things her way." His dirty-blond hair falls forward—the same color as mine. We used to pretend we were brothers when picking up girls. A childish game, but chicks dug it. And he's as good as family.

"I'm not getting in deeper just to have things implode," I say. "It's not fair to Jackson."

"Bullshit. The only person you're protecting is you."

I tug the thread at my fingers, rolling it around, faster and faster. I glare at him. "Leave it alone." My biting tone sucks the energy from the room, all casual banter gone.

His brows pinch closer and closer. "Is that what this is about? The Marina Incident? Please tell me that isn't what this is about."

Nico pushes through the door then, dark circles under his eyes. The guy probably hasn't slept in weeks.

He grunts, we nod, and Stella stands. "I'll leave you boys to it." Each click of her heels punctuates the somber mood as she heads to the door.

Nico sits in Stella's vacant chair, the framework groaning under his weight. "You guys ready to head out?" He rubs his eyes and blinks repeatedly.

Sawyer plants his hand on Nico's shoulder. "Looks like you could use a month of sleep. Any news on Josh?"

Nico huffs out a breath. "Nah. I've got something in the works. If it doesn't pan out, he'll likely get convicted. The little shit won't last a month in jail."

I try to catch Nico's downturned eyes. "Did he do it? Did he jack the car?"

A muscle in his jaw twitches. "Still trying to figure that out. Not sure if he's covering for one of his punk friends. Whatever. I don't want to talk about it. I need a mindless night of shitty beer and pool. Who's in?"

"Sounds good. Unfortunately"—Sawyer fans a hand toward me—"Debbie Downer here plans to grumble the rest of his way through life because he can't get over something that happened ten years ago."

Motherfucker. "Seriously, dude. Drop it."

Nico squints at us. "Someone gonna fill me in?"

Sawyer grins. "My pleasure. Let's roll back ten years to our first year at university. I was bagging chicks, and you, Nico, were taking my sloppy seconds, while our boy Kolton was pining for his high school sweetheart all the way in Calgary." Ignoring my *what a fucking ass*, he continues, "When the green-eyed monster got the better of our friend, he called his lovely girlfriend every version of insult in Jackson's *Urban Dictionary*, until she decided to prove him right."

I rip the thread from my chair and fling it on the ground. "I think we all know this particular bedtime story. Get to the punch line before I kick you both out."

Sawyer drags a hand through his hair, then settles forward on his elbows. "Okay. I'll stop playing around. The moral is this: Whatever happened with Marina happened ten years ago. *Ten years*. And you ended up together after the fact. I'd like to think you've matured a little in that time. You've raised a son, built a business. I think you can handle some time apart from the girl you're nuts over if it means having her in your future. But you split on her, didn't even look for middle ground. I mean, the stuff you did to get her on a date? That shit was epic. But you gave up. Maybe, if you hadn't spent the last month dragging your ass around like an extra from *The Walking Dead*, I'd chalk it up to a change of heart. You realizing you didn't fall for her like you thought. But this?" He motions loosely to my face. "I'm tired of looking at your depressed mug. You need to pull out your Prince Charming moves and get her back."

Nico picks up a pen from my desk and clicks the end of it.

Click

Click

Clickclickclickclickclickclickclickclickclickclickclickclickclickclick clickclick

Then, "Dude's got a point."

Nico's eloquent wisdom.

"Okay," I say. "Let's pretend for a second I do try this with Shay. When Marina and I were apart, I became a jackass—a controlling, jealous boyfriend who couldn't trust his girl—but Marina somehow forgave me, and I moved past what she did. If that went down with Shay, she'd bolt so fast the air would spin. Never in a million years would she put up with that kind of bullshit. Not with the way her ex treated her. And she shouldn't have to. Marina shouldn't have, either. So if this goes south because of me, there won't be a reconciliation. It won't play out like it did with Marina. Then I get hurt, Shay gets hurt, and Jackson gets dragged along for the ride."

I glance at the most recent photo on my desk. Caroline met Jackson and me at the library last week so I could head to karate. I didn't notice she had a camera, didn't know she took our picture. When she e-mailed it to me, I stared at the screen for five minutes. To anyone else, it's a sweet shot of me and my son going through his book of words—Jackson hunched over the table, me kissing the side of his head. But I know what page we were on. He had flipped back and landed on *glomp: an attack hug made of love.*

Shay's neat writing.

Jackson bit his lip and whispered, "I miss her."

I kissed his head, but couldn't speak.

I don't know why I put the picture on my desk, an invisible photo of Shay. She's absent yet fills the space, the way her presence invades every aspect of my life. All because of me. Because, too terrified to relive my past, I pushed her away. Because without risk, there's no loss. But there's no gain, either.

No late nights whispering in Shay's ear.

No mornings setting up pillow-barricades.

"Look," Sawyer says when he's had enough of me zoning out, "if this were just about you, I'd leave you to it. Let you wallow until you joined the land of the living. But Shay's a mess."

My eyes snap up to his. "What do you mean?" We've had a pact until now, the unspoken knowledge that all topics involving, concerning, or relating to Shay were off the table. Pact's over. "Did something happen at Concept?"

Nico shakes his head. "You really are dense, dude." *Clickclickclick*

Sawyer chimes in with, "Her job? Seriously?" He squints at me the way he does at reality TV, his *these people are dumber than glue* always following. "She's taken your self-pity act up a notch. If she runs any more, I think she'll snap her Achilles, and she's single-handedly keeping that cupcake shop in business. I'm pretty sure she regrets her decision, and the girls are worried. Lily's been on my ass to talk to you."

My heart knocks in my ears, the room around me spinning. Our last dinner date replays in my mind—Shay's excited squeals and infectious grin as she dished about her promotion. What's kept me marginally sane the past month has been that image. Knowing, believing, she's happy. That, although it wasn't her first choice, losing us but keeping her job would be enough for her. But if she's as miserable as I am, what's the point? "Why hasn't she called me, then? She knows how I feel. She knows I want her here." But our awful fight outside the opening and the words I didn't say stop me short. I never told her I loved her.

He scoffs. "You have met Shay, right? Hazel eyes? Curly hair? …Stubborn streak? Lily's not allowed to say your name around her.

Actually, that sounds kind of familiar." He raises his eyebrow, and I huff out a laugh. Then he adds, "You two were meant for each other. You both just need to deal with your shit."

Again, I think of Marina. Again, apprehension twists my gut. "What if we do it her way and it falls apart?"

Nico yawns into his elbow. "Don't walk away because you're a pussy. Take a chance. Try living for a change." He tosses my pen on the desk.

Sawyer jabs a thumb toward Nico. "What he said. This current situation you guys have going isn't exactly working, is it?"

Over the past month, I've found balance. Stella's taken on more of my workload, and Caroline babysits for Jackson a few nights a week, allowing me time for rock climbing and karate. Things I've missed. Still, I can barely keep it together. My temper flares at will. I even barked at Jackson the other day for asking me to watch a video. Without Shay, none of it works. Nothing settles me the way she does. And if she's sticking to her decision because she's too proud, then we'll both end up miserable.

I'm not the guy I was in university. I can learn from my mistakes. Letting fear dictate my life is as dangerous as running from the unknown. Fuck my baggage. Scratch that, *our* baggage. We both need to let go of our pasts and move forward. Together.

I sit up straighter. "You're right."

"Aren't I always?" Sawyer smacks his hands on my desk, and a stack of paper slides to the side. "Anyway, that's enough motivational bullshit for me. I leave the rest in your capable hands. Time to get Nico liquored up." He punches the big guy's shoulder, probably hurting himself more than Nico.

"Wait," I say as they stand.

They plop down and fold their arms simultaneously, one eyebrow cocked each.

I went to Toronto this summer with a plan: Convince Shay to go out with me. I knew what it would take, I didn't let up, and that first night together was worth the wait. She's worth the wait. The risk. It's time I prove that. "The Snow Show's in three weeks, right? At the Toronto Convention Center?"

Sawyer nods, still waiting.

"Last I heard, Shred pulled out, something about a disagreement with the organizers. Do you know the owner, Tom Sittler, well enough to ask a favor?"

He massages his chin. "Yeah. We've skied together a few times. Frequent the same bars. Why?"

The room is no longer spinning. It's vibrating. If I pull this off, if I make the impossible happen in three weeks, I could have Shay in my arms before winter hits. "Just ask him if he still has that glass dome he built for the Vegas trade show, the one that housed the indoor snowboard stunts. We need it. I don't care what it costs."

Sawyer salutes. "Oh, captain, my captain."

Too pumped to sit, I push off my chair and gather my things. I pause and look up at Nico. "You still speak with your buddy on the Toronto force?"

He grunts. "Greer? Yeah. We message from time to time."

"Perfect. I'll need you to get in touch with him. Do some smooth-talking."

He winks. "I'm practically Barry White."

Sawyer scoffs. "More like Pitbull."

Once the details are discussed, I blow past the guys and out the door.

I thought I was doing what was best for me and that Concept was enough to make Shay happy, but we're barely getting by, both of us pining for each other from across the country. I'm done playing it safe. Done letting unknowns determine my course. Jackson misses Shay, and I'm a mess without her. Pretending otherwise is a fool's errand. It's time for me to live my life, whatever the fallout.

Terminator Shay's about to get schooled in the art of wooing.

Twenty-six

Shay

I answer the door at Concept, and a thin-mustached delivery guy taps his toe, yawning, a small package tucked under his arm. "Shay Gallagher?"

I nod. "In the flesh."

A few leaves tumble from a nearby tree, oranges and reds spiraling to the ground. Another yawn, a scratch of his neck, then the guy holds out a computerized pad for me to sign. He lumbers to his van, and I walk back inside, box in hand, turning it over. No return address. No clue as to who it's from. I lean my hip into my mahogany desk and grab an X-Acto knife to pry the cardboard open. The rest happens in slow motion. Or maybe super-fast. It's hard to tell when your world flips sideways.

My lungs collapse.

I drop the package.

My stomach plummets, too.

Once in control of my motor skills, I pick up the DVD that slid out, knowing precisely who sent it. *The Terminator*'s dark imagery—black leather, sunglasses, and gleaming gun—screams Kolton. Like everything these days. I can't go into a convenience store for fear of seeing a PEZ dispenser. I can't look at word games, dictionaries, puzzles, or pottery without my throat burning—Jackson's sweet face always present in my mind.

I can't eat McDonald's.

There's no note in the box, but I know it's him. I look outside in case he's hiding behind one of the maple trees, watching me fall apart. No Kolton in sight. It's been almost two months without a peep. Forty-nine days. People say this type of thing gets easier, the pain less acute, but the hollow in my chest has only deepened. Widened. The Grand Canyon of broken hearts. Now I have to survive the rest of work before I can go home, watch this video, and figure out what the guy is up to.

Three agonizing hours later, I rush out, barely closing the door behind me as I hurry into my apartment and switch on the TV. I sit, pulse racing, until the DVD plays. In no time flat, a name rings from the speakers. A specific name: *Connor*.

Shaking, I hit pause.

For forty-nine endless days, I've dissected every conversation we had, every sexcapade, wistfulness and regret my constant companions. Why send this now? Why nose back into my life? With a video? I should toss it. It will only open festering wounds. But my curiosity wins. I need to know why he gave me that nickname.

So I watch it. All one hundred and seven minutes. (My life these days is measured in fragments of time, each nanosecond survived a victory.) At first, my irritation builds. Does he think I'm a damsel in distress in need of saving? With bad eighties hair? Is that why he called me Connor? By the end, when the credits roll, I lie on the couch and stare at my new chandelier, at the flat white discs layered in strands—my new paycheck getting a workout. Sarah Connor wasn't weak: She fought back. She became a feisty, badass, take-no-prisoners woman who fought for her life. She rocked.

And Kolton called me Connor.

My heart disintegrates, grief seeping through my chest like acid. This man who thinks so much of me wanted me to move with him to Vancouver, and I chickened out. The Toronto Snow Show is two days away, and a certain someone with the sexiest backside I have ever seen will be here.

In my city. The same time zone. And he's extended an olive branch.

I so badly want to reach out and grab it. Still, the way I've felt the past couple of months, if he's being nice because he knows Hilary and I are attending the show, because we'll no doubt have to see each other, I might run myself into the ground. Or eat myself into oblivion.

Whichever comes first.

My phone buzzes. Lily.

Come to O'Day's. Raven's on her way.

The last thing I feel like doing is putting on my social face. Recently, all I've done is decline any attempts the girls have made to get me out, shooting down invitations to bars and out shopping. Here I strike again.

Can't make it. I'm tired.

A pause, then: I really need to talk to you. There's a lot going on. Stuff with Kevin. Please come.

Not much I can say to that. I'm on my way.

* * *

I walk into O'Day's—a shitty-ass pub in a shitty-ass part of town—and I loiter at the door. To say this place is ten years past a much-needed makeover is being kind. Instead of doing my Etch A Sketch thing, erasing the stained green carpet and spindly wooden chairs in my mind, I shove my hands into my jean pockets. Redesigning this space, even figuratively, would take too much energy. Between my binge eating, my runs, and that video, it's all I can do to put one foot in front of the other.

The girls are in a booth, laughing, something I haven't done since Kolton walked out of my life. Sighing, I plod to the corner booth, pull a chair from a table, and sit at the end.

Lily pats my knee. "I'm glad you made it."

"Yeah," Raven says. "I'm surprised your apartment door still opens. Another few weeks, and I'd be coming by with an axe."

"Whatever," I harrumph.

A month ago, I had no idea *harrumph* was even a word, let alone the perfect description for my harsh and disapproving tone as of late. Taking a page from Jackson, I killed some time on the Internet, perusing words and guttural sounds that could describe my descent into the Land of Miserable. (Cruella ain't got a thing on me.)

I drape my purse over the back of my chair, the furniture wobbling as I shift my weight. Lily pushes a glass of white wine toward me.

I take a generous swallow. "Thanks. You okay?"

"Yes and no." The way she picks at her blue nails, I'd say the scale tips toward no.

Raven stays mum, so I nudge Lily's foot with mine. "Lay it on me."

Flecks of blue polish dot the table beneath her hands, accumulating by the second. Finally, she says, "I'm thinking of breaking up with Kevin."

Again, I glance at Raven, who shrugs. "Did something happen?" I ask.

Lily shakes her head emphatically. "No. Nothing specific. It's been rough for months. Years, if I'm honest. It's just so hard to let go. There's so much history. And I love him, I really do. But I'm not *in* love with him. I can't keep hoping it'll go back to how it was. It's hurting both of us."

Raven sips her beer, licks her lips, then leans on her elbows. "You know I'm all for you moving on, I haven't exactly been quiet about it, but you need to be sure. You guys have been together forever. There's fallout with that."

"Eleven years," Lily whispers.

My jaw drops. "Jesus. That's longer than most people stay married. I know you guys got together young, I just never calculated the time." Lily's attention stays fixed on her nails, so I place my hand over hers. "You can't force yourself to feel something that isn't there. It might hurt at first, but you'll both be happier in the long run."

I pull my hand back, taking a cardboard coaster with me. I rip notches into its edges, anything to keep my hands busy. My mind occupied. *Happier in the long run.* The exact opposite of my life.

"Yeah," Raven says. "You're not doing Kevin any favors by dragging things out. He looked like hell the last time I saw him."

Lily sighs. "I know. You're both right. I just keep thinking about our families, too. How close he is with my folks, how much I love spending time with his parents. His father wants me to design the shirts for his bowling team. How cute is that?"

Still picking at the coaster, I cross my legs. My chair tips back and forth. "Who knows, maybe you two can stay friends."

Raven snorts. "Like that ever works. But I need to ask, does any part of this have to do with Sawyer?"

A red stain transforms Lily's pale skin, a glow seeping from within. She scrapes her teeth over her bottom lip. "Yes, I'm curious about Sawyer. More than curious. We've spent a lot of time together the past eight months. I mean, he's gorgeous, and we get along great." She does some yoga breathing thing—deep inhale, a slow, hissing sound out. "But this isn't about him. I booked a trip to Belize for Kevin and me a while back, an anniversary gift. It's not until late December, but the more I think about it, the more I panic. I'm not sure I can go with him and pretend things are okay. Because they're not." Her pale eyes widen, her head slowly shaking. "I can't go with him," she says again, mouthing the statement a third time. "Right?" She looks to us for answers, but I can tell she's figuring things out for herself. "I can't keep doing this. Living a lie. I won't."

There's fire in her determined face, as fierce as the day she challenged our art teacher, claiming Raven's cubist sculpture deserved a passing grade. (The thing made Jackson's work look professional.) Her hand flies to her mouth. "Oh, my God, guys, I'm going to do it. I'm going to break up with him." She actually looks excited.

The other shoe will fall, her moment of clarity sure to falter when faced with the task. But it's our job to be the wind in her sail. I smile and raise my glass. "To Lily. You got this, girl."

Raven lifts her beer in the air. "To being brave. We're here for you."

Lily clinks our glasses and says something that doesn't register, because all I can think is: *brave*. Kolton's accusation that night in the alley invades my mind, the word haunting me like it has the past weeks. Lily doesn't look the part. Petite. Nail biter. Collector of recycled goods. Still, she's turning her life on its head, shaking things up. This girl who refuses to throw away her high school T-shirts is moving on from her high school boyfriend. She's the real Sarah Connor. Not me. I refused to let go of a promotion, because what? I might not find something as good? I might love Kolton so much I'd change aspects of my life to fit with his? Someone brave would revel in the risks. Someone brave would deserve the nickname Connor.

"Kolton sent me a video," I say out of the blue.

Raven raises one dark eyebrow. "Kinky. Is there some girl-on-girl action?"

My chair tips as I fling my shredded coaster at her face. "*Not* that kind of video. *The Terminator*." When both girls frown, I add, "It has to do with a name he used to call me. It's just, I don't know why he sent it." *Tick tock* goes my chair. "I think I messed up, like maybe made the wrong choice. I thought I was over everything with Richard, but I let that same stuff drive my decision with Kolton."

The promotion at Concept has been amazing. I'm challenged every day. Each project is daunting and exciting, my creative juices thriving. It's a kickass job, especially since Hilary hired Alec as her new partner—a sweetheart of a guy. What I've realized, though, is it's just that…a job. A nine-to-five that fulfills me in important ways, but it doesn't put the bounce in my step or the fire in my belly or the laughter in my life. It doesn't come with Jackson and his mad quirks. It certainly doesn't come with Kolton. I could design anywhere for anyone, but I thought this was it: my one shot at independence and advancement. My mistakes have become clearer over the passing weeks, but how do I apologize? What do I say to make things right?

"Then call him," Raven says. "He might not have used those three words, but he loves you. The video must be his way of reaching out. I bet he misses you as much as you miss him, although he might not be inhaling pounds of icing."

I ignore her jab. "What if he's tired of my crap? What if the movie last night was him mending fences so it's less awkward when we see each other? What if he attends the Snow Show with a date?"

I must turn a shade of green, because Lily's brow creases. "Are you feeling okay?"

I laugh—an abrupt, harsh sound. "No. I am far from okay. I haven't been sleeping much."

I grab a second coaster, and Lily says, "He doesn't have a date, Shay. I know he misses you."

Her intel must come from Sawyer, which means we're both drowning in our own sorrow, too afraid to take the next giant step, believing our histories are bound to repeat. The girls leave me be while I shred my coaster and rock on my chair and sip my wine, the whole while on the verge of tears.

How long can we go on like this?

Recently, not only have I dissected my surly self, learning descriptors like *harrumph* and *curmudgeonly*, but I've thought a lot about my stuttering. As a child, I was ushered to appointments, my prolonged stammering examined with a magnifying glass. The good moments, the ones where I'd channel my inner cheetah and chase sounds fluidly, happened around family or when I sang. The bad times, the absolute worst, were in school with my "peers." My syllables would whir in place, an endless skipping record. Through breathing exercises and articulation, I gained control over my voice. My folks bought Snoopy then and encouraged me to talk to him. My four-legged best friend. I did, for hours. No pressure. No judgment. No stammering in sight. Belonging to a ski team was the final push I needed. My fear of *the fear of* speaking dissipated. But it was a battle to get there.

Now, fifteen years later, I realize it still impacts my life. Like every obstacle I face is another struggle I must fight. And win.

But every challenge *isn't* a battle. My mistakes aren't life sentences. If I walk away from this job, another will arise, because I'm capable. I need to take a lesson from Lily and be brave, earn my nickname. Stop worrying about what-ifs and how to apologize. Stop assuming my talent is short-lived, every struggle a fight to the death. Just show up at Kolton's hotel tomorrow, beg forgiveness, and pray I'm not too late. *Brave. Brave. Brave.* I nod, as if the action will shake something loose in my obstinate brain, because—*fuck it*—I can get a job in Vancouver. Start over. With the man I love.

The girls are still chatting, shooting furtive glances my way. I grab my purse and put ten dollars on the table. "I'm heading home." I turn to Lily. "Call me if you need anything. I'm proud of you."

I'm about to leave when Raven says, "You normally take Bathurst Street, right?"

"Sometimes, why?"

"Bad accident earlier. It was down to one lane on my way here. I'd take Spadina."

It's a bit of a detour, but nothing's worse than sitting in traffic. "Okay, thanks."

With one last wave, I leave to spend another lonely evening in my apartment. Hopefully, Kolton's *Terminator* movie wasn't just a peace offering. Hopefully, it means he still wants to work on things. If not, tomorrow will be the start of an epic cupcake eating competition. Contestants: Me versus Me.

* * *

A few blocks down Spadina, my mind a thousand miles away, flashing lights flicker through my rear window. "Shit." As I signal and pull over to the side of the road, I mentally catalogue what infraction I could have committed. The needle on my speedometer's only a few clicks above the limit, my lights are on, and my license renewal is up to date. I don't have so much as a speeding ticket. Maybe there's an APB out for a depressed, cupcake-obsessed girl who can't get her life together.

A tall man approaches, his uniform blues highlighted by the occasional passing headlight. He raps his knuckles on my window. "Please step out of your car, ma'am."

Ma'am. I almost snicker, but I'm pretty sure he asked me to step out of my car. Not roll down my window or extricate my license and registration. Only felons and serial killers are asked to step from their cars. I flip my handle with shaky fingers, suddenly vulnerable on the side of the road. At night. Alone. "Is there a problem?" I ask once I'm out.

"Turn around and place your hands on the car, ma'am."

My hands? On the car? *Ma'am?* I glance around, wildly now, sure there's a hidden camera. A TV crew? Some sort of explanation. The nearest intersection is two blocks away, the sidewalk empty at this time of night. The cop's cap is pulled low, no hint of humor on his face. And there's no partner in his car. Don't all cops have to work in pairs? My gaze slides to the gun at his hip.

"Hands on the car," he says again.

Eyeing my purse on the passenger seat, I turn and do as instructed. I need to get my phone and call the girls. "I'm sorry. There must be some mistake. You must have me confused with someone else."

"Shay Gallagher?"

There goes that theory. "Yes," I say, drawing out the word. Maybe something happened at work. A break-in? Or Maeve could've faked evidence at a crime scene because she thinks I'm the reason she got fired. My stomach drops for a second, picturing my folks in an accident, but bad news isn't accompanied by the "hands on the car" routine.

Spots cloud my vision.

Before I stroke out, the cop reaches around my shoulder and places a piece of paper between my hands. "This is for you."

Pulse thundering, I unfold the sheet, only to be faced with familiar writing.

Un-freaking-believable.

Kolton's note reads: *If you're done pretending you can live without me, get in the car. Eric will be your chauffeur. The wooing will begin shortly.*

The relief is so palpable I drop my head forward onto the car.

Kolton wants me. He hasn't moved on. I don't have to chase him down tomorrow.

I'm not going to jail.

My determination doubles. It's time to strike a match to the girl who seesaws—knuckling under Richard one minute, uncompromising with Kolton the next. My career and independence don't have to be mapped out to fall in love. Doing things to make someone else happy doesn't mean I lose my true self. If mine and Kolton's connection is real, it should help me find it. Grow. But I've been too focused on doing things my way to see clearly. Me and my endless battles.

"Are you all right, Ms. Gallagher? Sorry for the show. Kolton can be persistent."

Chuckling, I lift my head. "You have no idea." Note in hand, I face him. "Let's do this. But what about my car?"

"Raven's on her way over. She'll drop it at your place."

Of course my friends are in on this plan, and I love them for it.

Eric helps me into the backseat and closes the door, my worry from moments ago now excitement. I adjust my leather jacket, wishing I weren't wearing faded skinny jeans and a white T-shirt, my beige bra way too ordinary for a Kolton reunion. Guess he'll have to take me as I am.

My knee bounces restlessly as Eric makes eye contact through the rearview mirror. "There's an iPod on the seat beside you. Enjoy the ride."

I slide the ear buds in and select the playlist titled *Shay*.

Four songs appear:

"Love Interruption"

"We Belong"

"Together"

"Just the Way You Are"

He was serious about the wooing.

Leaning back, I close my eyes as I listen to Jack White's "Love Interruption," his raw voice demanding love's pain. The torture. The sweet agony. That or nothing.

Kolton.

Pat Benatar's "We Belong" drums into my chest, her message loud and clear: For better or for worse, there's no denying love.

Kolton.

By the time Ne-Yo's "Together" plays, a tear slips down my cheek, his smooth R & B rhythm telling of devotion, lingering scars from past relationships, and healing.

Kolton.

Then there's Billy Joel's "Just the Way You Are."

Kolton. Kolton. Kolton.

As the last note plays, the car stops. Timed perfectly. I wipe my cheeks and sit up, full to brimming with everything I've denied myself the past two months. For a lifetime, really. It's dark out, but the Toronto Convention Center is recognizable, as is the outline of a figure by the entrance—hair loose to his shoulders, thumbs hanging on his pockets.

My heart skips. *Kolton.*

Twenty-seven

Kolton

The second the cruiser pulls up, I stop pacing. I was pretty sure Shay would play along—get in the car and listen to the playlist. With her, though, there's always a chance she could misinterpret my intentions. Write a paragraph between each of my lines. I can make out her profile in the backseat, but can't see her face. Eric helps her out and they exchange words. Then she faces me.

She bites her lip. I rake my hair. He drives off, leaving us.

I'm a patient guy, attention to detail my forté, but following through with the rest of my plan means not kissing Shay now. Not dragging her into a dark corner to show her how much she's been missed. Her curls are blowing in the wind, her brown leather jacket brushing the top of her tight jeans, and my willpower wanes. But she deserves everything. The full wooing.

She approaches slowly, her motorcycle boots loud on the pavement. She stops a foot in front of me. "Come here often?"

I step closer, until her lips are inches from mine, her hair within reach. "Only if feisty Irish chicks are lurking about."

"Looks like today's your lucky day." She glances down then, humor fading from her face. She closes her eyes, and her breath catches. "Kolton..."

A car drives by, its exhaust wheezing. Then, quiet.

"I know," I say. I take her hand, weaving our fingers together. "Will you come inside with me?" I grip her hand tighter, thrilled to be touching her again, but nervous, too. She may have come this far, but it doesn't mean she'll hear me out. When she doesn't answer, I say, "Maybe I should've paved the way with cupcakes."

"Such an asshole," she says, fighting a smile.

I tug her toward the entrance. "That's my bitch."

Once I've locked the door behind us, I lead her through the maze of booths—snowboards, skis, clothing, and gear lining each space. Our feet echo on the tile floor. The organizer, Jim, was true to his word that we'd be alone. It took some coaxing to get him and Nico's buddy to participate, but free ski jackets make for good bartering.

The Moondog section is around the next corner, my palms sweatier with each step. We round the bend, and Shay freezes at the sight. The company name is decaled on a large glass dome, the interior filled with evergreens and merchandise. A life-size snow globe.

Her gaze roams its girth. "Impressive."

"That's what all the ladies say."

She chuckles. "Still a child."

"Actually, what's impressive is getting that dome up and organized in three weeks. Sawyer did a lot of sweet talking. Lily helped, too." I start on my way, but she doesn't budge.

I'm about to get on bended knee and plead with her to let me say my piece, when she squeezes my hand. "I'm sorry." Her voice cracks, thick with emotion. "I mean, I'm still hurt you walked away, but I should have pushed you to talk it out. And I realize now that the job—"

I press a finger to her lips. Those soft, full lips. This isn't her apology to give. She was willing to give us a shot, eventually move her life for me, but I wouldn't meet her halfway, earning me the name Asshole. "We'll hash everything out," I say. "All of it. But there's something I need to show you first."

Her hazel eyes flick to the dome then back to me. "Okay."

Fingers intertwined, I lead, and she follows.

The second I open the glass door, Shay squeals. She tries to run inside, but I won't release her hand, so she jerks backward. Recovering quickly, she kicks the fake snow, scattering the calf-deep flakes. She jumps like Jackson. "How did you do this? It's amazing. Are those Lily's purses?" She's dragging me now, touring through the white-tipped evergreens and displays, thick "snow" fluttering with each step. Moondog jackets hang off giant molded icicles. Purses, hats, and scarves line iceberg-shaped shelves. "Seriously, it's beautiful," she says.

When she pauses in the center of the room, I pull her toward me, and finally, *finally*, weave my hands into her curls. "*You're* beautiful," I say.

Her eyes search mine, questioning. I'm not supposed to kiss her. Not yet. The plan was to wait until after the big finish, but I'm a man. Weak. Hungry for her. And not all plans are meant to be followed. I kiss her sure and deep, until she falls into me. Into us. I'm not tentative, in no way gentle. My frustration and angst these past weeks flow out. She grabs my neck, nails scraping my skin, and the more our tongues slide, the louder I groan, each pass shooting fire down my spine. I nip her bottom lip. "I've missed you, Connor."

She brushes her nose against mine. "I almost overdosed on cupcakes."

We kiss again. Once. Twice. A third time for good measure.

Then I square our shoulders and cup her cheeks, still amazed she's here. With me. In front of me. Hopefully, willing to accept my apology. "Here's the deal, Shay. I love you." I have to pause. Swallow. She grazes her teeth over her bottom lip. "I love you," I say again, because I have to. "I haven't said those words to a woman in a long time. It's not something I take lightly. You're it for me. You're stubborn and opinionated and smart and funny, and I don't want to be with anyone else. If you love your job at Concept and want to stay here, we can work it out. Do the long distance thing. I can come here in the summers when Jackson's off school. I'll fly you down during any and all vacation time you have. We'll do what we have to. I trust you, and I trust us. We can make it through."

I search her face for any sign she's still willing to do this, but it's hard to tell. I pushed her away. She told me she loved me, and I walked out the door. Unable to endure her silence, I go on. "For this to work, you have to be okay with us doing things for each other. I might watch a romantic comedy, and you might come rock climbing. And there will be times when we lose ourselves in each other. It happens to all couples. It takes effort to keep things fresh, to maintain our likes and dislikes. Our individuality." I release her face and, leaning to the side, I feel for the button I had installed on a nearby shelf. With one press, Van Morrison's "Sweet Thing" pipes through the speakers, his guitar strumming while the snow at our feet blows into the air. "When you become a snowball, we'll shake things up."

She tips her head back, individual flakes brushing her cheeks. A tear slips through her lashes, and my throat burns. I want so much for Shay. For her to shine, to believe in herself. To trust that, together, we can make each other better. If I can't do that for her, I'll walk away. Getting over her is a mountain I'd rather not climb, but I'd do it for her. I lean in and kiss her tear-soaked lashes. "Will you try this with me? Be apart but together? Always shaking things up?"

She winds her arms around my waist and rubs her eyes on my long-sleeve T-shirt, leaving a wet splotch on my shoulder. "No, Kolton. I can't."

The snow is blowing, billowing around us, her brown curls covered in flakes, and my breathing turns erratic, more oxygen coming in than going out. That's it. I fucked everything up. My fear over the past has ruined my future.

I move to pull away, but she lifts her head and slides her hands lower. Over my ass. I'm not a praying man. I didn't attend church like Caroline to ease my heart when Marina passed, but right now, with Shay's hands on me, I say a silent *please, God*, hoping this means she's not leaving.

Eyes still damp, she shakes her head. "I can't do long distance with you. It would be too hard. But I *will* move to Vancouver. I'll put my baggage aside and try, because…I love you, too. So much. Your temper and persistence, and"—she smiles as a snowflake lands on her nose—"the wooing. There's also the hair. I really, *really*, love your hair. And I miss Jackson like crazy. So, if choice A is still on offer, I'd like to try living out west."

My throat closes, disbelief and awe stunning me. Temporarily. Then I crush her to my chest and kiss her again, sealing our fate. She's coming home with me, risking everything for me. I press my forehead to hers. "You bet it's still on offer."

She tugs me closer. "I didn't hate *The Terminator*, by the way. I love the nickname."

I chuckle. "We can watch the whole series in Van. And I have a shit-ton of other action films you'll love to hate. And they have a cupcake store downtown you'll go nuts over. Oh, fuck"—I press my face into her curls—"wait until you see the pottery thing Jackson made. It makes the other pieces look professional. The kid will not be an artist." I sigh. "I can't believe you're coming."

She shrugs. "You had me arrested, made me a playlist, and built me a snow globe. Of course I'm coming."

I nip her bottom lip. "I love you," I say.

Then I hit the button again.

See the next page for a preview of the next book in Kelly Siskind's Over the Top series!

One

Lily

Whoever wrote the sixties song "Breaking Up Is Hard to Do" didn't
know the half of it. I've been living in Break-up Limbo for a year. A
quiet town, population: two. Three hundred and sixty-five days of in-
decision. Each month, I wonder when I'll find the courage to break up
with Kevin, crushing our eleven years together. Each month, my fear
and nerves and doubt feed my uncertainty. Then my design partner
and boss, Sawyer West, comes to town, and I'm a walking mess.

We stand back from the takeout counter, Sawyer with his arms
crossed, me biting my lip, while we examine the chalkboard menu
above. Normally, ordering lunch is a simple affair. I might take a
while deciding between a wrap or salad, sushi or dim sum, but I
don't stare at the menu as if the letters are rearranging themselves.

That only happens when I'm with Sawyer.

He squints at the scrawled letters. "I'm obviously getting the Pig Wrap. Chipotle bacon and porchetta were invented for me. You know what you want?"

You, I should say. I'll take all five feet eleven inches, the sandy hair, brown eyes, wide shoulders, and lean body to go. With an extra dimple and sexy smile on the side, please. Unfortunately, my boyfriend might put up a fuss when I show up with my purchase.

"Can't decide," I say. The theme of my life these days.

A month ago, I dragged Shay and Raven out for a girls' night. I was desperate to unload my dizzying thoughts about my stagnant relationship with Kevin. *We've grown apart*, I said. *I love him. I'm just not in love with him.* They were the same words I'd parroted mentally for a year. It all seemed clear in that moment. I was sure I'd march home and finally end things with him. But when I got there, he smiled at me from our couch, his nose poking above his book. "Your mom called. I told her I'd drive up north this weekend to help with that charity drive."

My resolve plummeted. *He's a good man*, I thought. *He loves my family as much as I love his. Why would I let that go?* Still, I went to sleep alone, the way I often do, and when he crawled into bed, we slept with our backs to each other.

Now Sawyer's in town from Vancouver, his first visit since that night, and I hate myself a little more for not doing what I should have done a year ago.

Move on with my life.

Oblivious to my turmoil, he says, "If you can't decide what to order, we'll have to break it down. Pros and cons." He steps behind me as a group of three squeezes past us to order at the counter. The toes of his shoes touch the heels of my ankle boots.

"Okay," I say all breathy, like I'm twenty-six going on sixteen.

"The Veggie Vixen is off the list for obvious reasons. Portobello mushrooms don't replace meat. The Napa Wrap could be decent since turkey is your go-to choice. The apple is a plus, and you eat kale like it's going out of style. But the blue cheese is a deal breaker."

"I like blue cheese."

"No, you don't. No one actually likes something that smells like ass. And the honey mustard dressing is questionable. If they use that Dijon crap, it's a hard no."

I tilt my head so he can see me roll my eyes, and my hair catches the stubble along his jaw. He brushes the strands away, grazing my ear.

My IQ joins my belly in a free fall.

It's been like this since Aspen, my feelings and attraction to Sawyer growing by the month. The week. The day. The minute. I often pick apart the domino effect that led us together, a string of innocent coincidences. If Shay hadn't stayed in her toxic relationship with her ex as long as she had, he wouldn't have dumped her, and we wouldn't have taken a girls' trip to Aspen with Raven. Shay wouldn't have skied into Kolton, and we wouldn't have knocked on his hotel door and met his friends. I wouldn't have looked into Sawyer's brown eyes as we talked design and clothing for five days, my *I have a boyfriend* keeping him at a platonic distance.

He certainly wouldn't have hired me to work freelance for his retail chain, and I wouldn't spend countless hours fantasizing about my boss and design partner.

While in a committed relationship.

Of eleven years.

Another couple hurries in, the man accidentally brushing us.

Sawyer tips forward, into me, and grips my waist to keep me from falling. The man apologizes and Sawyer replies, but I don't hear a thing. I may be wearing a thick peacoat, but I sense each of his fingers—his thumb on my back, his large hands curling around my waist, his index finger touching my ribs. I inhale deeply, and I swear his grip tightens. I'm on my feet, no chance of falling, but he doesn't let go.

"Back to the pros and cons," he says, his voice deep and heavy in my ear, weighing down my body. The rest of his playful menu descriptions barely register.

My life these days is nothing but stacks of pros and cons. Lists upon lists of break-up woe. It's time I end things with Kevin, but letting go of him is like letting go of everything I've ever known: my best friend, my neighbor who chased me around our joined yards tossing dirt at my head. My first kiss. My rock when my grandmother passed. My security when away from home for the first time.

Then there's Sawyer.

His lips are by my ear, his hands spanning my waist as he helps me decide what to order. Pros and cons. Kevin or Sawyer. Right now, like this, the choice is easy. All I want is to spin around and kiss Sawyer until the floor falls from my feet. Until I'm air and he's light and we're lost in space. The way he takes advantage of moments like this, touching me, talking close, I'm sure he wants that, too.

But I have a boyfriend.

"So, what will it be?" he asks.

"Sorry, what?"

He pauses, drops his hands, and steps to the side. No air. No light. Only confusion. "What will it be?" he repeats. "The offensive blue cheese wrap, or the Greek Chicken one with the olives and feta?"

Just like that, he flips us back to friends, coworkers, as though I imagined the heat between us. "I'll get the blue cheese one."

As he heads to the counter, he says, "If you're nice, I'll let you have a bite of mine when you realize you made the wrong choice."

I almost laugh. *Almost.* He has no clue how badly I want that bite. A lick. A taste. Because he's right. When I went home from the bar last month and didn't end things with Kevin, it was the wrong choice. It's not fair to Kevin. To me. We haven't touched each other intimately in close to a year. We don't cuddle anymore. No stolen kisses. No flirtatious games. We're roommates who are too comfortable to move on.

Sawyer's at the counter, grabbing our order, and I pick at my nails. If I do it, if I break up with Kevin, Sawyer and I would be free to pursue this thing between us. No more pretending or stepping away when the nearness gets too much. Would he book a flight right away? Wait a week? Would we say the things we've left unsaid at the end of each phone call? But there's a chance I'm wrong about him; his feelings might not run as deep as mine.

My blood rushes then, a tide of nerves flowing under my skin. It's a familiar sensation. One I haven't felt in a while. One I thought I'd overcome. I ignore the warning signs as he turns with our food. We remove our coats and sit at the counter. Immediately, he takes the radish garnish from his plate and sticks it on mine. I give him my pickle.

After a few bites of his wrap, he says, "This is amazing. How bad is yours?"

I pick up a piece of fallen blue cheese and make a show of placing it on my tongue. "Delicious."

"That's nasty. But I'm glad my pros-and-cons exercise worked.

When I go home and you get stuck making a decision, you should call me. I'll talk you through it."

That would be quite the conversation. "I'm capable of making my own decisions."

"Sometimes."

"*Sometimes?*"

"Sometimes." He swallows another bite and shrugs. "When it comes to work, you're a decisive champ. You play around with options until you nail an idea. But when we go out to lunch or you rent a movie—you know, the important, life-altering decisions—you freeze. That's where I come in."

That *is* where he comes in. Kevin often works late, leaving me time for evening "business" calls with Sawyer. My excuse to hear his voice. If I plan to watch a movie afterward, we sit on the phone while I scroll through listings, laughing at the options, me unable to decide. His voice fills me with static. Electromagnetic interference. If he were one of the comic book characters he obsesses over, he'd be Captain Distracto.

Kevin would be Dependable Boy.

Sawyer's powers are even stronger in person. Since he and Kolton opened their newest Moondog location in Toronto—another coincidence, fate guiding my life—Sawyer flies down from Vancouver monthly to check on the place. We review my sketches, and I try on sample clothing while we brainstorm. I often zone out, wondering how his stubble would feel against my inner thighs.

Static, static, static.

"I don't trust your taste in movies," I say. "You only like the Marvel Comics ones."

"Because they're awesome."

"Because they're juvenile."

He grins. "Juvenile is awesome, but these days, they're pretty dark and gritty. Also awesome."

I lick some sauce from my fingers and glance over to catch him watching me. His gaze lingers on my lips. Without warning, he reaches over and brushes his thumb across the corner of my mouth, those beautiful brown eyes turning midnight. His lips part. My pulse rockets.

He blinks and pulls his hand back. "Just a crumb," he says to the window in front of him and picks up his wrap. I love how his eyelids slant down at the sides, giving him a lazy look. Relaxed. Laid-back. Through the glass, pedestrians battle the wind, hunched forward as they hurry by. Sawyer eats quietly.

But I'm a tornado.

Kevin is the ground below me, Sawyer the sky above. If I don't detach from the comfort and familiarity of my relationship, I'll spin until I'm too dizzy to stand upright.

I can't keep living like this.

It's not a choice. It never was. It's about courage. I'm not in love with Kevin and haven't been for years. I have to break up with him. Finally. Not because of Sawyer, but because it's the right thing to do, and I have to do it tonight. Not give myself time to chicken out. Not allow my history with Kevin to undermine my intent. Sawyer is flying home this afternoon, so I won't get to tell him in person and see the look on his face. Watch as realization sinks in and he finally touches my lips with more than his thumb. I'll call him right away. God, that phone call. It will be wild. Crazy. Wild *and* crazy, hopefully. I'd rather not contemplate the flipside.

Suddenly parched, I grab my iced tea and smile at the four straws on our tray—three for me, one for him. The first time I stuck three straws in my drink in Aspen, he looked at me like I was nuts. I explained I like to get maximum suckage, not realizing how dirty it sounded until it was out of my mouth. He jumped on my faux pas and said, "I'm all for maximum suckage. Minimal suckage can be unsatisfying."

After a morning of skiing, the two of us went for an early lunch, one of the few times we were alone on that trip. Being with Kevin, I wasn't the type to enjoy harmless flirting with other men. I'd always excuse myself from an awkward conversation or clam up, but something about Sawyer was different. His unapologetic humor. The way we could spend hours talking about the cut of ski jackets and fabric trends. How I couldn't stop imagining kissing his full bottom lip.

Instead of shying away from the conversation, I said, "I agree. It's all about technique." That was as bold as I could get. If I were Raven or Shay, there would have been innuendo about where to place your tongue on the straw and how deep to take the plastic. I thought those things and likely blushed, but didn't say them aloud.

He must have read my mind, sifting through my unspoken banter, landing on the heart of things. "It's too bad you have a boyfriend," he said. "I wouldn't mind testing your theory."

My cheeks burned.

That was the only time either of us has mentioned being more than friends and coworkers. Boss and employee. That was nine months ago, but I never forgot. I often wonder if he has. Then we have moments like today when he stands close, leans closer, and touches me longer than a friend would.

I don't think he forgot.

We sit on stools at the counter, side by side, eating in silence.

Nothing has changed. But everything is different. His knee is touching mine, his elbow brushing mine, his space invading mine. If I follow through and break up with Kevin tonight, Sawyer could possibly be mine.

Static, static, static.

He wipes his mouth, tosses his crumpled napkin on his plate, then eyes my half-eaten wrap. "I told you not to get that one."

"It was good; I just wasn't hungry." For food, I don't add.

He checks his watch. "I should go. I have some things to do before my flight." He studies me a beat, his gaze roaming my face, then he leans in to kiss my cheek. So, so slowly. So, so softly. His lips press against my cheekbone, his warm breath and closeness overheating my brain. He lingers. A platonic friend wouldn't linger. A platonic friend wouldn't inhale my scent. Or maybe I'm overanalyzing everything he does.

A moment later, he pulls back. "You watching one of those stupid singing shows tonight?"

Still tingly and mesmerized by the small scar on his neck, I shake my head. "I need to spend some time with Kevin."

His jaw tics, and I want to eat my words. I want him to know I'm changing my life, that as of tomorrow things can be different between us. Instead, it sounds like I'm having a romantic evening with my boyfriend. Then he grins, big, bright, and carefree. Maybe his jaw didn't tic. Maybe the frown was nothing. Maybe he didn't notice my wording or doesn't care.

Or maybe he does.

"Send the revised purse sketch when it's done," he says. "And I used one of the last drafting boards this morning. You should order more and check our supplies." He puts on his coat and winks at me.

"See you at the Christmas party next week." Calm, cool, and collected, he leaves to catch his flight, treating me like the friend and coworker I am.

The rest of the day goes fast and slow, my nerves and excitement pushing and pulling me in a million directions. None of which allow me to focus on work. By the time I get home, my nerves win the battle. I don't go near the kitchen. I pace the floor in my bedroom, eyeing the clock. Kevin texted that he's running late. He works around his clients' schedules, using his honest character and trustworthy nature to sell life insurance; his sales are the highest in his region. Usually, I'm supportive of his long hours, but tonight they prolong my agony. I get jumpier. And jumpier. The enormity of the evening builds—my impending breakup and Sawyer's possible reactions warring. My heart and thoughts race each other, no finish line in sight.

Why did I let things drag on so long?

Poundpoundpound

Whywhywhy

It hasn't been this intense in ages, the rushing of blood in my ears. I focus on the silk robe I found at last month's flea market. The delicate fabric may hang loosely over my chair, but in my mind a woman fills its lengths, her imagined story sewn with every thread: *A new immigrant from Hong Kong clings to the last of her identity.* I drag my gaze to the wingback chair below it: *high tea and gossip slip across the leather, a besotted debutante dreaming about her betrothed.*

Pound

Pound

Why

Why

My discomfort eases some.

Then Kevin walks in the door.

As desperate as I was for him to get home, my courage falters. Eleven years of memories flood through my mind. I can't keep delaying my life, though. Being a tornado is exhausting. A deep breath later, I go into our open living room and force a smile. "How was your day?"

He hangs up his jacket with a sigh. "Long." His straight hair is neatly parted, his slight build accentuated by his dress pants and a tucked-in button-down. He's handsome in a sweet way—clean-cut, familiar. The opposite of Sawyer.

Where Sawyer is muscular, Kevin is slender.

Where Sawyer commands presence, Kevin blends in.

Where Sawyer lights me up, Kevin grounds me.

I stand by the couch, legs cemented, like a guest in my apartment. Kevin heads to the kitchen and opens the fridge, talking as he goes. "I spoke to my dad today. He's planning on doing that fishing competition this year. Your dad's going, too. He asked if we wanted to make a day of it like we used to. I think it would be fun." Jug of juice in hand, he grabs a glass, fills it, and drinks half in one gulp. "I also checked out some stores for snorkel gear. We leave for Belize in a month and should figure out what we need." He pokes his head back in the fridge, probably checking for our nonexistent dinner, then he shuts the door and leans on the counter. "Looks like an ordering Thai kind of night. Want me to call?"

His green eyes are soft, crinkled at the sides, radiating eleven years of comfort. Companionship. If I look closely, though, the dark circles beneath are unmistakable. Maybe he's ready to move on, too. Put an end to our fading relationship. But that means we won't go on our planned anniversary trip to Belize. We won't spend time with our families together. I could continue on and enjoy my life with Kevin, even though I'm not in love with him. Even though he doesn't create static. But I want more. I'm ready for more. No matter how hard it is, I can't keep living a lie.

He's relaxed tonight, the tension between us lately absent, smiling at me like I'm not about to rip the rug from under his feet.

That's when I say, "We need to talk."

Acknowledgments

Writing a novel takes a village, and my village is looking to acquire land due to overpopulation. Madeleine Colavita, editor extraordinaire, you are the filling to my Oreo cookie, the caramel to my Caramilk bar; you help make everything I write that much sweeter. Working with the right editor elevates your novel, and when that editor gets you and your humor, the work part of this job becomes fun. Also, if it weren't for Madeleine, my readers wouldn't know just how much chest hair Kolton has. All thank-you notes can be forwarded to her.

The team at Forever Yours has polished and buffed this sucker to make sure it sparkles. Brian Lemus has outdone himself with this stunning cover, and my copy editor, Rebecca Maines, has not only taught me that "blow job" is written as two words, but also corrects every wayward comma. A huge thank-you to these rock stars as well as everyone at Forever Yours for bringing *My Perfect Mistake* to life.

I wouldn't get to do this thing I love if it weren't for my agent, Stacey Donaghy. She's an entire cheerleading squad packed into one feisty woman who champions my work and has my back. Her voice messages keep me smiling, and her tireless support of my writing is unparalleled. I couldn't ask for a better partner to guide me through the publishing world.

My publicist, Tara Gonzalez, has dealt with my endless e-mails with grace and has helped spread the word about my novels, always coming up with innovative ways to market my work. You and the team at Inkslingers are a force to be reckoned with.

If it weren't for my critique partners, I would have overdosed on chocolate and gummy bears years ago. Kristin B. Wright, a day without our messaging is incomplete. You keep me sane, and your thoughtful critiques push me to write better. Esher Hogan, you get to see my words at their most vulnerable. I'd be lost without your honest feedback. Brighton Walsh, you helped bring out Shay and Kolton's softer sides. I'll never regret having your face tattooed on my boob. Marian Bartolome, thank you for finding time in your crazy life to work with me.

To my beta readers: Meggy Woodhouse, Celeste Grande, J. R. Yates, Heather Van Fleet, and Jacqueline Hughes, your comments were invaluable. Thank you for carving out hours to read Shay and Kolton's story.

The suburbs of my village are filled with writing groups that offer me emotional support and enough laughs to power a city. The ladies of the Life Raft are proof I'm not the dirtiest girl on the block. Mad love for each and every one of you. To the Den: there's only one word I want to write. You know what it is. This is me applying my often nonexistent filter.

To my family, a thousand thank-yous for always being in my corner. My husband, Steven, deserves a medal (and a properly cooked meal) for putting up with me. Even though I spend a lot of hours alone in my office, I couldn't do this without you. Thank you for your unending support, and for the constant supply of good wine.

Last, but never least, to my readers: Thank you for laughing and loving and swooning with me. Without you, Kolton and Shay wouldn't exist, and I wouldn't have the joy of creating more worlds and characters for you to savor. Here's to finding the perfect go-to bra!

About the Author

A small-town girl at heart, **Kelly Siskind** moved from the city to open a cheese shop with her husband in northern Ontario. When she's not neck-deep in cheese or out hiking, you can find her, notepad in hand, scribbling down one of the many plot bunnies bouncing around in her head. She laughs at her own jokes and has been known to eat her feelings—gummy bears heal all. She's also an incurable romantic, devouring romance novels into the wee hours of the morning.

Learn more at:

KellySiskind.com

Twitter @KellySiskind

Facebook.com/AuthorKellySiskind